THE WOLVES OF ROCKY FALLS

THE MALE LUNA

BOOK I

Vanna Bay

ISBN: 979-8-9988053-0-1 (Paperback)
ISBN: 979-8-9988053-2-5 (Hardback)
ISBN: 979-8-9988053-1-8 (eBook)

First print edition 2025.

www.vannabay.com

Dedicated to:

My Loving Spouse,
Who has endured many late-night ramblings
about the werewolf genre.

BRAYDEN

Sunday 6:37 am

I t's dark out.

The moonless sky coats the area in a thick blanket of darkness. Even though it is the early morning hours, night has not yet receded, and the area is still completely black.

That's how it has been for a while now. Dark, with a seemingly endless emptiness that engulfs anything within its clutches. No moon, no stars, just the night overtaking the area.

The only light at this time is the streetlamp, which contains a dull, flickering bulb. The illumination from the sputtering light is barely bright enough to give me enough details to see my surroundings and seems to make the darkness surrounding the vehicle appear thicker.

The remoteness of the small town also adds to the eerie atmosphere.

The last city I passed was several hours ago, and I haven't seen another car since. For a while, I could pass the time by looking for the large, random billboards that lined the streets of the rural

1

midwest, but even they have slowly disappeared. In their place, a thick forest soon begins to rise in the landscape, and with every mile, the canopy of trees seemed to become denser along the side of the two-lane road.

There was a brief reprieve from the feeling of isolation when I finally saw the welcoming sign at the town's city limit. The old wood, more grey than brown, and the letters of the town's name have been hanging at precarious angles. But it doesn't negate the relief I had felt when reading the words 'Welcome to Rocky Falls'.

The van is currently parked in front of the local grocery store. The pavement is worn, just like the rest of the roads, but the building itself looks decent. The paint has long faded from harsh weather but is free from any dirt or grime. The lights advertising the store name are all working, but faded.

I guess that could be said about the condition of the whole town—all the buildings, streets, and lights. Everything is clean and in seemingly altogether good condition, but everything is just worn, as if the town's energy has been slowly drained over the last decade leaving everything with an air of lifelessness.

I tiredly rub my burning eyes as I gaze out the windshield. As much as I want to succumb to sleep, I don't have the time. Twilight is just barely starting to light up the sky from foreboding black to a pale purple, and sleeping now would just cause discomfort after waking.

I let the early morning continue and begin fiddling with the temperature and fan knobs. The old vents pathetically sputter out some luke-warm air due to my fidgeting, and my hand finds its way subconsciously rubbing my now, dusty fingertips on the tops of my jeans.

Heaving a sigh, I try to distract myself with something, anything, just to help me stay awake a little longer. Glancing over, I see the center console is filled with various, emptied energy drinks and gas-station coffee cups that have accumulated over the long hours of driving. As quietly as possible, I reach over and gently shake some of the empty containers. I was hoping one of them has just a little more caffeine left at the bottom. After shaking the last drink, I let out a string of curses.

In frustration, I run my hand through my greasy blond hair. The dirty locks were a physical reminder of just how long we had been traveling and longer still since I had time to have a shower.

I sigh and lean back into the firm driver's seat as I try not to think too hard about the specifics of the situation I am in.

The entire journey has been difficult, although that was to be expected. The van I have been driving is stuffed. Old cardboard boxes are balanced on top of each other, while clothes of varying sizes are wedged in crevices. Empty chip bags and coffee cups are strewn over bundles of blankets. Not to mention the old car smell that has permeated the inside of the vehicle from having been full of warm bodies the last several days.

My fiddling continues until I adjust my driver's mirror before taking a moment to check over the other passengers along with me. Amidst the chaos, I could see four silhouettes. Stuffed between the suitcases, piled under blankets, with limbs spread all over each other are the animals otherwise known as my four youngest siblings.

While there are six of us in total, none of the children look anywhere near related. We are all half-siblings.

Although having kids is always an occupational hazard in mom's line of work.

Not liking where my thoughts are headed, I immediately try to distract myself from thinking about the topic which still causes my heart to clench. Instead of thinking about the past, I try to take a look at what our future holds.

I return my gaze out of my side window. Slowly, the sun starts to formally make its appearance, and dawn begins to break over the parking lot ahead of me.

As the sun rises, I rub a hand down my left leg and feel the familiar shooting pain in my upper thigh. The rough texture of my unwashed jeans begins to chafe my leg and irritate the skin underneath the fabric. I must not have been as subtle with my movement as I had thought as sudden movement from my side startles me.

The drowsy figure in the passenger seat begins to uncurl from the fetal position she was previously sleeping in. Long, stringy hair peeps out from under her dull hood, and thin legs stretch out in an ungraceful way as my younger sister tries to adjust her waking position. Pale skin, a small nose, with even smaller eyes hid underneath a curtain of straight hair, the lanky fifteen-year-old is slowly growing into her features.

"You're up early, you should try and get some more sleep before the rest of the gremlins decide to rise with the sun," I whisper, trying to be as quiet as possible.

She rolls her eyes tiredly, giving me an indecipherable grunt as her only verbal response, and casually flicks her hand towards the back seat as if to try and make the other passengers disappear with the action.

There's a moment of silence before she's awake enough to look over at me. With sharp eyes, her sudden gaze catches the movement of my hand on my leg, and she sends a worried glance my way.

"How's your left side?" she quietly asks.

"I'm fine, just the normal travel stiffness everyone gets," I reply, trying to subtly shift more to my right side and hide the tension the trip has put on my left leg and shoulder.

Kelsey scoffs, "I'm not an idiot Brayden. You're practically putting all your weight on your right side."

"I said I'm fine!" I whisper-yell, completely irritated and slightly embarrassed with the conversation.

From the corner of my eye, I see Kelsey flinch at my harshness, and I immediately regret snapping.

Rubbing a tired hand down my face I quickly try and rectify the situation. "I'm sorry Kels. I know you were just trying to be nice. It was very considerate of you to ask how I was doing, and you didn't deserve such a harsh response."

She merely shrugs her shoulders and curls in on herself.

I internally scowl, disappointed at myself for not watching my temper and letting unwarranted aggravation from the trip leak out.

I clear my throat in a sorry attempt to hide my guilt.

"In all honesty, it's hurting. Before going to our new home, I was planning on stopping at a grocery store for some food and necessities. I'll pick up some pain medication there," I say quietly.

After a moment Kelsey snorts softly and affectionately pats my leg.

"I suggest something stronger. You're a wuss when it comes to pain," she teases with a smirk.

I throw my middle finger up at her as we both chuckle and enjoy the quiet of the morning as the sun continues to rise.

Kelsey is us to my antics, and she takes them in stride as I was a clone of our mother.

Mom used to joke that it couldn't be helped that I turned out just like her. She taught me all the tricks she knew, ranging from her street smarts to street ways. I am the male version of her: straight blonde hair, bright blue eyes, and golden skin, a younger lithe body, just like her, who knew when to use it.

She used to proudly show me off to the world around her as she nurtured my existence. She was only sixteen at the time she became pregnant with me. She decided that since I was a strong enough swimmer to get past a condom, birth control, and day-after pill, then she'd raise her finger to mother nature by letting two versions of herself cause chaos.

My birth was a way of her taking control of the situation.

I clench my jaw and vigorously rub my face as I shake off my wandering thoughts. My vision is slightly bleary as I drop my hand and contemplate the coming cup of coffee I'm going to need.

There's a shuffling sound from further behind in the van, and my eyes immediately dart over to Kelsey. The young teen is already looking at me. Both of our eyes widen, and just as soon as we come to the same conclusion, the yelling starts.

"I have to pee now!" Charlie demands in a rage.

I spin around in my chair and try to keep my face calm.

The older of the five-year-old twins is sitting in his booster seat. His curly black hair is matted to his forehead, remnants from sleeping in the hot car. While his normally light cheeks are flushed a deep red that displayed both his anger and urgency to his request. He kicks his feet to display his earnestness to the situation and simultaneously hits the passenger next to him.

"Ow! Brayden, Charlie kicked me!" resounds a higher pitch squeal.

Charlotte is sitting next to her identical counterpart and has just become the victim of the swinging limb. Much like Charlie, Charlotte displays their father's Italian heritage well with her long dark hair and equally dark eyes, which are quickly filling with tears as she turns her doe-eyed gaze to me looking for support.

At her proclamation, Charlie is quick to retaliate and begins screaming his request. The younger twin decides to try and get her way through more tears.

Kelsey groans at the twins' arguing and is quick to curl back into her fetal position against the car door. Her avoidance of the situation isn't surprising given how early it is, and her introverted nature was taking over as a defense mechanism. Normally, Kelsey would be willing to lend a silent and firm hand to the kids when asked, but this was a lot to handle at such an hour, and I didn't blame her for wanting to avoid confrontation.

Before I can stop the ruckus, another voice groans from the backseat.

"Will you two shut up!" Marcus yells, his green eyes squinting as he blindly reaches around his seat for his pair of glasses. His mop of hair hangs limply over his ears, and he quickly brushes it away from his face. The normally bookish twelve-year-old already has frustration written across his thick eyebrows and scowling lips.

The twins pause their arguing with each other, only to begin another tangent at the newly awakened sibling. Marcus soon joins in, yelling his own frustrations at them.

With a sigh, I look over to the last passenger of the sibling bunch. With her bright red hair and puffy cheeks, baby Evie sits silently in her car seat. Her hazel eyes meet my gaze in the reflection of the mirror above her seat, and she quietly watches me with an unmoving stare.

The chaos continues in the car, and for a moment, I look out my front window.

The sky becomes more vibrant, and the area around the old van is slowly illuminated by the bright sun. I bask in the warmth the morning rays bring into the car. While the journey to get to our fresh beginning has been tough.

We had made it.

Everything is going to be fine.

BRAYDEN

Sunday 9:12 am

This was a mistake.

Currently standing in the middle of a grocery aisle, we were grabbing the last couple of things off of our list, and the supposed-to-be quick trip had quickly devolved into a horrific nightmare that seemed to never end.

Shortly after the kids had become more awake, it had been agreed that I would watch the three middle children while Kelsey took full responsibility for baby Evie. We had all discussed the rules of going into the store. The kids had even recited them back to me to prove they understood what was expected of them. While I had been tired, I was slightly optimistic that we could quickly get the necessities we needed before arriving at our new home.

It was a well-intentioned plan, but I was naive back then, full of high hopes and dreams.

Almost immediately after entering the store, Kelsey handed off Evie to me saying that she needed to go grab some personal hygiene products ASAP. I would have been a little more compassionate of her plight; had this not been the third week this month she had used that excuse on me to dodge helping me with the rowdy youngsters.

Kelsey's hasty departure meant that I was now in charge of the four youngest kids as well as obtaining the long list of items without any assistance. As it was early in the morning, I decided to first take the kids over to the deli counter. I had hoped that by feeding them they would be more likely to cooperate than if they were hungry.

This was yet another well-intentioned plan that had quickly become a nightmare.

Upon entering the food area, Marcus insisted he did not want a donut but wanted a burrito. After looking at the options he realized that all they had were cheese options and he started to argue with the counterman about his lack of accommodation for lactose-intolerant customers.

It didn't take long for the counterman to become visibly frustrated with my brother, and I had been I had tried to diffuse the situation by convincing Marcus that a breakfast sandwich was a superior choice to the burrito, all the while slipping a five-dollar bill into the tip jar for the glaring man.

Meanwhile, Charlie had somehow figured out that the donut cabinet could be opened. By the time I had taken care of Marcus, the twins were chin-deep in gooey sugary residue and were happily stuffing their cheeks with several handfuls of desecrated pastry. Having had enough, the cashier promptly threw us out of that section. This meant I was left without breakfast and ended up scavenging the remains of Marcus' mostly eaten sandwich.

The chaos continued throughout the shopping.

By the end of the trip, Evie had lost her left shoe, and Marcus had acquired a new comic, which Charlie had pointed out was not fair as it was not on the list. Charlotte had taken to playing with her hair and, in doing so, kept hitting Charlie in the face every time she tried to braid a new piece. Deciding that the safety of the store and my sanity were more important than getting a box of cereal, I made the executive decision to try and acquire the remaining items at a later time.

My frayed nerves were not helped by the locals. Even though it was rather early to be in a grocery store, we would pass by someone every other aisle or so. At first, I had thought the attention was due to the arguing kids around my shopping cart. The first couple of times someone had given us a curious or even outright disdainful look, I had ducked my head in embarrassment, and my cheeks had flooded with warmth at the judging stares.

However, my initial assessment had quickly been disproved the further we ventured into the store. In the produce section, a young lady had been quick to run over and snatch the last bag of apples that I had been reaching for. The bitch quickly scurried away with her prize at my stunned face. The bread aisle became a glare fest between myself and the older gentleman who kept purposefully blocking our route anytime I went to move the cart. These minor inconveniences were not terrible until the last offender in the cereal aisle. After the twins picked out the chosen sugary breakfast for the week, one local even dared to try and slyly take a picture of us.

At my harsh glare, and scowling face, the young man instantly flushed with embarrassment before quickly putting away his phone.

While I understood this was a small town, I had been optimistic about the new start awaiting us here in Rocky Falls. My opinion of the formerly quaint town began to diminish the longer we were in public. It was obvious there was a strong small-town mindset that disliked newcomers. The pinched faces of disdain began to overlap around us. The dividing line between newcomer and resident was getting deeper by the minute, and I couldn't quite push back the familiar feelings that came along with the purposeful segregation.

Having others look down on us was nothing new. Given mom's line of work, there was never a shortage of those who wished to constantly point out our inferiority to their supposedly superior living. Even on the streets mom was known to be somewhat of an oddity and played a dangerous game with each of her customers in the hopes they would be the ones to rescue her from her trapped life.

Mom used to say freedom was everything. She taught me that actions had no meaning to one's self if they weren't done freely. Once something came along to bind you up, your actions were no longer your own, but instead belonged to another, and once you were trapped there was never an easy way to escape. It was a harsh lesson, but one I quickly came to understand the sincerity of. Freedom was essential to maintaining one's identity, and freedom could only be maintained through control over one's decisions in life.

That was why this move was so important. A new job, a new house, a fresh start so far in the middle of nowhere and that the bindings of the past might just be too short to reach us. A place to have freedom.

It was almost automatic how my feelings towards the unwelcoming faces became nothing more than annoyance. I could feel the familiar walls being built back up, almost as if I hadn't taken them down in the first place. If people want to stare, let them. If they wanted to act like we were the first outsiders they had encountered for the sake of distancing themselves from us, fine. People were the same everywhere after all.

Fucking small town–everyone should just mind their own business.

A sudden scream startles me out of my wandering thoughts, and my attention is immediately brought back to my four youngest siblings.

Marcus is standing off to the side, one hand on the metal basket and one hand holding a new comic he had decided to read through while we were shopping. His face is completely obscured by his new reading, but every once in a while, a sharp quip is heard from behind the pages as he argues with the twins.

Charlie is crouched in the basket of the cart. His back is against the metal side as his knees were pulled tightly against his chest. His face is once again full of anger as he frustratedly pushed Charlotte's hair from his face as she purposefully tossed it over her shoulder. The little female devil sits in the official kids seat just above Charlie, and with every scream he gives of anger at her antics, she matches with her own volume of indignation.

"OW!" Charlotte yells suddenly, her tiny hands reaching for her scalp. "Charlie, stop pulling at my hair!"

Charlie looks up at his sister as he glares at her sudden complaint. "I'm not pulling! Your hair was in my face and I moved it so I could breathe!"

"You're both acting like babies," Marcus interjects with an annoyed huff.

The bickering and screaming from all three kids continued.

With a sigh, I adjust Evie on my hip as she limply hangs against my side in my right arm.

"Guys, stop fighting. We're going to the checkout now," I demand, with as much authority as I can muster.

There's no reaction, and the three of them continue their banter. I would have gotten more response had I been talking to a brick wall. My frustration levels hit their max as the crushing weight of the entire moving trip begins to take its toll on me. I have gotten six hours of sleep in the last three days. I am physically drained from all of my energy, and we still have to get home and unpack. Not to mention I begin my first shift of work this evening. I am absolutely *starving* and have been surviving on nothing but scraps from the kids' leftovers the last few days. My frustration finally peaked.

I close my eyes and take a deep breath...

"ONE!" I shout, my voice booming against the old tiled floor. My eyes are hard as I full-on glare at the children in front of me.

Silence follows my sudden proclamation, and all three of their heads immediately turn to me. Their wide-eyed stares and rigid bodies show me that I now have their full attention.

"Two," I continue the count of the kids, numbering from oldest to youngest. "Kels is in a different aisle."

"Three," Marcus nervously gulps, his previous comic now hanging limply to his side.

The twins count off their numbers of four and five, almost in sync, and all previous roughhousing has come to a complete stop.

"And six," I end the count while pointing to the infant in my arms. I take another breath, and slowly let it out as I try to regain control of my own emotions.

I'm not necessarily angry at my siblings; rather, I am just frustrated in general, and if I were to speculate I believe their current behavior represents something akin to what I'm feeling. I don't believe they are deliberately trying to disobey or misbehave, but after a lot of change in a very short amount of time, we have all hit our limits.

"Look, I know it's been hard," I begin with what I hope is a softer tone, "I know the trip has sucked, and that change itself sucks in general. I know this whole situation is different, and everyone is tired and energized at the same time."

I pause as I make eye contact with each kid, "But I need everyone to please just make it to the cashier. Then we'll head to our new house and you guys can tear up the yard as much as you want. OK?" I gently beg.

The kids solemnly nod, and I can see that the previous frustration levels seem to have gone down after my little talk. I sigh in relief as I begin moving the cart up to the front for checkout. We make it to the register and I keep the kids busy by having them unload the food onto the conveyor.

Upon our arrival, the cashier glances at us with a very bored expression covering his pale and sweaty pimply face, before half-heartedly scanning our items. While our groceries are being scanned, Kelsey joins our little group with one of the store's plastic bags already in her hand. She silently walks up to me as she places her newly purchased items in the cart, before joining the other children.

After getting everything unloaded without an issue, I tell the kids they can all pick out a drink for the road. In just a few seconds they happily scramble to the mini-fridge in the checkout and hand me their choices. I also grab myself a much-needed energy drink and hand them all directly to the cashier requesting they immediately be handed back.

As the kids are opening their drinks, I see a few people get behind us in line. Not paying much attention, I crack open my drink and quickly gulp it down, ignoring the dehydrated headache that will surely get worse after the energy drink hits my stomach. The cashier grimaces at my behavior and after taking a once over at my appearance grimaces even more.

Fuck you, I'm way out of your league. I just need a shower, I think to myself as I glare at the sweaty teen.

15

Although I guess I couldn't blame his initial reaction. My normally lustrous blonde hair is falling victim to gravity and the many layers of oil and sweat from days of moving and traveling. My skin felt thick with residue, and I could practically feel the bags under my eyes become darker by the minute. I'm sure my clothes also didn't help. As I wanted to be comfortable while traveling, I had started the journey with an old high school sweatshirt and gray sweatpants that both draped over my figure in an unflattering way. While I had good intentions of changing, I couldn't find it in me to care to switch outfits, meaning I've worn the same outfit for nearly three days now.

I don't even want to think about the smell...

With one last disdainful look, the cashier glances behind us and instantly straightens. His head drops meekly, focusing on his task with new vigor, but his hands begin to shake.

Curious at what caused his sudden change of behavior, I try to inconspicuously take a look at the group behind us. There were two guys, both very tall and very well dressed. Trying to not be too obvious, I try to make out their details from the corner of my eye, but can only see well enough to determine one is closer to their early forties while the other is in their early thirties.

Other than standing as if they arrogantly own this crap shop, they don't seem too special to me.

I turn to Kels, trying to give non-verbal signals for her to see if she notices anything odd between our cashier's behavior and the guys behind us.

She glances at the cashier, and then guys behind us, only to shrug just as confused as I am.

Suddenly there is a loud clanging behind me.

"What the fuck!?" a deep voice shouts from behind me.

Panicked, I quickly turn around and see little Charlotte trembling, staring wide-eyed at a tall man in front of her.

16

BRAYDEN

Sunday 9:54 am

Looking at the scene before me, I feel the blood quickly drain from my face. My brow begins to break out in an anxious sweat that coats my already grimy face.

Charlotte stands in front of me with an equally horrified expression. Her small lips begin to quiver and her big eyes fill with unshed, embarrassed tears.

Seeing Charlotte panic, my protective instincts kick in, and I quickly grab the scruff of her collar as I bring her to my side. She doesn't resist and merely lets out a soft whimper at my abrupt actions, digging her face into my shirt. My palm shakily rubs the top of her head in a failed attempt at comfort, as my brain tries to process what just happened.

The gentleman in front of me is glaring at us. He is tall, extremely tall, easily dwarfing my lean frame by a half foot or so. Although his impressive height isn't the only thing intimidating about this man. He is all muscle, from thick shoulders to even bigger arms, I could see his toned physique even through the sleeves of his tight dress shirt.

However, my attention is drawn to the dark black pants of his suit, pants that proudly held a name brand that would most likely charge me for just reading their logo, expensive pants that were now drenched in my sister's bottle of orange juice.

I watch in horror as the stain on the leg seeps into the material. The sticky drops of sugar roll from the very top of the pant leg all the way down to the ankle, gently beginning to puddle onto the dirty tile floor.

"I'm so sorry sir!" I nervously apologize, "She didn't mean it! I mean, I know that's not an excuse, but she's only five. We've all been cooped up in a car for the last few days, so there's a lot of pent-up energy… you know how kids can be…" I rambled, my voice slightly shaking as I nervously cleared my throat.

"You're right," the man angrily grits out, white-knuckling both his tan hands by his side. "That's no excuse for not being able to keep your kids in line!"

The deep timbre of his voice resonates throughout the small space of the checkout line. I flinch as the sound grates against my ears, his gravelly voice giving the impression the man is used to yelling for long durations at a time.

Embarrassed and slightly irritated by his response, I drop my head in order to hide my growing annoyance. I have never been a coward, but there is wisdom in knowing to engage or submit in a fight. Not only is the gentleman superior to me physically, but if the suit is any indication of his status in town, I didn't need to anger a well-known town figure on our arrival.

I do, though, make a mental note to never engage with this man again, as he is clearly not an individual who was compassionate towards kids.

I let out a very tired sigh. "Look, we just moved here, and I don't want the town to think we're a bunch of delinquents.

Charlotte will give a heartfelt apology, and I'm also willing to pay for the dry cleaning. Sounds fair?"

I give a mental plea for the man to say it is a fair deal because I most definitely couldn't afford to replace his clothes.

Having stated my proposition, I'm still not brave enough to look the large man in the eyes, and instead settle for raising my gaze to his chest. There's a moment of silence, and for a moment, I'm hopeful he is going to accept my offer.

"Fair!?" the towering man suddenly yells, "Just from looking at you, I can tell these pants are worth more than your miserable life!"

I wince as my ears ring his scratchy voice and barely have time to register the man getting out his phone.

"I'm calling the police for harassment," he says, his voice dripping with authority as he brought out his phone, "let this be a lesson to you and your siblings of what discipline and authority look like and the consequences of breaking it."

Anger immediately consumes me as the fullness of his response register within my tired brain. My irritation towards the unreasonable man before me triggers my pent-up emotions as my parental instincts turn on when he threatens my family.

"Now you listen here you over--pompous, cum-dump piece of shit! It's a piece of clothing! How small is your dick that you need to overcompensate so hard by calling the cops on a fucking five-year-old?!" I scream, getting as close to the monster of a man, without actually touching him. I have the urge to stick my finger in his chest but quickly think better of it as I don't want to actually break my hand.

Behind me, I hear the cashier gasp and from the corner of my eye see him visibly trembling. The poor teenager looks scared enough to wet himself and his previously sweaty face had turned ashen. The worker gives me a look akin to horror as if my actions toward the man in front of me were unfathomable.

The young worker's reaction further spurs my anger. It is obvious by now that the gentleman I am currently in the middle of a conflict with is an important town figure; however, I believe that any power the man does hold should be immediately revoked due to his boorish behavior.

It is absolutely appalling that he is getting worked up so easily and even more appalling is his attitude that he felt justified in his anger. His arrogance is unlike anything I have previously encountered, and he even had the nerve to threaten my kids.

I like to think I'm pretty patient, but my tolerance for others threatening my kids is very low. He has ignited my mama-bear instincts, and I am ready to hold my ground no matter what.

Done with trying to be respectful, I begin to raise my gaze, and my eyes wander up the man's body. His chest is bulky, and the coiled muscles underneath his shirt are just as impressive as the ones straining on his arms. He has a thick neck, and his Adam's apple bobs angrily as he continues to fume. Much like the rest of him, his jaw is strong, square, and covered in a five-o'clock shadow. His lips are pressed in a very thin line, the corners showing the very beginnings of aging, while the scowling deepened the grooves. His tan cheeks have turned an unattractive splotchy red from getting so worked up.

If the situation hadn't been so serious, I'd have the urge to laugh.

"How dare you!" The stranger seethes, "Submit, you piece of..." His speech slowly comes to a stop, and his volume quickly diminishes into nothing more than a whisper as his jaw goes slack.

I make eye contact with him...and notice they are brown.

Although, I guess brown would be an over-exaggeration. They are not deep and rich, nor an endless soulful black nor are they an exotic light hazel, nor caramel. They are more just kind of there. They are a murky brown, with a dullness reflected back at me that seems to mimic the same lifeless condition of the town we are in.

A clattering brings me back to reality, and I glance down to see the shattered remnants of the man's phone strewn across the floor. I eye the broken electronic apprehensive and briefly wonder if the tall man is going to now blame me for the broken item.

Taking advantage of the man's stupefied state, I turn around to see a scared Kelsey gripping the two boys' hands, who both wear equally horrified expressions. Not knowing how this situation is going to end, I don't want the kids to witness any more than they already have. They have seen way too much already.

Digging into my pocket, I fish out the car keys and hand them to Kelsey.

"Here, take the kids to the van. I'll be out shortly," I command, trying to keep my voice steady.

She gives me a nervous glance trying to protest, "Bray-".

"Go," I demand, leaving no room for argument.

I push Charlotte her way, but she doesn't let go of my shirt.

"Charlotte," I try to gently coax, "you need to go with Kels."

With great reluctance, her clenched fist releases the fabric of my top, but her head subtly shakes 'no' as repetitive whimpers of "I didn't mean to" trail her. Kelsey gives me one last worried look, seeing the no-doubt seething bull behind me, as she ushers the kids out of the store.

Having had a second to catch my breath, I'm suddenly reminded why I am resisting the urge to retaliate against the man when he first made a scene. The man iss huge and could easily beat me if this conflict became physical. A jolt of fear shoots down my spine as I realize just how fucked I might be.

Very slowly, I bend over and retrieve the remnants of the man's now destroyed phone.

"Um, here," I say, stretching out my hand for him to take it.

I jump in surprise as I feel his meaty hands grab my outstretched wrist. The shards of electronics fall back to the floor as I lose my grip due to his actions. The man's oversized palm doesn't loosen at the clattering sound, and instead, his grip tightens around my forearm in a sweaty hold.

Startled, and extremely uncomfortable, I look up and give him a glare.

The man's lips are slightly parted, his eyes seemingly glazed over with a look of something that I couldn't quite identify. By this point, I do not have the energy to assess the stranger anymore and could feel exhaustion beginning to creep back into my system.

"What's your name?" he asks, in barely a whisper. Eyes, rapidly darting over my face, trying to scan over all my features in quick, repeated succession.

I feel my face deepen into a frown. "Why, so when you call the cops they can put my name and face on the news?" I ask in irritation. The man still had me within his grip and I was now trying to wriggle my wrist out of his grasp.

The man's face immediately drops, and he has the decency to look ashamed.

"That wasn't...I didn't know...I mean there was no way to..." he stutters, sounding slightly out of breath.

I roll my eyes, not paying attention to whatever bullshit is spilling from his mouth, as I am more focused on trying to get my arm back into my possession. It surprises me just how strong the man was. As the seconds begin to pass my desperation to escape the stranger's grasp became more and more obvious until I am full-on jerking my body against his hold.

I wince at his strong grip and can't help but wonder what kind of extreme body-building regime the man must have been on.

Remembering there are two people in this group, I looked around the man's torso to try and make eye contact with the other individual. The guy's friend is equally as terrifying, with a large frame and tall build; he is just as physically impressive as the first stranger. The second individual is slightly older than his colleague. He has long hair that reaches the tops of his shoulders with smatterings of gray streaks on his head. Stranger two also has a very large scar obscuring most of the left side of his face that seems to have been from a very old injury. Although he in't terrible looking now, eliminating the wrinkles and the previous injury would suggest that he had been mainstream handsome in his younger days.

Unfortunately, the second guy's face is also trapped in a frozen state of shock watching the scene in front of him.

I sigh, realizing there is probably only one brain cell shared between the two men.

"Hey, buddy, could you control your friend here?" I ask, annoyed.

Snapping out of his stupor, the older man gently places his hand on the first gentleman's shoulder.

As soon as he touches the first man, the grip on my arm tightens painfully, and I find myself yanked forward. My head bangs harshly against the hard chest. My headache grows at the sudden force. With my ear pressed tightly against the man, I can also hear a rumbling, that shakes me to my core, emanating from his chest.

"Dude! Let go!" I yell, my voice muffled by the wall of flesh smashing my face. The man still has his grip on my wrist, but my other arm is now pinned to my side, and I find myself nearly immobile. Desperate to escape, I resort to just wiggling my whole body, thrashing around to try and get loose.

Feeling my distress, the man loosens his grip, and I jump from his hold.

"You think you can file for harassment over a spilled drink!?" I angrily yell, trying to straighten my shirt, "Wait until I get a chance to talk to the police because holding me without my consent, against my will is actual fucking harassment!"

I wait for the man to refute me and go on a tangent of his own, but the anticipated yelling never comes. Instead, he just stands in front of me. Silently staring, his eyes stare at me in bewilderment, and his arms remain slightly outstretched as if anticipating my return.

There's a moment of silence as both of us are frozen, not quite sure what the other's next move is going to be.

The stranger sighs and straightens himself up to his full height. He seems lost in thought as one of his hands runs through his black hair messing up his short curls.

"Um, I think there's been a mistake," the stranger begins, his voice much softer than it had previously been, "My name is Damien Rockwell, and my assistant here is Aiden Thompson."

I look warily at the man, Damien, really uncomfortable and confused by our entire interaction this morning. Deciding that civil is the correct response, I give a curt nod, "I'm Brayden."

Damien's lips widen into a large smile as his previously frowning face splits open into a toothy grin. The sudden mood swing causes me to shift uncomfortably from foot to foot, and I inconspicuously try to use the movement to put some space between us.

He seems to register my nerves, and his smile drops, his whole demeanor tensing at my subtle retreat, "Listen, the whole police thing was, uh, just a hazing for newcomers," he rushes out. His eyes are now frantic, and his palms face me as if he's trying to coax a scared animal.

I give another curt nod to signal I'm listening, although I find it hard to process the idea of threatening jail as a joke.

"And the pants, these things were from a second-hand store, they're worth practically nothing!" He continues, nervously chuckling. Behind him, his friend looks at him shocked and slightly confused by his last comment, and I make a mental note of their odd behavior.

I simply nod again.

Knowing this isn't going to lead to any actual fight or any authorities being called, my interest in interacting with Damien drops to zero. My attention returns back to the cashier, and after briefly looking down at the conveyer, I see that all the items are bagged and neatly loaded into the cart. I begin digging in my pocket to pull out my wallet but pause when I don't see a total displayed on the register.

"How much is the food?" I ask, looking at the teenager.

The kid's face is pale, and he is visibly shaking so bad the name tag on his uniform is rattling. Sweat drips down his plump face, and his pupils look dilated as he stares at me with growing horror.

"I-it's f-free Lu–I mean, it's f-free s-sir," he nervously stutters.

"Is this another hazing technique?" I ask with a scowl, "Am I going to be charged for theft if I walk out of the store with my cart and don't pay?"

Tired from the antics of the locals, I throw some cash on the counter giving the kid a harsh glare, "Nice try. The security camera will now see that I've paid whether you choose to take the cash or not."

Heat envelopes my back as I realize Damien has now pressed his front up against me. Looking back at him annoyed, I see he has matched my previous glare at the worker.

"Give him his money back," he demands coldly, through tightly clenched teeth.

A new wave of anger rolls through me, and I immediately seethe at the cashier, "Don't you dare touch my money!"

Stranger two, or Aiden, quickly rushes forward with a strained smile, "Uh, Brayden was it?" he asks quietly, eyeing Damien warily while sending a tentative smile in my direction, "This is part of the, uh, hazing you're right, but not in the way you think. You see, um...after a town member gives a newcomer a hard time they're supposed to do something nice so no one leaves angry," Aiden roughly grabs Damien's shirt, trying to yank him away from me, "So the groceries are being paid for by Mr. Rockwell here."

I can't help the urge I have to just say fuck it to this whole morning.

"Fine," I grit out stepping away from the keypad, overly dramatically presenting it to Damien, "Be my fucking guest."

While the younger man gets out his card, I start digging through the bags looking for the bottle of painkillers. With all the travel, childcare, and drama in the last hour, I am in a lot of pain. My head feels like it is going to split open down the center, and I swear every time I blinked my vision rattled. There is also the issue that my whole left side felt like it is on fire. Every time I move electric shock waves of pain angrily pulsed through the old injuries to my arm and leg.

Relief fills me as I find my treasure and quickly twist the top off. It only takes me a couple of seconds to dry swallow several and toss the bottle back into the bag. As soon as I'm done my body is spun around and caged against the counter.

26

I can't help but think this is an odd way to tell me he's done paying.

Damien towers over me holding the bottle of medicine in one shaking hand.

"What's this?" he barely chokes out, as if having to look at the bottle was more painful than *my migraine*.

Realization hits me, and I quickly begin digging through my wallet.

"Shit, I didn't even think of medicinal laws," I tried to apologize, immediately showing my license to the cashier, "but I'm a legal adult so don't worry."

I hear two incredulous gasps, and both Damien and Aiden's faces have turned white.

Everyone seems to be going pale around me. Maybe, I should hold my breath in case it's contagious...

"You're only *nineteen*?" Damien asks, eyes glued to my license looking like he's about to throw up.

"Yeah, I get that a lot," I reply, rolling my eyes as I put my wallet away, "but don't worry I didn't have a kid at four. I'm a guardian over my five siblings."

My joke seems to fall flat as no one laughs at my attempt at humor.

Honestly, Damien is confusing me or maybe this town is just shittier than I originally thought. Both Aiden and the cashier don't seem too concerned with the hazing, so maybe Damien is just following tradition, I mean he did just pay for a week's worth of groceries for a family of six...

I give myself a mental shake, deciding that one good deed was not enough to make up for his previously atrocious treatment.

My words must have finally registered with Damien as he straightens a little bit allowing me just enough room to scoot over to my cart. His eyes follow me creepily, and his mouth is slack in an almost dreamy smile.

"A family of seven..." he whispers through a crazed smile that seems to painfully be splitting his face in half.

Alright maybe he's not trash, maybe he's just crazy tripping?

"Right, because one plus five equals...seven..." I say, shaking my head in confusion. Not getting a response, I realize Damien is lost in his own little world, and I catch eyes with Aiden instead.

"Hey, when your friend is no longer high, let him know that if I ever see him within a hundred feet of my kids I'll start his balls on fire, rip them off, and shove their burnt carcasses down his throat."

His shocked face is my only response as I quickly push the cart out of the store and to the van.

DAMIEN

Sunday 10:31 am

I feel a hand grab my shoulder.

"Alpha..."

Whipping my head around, I see my Beta staring at me with shock and worry.

I couldn't blame him; with my actions this morning the pack might truly be fucked.

I look at my best friend and companion with desperation. "Aiden, what have I done?" I ask, barely able to rasp out my question.

I feel sick.

Worse than sick.

Turning away from Aiden, I start to dry-heave in the checkout line. My chest constricts, and my throat burns as bile tries to rise from within. Tears begin streaming down my face, although I don't know if it's from getting sick or from the horror of this morning's interaction. My knees turn to jelly as I can no longer hold myself upright. Grabbing the conveyor, I try to steady myself as my lungs go into overdrive with the beginnings of hyperventilating.

Like a bad tape, the terror and disgust from my soulmate's face has ingrained themselves into my head. The fear of my behavior. The actual, physical anxiety rolled off of him in waves. The way he stood in front of his children, to protect them from *me,* seeing me as a *threat* to his children. He even went so far as to send them out of my presence for their safety.

Strong hands grab my arm and try to help straighten my pathetic form up. Aiden lets me lean on him as all my strength has drained away..

"It'll be ok, Alpha," he tries to quietly comfort, "Luna did talk to you afterward a little bit, and he didn't immediately run away, so that's something."

I sag a little more against him, as I realize the bar for how I treat my soulmate is set at him not running from me screaming.

"Although..." Aiden trails off, his face pinches in confusion, lips drawn in a thin line, as his eyes look elsewhere in concentration. "was it just me, or did he look familiar?"

"He looked perfect," I reply, solemnly.

It is true. Everything about him seemed to glow: light skin, blonde locks, raging blue eyes just above his scowling pink lips. Even his oversized loungewear couldn't hide his striking appearance.

Aiden, shakes his head in dismissal, "Yeah, I guess I'm seeing things after a long patrol last night."

With a sigh, I stand up on my own. My body feels stiff as it finally begins to relax from the high tension it was carrying not moments before. I gently try to move my limbs and get the blood circulating again when I hear a rattle coming from my hand, and realize I'm still gripping the bottle of medicine.

Concern immediately fills me as I remember my mate taking a handful with earnestness.

My thoughts are immediately flooded with worry as I think about all the negative possibilities that could have caused my fated pair to feel unwell.

"He's sick," I rasp out, staring at the bottle with rage as if it was the fault of my mate's pain.

Aiden shakes his head. "I don't think he was sick, but he definitely looked to be in rough shape."

I nod gravely, gripping the bottle of pills so tightly the casing begins to crack, "I'll go see Dr. Monroe later today, so that he can keep an eye out for if my mate goes to the hospital and maybe obtain some more information about him."

With that, there is no longer any reason to remain in the store.

Walking out the door I can't help but think that we weren't even supposed to be shopping in the first place. Normally, groceries are delivered to me by another pack member, but today Aiden said that his mate had run out of eggs to make a new recipe and thought it would be easier to just run and grab it himself. I had offered to join him as it was a rare instance to discuss work on a Sunday morning.

I abruptly stop outside the store's entrance.

Sunday morning.

"Is the temple still in service?" I ask, looking out in front of me to the nearly empty parking lot of the store.

Trying to hide his surprise, Aiden simply nods his head slowly. "Service runs until noon."

Not needing any more encouragement, I quickly tear down along the sidewalk. If I had had more energy, I would have run towards the temple, but seeing as this morning has drained me I settled with a brisk walk. Unease fills me as we weave down the streets around town. My eyes shift as I look around the city I had been both born and raised in. While I have lived here my whole life, the familiar streets of Rocky Falls felt foreign. I find myself looking around with a new interest as I try to imagine what my mate's first impressions had been upon arriving.

I grimace as I take in the condition of the town and wonder if it looks as rundown to my soulmate as it currently did to me. The main street contains a small, two-lane road, and the paint of the divider was fading away on the grey concrete. The buildings themselves aren't in need of any repair, but all the one-story storefronts look bland with their beige paint and dusty window fronts.

I don't remember when everything had become so lifeless. It is as if I blinked one morning and suddenly everything had lost its previous colorful vigor. Quaint quickly turned to boring as monotonous days passed by in a blur. It is shameful, and in a way, I could see my own inner turmoil reflected back to me in the condition of the town.

I remember when I had first taken over as Alpha of the pack from my father. In my young twenties, I had been very hands-on in the remodeling and beautification of the town. It felt like a new park was being put together nearly once a month, and I can recall many occasions of celebrating a new business opening.

Main Street used to be colorful and full of excitement. Restaurants and shops lined the center street with welcoming lights and colorful signs as people bustled in and out from the varying storefronts. While I could still see that most of the buildings were still open and in use, there is a stagnant air throughout the town that hadn't been here a couple of years ago.

I watch my feet as they pad along the sidewalk and silently contemplate if my view of the rest of the town would be the same.

Branching from the main street, a gridlike network runs on either side of the center road. Off to one side of the town, the forest owned by our pack lines the city. Further still, deep within the trees, the Alpha's house resides nestled safely in the heart of the territory. On the other side of town, the commercial area quickly turns into the pack's residential area. Those living closest to town are the higher-ranking officers which included Aiden and his wife, our religious leaders, board members, and top warriors. From there, the residents who work primarily middle-class jobs live in the next section of homes, while the Omega District borders the woods just on the edge of the pack lands.

It is all so familiar, and while I would normally find the familiar comforting, today it feels suffocating.

I continue walking down the sidewalk lost in my thoughts, and Aiden quietly follows me. Our journey is a silent one as neither of us really has anything to discuss with the other. We are both trying to process what had happened this morning and how the past incident would soon change the future.

While Aiden is slightly older than I, he is still considered my closest confidant. As my second-in-command of the pack, he contributes a lot in the realm of helping me maintain the safety of our residents as well as the general upkeep within certain divisions. I have known Aiden for most of my life, although we have been working together for almost eight years. He has been the Beta of the pack right before my father had retired as reigning Alpha and has been vital in helping me understand some of the responsibilities of my newfound position.

Aiden had been born in the pack and had acquired his position as second-in-command the traditional way through the passing of the position from his father. He is an astute man, always putting his responsibility to the pack first. He understands the duty his position held and could often be seen putting business before any kind of pleasure. Logistics come first for Aiden as well as the following of certain protocols, but he is able to hold his position admirably due to these ideologies. His loyalty of service to the pack has gained him an immeasurable amount of respect not only from myself but also from the community he served.

I suddenly feel a hand grab me and realize Aiden is stopping me as I was about to walk past the temple.

While the temple is the traditional term, the building used for worship is very similar to a normal countryside church. White painted paneling that had begun to peel surrounds the structure. The front stoop is similarly weathered, with a long ramp zig-zagging into the front lawn, and a covered terrace giving shade on the front porch right before the two main entry doors. There is also a traditional steeple on the top of the bell tower which rang during ceremonial times or seasons of celebration. The crown jewel of the structure, though, is the large metal crest of the Goddess that hung on the front of the building.

It has been a long time since I have bothered to see the old worship center again and even longer since I contemplated attending a service.

"Are you sure you're ready?" Aiden asks, knowing what going through the doors would mean to me.

I grimly stare at the building, the source of many years of heartache and pain.

"Isn't it obvious?" I ask, numbly, "Today was a punishment for my neglect of the Goddess. I must now go and repent."

Without further thought, I rush up the stairs of the stoop and quickly enter.

The double wood doors bang open, and the sunshine behind me streams into the dimly lit sanctuary. It is almost surprising how very little had changed since I had last stepped through this entrance. The dark hardwood floors that cover the entirety of the sanctuary are scratched and lacked luster. Equally dark pews are lined on either side of the long, center aisle. The seats are cushioned with dark blue fabric, although the color is on the brink of fading and is beginning to wear along the edges.

The cathedral is magnificent. The same dark wood from the floors continues along the walls and in thick columns, paneled intricate archways cover the ceiling. There are tall windows in the back, framing the holy altar, of crafted colored glass that had been lovingly put together by pack members several generations ago.

At the back of the room is the altar that is raised slightly above the rest of the room by a few steps. The priestess stands above the attending members with her entourage of serving maidens. The holy women are all adorned in white robes that are lined with silver, and the dark emblem of the Goddess is worn proudly across all of their chests.

Upon my sudden arrival, everyone in the sanctuary immediately turns around, and loud, audible exclamations of shock echo in the chamber. My presence fills the building as I walk toward the Priestess. Everyone knows how much I detested this building. The service and worship are all a part of the support to the Goddess, whom I had long ago forsaken.

But it wasn't always like this.

I grew up attending the temple and served under the maidens every Sunday morning as my mother used to be a part of these serving women. I followed the Goddess until I was eighteen, volunteering for the construction and restoration of the building. I came to every mass, vigil, and holy day and sang out the rites of praise. I worshiped on the prayer benches until my knees were cramped, and my calves went numb from the time spent mumbling fervent prayers. I did this all for three decades. For thirty years, I was faithful to the Goddess, was a devoted Alpha and servant to her will, and what did I get in return?

Nothing.

I didn't complain when I didn't receive my destined soulmate at the expected age of eighteen. I was content at twenty-five to be a celibate Alpha, devoting myself to the upbringing and betterment of my pack. Then, on the eve of my thirtieth birthday, I had had enough. Declaring in drunken rage obscenities in the Goddess's name and the hoax of serving an image that was merely a decoration in most wolves' homes, I vowed to never step foot in her sanctuary again.

Two years later, I am here for my penance.

When I approach the altar, the Priestess has ceased her preaching and openly gawks at my form. Along with wearing the white robes of the other maidens, the holy leader also wears a dark blue sash and a traditional head covering. Silver cloth is draped over her head and rests lightly just above the tops of her shoulders, the fabric intertwining delicately with her long brunette hair with streaks of gray. Her silver eyes seem to pierce through me as her thin lips slightly part at my arrival. The tight lines around her mouth and eyes slowly begin to soften as her sharp features tried to hide her initial shock.

I immediately drop to my knees, my entire body lay prostrate before her and the altar.

"Oh, holy mother, I have sinned against thee. I request to embark on the journey of repentance for gaining our Mother's favor again."

There is another audible gasp around the sanctuary as I recited the words enacting the observance of millennia-old rites. The Priestess stares at me in horror, and rightly so. The words I had spoken were special. They signaled that the wolf had done something unforgivable, a betrayal of some sort, either to the pack or their mate...

The Priestess quickly comes to her senses and kneels next to me with tears in her eyes. She reaches down to her blue sash and pulls a silver handkerchief from it. Unfolding it carefully, she places it on my forehead.

"With this cloth, as a symbol of our Mother's forever comfort upon her children, I encourage you to seek her mercy, so that you can clear your mind to hear her plan for you."

After the Priestess anoints me with the cloth, I stand with my head bowed making my way over to the side balcony, a small wood gazebo of sorts, where my parents are currently seated. I walk up the steps to the sacred Alpha deck and take my place next to my mother. Tears stream down her cheeks as she lifts a shaking hand to my face. Her words are barely audible through the tremble of her voice.

"What did you *do?*"

BRAYDEN

Sunday 11:19 am

After our morning grocery run, the kids had been quiet while riding in the van, a stark contrast to earlier in the morning, or the entirety of the road trip in general. Instead of screaming at each other, the kids just looked through their windows and silently took in the details of our new town.

It didn't take us long to leave the commercial area and enter the residential zone of the new city. The sprawling neighborhoods, while cute, were a little confusing to navigate. The first streets of homes were relatively impressive. A collection of two-story buildings with sprawling yards made the area seem nice and put together. Behind these homes were similar, yet smaller versions, with paralleling smaller yards. Even farther behind that neighborhood a couple of streets of large one-story houses were built, and even farther still some nice duplexes stood.

We kept going in this same direction for about ten minutes as the houses became smaller, and the beautification became more sparse. There was a point in the drive where there weren't any houses and we were instead met with a stretch of open field lining the road. I became nervous that I might have gotten lost, but just as I began to worry, the sign for the trailer park stood among the overgrown grass on the side of the road.

Turning into our new residence the concrete road became nothing but gravel, and metal trailers were lined next to each other on either side of the dirt road. There were several rows of these small buildings, and behind the last plot thick woods boarded the premises.

After what felt like an eternity—days of travel, endless motel rooms, and even more car-sickness than should ever be humanly possible—I pull up in front of our assigned trailer and park the van right outside our assigned residence.

Almost immediately after parking, the twins jump out of the vehicle and begin to run around the premises. Excited noises soon fill the little yard as they explore every crevice of our new home. Marcus exits a little slower. His eyes were calculating as he looked between his two running siblings and the stuffed van. After a moment of deliberation, the pre-teen pushes his glasses up onto his nose and volunteers to watch the three youngest kids in exchange for not having to help unload.

I nod in agreement to his proposal, and everyone quickly went to work.

Kelsey and I began to tag team the unpacking. With the pain from travel shooting down my left side, it isn't long before I began to drop some of the heavier items. With a sharp glare in my direction and a motherly scowl, Kelsey quickly herds me inside our house before stating that she would be the one to grab the items from the car, and I could start putting the items away.

Our new home is small, very, very small, but it seems safe and clean. The outside of the metal complex looks to have been power-washed recently. There are dents in some of the folds of the plating, and rust lines the bottom edge near the ground, but it looks sturdy enough. Wooden steps lead to the small, faded porch in front of the entrance, and the ripped screen door opens with a loud creak.

The inside is similar in quality to the outside. The carpet is outdated by a few decades. The dark brown pattern flows throughout the main flooring of the living space and into the corresponding two bedrooms. The kitchen is clean although the old appliances looked to be just as old as the floors. After a quick inspection, the amenities are all still working, and none of the pipes are leaking.

There is also some furniture that had been provided, which I was extremely grateful for. A black futon is pushed against the back living room wall, while a small fold-out card table had been set up right beside the kitchen. Both bedrooms also come with a set of bunk beds and closets, which made the rooms feel more dorm-like than home-like.

Altogether, a much better home than where we had come from.

As the morning progressed, I watched through the windows as the other residents came out from the surrounding houses and tentatively made their way over to the kids. These more rugged folk were covered in worn clothes and dirty boots. Lines of age and wear danced across the faces of the adults, no matter the age of those surrounding us. In a way I felt a little better, these people were hard-working and had experienced the struggle of the world around them, maybe even felt the helplessness of hunger and cold similar to us.

I was inside setting down my load of boxes when the friendly group had begun to assemble in our yard. At the approach of the new adults, the kids had stopped playing, and I could see Kels introducing herself and the rest of our siblings.

Stepping outside, I join the little assembly. The twins quickly latch onto my legs, and their giggles can be heard as they peek back and forth from behind me to the strangers. While Marcus stood off to the side, shyly eyeing everyone as Evie squirmed in his arms. Upon my arrival, Kelsey took the liberty of introducing me to the neighbors who had assembled, and I smiled what I hoped was an appreciative smile.

"Hi, I'm Brayden. It's a pleasure to meet you all," I say with genuine happiness at their eagerness to greet us.

I look around the group and am surprised when the once-friendly faces of the surrounding adults slowly seem to dissolve at my greeting. Confusion creeps its way into the eyes of those around us, and the quiet chatter from the crowd quickly becomes silent. It took me a second to register that the confusion from the group had slowly turned into incredulous fear.

The strangers shift their eyes amongst each other before a woman steps out from the circle of people. She doesn't appear to be old, more bordering on middle-aged matron than anything else. Her amber eyes were a little too large on her face, just above a crooked nose and thin lips. She had unruly curls that covered her head and were held together with nothing more than a large clip.

With shaky steps she approaches me, her thin hands wring nervously in front of her, "I'm sorry, sir, but I don't think you're supposed to be here."

Confused by her statement, I chuckle nervously, warily eyeing her and the rest of the group.

"Um, this is trailer fifteen right?" I ask, trying not to show how nervous her comment has made me. For all I know she didn't mean anything negative but was referring to the actual trailer. Maybe we had begun unloading into the wrong residence.

The woman nervously squeezes her fingers in a vice-like grip refusing to meet my eyes, "Uh, yes it is that trailer, but are you sure you belong in the trailer park at all? The park is on the border of the land, so this is the Omega District."

I scan the rest of the crowd and realize everyone seems to agree with the woman. Fear ripples across the bodies of all those present. Most looked shocked that I seemed to be standing in front of them. Incredulousness passed the faces of the crowd, and I noticed some of the men trying to subtly put themselves between us and the direction of the woods that surrounded the park. The rest of the group is on defensive alert with wary eyes scanning us and the area around us.

Friendly smiles are gone.

The welcoming atmosphere is gone.

Courteous and open body language, gone.

I feel myself slowly becoming royally pissed off as I realize what is going on.

"Look, I don't know who you think we are," I grit out specifically eyeing those that have gone protective over their land around us, "but there is absolutely no need to feel as if we are a threat to your little community."

Everyone seems taken aback at my sudden outburst, and the woman immediately shakes her head in indignation. Her round eyes go wide, and her mouth opens and closes in surprise.

"NO!" she immediately gasps out, "That isn't what we meant by–"

"I understand there seems to already be a clique among the residents here, and with all of your defensive positions, it seems you aren't interested in expanding that circle, " I say, as I interrupt her rambling. "Message received, but me and my family have every right to be here as much as the rest of you, and I won't tolerate being forcefully socially secluded!"

I'm fuming and slightly hurt. This morning had already been full of judging stares and harsh treatment, the fact that our neighbors are already trying to distance themselves from us just puts a nail into my emotional coffin.

Kelsey has gone quiet at my defensive response, and the twins have fully hidden behind my legs. Marcus is nowhere to be seen, and I presume he had escaped into the safety of the trailer.

The faces around us paled and maybe even saddened at my response. Something close to pity is felt by the crowd as there is another moment of silence that surrounds us.

One of the men standing among those who have bordered themselves between us and the woods suddenly steps forward and stands next to the woman. The large man is about a decade older than the woman. Stringy hair is hidden beneath his old ball cap, which looks to be in an even more ragged shape than the man. Hard lines surround the man's face, from the corner of his eyes to the folds of his forehead, just above his sun-beaten face. He's around my height or slightly shorter, but his stocky frame doesn't do anything to hinder his presence.

With his dark eyes, he gives the woman an understanding stare. "Mary, why don't you go and get the cookies you had prepared for the newcomers," the man states in a deep voice that had a rough edge to it seemingly weathered with the remnants of age.

The curly-haired woman nods in agreement and takes the opportunity to excuse herself.

With the same impassive look that the man just gave Mary, he looks at me.

44

"I think there's been a misunderstanding," he begins in a slow drawl that has the remnants of an accent. "I'm Paul. It's a pleasure to meet you."

I nod but don't say anything in response, not trusting myself to reply without something snarky.

"Mary wasn't trying to say that you didn't belong here," he slowly begins to explain. "She was more just surprised at the presence of a young family in this area as you're the first to move in, in quite a while."

I take a moment to contemplate his words as I look around the group. All the people surrounding us seem to be middle-aged adults, and I realize that there is, in fact, a lack of children in the area.

I look at Paul's patient face, and my feelings of anger wane as humiliation begins to grow.

"Sorry," I mutter out slightly ashamed at my quick temper. "I didn't mean to jump to conclusions, it was just—"

"There's no need to apologize," the man quickly interrupts, "It seems you've had a hard time getting here, and we're all strangers to you so there was no way for you to know."

The surrounding crowd goes wide-eyed as Paul interrupts my apology, but otherwise remains silent during our transaction.

I give him an appreciative smile at his understanding.

No sooner had we stopped our exchange than I see Mary scurrying over to us at a rapid pace. Her layered skirts fluttered around her feet as her hands carried a paper plate covered in tin foil.

With a small smile, she approaches the group and hands me the baked goods.

"They're just chocolate chip cookies," she says a little embarrassed, "but if you ever need anything, please don't hesitate to ask any of us."

The rest of the group nods in agreement and the welcoming atmosphere from before slowly begins to return.

"We've all been in harsh situations," Paul says, gesturing around the group. "The only reason you're here isn't because where you've come from was easy," he makes eye contact with me and I can't help but swallow thickly at how accurate he has come to our situation. "we're here if you need us."

I'm taken aback by his earnestness but am deeply moved by his sincerity.

With a nod of agreement, and before anyone else can say anything else, I usher the kids inside our new home.

BRAYDEN

Sunday 7:33 pm

The rest of the afternoon and early evening seemed to pass by with a quick succession of mundane routines. It took Kelsey and I a little over an hour to fully unload everything from the van and get the necessities properly put away. After emptying the van, I had called the kids into the house for lunch and, like a stampede, they had raced inside.

The heat from the end of summer afternoon meant all of us were sweating from our varying physical exertions, and everyone was flushed as they came to eat. The three kids sat around the small kitchen table. They were happily chatting amongst themselves as they chugged multiple glasses of water and only paused their guzzling long enough to take greedy handfuls of freshly warmed chicken nuggets.

Off to the side, Evie was content in her chair. The little infant sat in confusion, as she swirled around the ketchup on her plate, before occasionally sticking a red-dyed hand into her mouth.

Kelsey had opted to sit on the futon and quietly munched on the few pieces of food she could get her hands on. Her small form was strewn across the furniture as she lazily reclined against the arm of the chair, and stretched out her legs.

I chose to sit on the floor; hoping the hard floor might bring some relief from the pain coursing through my left side.

My tongue briefly sticks to my mouth as I swallow a large bite from my peanut-butter sandwich.

"Anything you need me to pick up after work for your school tomorrow?" I ask Kelsey after I'm finished chewing.

She looks up from her plate as I talk before looking back down at her food. Her face scrunches in concentration as she seems to debate her answer.

"No, I think I'm good," she responds with a thoughtful look. "I'll pick my books up from the office in the morning, and besides that, I really only need one pencil."

She takes a bite out of one of the nuggets on her plate. "Anything else the school says I need is just a scam," she mutters through her full mouth.

I chuckle, not disagreeing with her.

"Don't let me forget the paperwork that I have to sign for the other gremlins," I say, picking up my cup of water. "If I don't drop those off with them tomorrow I'll be in a lot of trouble."

Kelsey nods her head, watching me as I take a drink. "Noted."

After lunch, the kids had gone back outside and continued to explore the new yard. The evening had quickly approached, and the small bodies of my siblings slowly became tired from all of the day's events. Dinner consisted of much less enthusiasm than lunch, although there was a brief argument over how many chocolate chip cookies everyone was entitled to after eating their portion of vegetables.

Later, the twins had begrudgingly done a rock-paper-scissors contest to see who had to take a bath first while Marcus passively waited for his turn to shower in our one and only bathroom. Evie had a quick rinse-off in the sink, and the rest of the bedtime routine commenced with angry shouts over toothpaste and giggles from pajamas accidentally put on backward.

The baby had gone down almost a half-hour ago, and the middle children were curled on the small futon watching a movie. It wasn't quite time for them to go to sleep yet, but everyone was ready for when their official bedtimes came.

I could vaguely hear the characters talking on the screen as I stand in one of the back bedrooms. Every once in a while I would peek through the doorway to make sure everyone was settling down, and from the droopy eyes and relaxed postures, sleep is quickly approaching.

"Alright, I left a list of all the scenarios that could go wrong on the fridge including all the cures for any of Charlotte's nightmares," I inform Kelsey as I carefully fold my work clothes into my backpack. "Oh! And don't let Charlie have warm milk when he comes out to ask for a drink, he's only allowed to have water. I should be back before Evie is awake and—"

"You act like this is the first time I've dealt with the circus of nighttime," Kelsey interrupts with a playful roll of her eyes.

My younger sister sits on the bottom bunk of her bed. Her legs crisscrossed under her as she mindlessly played with a pillow in her lap. She has changed into a pair of her pajamas, some bright fleece sweatpants, and an oversized screen t-shirt, while her hair is damp from the remnants of the shower she has just taken.

I sigh. "It's not that I don't know that you know how to take care of them Kels, it's that I feel bad that you have to. Especially with your first day at a new school starting tomorrow," I explain, picking up a couple of granola bars off the bed and tossing them into my bag.

She merely shrugs her shoulders as her hands go up and tighten her ponytail.

After Kesley was born, I remember mom, and my life had changed a lot. With another kid, there were suddenly more expenses, more responsibility, and even less time in the day to accomplish everything that needed to be done. Mom was spread thin with a new baby and a four-year-old. The chaos was more, but that meant the loneliness was less. I had immediately felt the protective instincts of brotherhood kick in at such a young age, and as we grew I became more and more determined to make sure Kelsey and the other kids would never have to have the same experiences I did growing up.

While the four youngest don't know the exact details of mom's previous job, Kelsey was never left in the dark.

Kelsey was the closest to me in age, and due to this, I had always felt we had a special bond. Not that we were closer to each than the other siblings, but the relationship with the other kids was just different in a way. Even when mom was alive, I had taken on the role of the second caregiver to the four youngest children. From enacting discipline when mom was at work, to taking care of their everyday needs of food and hygiene, I was always the second adult in the house no matter my actual age.

But Kelsey was different.

While I always kept an eye on her, she was much more independent compared to the rest of our siblings. Her keen eyes were aware of everything that went on in our house–consistently aware of the terrible chaos but never quite old enough to take matters into her own hands. Kelsey adapted to our situation by observing, and offering her input when necessary.

She knew exactly what happened behind closed doors and was even more aware that I took on some of the burdens of working to keep food on the table as more mouths to feed joined the family. In her own way, this made her more protective of me too. Although she couldn't take on responsibility as I could, she had decided a long time ago that taking care of me would be her task in the family.

When I was looking out for the kids and mom, Kelsey looked out for me. When I was too busy trying to keep our family afloat, Kelsey made sure to step in and alleviate the pressure where she could.

I guess we both had to grow up fast.

The teen huffs at my comment. "I'll be fine Bray, if it's too much on me tonight, we can discuss changing the schedule tomorrow. You can't work and watch the kids twenty-four seven. Something has to give," she glares, "and don't think I haven't counted up the hours you've been awake either."

Her dark eyes pierce at me with an edge of arrogance from her scolding, although underneath the iciness of her exterior I could see just how fragile she felt inside.

I shrug, helpless at the last comment. It's not like I want to miss sleep. I would love to pass out on the couch—hell on the kitchen floor—if I could at this very moment, but that is a luxury we couldn't afford. Because Evie is too young for school, someone has to be home with her during the day, and childcare is way out of our modest budget, which leaves the options for working hours to strictly the night shift.

"If there are any panic attacks tonight, do not hesitate to call. I don't give a shit what my boss says, if you call I know it's an emergency and he can suck it," I say, looking her in the eyes as I zip up my backpack.

51

"Stop worrying," Kelsey insists with a stern tone. "You should be more concerned about yourself," she says as she reaches across the bed to toss me a folder full of documents, "you almost forgot your morning sanity."

My eyes widen as I realized I had already closed up my bag and would have forgotten the papers I needed to sign for the kids' school. I send her a grateful smile as I reopen my pack and throw it in the folder.

I smile as I look at the currently glaring high schooler.

Yes, we have a special bond.

Glancing down at my now full backpack, I zip it up, ready for work.

"You know you're the best, right?" I say, gratefully hoping to express the gratitude I feel for her at the moment in just those few words.

She rolls her eyes and arrogantly grins at me. "Yep, now go. You don't want to lose your job on the first day."

BRAYDEN

Sunday 7:58 pm

My new workplace was nice. The building looked like a typical hospital that provided decent medical care. White speckled tiles covered the long hallways and easily echoed the steps of nurses who rushed past. A stray visitor lingered against the plain beige walls, and the smell was a familiar combination of sterile cleaning supplies overlaid with the scent of stale coffee.

Near the entrance, a greeting desk was set up, and I noticed one particular nurse. He was petite with large blue eyes, shaggier brunette hair, and seemed younger than the rest. His timid behavior and shy responses to those around him made him seem friendlier than the other workers, and I quickly decided to approach him.

"Um, excuse me, I'm a new hire here and was wondering where the bathrooms are so I can change into my uniform," I politely ask the brunette, "and if there were personal cubbies, we could put our stuff during our shift?"

The young man looks up at me, startled that I had approached him before he immediately starts blushing.

"Oh, of course, the bathroom is right down the hall," he shyly answers, clearly nervous as his large eyes hesitantly meet mine, "and I'd be happy to introduce you to Dr. Monroe, so he can direct where to put your stuff."

I internally smirk at his behavior and make a note that he was definitely into me. I'm not going to complain as the young staff is clearly adorable and relatively good-looking in a cutesy way; not to mention, I could practically feel the attraction he held for me as he stared at my body.

Yes, he'd be a fun colleague to work with.

With a nod of appreciation, I head down the hall and quickly find the bathroom to change my clothes. The uniform itself is really simple. A white, long-sleeve t-shirt that went under a set of matching white scrubs. It is a crisp look and would be easy to bleach later if anything were to spill on me during my shift.

The only problem I could see is my tattoos.

While the hospital didn't have a policy directly opposing them. I am still a little nervous about what my boss would say. Underneath the thin white material, anyone could see the dark swirling outlines that curved and twisted along my skin in a thick black pattern. They start from the bottom of my wrist, go up to my arm and shoulder, continue down the left side of my chest, and then end on my upper left thigh. Granted, it is harder to make out under the two-layered part of the uniform across my chest, but on my leg and arm, the ornaments are pretty clear.

I step back into the hall and am relieved to see the same young man waiting for me. I immediately begin to approach, and the young nurse starts to nervously shuffle his feet.

"So, I'm Brayden," I say with a kind smile, as I stick my hand out in greeting, "I'm a new hire here. What section do you work in?"

The young man blushes and tentatively takes my hand.

"I'm Travis. I'm a senior and work under the hospital's 18+ program," he quietly mentions, making deliberate efforts to not look me in the eyes, "it allows adult students to intern."

I notice his reluctance at making eye contact and get excited as I realize he's a sub.

There is an art in being able to read potential prey.

Mom used to say that I had an unnaturally keen eye for being able to know a person's exact wants. I was good, no, I had always been great at this skill. The ability to read a person came naturally to me.

Mom treated pleasure as an untapped economic resource, and as her oldest, she found it her duty to hand down her trade to me. After years of teaching, the response was now automatic. Even other field workers, who had been a part of the craft for decades longer than myself, were astonished by my innate intuition.

I was the best because I had never failed at reading someone's desires.

I analyze my new mark. My body instinctively responds to the subtle sexual signals he gives out, the small clues as to what he likes and dislikes–gathering the information of what would make this little mouse thrum. I straighten my shoulders and harden my stance, making sure to give a dominant presence.

Looking at Travis, I am not necessarily looking at a client as that was a part of my past that I was glad to leave behind. No, the little nurse is a definite booty call. Someone I could fuck in the janitor's closet for a quickie a couple of times a week.

Not wanting to scare him, I soften my gaze as I lean forward into his personal space.

"Lead the way," I demand.

Travis shivers at the new change in my actions. Our interaction has turned intimate under my careful guidance.

Hot air suddenly streams down the back of my neck and a deep rumbling shakes my bones. Spinning around, I immediately scowl at the culprit. His tall and dark demeanor, not to mention his unfriendly attitude, is something I wished to never meet again Damien Rockwell.

I can't help but grimace as my attention is locked on his hard and angry face. His eyes are glaring in front of him, and his jaw is set in a seemingly permanent snarl. The lines on his neck and shoulders spread his shirt taught as his muscles seem to be straining and flexing against the fabric.

My attention is fully on Damien, but he is focused on the little nurse, Travis.

"You'll do well to remember your place pup!" Damien hoarsely seethes to the shaking brunette, "I will be having a word with Dr. Monroe on your behavior. This is your only warning," he all but barks out in anger.

Towering over the cowering figure, the older man's fists are clenched at his sides, looking as if he's restraining himself from hitting the younger worker.

Travis is a sweating mess as his small form trembles in place. He vehemently nods his head, mumbling apologies, and all but runs away.

I frown at his quick departure. My disdain for Damien grows, as I realize I'll need to now start my intimate interaction from square one the next time I see Travis.

Although my future seduction seems to be the least of my worries as now that Travis is gone, the large man's attention finds itself solely on me.

Once we're alone, Damien's entire demeanor seems to change. His once firm face immediately lifts into a bright smile that stretches painfully across the center of his face. The once tense shoulders loosen up, and his clenched hands have relaxed at his sides; although they seem to twitch in my direction every couple of seconds.

The sudden change spooks me more than his previous display of anger.

Beaming down at me, he leans into my personal space trying to press our bodies as close to each other as possible. I can feel the heat from his body, and his shirt almost touches my skin. The close proximity feels overbearing, and the scent of his strong cologne immediately begins to overwhelm my senses, stinging my nose.

"Hi!" he happily greets me. All his teeth are on display in a very toothy smile.

Disgusted by the man's unabashed play at familiarity, I simply give a curt nod and take a step back.

"Mr. Rockwell," I reply, coldly.

I don't want any confusion about my opinion of the man, although I am trying my hardest to remain cordial, especially when future co-workers are potentially watching. Therefore, I simply keep my back straight, and my face passive; blank from any negative emotion.

The giant's smile falls at both my step back and short answer before his beaming face morphs back into a scowl.

"So you're fine to get close to a stranger but refuse a closer greeting to someone who you've already met?" he growls out, taking a step forward. His face crinkles with anger and the veins on his arms begin to show, as a new round of anger begins to take over his features.

Annoyed by his dizzying mood swings, I decide to just put an end to our conversation.

"I don't mind getting closer to someone who I'm trying to fuck," I say with the same passive tone as my previous reply.

The intention with that one-liner was to stun him with my unabashed nature and give me time to walk away, or maybe he'd be somewhat embarrassed and realize how rude he was being by trying to butt into a conversation he wasn't invited to join in the first place.

At my declaration, the once bustling hospital floor stills. The shuffling of feet stops. The rolling of carts stops. No sound could be heard, and everyone freezes.

Shocked by the reaction, I carefully take a look around, openly gawking at the frozen room.

"What the hell..."

I'm smashed into a hard chest, and I can't help but feel a sense of deja vu.

Aw, fuck not again.

Damien's arms are tightly wrapped around me. The same rumbling I had heard earlier this morning is back again only this time ten-fold. The reverberations echoes in my ears, and the sound is even more amplified around the tiled lobby. The man's chest feels like a brick wall, and his beefy arms are snaked around my torso in a vice-like hold.

It is hard to focus on anything else as his tight grip only becomes tighter.

Every inch of me is touching this monster of a man. I could feel the heat of his skin seeping through his thin dress shirt, and my nose is squished against him.

And the shakes.

His whole body feels as if it is shaking, rattling me to the core.

From a distance, I could hear men yelling, which causes the beast's grip to become tighter around me.

I am trying to get away, I really am, but his goddamn grip is too much. No matter how much I thrash, kick, or yell into his chest, all my struggling only seems to make his grip on me tighter.

"Let me go! Let me go!" I repeat over and over in frustration.

His grip becomes painful. I can feel my ribs shift slightly, and my breathing comes out in gasps. It's not too long before I can't even yell at the man, and my only focus is instead on trying to breathe.

I feel several other hands try to dislodge his grip but to no avail. The top of my head becomes warm, and I can feel his mouth nuzzling into my hair as he mumbles incoherently, and it only takes a couple of seconds for his affection to move to my neck.

Damien's mouth scrapes against my neck as his mumbling becomes a little clearer: "Mine, mine, mine..."

My cries for help begin to match my internal screaming as I beg him to let me go.

My vision starts to go dark around the edges. My lungs are screaming at me. Just when I think my ribs will crack, I hear another voice say something indecipherable to the monster before his grip loosens around me.

I instantly take the opportunity to shove his arms off of me, jumping out of his reach.

Losing my balance, I desperately try to grasp for something stable. My flailing hand finds the stone wall of the building. Leaning against the cool surface, I begin coughing and hacking as my lungs overcompensate from the previous loss of air. I'm gulping oxygen like a fish out of water, not able to focus on anything else other than trying to stop the burning in my lungs and ribs. My vision continues to darken and I feel myself panic. From the quick breaths to the high adrenaline of being held, I can feel myself start to hyperventilate, on the verge of a full-blown panic attack.

The shouting, the banging, the shouting, the banging!

I cover my ears with my hands as memories forcefully take over, and I'm suddenly five years old again...

...I flinched, the sound of another scream piercing the flimsy barrier of the hall closet door. My current sanctuary – a precarious pile of dirty laundry shoved into the back – offered little real protection. The rickety folding doors wouldn't stop a determined toddler, let alone... him. But some illusions of safety were better than none.

Another shout ripped through the thin walls, followed by a sickening thud that rattled my makeshift hideout. I jam a stray shirt between my teeth, desperate to stifle the sobs that claw their way up my throat. My face felt slick and hot, a disgusting mask of old and new tears. The argument raged on, a brutal soundtrack to my terror.

"You fucking bitch! This was a baby trap, wasn't it?" His voice, thick with rage, slammed into me, punctuated by another heavy thud.

You said you wanted a family with her; a treacherous voice whispered in my memory.

"I swear, I've been on the pill!" Mom's weak gasp was barely audible above the shouting.

You said you'd give him anything as long as he'd take us away from here; the hopeful echo returned, laced with bitter irony.

"I have a goddamn family of fifteen years! You think I'm going to give that up for your whore ass?" He spat out, the words choked with a guttural sound.

You said you'd leave them for her; the broken promise hung heavy in the air.

"I'm sorry! Just tell me what you want. We can fix this!" Mom's desperate plea ended in a sharp smack that reverberates through the small apartment.

You said you wanted nothing but her devotion; a naive belief shattered by reality.

"There's nothing to fix. You were a cheap ride, and I'm done with my test drive." The sickening thud of a body hitting the floor followed his cruel dismissal.

A tremor ran through me as the slow, heavy stomp of boots drew closer to my hiding place. The sliver of light beneath the closet door dims as his shadow fell across it, a looming darkness that stole what little comfort I had.

"Don't you fucking touch him!" Mom's desperate scream coincided with the sudden flood of light as the closet doors are yanked open.

You said you'd always protect me; the final, devastating whisper...

...I can't tell if my eyes are open, or is it just dark because my hands are over my face? Is that air I'm breathing or have my lungs stopped working? Does anyone else feel like there's an earthquake happening or is that just my own shakes? Is it just me or is anyone else sweating and freezing at the same time?

There is a lot of noise in the background, and it sounds kind of like a fight has broken out. All the voices in the room are muddling together.

"...he said he'd fuck another..." "...calm down Alpha..." "...he's injured..." "...didn't mean to..." "...let me hold him..." "...he'll phase if we force him to leave the room..." "...MINE!"

Unable to see or comprehend what is happening, I suddenly feel a set of hands grab either side of my face, forcing my head up. The same hands begin to poke and prod at different areas on my sides, although the shock I feel prevents me from moving.

While the hands continue their searching, I can't help but wonder when I ended up on the floor.

"The air was knocked out of him with a high probability of bruised ribs. He's in the beginning stages of hyperventilation, and on the verge of a panic attack," I hear a gentle voice say in a business tone.

The same voice begins counting back from a hundred and the same hands from before hold me steady. The rhythmic and calm voice gives me some stability in my teetering world. By the time the voice reaches twenty, my breathing is almost back to normal.

Looking up, I realize I must have made quite a scene as many of the staff and nurses surround me with various pieces of medical equipment and nervous looks on their faces. I also notice that the room has gone mostly quiet again.

Taking a look at the man in front of me, I see he's in his late forties. Graying black hair and a pair of glasses adorn his round face. He's wearing a lab coat, and upon further inspection, I see his name tag that says "Dr. Monroe."

I instantly tense realizing that the previously unknown man is my new boss, and he is witnessing me have a breakdown before work has even started. Trying to appear nonchalant, I immediately stand up ignoring the dizziness that rips through my skull. The doctor quickly follows suit, not removing his hands.

"Take it easy and don't move too fast," he gently orders as he looks at me with concern.

I begin to mentally curse as I try to cool my features, embarrassed my boss was here during such a scene. Although Dr. Monroe doesn't look too angry, it could just be medical professionalism.

Getting a little more stable on my feet, I peer around the wall of hospital staff and instantly feel my body tense. Behind the crowd stands a very distraught Damien Rockwell.

His hair is completely in disarray, standing in every direction on top of his head. The once nicely pressed shirt and pants are now wrinkled and ripped beyond repair. The man's face is almost ashen instead of his normal tan complexion, and his eyes are full of worry, solely focused on me.

Noticing that I'm looking his way, Damien immediately starts making his way toward me. My eyes widen with fear at his approach, and I can feel my heart rate begin to pick back up. I subconsciously lean towards the doctor as the terror of having to be within the proximity of the psycho in front of me scares me to my core.

Seeing my reaction, Damien freezes and looks to be on the verge of tears. His arms are slightly outstretched towards me, only to quickly drop back to his side.

There's a heavy silence as nobody makes a move.

Dr. Monroe clears his throat from beside me, and I whip my head towards him, thankful for the distraction.

"Why don't we take this to the privacy of my office?"

BRAYDEN

Sunday 8:38 pm

I was currently sitting in a square armchair. My back was straight as a board, and my hands were folded meekly in my lap.

Dr. Monroe's office was organized, and everything was neatly put in its place. From the books lining one of his back shelves to the perfectly symmetrical degrees hanging on his wall, there was precision in all his decor. He was currently sitting in front of me, behind the fortitude of his large wooden desk. Looking at me slightly over the rim of his glasses and tapping his fingers.

This was supposed to be a protocol meeting. He was to give me the specifics of how the hospital and go over the policies of their establishment. Then we would end with a brief tour of the floor I had access to. Instead, the room was filled with a high amount of tension; the air was thick enough that it was almost hard to breathe.

The creaking of a chair to my right reminded me why the night had taken a turn.

Mr. Rockwell was also sitting, but instead of matching my stoic demeanor, the man kept moving. First, the tapping of his feet. Then, the crossing and uncrossing of his legs. Next, the shifting of his hips, as if he couldn't get comfortable in his chair. One arm up on the armchair, then back down, and then the other arm up on the other armchair. His eyes were shifting uncontrollably, glancing everywhere around the room...until finally landing on me.

For a split second, I'm caught. Damien locks eyes with me and his whole body ceases its previous fidgeting. If possible, the air becomes even thicker with tension as neither of us looks away.

The clearing of a throat has me looking at Dr. Monroe, and a slight whine is heard the minute I turn my attention away from the man seated next to me.

"I would like to begin this meeting with the clarification that its purpose is to clear up some previous misunderstandings," Dr. Monroe's voice is firm but very soft, almost as if he's scared of either me or Damien cracking if he speaks too loud. The doctor sits back in his office chair putting on the facade of ease, but his posture is rigid, and his fingers seem to have a slight shake to them.

The nerves my boss was trying to hide slightly confused me. If anyone should be shaking it should be me.

Dr. Monroe turns his attention to me, "Brayden, what is said in this meeting is strictly confidential. If any of this information reaches the public, it could be detrimental to the hospital and all of our work here."

I'm slightly taken aback by his statement, and my eyes widen in shock.

"Uh, of course, sir," I mumble, more curious as to what is happening.

Sending a quick glance to Damien, I see his focus is off of me for the first time and instead on the doctor. His eyes seem to be sending piercing daggers at the man across the desk, and if I were to guess, there is a warning to his glare.

I am not the only one who seemed to notice this intensity as Dr. Monroe once again clears his throat and adjusts in his seat.

"A few weeks ago Mr. Rockwell was in an accident," the doctor says with a slight tremble in his voice, "More specifically, he was attacked by a wild wolf. While the physical injuries have healed, he has retained some… mental injuries that we are still working through."

My eyes widen into saucers.

Holy Shit!

I turn my astonished gaze to Mr. Rockwell. His body is rigid, and he refuses to look at me. Instead, he stares straight ahead, muscles coiled tensely while his hands are clenched tightly at his sides. He seems angry as if he's trying to physically restrain himself from attacking the doctor.

I feel a tweaking in my consciousness as I realize the man must be embarrassed about having to share such private information with a complete stranger.

Still kind of shocked, I blurt out the first thing that came to my mind.

"You lost a fight with a wolf and fucking lived!?" I ask.

Damien immediately turns to me. His eyes flashing with anger and his chest heaving with furious breaths, "I did NOT lose-"

"That's really impressive," I murmured, lost in thought.

While I knew he was fit for a man and in incredible shape, a wolf is still a beast, a wild anomaly of nature with its only intent on killing whatever gets in its way. The fact that he was in an altercation with one and lived is a feat, and according to the doctor, he didn't even have any physical injuries! At that realization, I am suddenly all too aware of my own abundant scars, and the fabric on my left side seems to suddenly scratch at the sensitive skin.

My comment seems to have taken Damien by surprise as he sits up a little straighter in his chair, and his previous anger at my comment immediately vanishes.

"You're impressed?" he asks, his eyes imploring me with veiled excitement hidden behind a flickering smile. His body is not as defensive as when the doctor is talking and is now leaning towards me.

Noticing his eagerness to hear my reaction, I realize that I should have just kept my mouth shut. With one positive comment, I don't want Damien to get the wrong impression.

"I'm impressed by the fact that your body didn't stop ticking. I'm not impressed by you," I state rather shortly, turning back to Dr. Monroe just as Damien's body seems to deflate.

"I'm sorry, that situation sounds unfortunate, but I do not see why that has anything to do with me," I say, curtly to Dr. Monroe, trying to ride the line of being respectful to my boss, while also not being pushed around.

"As I said earlier, Mr. Rockwell's condition is now mostly mental," my boss replies, "You could say we are working through the last remnants of symptoms akin to PTSD. Mr. Rockwell's triggers include but are not limited to someone or something new to his otherwise normal life and/or routine," Dr. Monroe pauses and gives me a pointed look.

I don't meet his eyes as I realize that my new presence in the town would definitely qualify as something new to Damien's routine.

"After being triggered, symptoms such as agitation or anxiety are displayed through a range of sudden acts of anger, domination of those around him, all the way to even extreme affection," Dr. Monroe continues.

He seems rather uncomfortable. While all of his answers make sense, I can't help but feel as if I'm watching a newscaster repeat a story, as if he is reading or reciting a script, but the whole time he has been looking at me.

I shift uncomfortably in my seat. My eyes dart between an increasingly stressed doctor and Damien, who now seems to be back to intently staring at my boss. It is creepy, almost as if there was an unbreakable tether connecting the two men, ike an invisible line that Damien was somehow using to control the actions of the doctor.

Great, now sleep deprivation has caused me to hallucinate.

I give my head a subtle shake, clearing my mind.

"Listen, I'm sorry about the accident, I truly am, but I have kids, and things like this can't keep happening," I say sternly, "my two five-year-olds had to be reassured the mean man from the store wasn't going to find us before they would get into their beds."

I see Damien flinch from the corner of my eyes.

"I grew up on the roughest part of streets and haven't been physically assaulted in one day as many times as I have on my first day in this city," I pause and turn to Damien, locking eyes with him, "I sympathize with your condition and process of healing, but if I'm a major trigger and hindering your recovery, I think it would be in both our best interests for me to file a restraining order so that we can keep as much distance from each other as possible."

I think this is a great compromise, but apparently, Damien does not. After my declaration, I notice his whole body goes rigid and almost seems to expand, as if his muscles were straining and swollen after a long workout. His hands grip the arms of the chair in a death hold and the whiter his knuckles become, the more sure I am that I could hear the cracking of wood. He also refuses to look at me. Instead, his clenched jaw and intense stare are once again directed to poor Dr. Monroe.

The man sits behind his desk, and while his professionalism has remained strong throughout the meeting, he was starting to break. His hands and arms are now visibly quivering, and sweat had broken out on his forehead. As if straining under some unseen weight, Dr. Monroe looked at me.

"Uh, well I don't think that is such a good idea," he weakly mutters out, "you see, Mr. Rockwell is a very important and prominent figure in our community. As his condition has not been made public, it would be in our best interest to not cause negative attention to be drawn to him."

I scoff, trying really hard not to be offended, or show my anger at the obvious favoritism to the treatment of a local versus an outsider.

The blatant discrimination made my blood boil, but what else could I expect from this small town's rural dynamic?

"Not trying to be rude or disrespectful, but how important could you actually be?" I ask, trying to keep my voice steady as I seethe.

Dr. Monroe visibly flinches as if struck with a jolt of pain, and the same low growling that seems to have followed me around town can be heard again. I begin looking around in confusion as I only see a distressed doctor and intense Damien.

"Hey did anyone else hear—"

"Mr. Rockwell is the owner of the hospital!" Dr. Monroe gasps.

I'm once again stunned into silence as my wide eyes seem to assess Damien for the first time.

Fuck.

The guy I had an altercation with was my boss. The guy who I accused of being high is supposed to sign my paychecks. The guy who caught me trying to get with a future colleague is my fucking superior's superior!

I try to hide how nervous I am and warily keep my eyes on Damien. As if sensing my stare, he turns to me, and I hear an audible sigh of relief from the doctor once the larger man's focus changes to me.

"Not only that, but Mr. Rockwell also owns most of the businesses in town and is considered the town's Mayor," Dr. Monroe adds in a tired voice.

Double Fuck.

"However," the doctor continues, "while I appreciate your reason for wanting to limit your time with Mr. Rockwell, it would actually be in his recovery's best interest to see you. Since he is triggered by anything new, getting more familiar and acquainted with your presence would certainly be going in the right direction."

I see Damien smirk at this comment, and if I didn't know any better I'd say he was trying to hide a laugh, as if the doctor had just made an inside joke that I'm not a part of.

I frown slightly at this information and am not pleased that both of my bosses seem to be in favor of me spending more time with the large, scary man.

"Yeah, I can see what you mean," I relent, not quite sure what my other options are. If I deny, I would probably be fired, and the whole domino effect of me not having a job is too much to think about.

Damien leans forward towards me.

"I would like to formally apologize for my previous behavior. Our only encounters together have been what can only be described as negative, at best. I think you will make a great asset

71

to this hospital, and you and your family will be a wonderful addition to our community," he says, reaching his hand toward me, obviously intending for me to shake it.

I eye his hand warily, not comforted by the fact that the man seems to believe all of his wrongs can be forgotten with a handshake.

With much reluctance, I find myself slowly extending my own hand in acceptance. Before I get it even a few inches from my body, it is eagerly engulfed by the beast in front of me. Damien's eyes lock with my wary ones.

Our handshake lasts for a few seconds...then a few more...

I try to subtly pull my hand, but Damien seems content to just stare at me while keeping my hand captive. Just before I really start struggling, Dr. Monroe loudly claps his hands together, startling both Damien and me, which allows me to get my hand back into my possession.

"Since that's settled, on with the tour!" the doctor excitedly exclaims.

DAMIEN

Sunday 11:01 pm

I watch as my sweet mate saunters out of the office. Even with his back turned, he is unable to hide his irritation and displeasure at the outcome of the meeting. Sighing, I turn to Monroe, who looks as exhausted as I feel. While his clothes are still pristine, he couldn't hide his physical exhaustion. His cheeks are flushed, and perspiration drips down the side of his face. The poor man has gone through something extreme and rarely done.

Through heightened intuition, the ability to hear one's blood pressure or breathing pattern, and sense of smell in order to better determine one's natural pheromones and emotions, it is no wonder why the myth of werewolves has become one of reading minds. Although as an Alpha werewolf, I have the unique ability to infiltrate pack members' minds for a short duration. I used this ability the moment I saw my mate's face and sent his image to every pack member, so they were aware of their Luna. There is no such thing as open mind-links or talking to each other through our thoughts. It is not so much as open telepathy, but more of a skill through pack mentality that has evolved through the evolutionary DNA of werewolves. Wolves in general can sense a lot more about an individual than humans can.

Especially if you are the Alpha.

As an Alpha, part of my job is to strengthen the pack, both physically and mentally. Therefore, brief snippets such as a mental picture of an area, a telling of a location, or a warning of danger, is all the information I can invade into the minds of my pack–up to a short distance. However, what I did today with doctor Monroe is more extreme, even in the world of supernatural beings.

The original intent of the meeting was to calm Brayden down and reassure him I was normal. However, after sitting down for a short while, both the doctor and I could smell my mate's growing apprehension at my presence and palpitating heartbeat. I had resigned to letting Dr. Monroe lead the meeting but quickly regretted it the more he kept talking. After only a few seconds of smelling the stench of fear emanating from my mate's disheveled state, my instincts took over. Reaching through my animalistic connection to Dr. Monroe, I pulled at the ancient strings that connected us as pack members and leaders. I will give it to the doctor; he did a good job at not appearing startled when he felt the connection being tampered with. I coaxed the words through his mouth and guided what he was saying. This took a lot of extreme focus on my part, and this type of use of pack bonds was very rarely used as such control and authority over pack members' links was a powerful skill. Not all Alpha's are even able to do it, especially for the duration of the conversation we just had, but I was desperate.

And now I'm exhausted.

I slowly stand up and feel the extent to which the bond control has taken on me as my joints are stiff seemingly everywhere. Raising my hand, I rub the back of my neck and try to stretch out my sore limbs, feeling as though my whole body has been straining, holding up an immense amount of weight for the time of our meeting. Monroe is also shaky as he stands, heavily leaning on his desk as he slowly walks around to where I'm standing.

Gazing at the door to the office solemnly, I can't help but feel somewhat excited about the tour and being close to Brayden but also nervous as I know I will have to no doubt endure the cold shoulder treatment, and that shit hurts coming from your soulmate.

"Did you really have to tell him I lost to another fucking wolf?!" I growl lowly to Monroe, angry enough by that particular comment to let my Alpha pressure drape over him. For whatever reason, while I had tried to push the word "bear" through his mouth, the doctor had fought back, and the word "wolf" came out instead.

He has the decency to flinch and bares his neck to me while his eyes remain on the carpet of his floor. The top of his graying head bowed to me.

"I'm sorry Alpha, my intent with the wolf attack was not for him to think you weaker than the opponent. Rather, I thought that if wolf vocabulary accidentally slipped among pack members while he was around, he would have no reason to be suspicious, and the reason they were talking about nearby wild wolves." He gasps out, no doubt ashamed at having disobeyed a direct order.

I grunt, not liking that his reasoning makes sense, and not at all in the mood to acknowledge him.

"Let's just get on with the tour." I gruffly grit out already heading to the door and opening it.

Stepping out of the office, my nose is immediately assaulted by the smell of harsh cleaning chemicals and the sounds of people hurriedly moving about, but I pay them no mind as I search for my mate. Darting my eyes around, all I can see are pack members working and the usual pushing of hospital carts. I become more desperate as I can't smell Brayden's delectable scent, and my shoes squeak against the floor as I begin turning around to catch a glimpse of him. Finally, I see a familiar head of golden locks exit from the gift store. Not noticing me yet, I take the rare opportunity to just gaze at my mate.

Unlike this morning with his disheveled appearance, he looks much better this evening as it is abundantly obvious a shower had done him absolute wonders. His hair is now a bright golden yellow, cut in such a way to accentuate the soft texture of his locks, that seem to have been styled by nothing more than his fingers running through the top of his head a few times. And his eyes, by Goddess his eyes! Who knew such an icy stare could be found on any living thing. Frozen blue lakes that could stop anyone in their tracks surrounded by thick, dark lashes. While there are still the remnants of bags under his eyes, his skin does not hold the same pallor as this morning. No, much like his hair, his lean form is covered in a light tan, adding to his alluring overall golden form.

Coming out of my stupor, I embarrassingly realize that my little Adonis is standing right in front of me and looking at me with a rather bored expression. Caught off guard by his sudden closeness, I reflexively inhale in surprise and am rewarded with a lungful of his addicting scent. He quirks a perfect eyebrow in response to my reaction before rolling his eyes.

"I take it you didn't hear me?" He states, more than asks in a monotone voice.

Hear what?! He voluntarily said something to me, and I missed it?!

"I...uh, yeah...I mean..." I stutter, trying to think of something that will show that I am engaged with him, yet didn't hear what he said.

Apparently not interested in my rambling, Brayden turns and begins walking away from me.

"I said the tour is starting, and Dr. Monroe said you should come along."

The tour has gone fairly well. Although anytime in the presence of my mate is a good time, it could definitely be going better. So far, Brayden has made sure to stick close to Dr. Monroe giving the man his full attention as every inch of the hospital is being explained to him. While I'm thankful to the doctor for giving us the full tour, as normally new hires would only be shown the sections they're working in, I can't help but feel jealous at Brayden's undivided attention being elsewhere.

Walking through the halls, I have been content to be slightly behind Brayden as he and the doctor engage in conversation about different protocols and policies. However, as the evening continues, I become more and more agitated. Every now and then, I'll try to engage in what they are talking about, as I am the owner of the establishment, but very quickly the conversation becomes one between just me and the doctor. After entering the conversation, Brayden will immediately fall silent, refusing to participate.

But now it is different.

Now is my chance to have a normal conversation with him.

Dr. Monroe is currently off to the side of the hall, talking to a nurse who needed his immediate attention on how to handle a critical patient. Leaving just me and my mate standing nearly shoulder to shoulder in the otherwise silent corridor.

I straighten myself and look over at the perfect young man next to me.

"So, I see you have some tattoos?" I ask, having noticed the dark pattern underneath the thin lining of his shirt and pants. And how could I not? The entire time he has walked in front of me, the intricate lines tracing along his delicate skin taunted me in a torturous way. My eyes have greedily looked over the pattern wondering just where it began, and how far down it stopped on the parts of my mate's body that I couldn't see.

Couldn't see yet.

Brayden absentmindedly looks around the hall, although it is painfully obvious that there is nothing to distract his line of sight, and he is just avoiding looking at me.

"Yeah." He mumbles, his pink lips barely moving as the rest of his body tries to angle itself slightly away from me.

I try to appear nonchalant and put my hands in my pockets. My back straightened and chest-puffing out slightly, straining against my shirt, hoping to get Brayden's attention on my looks. While I have never been vain, I do know I'm in good shape and wouldn't mind at *least* a millisecond of appreciation from my mate for my physique.

"Do they mean anything?" I ask.

Isn't that what young kids like doing nowadays, discussing tattoos?

Hoping this is a safe topic, while simultaneously running my fingers through my hair hoping he notices my arms, or hair, or face, or *anything*!

"Excuse me." Brayden shortly replies.

I begin to panic. The topic must be a personal one. Do I apologize? No, that would look desperate. Do I push? No, that would be overbearing. Do I change the question? No, that just seems ditzy.

By the time I make up my mind, I notice Brayden is no longer standing next to me. Immediate panic engulfs my body, and I uncontrollably begin to release my dominating Alpha pressure to the surrounding area. This is an instinctual action; if there was an attacker in my close vicinity, such a dominating presence of aggressive pheromones would be enough to knock them to the ground. I see Dr. Monroe and the nurse lean against the wall under my dominance, but I refuse to stop and nervously continue to scan the area. Almost as soon as I do, I let up my presence as I see Brayden kneeling next to a little girl who is sitting outside a lab with her parents. I quickly recognize the family as regular ranking pack members and the owners of the town's small hardware store.

Quietly making my way over, I hear Brayden gently talking to the little girl.

"What? They said you *had* to get your blood drawn. Did they not tell you that you *get* to?" He asks with false surprise.

The girl looks at him in confusion. The still-wet tear stains along her flushed round cheeks make it obvious that she is not happy about being there. With one pudgy hand, she wipes at her dark eyes, not taking her gaze off my mate.

"What do you mean *get* to?" She asks in a soft, trembling voice, her lip quivering slightly.

Brayden gives a blinding smile and leans in closer as if he was about to tell her a secret, "Well, only some people are chosen to get their blood drawn, and that's because the person always gets a prize when it's over."

Her once wet eyes take on a new light, and she sits up a little straighter.

Noticing her excitement at a prize, Brayden digs into his pocket and pulls out a handful of brightly colored keychains with a small stuffed animal attached to them. He holds his hand out to the little girl as she greedily shuffles through her options before deciding on a sparkly, purple cat. Quickly grabbing her new toy, she hugs it to her chest as her parents give continued thanks to Brayden for calming her down.

Watching the family get up and leave, I can't help but stare at my mate in awe.

"That was really impressive how you handled her." I praise him, knowing full well this incident will be reported to other pack members, and his positive reputation as Luna will quickly spread.

Brayden merely shrugs his shoulders, "I didn't know if I would be handling kids tonight or not, but I stopped at the gift shop just in case. The five I have always love a prize when they're doing something they don't want to, so I figured it might work with other kids." While he tries to brush off my compliment, he isn't able to hide the bright flush steadily creeping up his neck until reaching to the top of his high cheekbones. Very nearly touching his luscious pink lips.

Oh Goddess, let me fuck you!

BRAYDEN

Monday 4:46 am

My first shift at the hospital had thankfully been pretty mundane . That is, if you ignored my evening run-in with Mr. Rockwell, whose presence during the tour was about as welcome as a sunburn on vacation.

God, that man was a walking, talking migraine.

While Dr. Monroe droned on about hallways that already blurred together, policies that seemed designed to confuse, procedures that felt like ancient rituals, and the occasional name that immediately evaporated from my brain, Damien was a persistent, breathing distraction.

It was like he was playing some bizarre game of tag, only the goal was to see how intimately he could occupy my personal space without actually touching me. I'd be trying to absorb vital information about, say, the location of the linen closet, only to feel the radiating heat of his oversized body practically branding my back.

Shuffling to the other side of Dr. Monroe became my new Olympic sport, and while the game of cat and mouse annoyed the shit out of me, it was nothing compared to Mr. Rockwell's *eyes*.

Mr. Rockwell had bestowed upon me a look that could melt glaciers and probably curdle milk. Bedroom eyes. The full, unadulterated, "I want to ravish you on these dirty tiles" stare.

I snorted, the sound echoing in the quiet corner of my brain. Please. I've been fluent in the language of lust since I was twelve. Damien's attempt was so hilariously obvious it took all my willpower not to burst out laughing in his face.

Okay, fine, the man was objectively attractive. Built like a brick shithouse in all the right places, tanned, dark-haired – the whole dominant bad-boy cliché package. But a good body was about as rare as pigeons in Times Square, a lesson Mom had inadvertently drilled into us with her... varied clientele. Money and status? Those were usually the opening lines to getting a free drink, not a panty-dropper.

However, everyone knew a good client was a reliable one. If this was a year ago, and wintertime, and our family was starving for more food and heat, Mr. Rockwell's inconsistencies and sporadic mood shifts would be enough of a turn-off for me to not add him to my rota.

Then there was the virgin thing. It practically radiated off him. The way he moved, spoke, even breathed – it was like a giant, neon sign screaming "INEXPERIENCED!" What was a grown-ass man doing still rocking the V-card? Maybe that church on the edge of town had a stricter membership policy than I thought.

Mom's golden rule: never tap a cherry. Too much potential for clinginess, unrealistic expectations, or, let's be honest, someone getting accidentally maimed during some ill-advised exotic roleplay without a safe word. So, yeah, Damien was about as appealing as a root canal without anesthesia. Attractive now, maybe, but the dude was aging.

The least he could offer was some damn experience.

His lingering gaze, though, that familiar weight of being appraised, stirred that old, unwanted instinct. Even though I wasn't actively turning tricks anymore, the whore training Mom had inadvertently instilled ran deep. Spotting a mark, knowing how to become what they desired in bed – it was practically muscle memory. My childhood was a fucking circus.

Mom's mantra: sex was never about you. You were a blank canvas, ready to be painted with their desires. Pleasure was permissible, but secondary. Survival was the primary objective. It was a lesson etched into my bones, leaving me with this constant, low-level hum of feeling like I was perpetually in some awkward, unspoken foreplay with everyone I met.

Sex is not personal. Sex is not emotional. Sex is used for survival.

My shoulders droop as my mind repeats that old mantra of Mom's. I'd hoped a new town meant a new me, a chance to build a life I could actually be proud of, to shed this skin of being seen as… less.

Apparently, optimism was a luxury I couldn't afford.

I'm not saying that I wouldn't be interested in sleeping around. I did make a move on Travis this evening, but mutually agreeing to a no-strings-attached sex partner is different from strict objectification or perceived ownership over my body. But that was a far cry from the possessive vibe I was getting from Mr. Rockwell, and ownership was one thing I was officially done with.

Shaking off the unwelcome wave of self-pity, I trudged towards the flickering neon glow of a diner. My shift had ended half an hour ago, and the clock was inching towards five a.m.

Barely enough time to grab a questionable cup of coffee before the kid-wrangling stress began. I had debated sleeping in the van for that time as I didn't want to accidentally wake any of the kids upon me entering the trailer. But the luxury of sleep once again evaded me as I remembered the pile of papers that needed to be signed for the children's varying school administrations.

The diner's facade screamed "local institution." Worn wood that had seen better decades, a slightly off-kilter charm that probably didn't entice tourists, but clearly catered to the regulars. The buzzing neon sign in the window declared they were open, even at this ungodly hour.

I needed caffeine…by the gallons.

Walking through the glass door, a little bell alerts the restaurant to my presence. Taking a look around, I instantly see some faux leather booths lining the front of the diner, partially blocking their windows. Their faded maroon coloring, almost as terrible of a design choice as the faded green carpet tiles, clashed with the chrome sit-in bar that opens to a cutout window, letting customers see into the kitchen.

Seeing as I am currently the only customer here at such an early hour, I take a seat in the farthest booth away from the door and sit closest to the full wall window. It's still dark outside, and there isn't anyone walking along the sidewalks yet.

Maybe after dawn breaks, more people will show up.

Backpack dumped on the seat beside me, I wrestle out the dreaded paperwork. A dejected sigh escapes my lips as the towering pile of forms mocked me from the plastic tabletop. After a few illegible signatures, the sheer emptiness of the diner begins to feel less peaceful and more… ominous. The only sound is the rustling of my bureaucratic burden.

Where the hell was the coffee fairy?

A quick scan reveals a plump, older woman stationed near the counter. My eyebrows shoot up. She is already staring at me, a dirty blue apron clinging to her form, a dingy silver name tag glinting under the harsh fluorescent lights. Just standing there, hands clasped and wrung, a silent, unsettling vigil. We lock eyes for a beat too long before I, thoroughly bewildered, give her a hesitant wave over.

Instantly, she practically sprints over, a blinding smile plastered across her face.

Is she seriously waiting for permission to approach?

"Hi! My name is Marge, and I'm the owner of this diner!" she chirps, the smile stretching a little too wide, a little too enthusiastically. "Welcome to the Old Oak Cafe, what do I have the honor of serving you today?"

My eyes are still wide with surprise at her strange behavior, and I find myself leaning back a little bit to put some distance between us.

"Uh, I'll just take a pot of coffee, please," I manage, my internal alarm bells starting to ding.

"Of course, sir! Coming right up! Please don't hesitate to ask if you need anything at all while you're here. It would be my absolute pleasure to serve you!" she gushes, before practically teleporting back towards the kitchen.

What in the actual fuck?

Small-town hospitality? Maybe. But the sheer, unadulterated eagerness feels… off. My cynical brain immediately jumps to the conclusion of an impending, aggressively suggested tip.

Before I could even contemplate the mysteries of Marge's overzealous welcome, a shadow falls across my table.

"Is that seat taken?" a soft, woman's voice inquires.

Before I can answer the woman, she quickly makes up her own mind and sits in the booth across from me.

"Uh, sure..." I mumble, not quite knowing what to do as she is already sitting. Unless I wanted to make a scene, I guess she could sit here.

She is older, looking to be in her late fifties. Her long hair drapes elegantly over her shoulders, the color now turning what could be considered grayer than what appears to have been black. Her face is pretty, in a mature way. Wrinkles line her face but do nothing to take away from her high cheekbones or otherwise blemish-free skin. Her skin is darker, with equally dark eyes to match. She is petite in frame, shorter, and almost willowy.

There is something familiar about her.

Figuring I have the right to ignore her, I resume my task of painstakingly filling out forms. I quickly get lost in the rhythm of answering repetitive questions such as the age of the kids, height, etc. After what feels like a short while, a steaming white mug is placed on the edge of the current paper I'm reading. Looking up in confusion, I see that the woman across from me had pushed a filled coffee mug in my direction and is currently filling one for herself.

"Marge came over a few minutes ago, but you were so engrossed in your work that I told her to just set it down." The mysterious woman says with a soft smile.

I squint my eyes at her, not yet understanding what her motive is.

"I'm sorry, but are we supposed to know each other?" I ask, rather bluntly.

The woman gives a long sip of her mug before, once again, giving me a soft smile with her pale lips. "Not yet, but I would like to get to know you a little better. I go by many names and titles in this town, but for now, you can just call me Lou."

I give her a bored look, "I don't know why this couldn't have been a handshake rather than you inviting yourself to my table and drinking my coffee." I say with a slight edge to my voice.

Undeterred, Lou simply takes a sip of her drink while raising a dark eyebrow before answering.

I flinch, my carefully constructed wall of indifference cracking. My eyes dart away from hers, finding a safer focus in the inky blackness beyond the diner window.

"So next you're going to pull some therapist bullshit about seeing my 'inner turmoil' from across the room?" I ask, my voice trying for a casual roll but landing somewhere closer to a nervous tremor. I stubbornly refuse to meet her gaze.

I hear her sigh, and in my mind's eye, I can picture that same soft, almost maternal smile gracing her lips. "If something is broken, it implies a state of irreparable damage. No, Brayden," she says gently, using my name with a familiarity that both unnerves and oddly comforts me, "I didn't recognize something broken."

I startle, a jolt running through me as her hand, surprisingly warm and firm, closes over mine on the tabletop. My breath hitches in my throat.

"I recognized something strong," she continues, her voice low and steady, "because true strength is only visible when it's under immense strain."

Lou seems to sense my internal flinch, the ingrained reflex to pull away from any perceived vulnerability. Her hand gently retracts, leaving a phantom warmth behind.

"I know what you might be thinking – that this is some elaborate sales pitch for my services. But in all my years, I've never asked for payment from those who've chosen to confide in me." Her gaze is direct, unwavering. "If you'd like, I'd like to offer you some of my time. I'm still licensed, so anything you say will stay between us." A quiet chuckle escapes her lips. "And as you can see, my morning is rather... open."

I'm stunned into a silence that stretches, thick and heavy. A tightness begins to bloom in my chest, and against my will, my eyes prick with unshed tears. How long had it been since someone had truly *seen* the strain? How long since someone hadn't tried to diagnose and fix the 'broken' parts, but had simply... acknowledged the weight? How long since someone had genuinely cared?

The carefully constructed dam of my composure finally gives way, and the words begin to tumble out, a torrent of unspoken burdens finding their release.

Once the dam opened, there was no holding back. I don't know how long I talked, what I started talking about first, or what I eventually ended on. Time continued to flow in waves matching the torrent of emotions that seeped out of me. I'd find myself speaking fast, stuttering over words during some moments, while other times a long stretch of silence would weigh down on the table as my thoughts would engulf me in past memories.

I clear my throat, a rough, involuntary sound, and swipe at the stray tears that had betrayed my carefully-constructed composure. I hadn't meant to crack that much, to let so much of the past bleed into the present. Now, the awkward silence hangs heavy, and I brace myself for the inevitable recoil.

Grabbing my mug, I tip back the remaining coffee which offers a small, but welcome, burn as it slides down my throat.

"So," I ask, forcing a chuckle that sounds more like a strangled crow, "you're still sticking with the 'not broken' diagnosis?"

Lou is sitting across from me, her presence a calm anchor in my internal storm. To my surprise, that same soft, knowing gaze hasn't wavered. She looks as poised and serene as when she'd first settled into the booth.

"Brayden," she begins, her tone gentle but firm, "I appreciate you feeling comfortable enough to share some of your past with me." She pauses, her eyes finally leaving mine to rest on the worn

Formica tabletop, as if contemplating something profound etched within its surface.

A familiar instinct kicks in, and I felt myself retreating, the hardened walls I'd painstakingly built rising once more.

Idiot. Fucking idiot.

This woman is a complete stranger. I haven't even bothered to check for a laminated "Dr." on her name tag before spilling my guts. Any second now, she'd be making a hasty exit, ready to recount the sob story of the pathetic newcomer to her undoubtedly more well-adjusted friends.

"I couldn't help but notice," she continues, her gaze returning to mine, perceptive and unwavering, "that you kept referring to your mother in the past tense."

I offer no response. What was there to say? Her observation isn't wrong, but the topic of Mom's passing remains a raw nerve, a minefield I never quite know how to navigate.

Lou takes another delicate sip from her mug, the clinking of ceramic against ceramic the only sound in the quiet diner. "I've also heard that a young gentleman with five children recently moved into town. I want you to know that my specialty is helping children work through their trauma. While I won't presume their experiences mirror yours, the loss of a parent is a significant trauma at any age."

She reaches into her purse, a worn leather satchel, and hands me a simple white business card.

"Think it over," she says, her voice offering quiet reassurance, "but that's my number for if or when you decide they need some counseling. I'll make room in my schedule, no questions asked."

A weight I hadn't even registered carrying suddenly lifts, a phantom burden released into the quiet air. The offer of genuine, selfless help for my family feels so foreign, so unexpected, that my brain struggles to process it. And she is right. The kids *are* struggling.

Evie, once a champion sleeper, now wakes every few hours, her small cries echoing the emptiness Mom had left behind. Charlotte is plagued by night terrors, vivid scenarios of our fractured family being torn apart further, finding solace only in rigid routines. Charlie, bless his superhero-obsessed heart, refuses any clothing without a logo and occasionally insists on leaving the house in full costume during meltdowns. Marcus's sudden aversion to certain foods is a silent scream of anxiety, and Kelsey has retreated into a shell so thick I barely heard her voice anymore.

I've been doing my best, patching their wounds with my own frayed edges, but I am no damn professional. I know, with a certainty that settles deep in my bones, that I would be calling Lou.

"And," she adds, her gaze softening further, "if you'd like, I would also like to continue seeing you. To work through some of what we've touched on today, or anything else you feel comfortable sharing."

I consider it for a beat, the warmth of the coffee mug a small comfort in my suddenly vulnerable state. I pour myself another cup, the dark liquid swirling like the thoughts in my head.

"Well," I say, attempting a casual shrug that hopefully masked the sudden surge of something akin to hope, "the coffee here isn't terrible. So, yeah. I'll probably swing by again after my shift tomorrow." I don't want to appear too eager, too desperate for the lifeline she was offering, but the thought of turning her down feels inexplicably wrong.

A genuine smile finally breaks through Lou's composed demeanor, reaching her kind eyes. "Then," she says, a quiet promise in her voice, "I'll see you tomorrow."

BRAYDEN

Thursday 11:33 am

It didn't take long for the six of us to stumble into something resembling a routine in Rocky Falls. After the chaotic move-in on Sunday and my equally chaotic first shift that night, Monday dawned with the glorious promise of the kids' first day of school. That morning was a special kind of hell, a symphony of tears, misplaced homework, and frantic searches for forgotten gym shoes, and I spent the better part of the day playing a frantic shuttle service with Evie as I ferried forgotten necessities to various school buildings.

The next couple of days thankfully mellowed out. Mornings devolved into a slightly less chaotic circus, and I even managed to wrestle open most of the boxes while tackling the ever-growing list of household chores.

But today, today had been rough. The kind of difficulty that made me call it quits by eleven and decide that Evie and I desperately needed some fresh air – and a visit to Kelsey during her lunch break.

It is now the glorious midday hour of Thursday, and I find myself walking down the quiet halls of a stale-smelling high school. The fluorescent lights hum with a lonely buzz, casting long, skeletal shadows down the deserted high-school hallway. It is well past dismissal, the usual teenage cacophony replaced by an unnerving silence that amplifies the echoes of my lone footsteps. Each click of my worn sneakers against the linoleum feels significant, a solitary rhythm in the stillness.

Most of the hallway doors are shut, locked until the following period, all but one open classroom door. Very briefly my eyes glance into the room, and my feet involuntarily stop their movement.

The interior is bathed in the pale afternoon light filtering through the dusty windows. Rows of empty desks sit in regimented lines, their surfaces bare and silent. A forgotten textbook lays open on one, its pages ruffled by a nonexistent breeze. The scene, so ordinary and yet so devoid of life, snags something in my chest. It isn't the emptiness itself, but the *potential* within that emptiness – the echoes of youthful energy, the murmur of voices, the weight of unspoken anxieties – that suddenly twists my gut. The mundane image flickers, the edges blurring, and the sterile quiet of the hallway begins to warp, the hum of the lights morphing into a different, more oppressive sound.

I find myself returning to senior year…

…The sterile air of the classroom suddenly felt thick and suffocating.

I was perched on an unforgiving plastic chair, the expanse of my Physics teacher's cluttered desk a vast chasm between us. Between juggling extra shifts at the club to keep our meager finances afloat and the relentless training schedule for track, I guess a few… other things had slipped through the cracks.

"Brayden," Mr. Henderson said, his voice carrying a weary weight that mirrored my own internal dread, "you and I both know this isn't good."

I was trying to project an air of nonchalant concern, but inside, a full-blown panic attack was staging a hostile takeover. This year, track had been my laser focus, my Hail Mary for a scholarship, a far more attainable goal than anything purely academic. I wasn't a *terrible* student, but straight A's were a foreign language to my transcript.

But *this*… this was a five-alarm fire. The sheet of paper clutched in my trembling hands screamed its failure in a bold, accusatory red F.

Failing Physics. Not just some elective, but a goddamn *required* class for graduation. And with senior year's final semester ticking down like a doomsday clock…

"I… uh… are you sure this is my grade?" I stammered, a pathetic sliver of hope clinging to the possibility of a clerical error. "I thought I was… holding steady at a C-." Please, please let there be time to fix this catastrophic screw-up.

Mr. Henderson's sigh was the sound of my dwindling hope being slowly deflated. "You were, Brayden. Until you took the final exam."

My stomach plummeted, a lead weight dragging down my insides. My gaze locked onto the worn fabric on my thighs, as the pressure in the room continued to build, gluing me down into my seat.

"Look, I know you're not a bad student," Mr. Henderson continued, his tone surprisingly calm amidst my internal chaos. "I've actually spoken with some of your other teachers, and your overall average is a solid B." The squeak of his chair against the linoleum punctuated his words.

"I also know," he added, his steps slow and deliberate as he rounded the desk, the echo of his worn shoes against the tiled floor growing closer, "that you and a group of your friends have been accepted into the same college."

My hands, already clammy, began to tremble more noticeably in my lap. I could feel the subtle shift in the air, a creeping unease settling over me. The atmosphere continued to press me deeper into my seat. Invisible ropes seemed to tighten around my chest the more he talked.

"And lastly, Brayden," he murmured, his hot breath ghosting against the back of my neck, sending a shiver of something cold and deeply unsettling down my spine. "I also know that I wouldn't be the first in this school to have... heard whispers... about the particular skills pertaining to your... 'family business'."

My throat tightened. My heart hammered against my ribs. The air in the small classroom felt thick and heavy, charged with an unspoken understanding, a dangerous acknowledgment. A predator watching its prey succumb to its fate.

He had complete control. I was trapped.

"So," Mr. Henderson whispered, his voice low and conspiratorial, "how about you and I make a deal?"...

...Opening the doors, the familiar cacophony of cafeteria chatter and the distinct scent of greasy food immediately overwhelms my senses. Stepping through the double doors, I scan the crowded room until my eyes land on a familiar figure hunched over by herself in the back corner. With Evie balanced on my hip and a bag of tacos clutched in my other hand, I begin to navigate my way through the maze of tables and bustling students.

I try to ignore the way the noise level in the cafeteria seems to diminish with each table I pass. I mean, I am well aware that my high school days are behind me, but I hadn't anticipated being enough of an anomaly to silence an entire room upon entry. I am only nineteen, for shit's sake. Although, with the big two-oh looming on the horizon, maybe my coolness factor isn't as potent as I liked to believe? Do I look like one of those tragically weird parents awkwardly visiting their kids? I certainly hope not.

In my mind, I am channeling older brother, not awkward dad. I had even attempted to tie my whole ensemble together with a pair of dark sunglasses.

Ah, that's it!

Realizing my sunglasses are still down over my eyes, I quickly push them up on my head.

There, I bet that's what is so weird.

My embarrassing mistake rectified, I approach Kelsey from behind. I notice that her earbuds are firmly in place, effectively blocking out the surrounding chaos. Seizing the opportunity for some classic sibling torment, I reach out with my free hand and deliver a swift pinch to her side.

"Ahhh!" she shrieks, whirling around and swatting my hand with surprising force. Her eyes are wide with startled panic, and strands of her dark hair peek out from her gray hoodie in a frazzled mess. Her reaction is even more satisfying than I anticipated.

I begin to laugh my ass off, struggling to maintain my balance with Evie on my hip and avoid dropping the precious bag of food.

Kelsey's cheeks flame with embarrassment. Her brown eyes narrow with contempt, and her mouth twists into a deep scowl.

"What the hell, Brayden!" she spits out, her hands balled into fists at her sides.

I try to catch my breath, but the laughter has me painfully hunched over. I have missed this back-and-forth with Kels. Being the closest in age, we used to engage in the typical older-sibling dynamic. Teasing and annoying her was practically a cherished tradition. But in the last few months, we have both been forced to shoulder the responsibilities of semi-parents. This return to our familiar banter, this light teasing, feels surprisingly good.

Just as she looks ready to take a swing at me, I quickly hold up the bag of fast food as a peace offering.

"Wait! I came bearing gifts!" I yell, using the paper bag as a makeshift shield.

Kels's arm freezes mid-air, her squinty gaze shifting from my face to the enticing aroma emanating from the bag. With a swift motion, she snatches the bag for herself.

I give her a taunting smile before joining her at her table, gently settling Evie onto my knee and bouncing her slightly.

"Yours are the tacos, and mine is the cheese quesadilla," I announce, while Evie decides to stick my fingers into her mouth.

Kels locates her tacos and tosses the quesadilla my way before eagerly digging in.

"So, what, you just missed my sparkling presence so much you decided to bring me tacos?" she asks, her mouth partially full.

"You wish," I retort with a mouth full of sticky baby fingers, "-No, today, while I was attempting the monumental task of laundry, the ancient washing machine decided to stage a water revolt."

I sigh, the memory of the morning's soggy chaos still vivid. None of the trailers have built-in laundry facilities; instead, we have a small, slightly dilapidated communal building. I had foolishly tried to cram a week's worth of clothes into one wash, and the aging machine had overloaded.

Kelsey starts laughing, and I frowned, now finding myself on the receiving end of her teasing.

"It's not funny! The whole damn room was flooded, and Evie kept trying to drink the dirty floor water. So, naturally, I had to make a heroic dash to rescue her, only to trip over a rogue bottle of detergent, turning the floor into a slip-n-slide," I explained. "Apparently the Landlord was called, and he has a plumber coming out to fix it later this evening."

She smiles at me from across the table, a mischievous glint in her eyes. "So, a taco remedy then?"

"Basically," I chuckle, digging into my lunch with one hand. Before I could even take a bite, Evie begins trying to stand on my leg, her tiny hands reaching for my food. I gently try to push her back down, but she responds with a high-pitched squeal as I dare to pull the quesadilla out of her reach. Sighing, I begin tearing off small, manageable chunks and feeding them to her.

"Does Lou have any idea what she's walking into tomorrow?" Kels asks, her gaze pointedly fixed on the little devil currently occupying my lap.

I nod, as I continue to hand Evie the food.

My mornings with Lou had become a surprisingly welcome routine this week. I genuinely liked her, and she seemed to possess an uncanny ability to understand me in ways that sometimes even I couldn't articulate. Because of this connection, I had tentatively suggested that she meet the kids. Wanting to ease them into the idea and avoid any intimidation, she had casually proposed that we all go over to her house for dinner. That way, the kids could get familiar with her in a relaxed setting before any formal therapy sessions. I had warned her countless times that inviting my siblings over, especially in the evening, was akin to releasing a pack of uncaged wild animals, but she had simply laughed it off, claiming she was more than ready to have her house full again.

Famous last words.

"Are you actually going to have the kids see her?" Kels asks, her gaze not quite meeting mine. I knew what she was really asking, but I decided to answer the question she had voiced first.

"I think so. Tomorrow's dinner is essentially a chemistry test to ensure there's a good connection between the kids and her. But seeing as she's the only young child therapist in this area who doesn't look like they moonlight as a taxidermist, I'm not overly worried about her handling them," I say, continuing to tear apart my now half-eaten lunch for the awaiting mouth of the infant. "But that doesn't mean that you have to like her." Kels finally looks up at me, a flicker of something hopeful in her eyes.

"You're not going to force me to see her?" she asks, the relief evident in her voice.

"No," I say, treading lightly, "I am not going to make you see Lou if, for whatever reason, you don't connect with her. But I am going to say that I think seeing a therapist would be beneficial. So, if Lou isn't your cup of tea, we'll find someone who is."

Kels looks away for a moment, seeming to mull over my words, before offering a soft nod.

"Okay, that sounds fair," she agrees, finally meeting my eyes.

I let out a breath I hadn't realized I had been holding. While I have somewhat gotten the hang of being the "parent" to the rest of the kids, I never feel like I hold that same authority over Kelsey. With us being so close in age, we have always acted more like siblings and team caretakers when Mom was out. Adjusting to this new dynamic has been challenging, but overall, we have managed to find a pretty good balance.

All of a sudden, I feel teeth digging into my right hand.

"OWW!" I yelled as instant pain enveloped my hand.

Looking down, I see Evie happily munching on the side of my palm. Apparently, I had taken too long to give her more pieces of the quesadilla, and she was letting her starvation be known. I quickly try to use my left hand to gently squeeze her cheeks and release the pressure from her jaw.

"Evie, let go! No biting!" I tell her, as the little gremlin has the audacity to glare up at me.

When I am finally able to pry her mouth open, she lets out a frustrated squeal of her own and grits her tiny teeth at me.

Not one to be outdone by an infant, I bare my teeth at her in what I hoped was a slightly menacing grimace. "Don't even start with me, little girl. My bite is much bigger than yours." She remains completely unfazed and instead giggles at my now undoubtedly goofy expression, which is supposed to be slightly intimidating.

I hear Kels chuckling across the table, thoroughly amused by my inability to intimidate a fifteen-month-old.

But I couldn't help but notice that that was the only sound I could hear.

Looking up, I turn to view the rest of the cafeteria and see that every single student has stopped talking and is staring directly at us—not just a few curious glances, but all eyes in the cafeteria are glued to our table. And not a single person is saying a thing. I also notice that several of the students seem frozen mid-step in our direction as if a couple of them had been sprinting over but had suddenly stopped.

Not taking my eyes off the unnervingly silent crowd, I lean closer to Kelsey. "Uh," I whisper, a prickle of unease crawling up my spine, "is that normal?"

BRAYDEN

Thursday 11:45 am

Another moment of silence hangs heavy in the air as the frozen crowd continues their unwavering stares. Then, as abruptly as it began, the strange stillness dissipates, and everyone seems to snap back into their previous conversations and activities.

"Maybe they heard you were gonna do a strip show?" Kels quips, a mischievous glint in her eyes as she tries to inject some levity into the bizarre situation.

I give a dry, humorless laugh. "Bitch, do *not* joke about testing my lack of inhibitions, because it doesn't take much to break what little resolve I do have."

My gaze drifts towards the corner of the bustling cafeteria, where a brightly lit soda machine hums invitingly. The thought of a sugary, caffeinated energy drink suddenly sounds incredibly appealing. Scooping up Evie, who was still happily gnawing on her fist, I deposit her onto Kelsey's lap.

"Here, take the beast. I'm going to quickly grab an energy drink," I tell her, already digging into the depths of my pocket for my wallet.

Kels shoots me a glare. "How many energy drinks have you had today, Brayden?"

I offer a nonchalant shrug. "This is only my second one."

Her glare intensifies.

I sigh, the guilt gnawing at me. "My second *this hour*," I mumble under my breath.

Her eyes widen in anger. "Brayden! You're going to give yourself a heart attack if you don't slow down!" she scolds, her voice a low hiss.

I just wave off her concern as I stand up, not wanting to get into another argument about my poor sleeping habits or newfound addiction to caffeine.

The last few months I had really increased my intake of caffeine products as my time for sleep had slowly been diminishing. Kels has tried to offer help, or provide me with supplements, but what I really needed is more time. There just never seems to be enough time in the day to do all the jobs I am currently doing. If I could just clone another one of me, then maybe I could finally get some sleep, or having someone else able to take on a part of the parenting load, would be ideal.

I begin to slowly saunter across the expansive cafeteria floor towards the soda machine and carefully weave my way through the numerous round tables scattered throughout the room. It is a typical high school cafeteria. The clatter and clanging of the food service line on one side and the dreary puke-ish brown of the painted cinder blocks lined the other. The only real pops of color comes from the familiar brightly colored plastic seating, a stark contrast to the otherwise dull and utilitarian space.

I also couldn't help but notice that each large, round table seems to be occupied by a distinct clique, a silent testament to the social hierarchy of high school. This last observation tugs at a string of sadness within me as I realize it likely meant Kelsey hasn't yet found her own niche. While she is generally content in her own company, it is always nice to navigate the choppy waters of being an outsider with someone else by your side.

Unlike my initial entrance, everyone now seems engrossed in their own conversations, and I reach my destination without further incident. It doesn't take long to locate the sugary, caffeinated elixir I crave. I pull out a crumpled dollar bill and eagerly insert it into the machine. While I wait for the satisfying whir and clunk of my drink being dispensed, I notice a tempting display of peanut butter crackers and briefly debate whether or not to indulge. Considering Evie had effectively devoured my lunch, my own stomach is beginning to rumble in protest. Glancing back at my wallet, I realize with a sinking feeling that I didn't have another dollar bill.

Guess it is just going to be another meal of pure, unadulterated caffeine then.

The sputtering sound of the machine catches my attention, and I watch with dismay as my dollar bill is promptly rejected.

Goddamn it!

Taking the bill back, I meticulously try to smooth out any creases or wrinkles before carefully attempting to slide it back into the slot.

It goes in, but my drink remains stubbornly out of reach. The machine whirrs and clicks mockingly, but nothing is dispensed.

Fuck, it just stole my money!

I groan in frustration, knowing full well that Kelsey never carries cash. Looking around the crowded cafeteria, I am pleasantly surprised to spot a familiar face sitting at a table not too far from me. Without much more thought, I quickly walk over, offering a friendly smile.

"Hey, Travis!" I say with a casual wave. The younger man's eyes instantly widen in surprise at my approach.

Over the past few days, Travis and I have worked several shifts together and have gotten to know each other reasonably well. I have quickly discerned that he was naturally timid but rather vocal in the fact that he enjoys my company.

As I draw closer to his table, I notice that his group of friends also seems taken aback by my presence, and an awkward silence descends over their conversation.

"O-oh, hey Lu-Brayden," he stammers shyly, his eyes nervously darting around the room. His pupils are wide, and a familiar blush begins to creep up his cheeks.

"Listen, the soda machine over there just ate my dollar," I explain, gesturing vaguely behind me. "You wouldn't happen to have four quarters on you, would you? I can pay you back at work tonight."

His mouth opens and closes in a silent expression of shock before he frantically begins digging into his pocket and pulling out his wallet. He shuffles through the contents for a moment, his movements becoming more frantic as his search appears to be fruitless.

"I don't have any," he finally says, his gaze shifting to those seated around him.

"Damn it," I mutter under my breath, shooting a frustrated glare at the machine. First no lunch, now no caffeine. This day is rapidly spiraling, and I am going to need something significantly stronger than a soda by this afternoon.

"Alright man, thanks anyway," I reply, turning my attention back to Travis. My eyes widen in surprise as I notice not only

Travis's open wallet lying on the table, but all the other students sitting with him have also begun searching through their own. A flurry of overlapping, nervous chatter fills the air, making it difficult to follow any single thread of conversation.

"Don't have enough... I only have three dimes... what if I throw in my six pennies... it took money from *him* of all people..."

Shocked by the unexpected commotion I suddenly caused, I quickly try to diffuse the anxious atmosphere.

"Uh, guys, it's totally fine. I don't need a drink that bad..." My attempt at reassurance is abruptly interrupted when one of the girls at the table stands up with surprising speed and quickly runs out of the cafeteria.

Shock quickly morphs into worry at her hasty departure. "Is she okay?" I ask, my confusion growing with each passing second.

"What brings you two here today, Brayden?" Travis asks, completely ignoring my previous question. It taks me a moment to register the abrupt and rather bizarre change in topic.

"Oh, uh, I'm here visiting my little sister," I explain, gesturing towards the back of the cafeteria where Kelsey is still wrangling Evie.

He turns around to look in the direction I have indicated, and the other students at the table follow suit before turning back to face me.

"Kelsey's your sister?" he asks, his voice laced with disbelief. Murmuring ripples through the group once more.

"The new girl... thought she was a nobody... no one's even approached her yet... heard she was rejected from the photography club for being human... whose idea was it to ignore her... hope we don't get in trouble for not reaching out yet..."

"Yeah, by about four years, and the baby she's holding is our youngest sister," I reply, trying to make sense of their strange reactions.

"But you don't look anything alike," he blurts out, his tone bordering on defensive.

I merely shrug. "We're half-siblings."

Before he could inquire any further, the doors to the cafeteria burst open with a loud bang, and the girl, who had dashed out earlier, re-enters, accompanied by an older man. The gentleman appears to be in his early sixties with scraggly white hair clinging precariously to his mostly bald head. Round glasses perch on his small nose, making his beady eyes look even smaller on his otherwise large and chubby face. He is dressed in a dark brown suit and is panting as if he had been running in his formal work attire.

The two of them quickly approach the table where I am standing, and the short, stout man positions himself directly in front of me. He is breathing heavily and quickly grabs a pristine white pocket-handkerchief to dab at his profusely sweating forehead.

"Uh, I am Principal Eisenhower. It's a pleasure to meet you, sir," the aging man stammers, offering a slight, awkward bend at the waist.

"Likewise," I reply, completely bewildered as to why the school principal is addressing me. My first thought is that I was somehow in trouble. Some schools require visitors to obtain a pass before entering the building.

Shit, I hadn't even thought to grab one earlier!

To my utter surprise, the principal instead digs into his pocket and pulls out a crisp dollar bill.

"I was informed by a student that one of our vending machines was not functioning properly," he explains, extending the dollar bill towards me. "I just wanted to personally apologize and assure you that our school strives to portray a certain image of efficiency and service. The negligence in failing to promptly fix that machine is by no means representative of how we conduct our school. So please, accept this dollar as appropriate compensation for the inconvenience."

Oh, oh boy. Please, let the earth open up and swallow me whole right now.

"Uh, it's fine," I stammer, my hand awkwardly coming up to rub the back of my neck. "Things like this happen all the time." I try to downplay the situation and subtly shuffle away, eyeing his outstretched dollar bill with a mixture of contempt and sheer awkwardness. "You can keep it. I don't need it that bad."

I mean, technically, I *did* need it, considering the machine had just stolen my last dollar, but if accepting it means prolonging this increasingly bizarre interaction, then going without a caffeine fix is a small price to pay.

The principal's eyes widen with a hint of panic at my obvious discomfort. "Oh, I didn't mean any offense by this! I am just trying to-"

"Hey Brayden, I think Evie is ready to go," Kelsey's voice cuts through the awkwardness like a knife.

I spin around to see Kels standing right behind me. Looking down at her arms, Evie appears perfectly content, happily still chewing on her own hand. I meet Kelsey's gaze, and she subtly tries to shift her eyes back and forth between the flustered principal and the seemingly innocent baby.

"Oh... OH!" My eyes widen as the realization dawns on me, she is giving me a golden opportunity to make a swift exit. "Yeah, you know, it's almost her nap time, and I completely lost track of time." I quickly ramble, swiftly gathering Evie back into my arms. Turning back to the principal, I offer a respectful nod.

107

"Mr. Eisenhower, it was a pleasure to meet you, but I really should be going now," I say, already fully turning away from him.

"Wait-" he desperately yells after me, still clutching the offending dollar bill.

I lean over and gave Kelsey a quick side hug. "I'll see you after school. Try not to do anything I did in high school." She abruptly shrugs me off with a scoff, before I begin to speed-walk out of the cafeteria, the principal's bewildered calls fading behind me.

BRAYDEN

Thursday 6:50pm

"No, don't let him get me!"

"Stop! Stop, I surrender!"

"AHHHH!" Charlotte's delighted shriek pierces the tranquil evening air.

"Hahahaha, Kelsey help us!" Charlotte's plea echoes across the lawn as I swoop her up, hoisting her high above my head. With a swift, practiced maneuver, I pin her against my chest with one arm, my other hand already zeroing in on her ticklish sides. A torrent of high-pitched laughter and squeals erupts from her small form.

From her relaxed position across the lawn, Kelsey lazily glances our way before returning her attention to the crawling infant on the ground. "You're all on your own over there, I'm officially on baby duty," she declares, her tone implying a complete lack of sympathy for Charlotte's plight.

Suddenly, a small but determined weight slams into my back, knocking the breath from my lungs. The unexpected impact causes me to stumble, my knees hitting the soft grass. As I gasp for air and struggle to regain my balance, Charlotte seizes the opportunity to try and make her escape.

"I got him, Charlotte, run!" Marcus yells directly into my ear, his hands trying with surprising strength to push me closer to the ground. My back protests against the onslaught, but my grip on Charlotte remains firm, for now.

From my side, I feel another set of smaller hands joining Marcus's efforts, just as earnest in their mission to bring about my downfall.

"Yeah, we got him! Run!" Charlie encourages, now shoving his entire shoulder into my side.

With the combined efforts of the two younger boys successfully distracting me, Charlotte sees her chance. With a final push against my chest, she wriggles free and darts away, her giggles trailing behind her.

The boys erupt in triumphant yells as she ran, and I finally succumb to their combined weight as I collapse into the soft grass. My own laughter joins their victorious shouts as their small bodies topple me.

It has been a truly idyllic evening. Dinner is finished, the remnants of the day's warmth still lingering in the air as the sun dips towards the horizon, painting the sky in soft hues of pink and orange. Scattered across the lawn, the first of the night's fireflies blinks into existence, their tiny lights dancing in the twilight, accompanied by the soothing chirping of crickets in the background. A gentle coolness is beginning to creep into the air, a welcome contrast to the day's heat.

It is magnificent.

Kelsey is quietly occupied with Evie near the front door of our humble abode, patiently guiding our youngest sibling in her clumsy pursuit of the wandering fireflies. Holding Evie's small hands, Kelsey practically lifts her by her arms, helping her reach for the fleeting lights. Occasionally, a firefly would land on Kelsey's hand, which she would then gently try to offer to Evie, only to be met with a startled scream at the touch of the tiny insect, quickly followed by excited squeals for more once it had flown away.

The twins, Marcus, and I have engaged in a lively game that is a chaotic blend of tag and wrestling. We have been chasing each other across the yard for what felt like hours, sometimes sprinting, other times simply rolling around in the grass in fits of laughter. The four of us are thoroughly covered in dirt, our hands and feet coated in a fine layer of earth from our playful skirmishes. Vivid grass stains adorn all our clothes, and the twins even sport streaks of green across their foreheads. Everyone's hair is a dry, tangled mess, sticking out in all directions with stray blades of grass and other debris caught in the knots. The kids' cheeks are flushed a healthy red, their sweaty smiles punctuated by the happy pants of exertion.

Even with my old injuries rearing their ugly head, the usual chains of pain, forever tightening around my bones. A normally heinous reminder of forbidden memories, couldn't dampen the night.

It is one of those precious moments I desperately wish I could freeze in time, or even better, carefully preserve and tuck away so that when the inevitable hardships of life strike again, I could revisit this simple scene of peace and pure familial love.

Startled, I whirl around to see a large figure lumbering towards me at an astonishing speed. The setting sun casts long shadows behind him, making it difficult to discern his features, but his silhouette holds a vague familiarity. As the man drew nearer, recognition dawns, and my eyes widened in shock.

"Uh, good evening, Mr. Thompson," I say awkwardly. I had only met the man once, and frankly, that was more than enough for my liking. While he had never been outwardly rude to me or the kids, his direct affiliation with Mr. Rockwell is a glaring red flag, prompting me to maintain a healthy distance.

As he closed the gap, his features become clearer. His towering frame is clad in what appears to be sturdy work jeans and a short-sleeved button-down shirt. His long hair is pulled back neatly from his face in a short, low ponytail.

Standing directly in front of me, I notice his eyes flick rapidly from my face to the dense woods bordering the trailer park behind me.

"Why do you live here?" he asks abruptly, his gaze fixed on the perimeter of the lot, not meeting mine.

Taken aback by his blunt question, I struggle to find an appropriate response. "Uh… excuse me?" I ask, my voice taking on a defensive edge at the man's abrasive tone.

"I said I didn't know you lived here," he repeats, his dark eyes finally snapping to mine.

"Oh, yeah, we've been here almost a week now," I offer with a nervous chuckle, trying to mask my embarrassment at my sharp initial response. "What, uh, brings you here?"

Mr. Thompson, or Aiden as I vaguely remember his name, gestures towards the dilapidated communal building. "There was an accident in the communal building, and I had to come here to meet with the plumber."

My eyes widen slightly. "O-oh yeah?" I ask, trying to inject a note of surprise into my voice. "Are you the landlord?"

Aiden shakes his head. "No, Mr. Rockwell is, but he's preoccupied at the moment, so I stepped in."

"Cool, cool," I mumble, a wave of irritation washing over me.

Goddamn it, of course that bastard takes my rent every month! It is bad enough that he is the one signing my meager paychecks; now he is also the one who held the power to kick us to the curb.

An uncomfortable silence stretches between us, neither of us knowing quite what to say.

I nervously clear my throat. "Well, I guess I'll see you around—" but Aiden quickly cuts me off.

"Have you noticed that there aren't any other families with kids in this residence?" the man asks, his dark eyes locked intently on mine.

I pause again, not quite understanding why he is stating the obvious.

He doesn't wait for an answer.

"You see those woods?" he asks, pointing over my shoulder towards the dense treeline.

I glance back briefly before nodding.

"There are wolves in there."

A sharp intake of breath escapes my lips as his words sank in.

Holy shit! Those have to be the same woods that Damien had been in before he was attacked!

Mr. Thompson continues, his voice low and serious. "This is why families with children aren't normally approved to live on this side of town, seeing as it directly borders some dangerous land."

I frown, confusion and a growing sense of unease swirling within me. "Wait, when I applied to move here, I was very clear that children would be living with me."

For the first time, the stoic man's facade breaks. It is now Aiden's turn to look uncomfortable and somewhat ashamed. He breaks eye contact and swallows thickly.

"Yes, well, the circumstances were… different before you arrived," he replies, shoving his large hands into the front pockets of his worn work pants.

Squinting my eyes, my brain struggles with the implications of what I was hearing. "Are we getting kicked out?" I ask, the back of my neck already prickling with a cold sweat at the thought of facing homelessness again.

Mr. Thompson clears his throat. "Not kicked out. I am merely here to offer you the opportunity to relocate to a residence in a safer part of town. While this issue should have been flagged earlier, I suppose we can just chalk it up to a… loss of paperwork."

I jerk back at his casual explanation. "Hold on. If these woods are so dangerous, then why was this area even zoned for residential living in the first place? And why haven't the residents who are already living here been evacuated if there have been recent sightings of *active* wolves?" My anger begins to simmer as my brain finally catches up, rationalizing the absurdity of the situation. "In fact, the woman I spoke with when I applied made it very clear that there weren't any other available places to live, and that this was the *only* option for anyone new coming into town!"

Aiden seems genuinely taken aback by my pointed questions and rising frustration.

"U-uh well," he stammers, his gaze darting nervously around, no longer willing to meet my accusatory stare, "the residents here are normally… from out of town." He begins, his voice hesitant, as if he is carefully calculating each word. "Most of the residents come here because they have been… rejected by other… towns. They are normally fully aware that per this agreement, they are not afforded some of the same luxuries as other… town members who have lived here their whole lives. This includes, but is not limited to, the location of their housing."

"What the actual fuck kind of classist bullshit is this?!" I yell, unable to contain the disgust that welling up inside me.

Mr. Thompson's eyes widen, and he seems genuinely startled by my outburst. "It's not classist! It's simply a hierarchy of living. Everyone in town agrees to it, including those living at this trailer park," he tried to defend, his voice laced with a hint of both desperation and rising anger.

I glare at him, my fists clenching at my sides. "I did *not* agree to live in a place that was unsafe for my kids! I was told I *had* to live here."

Not that I could realistically afford anything different, but that is beside the point at this particular moment.

Aiden sighs, running a large hand through his short ponytail. "Those who live here don't have a problem with it, and in our defense, your kind doesn't normally—"

"My. Fucking. Kind?!" I shout, my voice raw with fury, my fists now balled so tightly my knuckles are white.

Holy fuck! That was wrong, so much wrong, all the fucking wrong with that statement!

The older man stumbles backward as if the force of my anger had physically struck him. I could see a sheen of nervous sweat breaking out on his temple, and his breathing has become rapid and shallow. I notice his hands are trembling slightly, and his knees seem on the verge of buckling, as if an invisible, heavy weight is suddenly pressing down on him.

"I don't think I'm explaining this properly—" he quickly gasps out, his eyes wide with a strange mixture of fear and something else I couldn't quite decipher.

I cut him off, utterly done with hearing any more of this idiot's condescending bullshit.

"Is my family safe here or not?" I ask through gritted teeth, my entire body thrumming with barely contained rage. I am so furious I feel a flush of heat spreading through me, my muscles coiled tight with adrenaline.

He pauses for a tense second, seeming to carefully consider his answer, before giving me a slow, deliberate nod.

"Yes, you and your family will be safe to live here," he says softly, his gaze lowered slightly.

I narrow my eyes, still not entirely convinced. "And what about the wolves?"

"We'll increase patrol– park ranger surveillance to make sure this area of the woods is secure," he concludes, his head slightly bowed towards me in what might have been a gesture of appeasement.

I take a deep, shuddering breath, trying to quell the sudden rush of rage that had coursed through me. A few seconds ticked by, and as I feel my anger begin to dissipate, I notice Aiden simultaneously begins to straighten his posture, the strange tension seemingly leaving his body.

Our strained silence is abruptly shattered by a shout from behind me.

"Brayden, catch!" Marcus yells.

Instinctively, I spin around, just in time to be struck by a small, soft object. Scrambling, I flail my arms in a desperate attempt to catch it, but it instead ends up fumbling and dropping the item. I sigh in exasperation as I recognize my wallet lying on the ground, its contents spilled across the grass.

I look up to see Marcus standing a few feet away, a picture of innocent indifference on his face. "It had fallen out earlier, and I figured you didn't want Charlie to get it," he says with a shrug before quickly running back to resume his game with the others.

I let out another weary sigh and turn back to gather my scattered belongings, surprised to see them already gone. Confused,

I look up and notice that Aiden has already collected everything, most of the items held precariously in one of his large palms. Reaching out, I quickly grab my things and begin stuffing them back into my wallet.

"Uh, thanks," I mumble, trying to get my cards and cash back in order. It isn't until I have everything mostly straightened that I realize something was missing. A knot of anxiety tightens in my chest as the realization dawns.

Of all the items to lose, it had to be that one.

"Listen, you wouldn't happen to have seen—" glancing up, I feel my anxiousness begin to fade as my eyes land on the missing item. "Oh, there it is."

Clutched in Aiden's other hand is an old, worn photograph. The edges are softened with time, and multiple creases run down its center. The picture itself isn't particularly good quality, so I am confused as to why Aiden's eyes are glued to the faded image.

"What is this?" he asks, his voice barely audible as he continues to stare intently at the photograph.

"Uh, that's a picture of my mom and dad," I reply, a hint of confusion in my tone.

His eyes snap to mine, and all the color seems to drain from his face.

"Your *what?*" he chokes out, the hand holding the picture beginning to tremble visibly.

"Well, my mom and sperm donor," I clarify with a roll of my eyes. "My mom liked to keep that picture in her wallet. She used to joke that it was our first family photo," I add with a small, wry chuckle.

Mr. Thompson doesn't seem to find the humor in it.

"You know, because the picture is taken right after they… you know," I try to explain, gesturing vaguely.

His breathing hitches, and his eyes dart rapidly from the photograph to my face, then back to the faded image.

"You're positive this is your father?" he asks, his voice strained.

I nod. "Yeah, apparently Mom had been grounded for the two weeks prior to that bonfire. She snuck out to go to the party but was caught returning home and was grounded for another two weeks. By that time, she had started puking, and the rest is history," I say with a shrug, the details of Mom's teenage rebellion a familiar, if slightly embarrassing, family anecdote.

I honestly couldn't fathom what is so captivating about the photo. It is a grainy, poorly lit image, no doubt taken by someone who was far from sober. In the photograph, Mom sits on a beat-up old couch, a half-empty beer bottle clutched in her hand, while the guy next to her has a drunken arm lazily draped over her shoulder. The guy's face is slightly out of focus, a blurry smudge, so I wouldn't recognize him if I passed him on the street. The only thing I know for sure is that I haven't inherited any of his features.

Aiden gasps, his eyes searching my face with an intensity that made me deeply uncomfortable. "You're… you're my—" he abruptly shoved the photograph into my chest.

"I need to go." And just as abruptly as the man had seemed to materialize out of the twilight, he turns and practically bolts, disappearing into the growing darkness.

I only have a fleeting moment to stare at his quickly departing figure before Kelsey's hand landed on my shoulder to hurry me back towards the trailer and remind me that it was almost time for my shift.

BRAYDEN

Thursday 1:50am

I can't breathe.

And it's wonderful.

Strong hands seize the nape of my neck. The rough callouses of his palms scrape against my skin before his powerful fingers dug into the tight cords of muscle at the base of my skull. The blunt tips of his fingernails undoubtedly leave angry red tracks as they clawed into me. The slightest shift of my hair sends jolts of pure pleasure down my spine.

My body blazes.

Every nerve ending screamed with heightened awareness. A surge of energy coursed through me. My limbs tremble with adrenaline, and a lustful shiver erupts across my skin in the stifling heat of the supply closet.

How had we arrived here?

The thought flickered briefly through my mind amidst the escalating passion. It was a hazy recollection, piecing together the fragmented moments leading to this cramped space. One instant, my break had just begun, and I was walking down the sterile hospital hallway; the next, I was abruptly pulled into this small enclosure.

Perhaps I should have seen it coming. The undercurrent had been palpable all week. With every encounter, the tension of suppressed sexual desire continued to grow. The game of hot and cold between the two of us could only be played for so long. Both of us knew this was going to happen eventually, I just didn't think it was going to be this soon.

I'm suddenly pushed into the shelves lining the wall, and I let out a grunt as my back takes on the brute force of our combined weight. I vaguely register the sound of bottles falling over, but the disruption doesn't hinder either of our earnest movements.

Maybe, I should've played hard to get a little longer?

Our mouths crash together, a savage claiming rather than a tender exchange. Neither of us leading; rather, both of us just ravenously devouring the other.

A better question: why had I waited so long in the first place?

His lips are full and demanding. The soft skin of his mouth presses almost painfully into mine as we both stubbornly refuse to break the seal for air.

Another involuntary grunt escapes me, this time a pure expression of pleasure, as my own hands find purchase at the base of his neck, tangling in his hair. My fingers deftly trace circles at his hairline before creeping further upward. When my hand is full of his dark locks, I give a sharp tug.

God, his hair is so soft.

I'd worried the height difference would be an obstacle, but it seems my impromptu maneuver has been executed flawlessly.

A guttural moan rumbles from his chest in response, breaking our breathless kiss for the first time in what felt like an eternity.

The sliver of light beneath the door allows me a fleeting glimpse of his face, his eyes squeezed shut in ecstasy as my grip tightened on his head.

We are both a panting mess, only the sound of our ragged breaths mingling in the confined space.

The heat radiating from our bodies has transformed the small closet into a sensual furnace. Sweat slicks my skin, my breath comes in gasps, and a tingling arousal pulses through every inch of me.

Just as I feet his body begin to relax, I reclaim his mouth.

His startled gasp allowed me to plunge my tongue deep into his mouth. An immediate warmth blooms on my lips as our tongues intertwine. Our open mouths are hot and wet, a heady mix of fresh mint and the salty tang of perspiration.

Almost instantly, his body begins to grind against mine. While our mouths engage in a wet whirlwind of passion, our bodies echo the same urgent need. His hands roam over my damp shirt, his palms sweeping across the contours of my torso. His fingers explore every line of my chest and back, leaving a trail of goosebumps with each desperate pass.

Instead of mirroring his exploration, I plant my hands firmly on his shoulders, anchoring us both in this frenzied dance.

I decide to escalate the encounter. With a guttural groan, I slam my hips against his. He responds in kind, our hardened cores colliding in a sensual rhythm of pure lust. Soon, we are locked in vigorous, clothed thrusts, a raw expression of our pent-up desire. The closet became a symphony of moans and whimpers as we both seek solace in the intimate friction of the other's body.

All too soon, the shrill ring of my phone alarm slices through the haze, announcing the end of my break. A long pause hangs in the air as we slowly unwind our limbs from each other's embrace.

"That was..." His voice is thick and raspy, undoubtedly strained from the recent peak of our shared intensity.

I chuckle, a smugness lacing my tone. "You sound surprised. Weren't you the one who dragged me in here?"

While the darkness obscures his features, I could almost see the embarrassed flush creeping up his neck.

He clears his throat. "Yeah, but... I never imagined you'd be that good." The dazed quality of our encounter still clings to his voice.

A smirk stretches across my face, and a soft laugh escapes me.

"Maybe next time we can plan this in advance," I suggest, half-heartedly straightening my wrinkled shirt. "That way, I'll know to bring extra deodorant—"

My words are cut short as the front of my shirt becomes instantly soaked, the pungent smell of cleaning supplies assaulting my senses.

"What the fuck, Travis?!" I exclaim, shock and irritation lacing my voice as I look up at him holding an empty cleaning container.

"I-uh-it slipped, sorry..." he mumbles weakly.

Not wanting to let the unexpected shower ruin the afterglow of a pleasant make out session, I give a small nod. "Yeah, sure, just be careful next time. This is my only set of work clothes," I mutter, trying to wring out the sticky liquid.

Not to mention, the clothes I'll have to wear home, since I hadn't thought to bring an extra set today.

I hear Travis shuffle his feet. "You're uh, not going to tell anyone about this, are you?" he asks, his voice laced with nervousness.

Surprised by the question, I look up at him. "No, it's nobody else's business what I do," I reply, a hint of confusion in my tone.

A sigh of relief escapes him. "That's good. People in town tend to disapprove of having, uh, intimate relations before uh..."

"Marriage?" I supply.

"Yeah," he responds, sounding slightly embarrassed, "and I would get a lot of harsh backlash if they found out I have had sex and other intimate sessions before finding my ma-lifelong partner."

I reach out and gently squeeze his shoulder. "As I said, I won't say anything to anyone, and this is a no-commitment thing. Whenever either of us is done, we can call it quits, no hard feelings." My hand slides up his neck, my fingers wrapping around the sensitive skin. "But," his body gives a slight tremor as I apply a gentle pressure, "there are some things I'd like to explore before that happens."

A soft whimper of pleasure escapes his lips before I release him and step out of the cramped closet.

BRAYDEN

Thursday 4:02am

Besides the uncomfortable feeling of wearing damp clothes for the remainder of my shift, work was relatively boring the rest of the evening, and I was relieved when it came time to go. I quickly gathered my stuff together, eager to clock out and get some breakfast. Just as I was about to drop off my work stuff, I felt a buzz from my pocket.

Reaching in, I get worried as the message is from Dr. Monroe.

Dr. M: Could you head up to room 1001. There is a distressed young boy who is inconsolable. I thought maybe you could calm him down.

Me: Sure.

I reply, trying not to get irritated as the front door is only ten feet in front of me. Resigning myself to some overtime, I make my way to the top floor.

As I continue my slow ascent up each floor, I couldn't help but question why a kid is roomed so high up. As far as I knew, the top floor is rarely used, its access restricted to specific personnel.

The elevator ascends slowly, each floor a drawn-out delay. When the doors finally slide open, I hurry down the deserted corridor. Alright, I'll go in, give the kid the toy, and hopefully be out in a couple of minutes.

Scanning the hallway for room 1001, I am surprised to find only one patient room number on the directory. Looking down the hall, a single door glows with light, and I assume that was my destination. As I approached the open doorway, the murmur of two voices drifts out.

"Are you sure?"

"Positive! How the fuck did this happen!?"

"Well, when a man and a woman—"

"This is no fucking time for jokes! How the fuck am I supposed to tell Olivia?"

"Listen, I have my own troubles to deal with—BRAYDEN?!"

I stand frozen in the open doorway, partially concealed by the doorframe. A small metal plaque beside the door reads "Room 1001." Inside, the familiar figures of Mr. Thompson and Mr. Rockwell break off their heated conversation, their expressions shifting to stunned disbelief as they stare at me.

Fuck my life.

I can't believe this.

My hand instantly digs into my pocket, and I reread the last message sent to me. My eyes flickered rapidly from the message to the door plaque, then to the two men standing in the room. I am certain my face mirrored their expressions: a chaotic blend of confusion, surprise, and a growing sense of unease.

My eyes first dart over to Mr. Thompson. The man is standing, his arms crossed over his broad chest. Unlike earlier, his once-crisp button-down is now a crumpled mess, dark sweat stains blooming around his collar and down his chest. His usually neat hair has come undone, the salt-and-pepper strands now a tangled wave above his shoulders. A stark look of fear seems to have settled over his features.

Beside him, Mr. Rockwell is, surprisingly, sitting on the edge of the hospital bed. He is bent forward, his hands paused mid-motion as if he'd been tying his shoe. The bedsheets behind him are rumpled, suggesting he'd recently been lying there and was preparing to leave. The man exudes his usual intimidating aura, but a flicker of genuine happiness crosses his face at my arrival.

"Brayden, what are you doing here?" Damien asks, his expression brightening with each passing second. "Are you here to visi—"

"I think there's been a mistake," I quickly mumble, already tapping out a reply to Dr. Monroe's previous message.

Me: In room 1001, but there isn't a child. Mr. Rockwell and Mr. Thompson are here.

Dr. M: Odd...what do his patient forms say?

Stepping fully into the room, I deliberately ignore the two men as I move closer to the clipboard hanging next to the hospital bed, refusing to meet either of their gazes. From the corner of my eye, I see Damien immediately straighten as I approach, only for his large frame to deflate slightly as I don't so much as glance in his direction. The placement of the clipboard forces me to stand directly between the two men, bringing them far closer than I would have preferred.

"How was your day?" he asks softly.

My hand grips the report tighter.

"Were you told I was here?" A note of hopeful anticipation colors his voice. The bed creaks as he shifted his weight.

I flip through the forms, my eyes skimming over the various charts and details, not truly absorbing the information but searching for something specific.

"How was work?" His voice is closer now, and I notice that he has scooted further along the bed, narrowing the space between us. Still pointedly ignoring him, I finally find the page I am looking for and frown in confusion.

A frustrated sigh escapes me, the absurdity of the situation weighing down my patience. "This is bullshit," I mutter under my breath, digging into my pocket for my cell phone.

I am beyond done with this unexpected detour, and eternity seems to drag on the more I have to deal with the situation. I quickly find Dr. Monroe's contact and tap the call button. As the phone rings, I feel the soft brush of Damien's leg against mine.

I glance up to see an eager expression on his face, clearly pleased that his proximity has finally caught my attention. I scowl, and watch as a look of hurt washes over him before he slowly scoots away.

"Hello, Brayden?" Dr. Monroe answers, a note of confusion in his voice.

"Hey, I know this isn't proper protocol, but there seems to have been a major mistake," I explain, my gaze fixed on the last page of the clipboard. "According to his papers, Mr. Rockwell has refused further medical treatment and is currently waiting for release."

A heavy sigh emanates from the phone. "This is my fault. At the same time I was messaging you about the child, I was also messaging an RN about Mr. Rockwell. I must have mixed up the room numbers."

It takes every ounce of my self-control to suppress an audible groan... or a full-blown scream.

"Okay, well, I'll head out then and..."

"NO!" Dr. Monroe's sudden yell through the phone startles me, causing me to instinctively pull the device away from my ear.

Looking up, I see both Aiden and Damien flinch as if they could hear the man's booming voice from across the room.

I sigh, the weight of the situation pressing down on me. "Sir, my shift is over. I need to go home."

"Brayden, given the situation with Mr. Rockwell, I feel it's best if I handle this personally. Please stay there until I can get up to his room. I can be there within the hour," Dr. Monroe states with finality before the line went dead.

"Fuck!" The word slips out under my breath. My thumb and forefinger pinch the bridge of my nose as I fight to regain my composure. With a heavy sigh, I glance down at my phone, noting the time. Disappointment washes over me as I realize I'd have to miss my daily breakfast with Lou, but at least I'd likely be released before the kids woke up.

"Is everything alright?" Damien's concerned voice reaches me from across the room.

I plaster on a fake smile. "Yep," I reply, making my way over to the two men. "So, there's been a slight misunderstanding. While you had requested to be released, I was the one who was accidentally told to come up." I catch Aiden trying to stifle an amused huff. "However, I don't have the authority to release you, so Dr. Monroe will be up shortly. In the meantime, I'll be right outside the room in case you need anything."

I start towards the door when Damien's voice booms after me.

"Wait! Didn't he also say *you* needed to stay here?" he asks, his hand reaching out with a desperate urgency, as if to physically restrain me.

"He did..." I reply slowly, a prickle of unease crawling up my spine. "But how did you know that?"

"Your phone's volume is way up; anyone could have heard your conversation," he answers smoothly. "The way I see it, how would I be able to tell the doctor that you stayed like you were supposed to if I can't see you?"

I am seconds away from putting my fist through the wall. Having to stay because a child needed help was one thing, a noble cause, but being forced to remain in the suffocating presence of someone who couldn't even execute a decent "accidental" leg touch without looking like a clumsy toddler fills me with a simmering rage that threatens to boil over.

I shoot him a glare that could peel paint, but his face remains infuriatingly blank.

Fuck him and his pathetic attempts at control!

"Of course, I'll remain here," I respond, my voice dripping with sarcasm. Tossing the clipboard carelessly onto the edge of the side table, I take up from my designated position, leaning against the wall directly facing the bed. A long, heavy silence descends upon the room. The two men exchange uneasy glances before their eyes settle back on me. Damien, noticeably less self-assured than I'd previously witnessed, abandons his earlier attempts at conversation and simply stares at me, a look of contemplation clouding his features. I welcome the quiet, letting my gaze drift around the sterile room, but Mr. Thompson clearly hasn't grasped the unspoken plea for silence.

"Do your tattoos have meaning?" the man asks, a nervous tremor in his deep voice.

Yes, they do, but that's none of your goddamn business.

"Not really," I answer, keeping my voice as flat and devoid of inflection as possible.

Aiden shoots Damien a look that is clearly a silent plea for help. Damien simply shrugs in response, looking just as lost. The two men stare at each other for another awkward moment before

Damien turns back to me, clearing his throat and offering what I could only assume is meant to be an inviting smile.

"Did you always see yourself working in the medical field?" Damien asks.

Never, but it was the only job I could find.

"Not really," I reply. Looking down at my hands, I begin to pick at the skin around my thumbnail in boredom.

Ugh, I could really use some lotion.

Damien's face falls at my answer, although it's obvious that I am beginning to annoy him just a little bit. While he is still sitting on the bed, his form has begun to tense, and his hands clench at his sides.

Mr. Thompson gives a strained smile, his hands shoved deep into his pants pockets. "Do you have any hobbies outside of work?" His tone is a little too tight to be considered friendly.

I used to love running.

"Not really."

Both men seem to be getting angry now, and I hear that familiar rumble emanating from Mr. Rockwell. Just as I think I have taken things too far, my phone goes off. Quickly taking the opportunity to not converse with the men, I dig out my cell and am pleasantly surprised to see who it is.

Lou: Is everything OK? You didn't show up this morning.

Me: Sorry, I had to stay late for work.

Lou: Are you still there?

Me: Yeah, I'm having to wait with a patient until the doctor comes.

Lou: I'll bring coffee and breakfast. Let me know the room number.

I fight back a grin at Lou's text. She knows me well enough to understand that directly asking if I wanted breakfast would result in an immediate refusal. Instead, she simply took action, recognizing my unspoken need. That is what I cherish about her, her intuitive understanding of when to nudge and when to give me space. I quickly type out my current location before turning off my phone.

Looking up, I find Damien's eyes already fixed on me, but this time he was standing beside the bed.

"You seem happy," he states, his tone not accusatory but rather a cautious observation.

I shrug. "Yeah, my friend Lou is bringing me breakfast."

A sharp intake of breath reaches my ears, followed by the sound of approaching footsteps. Startled, I realize Damien is rapidly closing the distance between us. Before I can fully react, I find myself pressed back against the wall by his imposing presence.

His toned chest is inches from my face, his body heat enveloping us in a warm, confined space. The distinct sharp scent of his strong cologne fills my nostrils once more, though thankfully it is less overwhelming than before. While he stood directly in front of me, he makes no move to touch me, keeping his arms firmly at his sides as his dark eyes peered down at my smaller frame.

He tilts his head downward, taking a deep inhale through his nose. His black hair falls across his forehead with the movement, and his tan face seems strained as he takes a few more deliberate breaths. After a moment, I notice his entire body appears to relax. Opening his eyes, he gives me one last intense look before straightening up and taking a small step back.

Well, that was new. I guess his therapy must be working.

"And who might Lou be?" he asks, his voice surprisingly devoid of any discernible emotion.

Taken aback by his unexpected calmness, I open and close my mouth, a subconscious feeling of having been caught doing something wrong washing over me.

"Uh..." I mumble dumbly, before a knock on the door provided a welcome interruption. I breathe a sigh of relief as I see who walked through the door.

It's about time.

Mr. Rockwell also seems shocked but not as shocked as I feel once Lou enters the room.

BRAYDEN

Thursday 5:22am

Lou strolls into the room, bypassing the formality of a knock, although I couldn't blame her as the door is technically already open. Her gray hair is neatly styled in a bun today, with a few stray strands softening her round face. She wears no makeup, and her attire is simple yet remains elegant, a consistency found both on her outer wear and inner personality.

The moment I see her, I gently push Damien aside.

"Lou!" I greet with genuine happiness, eagerly reaching for the bag of food she carried.

She smiles warmly at me, a slight shake of her head acknowledging my eagerness.

Rummaging through the bag, I quickly locate an egg sandwich. The aroma of slightly burnt, deliciously greasy food instantly makes my mouth water. Over the crinkling paper, I hear Lou sigh at my enthusiastic handling of the bag.

"Did you eat today?" she asks, her tone laced with concern.

I glance up at her, rolling my eyes as I begin to stuff a large bite of the sandwich into my mouth. Grease smears my fingers and face as I devour the food.

"Define today," I mumble through a full mouth, simultaneously reaching for one of the paper coffee cups in her hand. She gives me a pointed look, her lips pressing into a thin line as she deliberately pulls her hand out of my reach. I make a small noise of protest at the denied caffeine.

"We've talked about this, Brayden. You can't just live on caffeine and expect to function properly," she gently chides. I avoid her gaze, not wanting to see the disappointment I know would be there.

"It's not my fault!" I quickly defend myself. "Evie ate my lunch yesterday, and during dinner, Charlie dropped his peanut butter sandwich on the floor and refused to eat it. I offered to switch with him, but after I handed him mine, Charlotte spilled her orange juice all over the floor, soaking the food!"

I could see she wants to stay mad at me, but the bright sparkle in her eyes and the faint crinkling around the corners of her eyes betray the laughter she is trying to suppress. With a resigned huff, she finally hands me my coffee.

Taking a grateful sip, I hear Damien clear his throat, and for the first time all night, his intense gaze isn't directed at me but at Lou.

"How do you know him?" Damien asks, his voice gruff. His tense posture and clipped tone does little to conceal his irritation towards her.

Lou turns her attention to Damien, her expression cool and assessing.

Wait... is she actually glaring at him, or is that just my imagination running wild?

"It's none of your concern whose company I keep. Let alone how we met," she responds with a dismissive huff.

My eyes widens at her audacious act of defiance.

Did she just blow him off? The guy everyone in this town seems to treat like royalty?

I take a slow sip of my coffee, my eating pace slowing down significantly as I watch the scene in front of me. It is almost comical. Lou, a petite woman barely five feet tall, stood utterly unfazed in front of the towering figure of Damien Rockwell. The standoff is intense, neither willing to yield, the tension in the room thickening with each passing second their eyes remain locked. It is a silent battle of wills.

I take another bite of my sandwich.

Lou is the first to break direct eye contact, but it doesn't appear to be submission. Instead, she turns her full attention back to me, completely disregarding Damien's brooding presence right behind her.

"Any other dietary restrictions I need to know for tonight?" she asks, her tone casual as if Damien sn't even in the room.

I pause, considering. "Well, in terms of diet, you already know I'm vegetarian, but the other kids aren't. Marcus is lactose intolerant, though," I answer, mentally sifting through the details.

Lou looks thoughtful. "Hmmm, if it's alright with you, I think we'll just grill hotdogs and burgers. We can then throw on some veggie options for you and have a variety of sides."

I nod. "Sounds good to me. Want us to bring anything?"

Lou laugh. "I think bringing the kids will be enough of a handful for you."

I let out a grunt of agreement.

"What the fuck is going on here?! He's going over to your house for dinner?"

I flinch as Mr. Rockwell's voice echoes through the hospital room. He stands tall in front of Lou, but his body isn't trembling with anger. Instead, he is rigid, stiff as a board. His frustration seems to have reached a boiling point beyond mere anger.

Lou simply lets out an annoyed sigh.

My eyes dart between the two, a sense of anticipation bubbling within me.

O-my-god, shit's about to get good.

Lou turns stiffly to Mr. Rockwell, straightening her spine. "Damien..."

My eyes widen. She hasn't addressed him by his last name, unlike everyone else in town.

That's it, Lou, show this arrogant ass his place!

"...as I said before, I do not have to tell you whom I socialize with. Frankly, I don't understand why you're so concerned," Lou replies firmly.

I take another large gulp of my coffee, my attention completely riveted on the unfolding drama.

Damien's shadow falls over Lou as he glowers down at her, his imposing form completely dwarfing hers.

"I think you know why this concerns me, mother—"

A mouthful of hot coffee erupts from me, spraying across the room. I immediately clap a hand over my mouth, a futile attempt to contain the damage. I feel the sticky liquid soak into my sleeve. The realization of my messy predicament only exacerbates the situation, triggering a violent coughing fit. My lungs constrict, and I bring a fist to my chest, pounding desperately for air.

A pair of warm hands gently yet firmly pats my back until the hacking begins to subside. Looking up through watery eyes, I see Damien softly rubbing my back, his expression etched with concern. The moment I register his touch a jolt of surprise shoots through me, and I quickly recoils from his grasp.

Turning to Lou, a whirlwind of conflicting emotions churns within me, my thoughts spiraling into suspicion. Has she been manipulating me all this time? Damien's obvious interest in me hasn't gone unnoticed. Is she relaying everything I confide in her, using it as leverage for some future scheme? I am sure the betrayal I felt is evident on my face, yet I couldn't seem to harden my gaze as I looked at Lou.

"Brayden, I want you to think for a moment," Lou says gently, her tone the same soothing cadence she used when I teetered on the edge of a panic attack during our sessions.

"Damien didn't know that we knew each other," she states firmly, her eyes flicking a sharp glare towards her son. Looking between the two now, the resemblance is undeniable. While Damien's build and features differed from his mother's, he has inherited her coloring.

"And for good reason," the sound of a low growl seems to echo in the small space as she continues.

"I can see the suspicion in your eyes, and I want to assure you with absolute certainty that your fears are unfounded." She sighs, the rigid set of her shoulders a familiar sign of her unwavering principles. "I have taken a legal oath to maintain complete confidentiality regarding anything an individual chooses to confide in me, an oath I have never broken in over thirty years of my work." Her eyes are soft with understanding, yet her gaze holds a steely resolve. She says nothing more, allowing her words to settle and my own thoughts to process them.

Lou's voice resonated with unwavering conviction. There was no hint of rehearsed lines or the tell-tale signs of a hastily constructed lie. My own carefully honed instincts for detecting deception, a skill I'd diligently cultivated, registers no red flags.

With a sense of certainty settling in my mind, I nod at her, silently conveying my belief.

A small smile touches her lips before her expression cools once more as she turns to Damien. "Brayden's shift is over. He'll be going now," she states matter-of-factly.

My eyes widen at her audaciousness.

"Uh, Lou, Dr. Monroe told me I needed to stay..." But she cuts me off, holding up a palm to silence me.

"Dr. Monroe works for Damien, so I'm sure that once he finds out that you were kept here after an already overlong shift..."

Damien's gaze flickers to me, a flicker of concern in his dark eyes.

"...that before I came here you were eating your first proper meal in nearly two days..."

A soft whimper escapes Damien's lips as he takes a step closer. I narrow my eyes at him, warily watching his hand twitch in my direction.

"...and that by staying late you now won't get any sleep today. He'll be more than inclined to release you from your shift," she finished, directing a disappointed glare at Damien.

For some reason, the imposing man looks genuinely ashamed. He reaches out a hand as if to offer a comforting touch, but I instinctively dart behind Lou. It might have seemed illogical to seek protection behind the smaller woman, but she is the only person I've ever witnessed stand her ground against the behemoth. Damien gives me one last sorrowful look before his hand drops to his side, his gaze fixed on the floor.

"You're released to go," he mumbles, his voice barely audible, perhaps tinged with guilt.

I look at him oddly before cautiously sidestepping towards the door. Just as I cross the threshold, I turn back to Lou. "Bye, I'll see you tonight," I say before finally heading out.

DAMIEN

Thursday 5:39am

The air in the room crackled with a sudden, charged silence after Brayden's hurried departure, his absence leaving a void that seemed to hum with unspoken tension. It was just the three of us now: my mother, Aiden, and myself, and the remnants of the morning's chaotic encounter seemed to hang heavy in the sterile hospital air.

"You're not coming tonight," my mother declares, her voice a low, unwavering pronouncement. Despite her petite frame, she stands before me like an unyielding fortress. Her gaze locks onto mine with an intensity that belies her size.

"The fuck I'm not," I bite out. The words are laced with frustration that has been simmering beneath the surface all morning, threatening to boil over.

Her lips tighten into a thin, disapproving line, and a flicker of pure anger flashes in her usually warm brown eyes. "You are not invited."

A deep, guttural growl rumbles in my chest, a sound that vibrates through the very air around us. The primal, animalistic part of me, the wolf that is intrinsically woven into my being, stirs restlessly, demanding acknowledgment after hours of forced restraint.

The inner beast. A concept that danced on the fringes of human understanding, an anomaly to their structured world, yet a persistent shadow in their collective unconscious, fueling unspoken nightmares. Creatures woven into the very fabric of their history books, whispered in hushed tones through high tales passed down over millennia. The enduring myth of a man and an animal locked in an eternal coexistence, sometimes portrayed as a terrible curse, sometimes as a potent blessing, yet a narrative that stubbornly refused to fade entirely, even in the face of their increasingly rational and mundane world. The primal fear, the untamed power, the inherent duality, it resonated too deeply within their own complex natures to ever truly vanish.

However, it isn't as simplistic as the human fantasy like to portray. No, it is not a constant battle for dominance within one body, a mythical war between man and beast. We are not some clumsy amalgamation of two separate entities. We are something far more complex—a distinct, evolved species, gifted with the ability to navigate both the wild heart of the forest and the intricate complexities of the human world. Our emotions aren't mere triggers that flip some internal switch to a "wolf mode"; they are the heightened, often volatile sensitivities of a predator, our very DNA shaped by the holistic reality of our existence, not a clumsy duality.

"I don't need to be invited to my own fucking house for dinner!" I roar, the sound echoing off the bare walls of the hospital room, my voice raw with a possessive fury.

And it is the truth, a deeply ingrained fact of our pack's history and traditions. The grand, sprawling house my parents currently occupy, with its sturdy timber frames and the scent of generations clinging to its very foundations, is the ancestral home of our Alpha lineage. It has sheltered countless leaders and their families, its history intertwined with the very fabric of our pack. With each succession, as the new Head and their chosen mate establishes their own family, the house, a silent witness to births, deaths, and the intricate dance of pack politics, is passed on.

Tradition, a powerful force in our world, has dictated that after my father relinquished the Alpha title to me, my parents would gracefully retire to a smaller, more manageable dwelling on the outskirts of our territory, while I, the newly instated Alpha, prepare the grand estate for my future mate, a space filled with both anticipation and a gnawing sense of loneliness. However, the crushing weight of my nervous breakdown at thirty, a dark period I still struggle to fully comprehend, has shattered that carefully laid plan. In the suffocating grip of my despair, the vast emptiness of the Alpha house had become an unbearable symbol of my solitude. In a moment of raw, uncharacteristic impulsivity, I had hurled the heavy, antique keys at my parents, the cold metal clattering against the worn wooden floor, demanding their smaller, more intimate home, a space where the silence wouldn't feel so deafening.

My mother's glare intensifies, a laser-like focus that seems to pierce through my many rumbling emotions. "That is your father's and my house until you are mated, Damien. Until you bring a Luna to its hearth, it remains our roof and under our rules."

I throw my head back in frustration, the heat of the argument flushing my skin. "Which is why I need to be there when my mate is there!" I yell.

143

A pang of guilt twists in my gut at losing my temper with my mother, but the circumstances feel dire, a betrayal on a fundamental level. She knows the significance of Brayden to me, hell, the entire pack recognizes the bond that was forming. Yet, she has deliberately kept her interactions with him secret and led to a growing connection between them, without my knowledge or consent. I rake a hand through my already disheveled hair, the strands tangling between my fingers and squeeze my eyes shut in exasperated disbelief.

"Damien," my mother sighs, her voice softening slightly as she reaches out a small hand to touch my arm. I flinch at the contact, but I don't pull away as she gives my forearm a brief, comforting squeeze. "Tomorrow's dinner is not social. While it will take place in a social setting, the purpose is professional. I need to assess if I am a suitable support for the children."

She offers no further explanation, and none is needed. The only professional capacity in which my mother would interact with a group of children is in her role as a pack counselor.

A furrow creases my brow, a knot of concern tightening in my chest. "Are they alright?" I ask, the protective instincts towards the young pups, whom I already envision as future additions to my small, solitary world, rising to the surface.

"They are just fine, Damien, but everyone can always benefit from a little extra help," she explains cautiously, her tone measured.

My irritation flares anew, fueled by her evasiveness and the gnawing anxiety about Brayden's past. "What's going on with them, Mom? Why have you been seeing Brayden every morning?" My voice remains steady, but my palms feel clammy, a physical manifestation of the unease that gripped me.

What shadows linger in my mate's history that required such discreet intervention?

My mother's hand instantly withdraws from my arm. Her lips harden into a firm scowl. "You know better than to ask me a question like that, Damien."

I meet her angry gaze head-on, my own frustration now overtaking the ingrained respect I hold for her. "And you should know better than to withhold information about someone else's mate. That treads dangerously close to violating pack law."

To a degree, my statement holds true. The sanctity of the mate bond is paramount in our society and is built on a foundation of unwavering trust and open communication. Secrets between mates are a corrosive force, eroding the very essence of their connection. While individual confidences with unmated adults are commonplace, discussions about one mate without their partner's knowledge is a transgression.

The emotional resonance between bonded individuals is too strong; prolonged secrecy would inevitably breed fear and anxiety, a palpable tension that neither could ignore until the truth is brought into the light, typically within a day. Furthermore, acting as a sole confidant in significant matters concerning another's mate is considered a form of emotional infidelity, a breach of the sacred trust inherent in the bond.

While Brayden and I aren't yet officially mated, the undeniable pull between us, the undeniable truth of our destined connection, places my mother on a razor's edge. Her commitment to confidentiality teeters dangerously close to a violation of our most fundamental laws.

My mother stands firm, her voice unwavering. "He is not your anything *right now*, Damien, and therefore, within his wishes, I am well within the guidelines to be his sole confidant."

Her words land like a physical blow, a cold weight settling in my chest. "It's not my fault," I defend weakly, my emotions a turbulent storm. One moment, I am consumed by righteous anger, the next, the implication of Brayden seeking solace in someone else sends a wave of crushing sadness washing over me.

My hands clench in my hair, pulling at the strands as I lean forward, a strangled cry escaping my throat. "It shouldn't be this hard!"

Hearing the raw emotion in my voice, my mother is instantly by my side. Her small, familiar hands gently cup my face, guiding it to rest against her shoulder. Her touch, a comforting anchor from my childhood, soothes the frantic energy thrumming through me as she begins to rub her hand up and down my back.

"Shh, shh now. It's alright," she whispers into my ear, her voice a balm against my unraveling composure.

Once the dam had broken, the words pour out, a torrent of insecurity and longing. "When he saw me for the first time, I should have been enough. Even though we met arguing, my apology should have been enough. When he's near me, he shouldn't need to confide in another; *I* should be enough. When he seeks intimacy, I. Should. Be. Enough!" My voice cracked with unshed tears, a burning ache in my throat. I sagged against her, clinging to the familiar comfort of her embrace as my desperate rant continued.

"Why am I not enough?" I gasp out, my voice barely a whisper as I bury my face in the soft fabric of her shoulder, seeking solace in the nostalgic scent of parental care.

That question has been a relentless tormentor since the moment I first laid eyes on Brayden, its sharp claws reaching into every corner of my mind. I have dissected myself relentlessly over the past week, picking apart every perceived flaw, watching the list grow with each agonizing self-assessment. Every glance in the mirror, every meticulously planned schedule, every carefully curated social interaction becomes a source of scrutiny.

If I could just find all the flaws and fix myself, then… then I could be enough.

"Oh, honey, I don't think you're not enough," my mother soothes, her hand continuing its comforting rhythm on my back. I only burrow deeper into her shoulder, the familiar scent a temporary reprieve from the storm within.

"You're just… you're…" she hesitates for a fraction of a second. Her momentary struggle with words only deepens my sense of inadequacy. "You're everything in a mate that a human wouldn't naturally gravitate towards in a relationship," she finally explains.

I jerk back, pulling away from her embrace, my eyes wide with surprise. "I'm what?" The statement stings, a confusing blend of offense and bewilderment.

My mother looks at me, her eyes filled with a love that transcends my current turmoil. One of her hands rises to cup my cheek, her touch gentle and familiar. "Oh, my sweet Alpha wolf," I scowl at the endearment, a childish habit resurfacing, but a warmth spreads through my chest at her motherly touch. "Think about it for just a moment, Brayden first met you in a store, and you wielded your power like a weapon. He then discovered you were not only his boss but also his landlord. Power, something instinctively attractive to a werewolf, is often a barrier for humans."

I stare at her, still struggling to grasp her meaning.

She sighs, a gentle exasperation in her tone. "You're expecting too much of your mate, Damien." She pauses, letting her words sink in. "You're expecting him to react like a werewolf, to be drawn to your position and power within the pack. But for humans, those very positions can create distance. You holding those roles is likely causing him to instinctively create space between the two of you, a matter of proper protocol in his mind. He also doesn't understand what a 'mate' truly means in our world and, therefore, doesn't grasp his significance to you. If he were to step out of line, he understands that you are the one who enforces the rules, the one who would mete out the consequences. From his perspective, limiting his interaction with you as much as possible is the safest course of action."

I frown, the implication of her words grating against my very being. "So you're saying I need to change who I am? I *am* an Alpha. That's not a switch I can simply flick off. The need to lead, to enforce, to protect – it's ingrained in my bones. I'm a werewolf; I can't just *act* human."

While I've heard whispers of human mates finding werewolf culture barbaric or illogical, it's the very essence of our existence. We aren't human. Our species thrives on structure, on a clear hierarchy. Where humans might crumble under such rigid order, werewolves would equally disintegrate under the chaotic weight of pure democracy. History is littered with packs who had attempted to live without an Alpha or Alpha pair, only to eventually collapse under the strain of self-governance.

My mother levels another stern look at me. "I do not expect you to act human or to cease being an Alpha, Damien. Nor would I ever wish such a destabilizing fate upon our pack. We are werewolves, not humans," she pauses, her brow furrowed in thought as she carefully chooses her next words. "Humans fall to greed, wolves fall to instinct, and werewolves fall to complacency."

She leans up and presses a soft kiss to my cheek, a rare display of affection that warms the tension within me. "You need to remember that you are an Alpha leader, not a leader *led* by your Alpha instincts alone. When you truly grasp that, you will inevitably shift your perspective on how you lead, enforce, and protect. Your relationship with your mate will then have the space it needs to flourish."

A wave of relief washes over me, a weight I haven't even realized I am carrying suddenly lifted. I immediately pull my mother into a tight hug, the familiar scent of her a comforting balm. It has been too long since we'd had one of these heart-to-hearts.

From behind us, Aiden clears his throat, a polite interruption.

"Uh, Luna," Aiden begins hesitantly, "Olivia mentioned you might have one of her pans, and perhaps tonight we could swing by—"

My mother's warm expression vanishes, replaced by a glacial stare. "Do not start with me, Aiden. I've seen the picture. You are also not welcome tonight."

He looks genuinely shocked, a flicker of guilt crossing his features. "I, uh, just thought that..."

My mother releases an exhausted sigh. The weariness of potentially counseling a third troubled soul before the dawn is etched on her face. "Aiden, you first need to be completely honest with Olivia about Brayden. Only then can we schedule a time for the three of us to talk. After that, you will need to tell Brayden that you are his father. If you would like me to mediate that conversation, I am willing, but neither of you will be socializing with him under my roof tonight. Understood?"

Aiden's displeasure is palpable, though understandable given the emotional turmoil he'd endured all morning. The shock of this revelation is evident in his rumpled clothes and strained voice.

Earlier, he had burst into the hospital room, a whirlwind of frantic energy as he recounted his entire unexpected encounter with Brayden.

He remembered Brayden's mother vividly.

Aiden had been on a business trip with his parents and had quickly caught the attention of the local highschoolers. They had eagerly invited him to attend an impromptu bonfire that night.

Aiden had gone, eager to showcase his legendary tolerance for alcohol, only to far exceed his limits. Later, an equally drunk, buxom blonde had approached him, and in his inebriated state, he'd succumbed. She was the only other female he'd ever been intimate with besides Olivia.

Immediately after meeting Olivia, Aiden had confessed his indiscretion, and they had agreed to leave his youthful mistake in the past, a secret shared only between them. Olivia, though hurt, had been remarkably forgiving, but he'd worked tirelessly to earn her complete trust.

But Olivia harbored a secret of her own: she was infertile. Always had been, always would be. The human doctors had described it as a "barren womb." As the mate of a Beta wolf, there were unspoken expectations of producing a biological family.

However, couples facing fertility issues weren't unheard of. It was sometimes interpreted as a sign from the Goddess that another pack might possess two Beta-gene wolves, providing a space for a future integration. Similarly, if an Alpha couple couldn't conceive their own biological heir, it was seen as either the Goddess's signal to introduce a new Alpha lineage or an opportunity for two packs to merge.

But the circumstances are different now, Aiden had a biological son. The looming concern is the pack's change in reaction. He had essentially disregarded the sacred bond with Olivia early on and impregnated another woman. Olivia's infertility, instead of being viewed as a potential sign of future pack dynamics, could now be twisted into a divine punishment for his past transgression, a consequence of his youthful indiscretion.

"Listen to me, both of you," my mother commands, snapping us back to attention. "Aiden, you are not to come tonight. You need to focus on repairing things with your mate before even considering building a relationship with your son. Damien, you are not coming tonight because you need to address the expectations and hurt you have inflicted on Brayden before you even think about a relationship with him." My mother pauses, taking a deep, steadying breath. Her fingers smooth a few stray strands of hair that had escaped her elegant updo as she finished her pronouncement. "Do you both understand?" she askes, her gaze sharp and pointed, a rare hint of being overwhelmed flickering in her eyes.

Thoroughly chastised, Aiden and I both nod our heads in silent agreement.

Oh, I understand perfectly.

A plan already beginning to form.

BRAYDEN

Thursday 6:52 pm

It took a while, but the kids had finally been loaded into the van, and we were successfully headed to the Rockwells. Both Kelsey and I had tried to drill into the younger kids' brains to be respectful and calm. In all actuality, the kids were a pretty well-behaved bunch considering their ages and the strain they've all endured. But my kids were full of energy and rambunctious to the core and that accelerated my anxiety. The fear that if the kids did become a handful, people wouldn't understand, or they would think that I'm a bad parent because the kids weren't sitting meekly with their hands folded in their laps.

This fear was specifically coming from the fact that I didn't know much about Lou's husband. Lou had been adamant that her husband loved kids, but it was hard to believe that when Damien had to get his horrid behavior towards children from somewhere, and it was obvious that he didn't get it from his mother.

Therefore, I was a little nervous that maybe Mr. Rockwell senior was one of those people that just didn't get along with children. And that would be fine, nothing said he had to like my kids, but that nagging anxiety just added to the fear of the evening. It had taken almost twenty minutes to drive to Lou's. Even though the town wasn't that big, the Rockwell's house was on the other side of the small city, deep in the woods. While the scenery was pretty, both Kels and I had given each other wary looks as our old mini-van bumped along the dirt road of their driveway. The entire frame of the old vehicle shook with the unevenness of the road, and I could do nothing but hope that the engine wouldn't shake loose from the frame.

When we finally arrived, I was a little shocked to see a large wooden cabin. It wasn't a mansion, but the house was very impressive in its size and quality. The old wood looked to be freshly sealed so that the siding of the cabin had a rich, shiny finish to it that stood out among the towering old trees.

It was two stories tall with a very high gable, and several dormers built along the roofline. There was also an impressive amount of tall windows lining the front side of the house that led out to a massive wrap-around porch.

The kids were immediately in awe of the house, and Kelsey had even quirked an eyebrow at the structure. My reaction wasn't so positive.

Fuck, I bet there's a lot of expensive, breakable shit inside.

Upon arriving, it was a quick whirlwind of activity. Lou instantly ran out to greet us and ushered the kids to the backyard where a lot of outdoor games and toys were set up for them. I had immediately reminded her that she wasn't supposed to go out of her way to accommodate us or the kids for the evening, but she had just smiled and said that she hadn't, her husband, Al, had.

Al was tall, and it was easy to see where Damien had gotten his build and bulk from. Although Al was no longer as hard-bodied as his son, he was still in decent shape given his softening form. His hair was a bright shade of white, and his face held deep lines on his forehead and around his mouth, and he wore some glasses that framed his blue eyes, but they seemed to match the aesthetic of his old wool sweater and pleated pants.

Upon arriving, the older man's enthusiasm was so lively it was almost contagious. A wide smile had stretched across his face, and he had eagerly shown the kids the different setups in the backyard. Although Al was in his early sixties, he was able to keep up with the kids' roughhousing. Even little Evie had taken a liking to the energetic giant as she toddled next to him, laughing with the other children.

While Al keeps the four youngest busy, Kels, Lou, and I are on the back deck as Lou grills our dinner. Every once in a while the matron of the house would shout to Al to not wear himself out, but the large man would simply grin and continue his running while wiping a wrinkled hand along his sweating forehead.

"I figured Al would've preferred to grill, and you would've played with the kids," I comment as Lou flips a burger.

She shrugs her shoulders with a smile. "Al isn't allowed near any cooking implements. The man would burn down our house and somehow leave the food raw if left unsupervised," she gazes at the yard and the laughing kids as Al continues to try and keep up with them, "besides, the poor man has missed the sound of little feet in the house."

Kels looks at Lou, intrigued by her last comment, "Is he getting grandkid fever?" She asks with amusement in her voice as she leans against the deck railing.

Lou doesn't take her eyes off of the food. "I suppose you could say that," she answers calmly, her interest in the food had gotten very intense. "We're both getting to the age where it's more on our minds these days."

I watch curiously as Al's smile doesn't waver with the kids hopping around him.

"You know, I thought, given his size, Al seems more like the stern type than the kid-friendly type." I try to play my comment off as casual, but it was very obvious what I had been refraining from saying.

Given how Damien doesn't seem to take after you, I figured his brutish personality came from his father.

Lou looks up at me and quirks her eyebrow, no doubt able to read between the lines of my comment.

She sighs, "Al's personality has always been passionate and expressive. He's more extroverted, and he's always been a people person," she pauses for a second and slowly turns over another burger. "As he used to be Mayor, it helped in areas of alliances with other cities or forming a coalition with certain community projects. However, a high amount of passion also meant that he used to have a short temper."

Another burger flip.

"I have always been a bit more reserved. While I'm good at helping other people understand what they feel, I've never been very good at expressing myself." She looks at me, and I try not to feel uncomfortable at the intensity of her stare, "I guess Damien got the short end of the straw from both of us, he's passionate and doesn't know how or when to express that passion."

A beat of silence hangs in the air as I process Lou's cryptic comment, while Kelsey simply wears a mask of bewildered confusion. Her gaze darts between Lou and me, a silent question mark hanging over her head, until a dawning realization hits her.

"Oh yeah! The boor from the grocery store is your son, right?" she blurts out to Lou, her tone as casual, as if discussing the weather.

My eyes widen in horrified disbelief at her sheer audacity. "Kelsey!" I hiss sharply. My gaze flicks between her and Lou, and I brace myself for the inevitable offense.

But Lou simply chuckles softly, a warm, surprisingly unbothered sound. "Yes, the boor is my son."

I shoot Kelsey a warning glare, but she merely shrugs, adjusting her gray sweatshirt with an air of complete indifference to my heated disapproval.

Lou, with silent amusement playing on her lips, defuses the tension by thrusting full plates of food into our hands, effectively breaking our staredown.

"If you two could please set the table, I'll wrangle up the wild ones," Lou instructs, a fond exasperation in her voice as she places lids on steaming serving dishes.

It didn't take long to gather everyone inside for dinner. Kelsey and I instinctively settled on either side of Lou at the long, rustic wooden table, while Al took the head, the other kids scrambling to secure spots as close to him as possible, their faces alight with affection.

I am just settling a wiggly Evie onto my lap when the sharp chime of the doorbell echoes through the cozy cabin. My brows furrows in confusion, and I quickly glance at Lou, whose expression mirrors my own surprise.

A knowing look passes between Lou and Al, a silent communication that excluded the rest of us. Lou takes a deep, audibly annoyed breath before peering out one of the large front windows. Very slowly, Al pushes back his chair and casually tosses his napkin onto the table.

"I'll go see who it is," he announces with a reassuring smile directed at his wife, "I'm sure it's just business."

Lou's tense shoulders relax ever so slightly, and she nods in agreement, a quiet murmur escaping her lips. "He couldn't be that stupid," she mumbles, her voice so low that I only catch the words by virtue of sitting right next to her.

Suddenly, Charlotte bounds out of her chair and rushes around the table to where Al is standing.

"I'll help!" she declares, a wide smile already illuminating her face as she reaches out to grab Al's hand. He chuckles at her enthusiasm, his eyes crinkling at the corners. The two of them walk out of the dining room as the doorbell rang a second time, its insistent chime adding to the growing sense of unease.

I look over at Lou, my confusion deepening with each passing moment. "Were you expecting anyone—"

"Ahhhhhh!!!" Charlotte's piercing scream rips through the air, cutting off my question mid-sentence.

Without even a flicker of conscious thought, my protective instincts surge. I immediately pass a startled Evie to Kelsey and bolt out of the dining room, my feet pounding on the wooden floor as I race towards the front door.

"Charlotte?!" I yell, a cold grip of worry tightening around my chest at her sudden, terrified cry.

I skid to an abrupt halt just shy of the front door as Charlotte's small, shaking form tumbles into my legs. Without hesitation, I scoop her up into my arms. She instantly buries her face in my shoulder, her small body trembles with harsh, ragged sobs, her hot tears soaking through the fabric of my shirt. I gently rub her back, hoping the motion conveying some semblance of comfort, and looking up, my eyes desperately searching for the source of her terror.

My breath hitches in my throat. My muscles instantly stiffen at the sight that greeted me.

In the open doorway, Al stood locked in a heated, hushed argument with an unwelcome guest, both men leaning in, their voices tight with suppressed fury.

On the other side of the door's threshold stands the monster himself.

Damien fucking Rockwell.

The familiar, imposing figure of the devil himself stands before his father, his expression a thunderous mask of anger.

He is dressed in his usual formal attire, a crisp white button-down shirt stretched taut across his broad chest, the top two buttons carelessly undone, offering a tantalizing glimpse of sculpted pectoral muscles against his bronzed skin. Dark dress pants encase his long legs, and his dark, tousled hair is swept back, the unruly curls framing his face with a casual elegance.

My presence brings their heated argument to an abrupt halt, an unnerving silence descending upon the doorway. Damien's gaze locks onto mine instantly, his face etched with a desperate plea as his eyes dart between my protective embrace of a trembling Charlotte and my own furious expression.

A grimace twists his features, the lines around his eyes deepening with a visible wave of regret.

Seeing him, a glacial fury washes over me, my breath catching in my throat. My arms instinctively tighten around my sister, shielding her from his unwanted presence.

I turn to Al, my voice a low, seething growl. "I thought he wasn't invited?"

Damien's jaw clenched at my accusatory tone, but he offered no other outward reaction.

"He wasn't," Al deadpans, attempting to physically steer Damien's large frame back out the doorway. But the younger Rockwell stands his ground with surprising ease, his dark eyes fixes on me with a solemn intensity, the creases on his forehead hinting at a profound weariness.

"I wasn't going to stay. I was just trying to drop this off..." Damien replies quietly, gesturing to the overflowing plastic bag clutched in his hand. He eyes Charlotte warily, as if her terrified reaction had completely deflated his bravado.

"Stop looking at her!" I spit out, my grip on Charlotte tightening almost imperceptibly.

At my sharp outburst, I feel Charlotte's head turn, her face no longer buried in my shoulder. Her small hands suddenly push against me, her attention now fixated on the colorful contents of the bag in Damien's grasp.

She wipes at the tears still clinging to her eyelashes, a sniffle escaping her as a bead of snot glistened on her upper lip. Her gaze flickers between the bag and me before she leans in close, her voice a mere whisper against my ear.

"Is that a crown?" she asks, her breath warm against my skin.

I finally register the contents of the bag for the first time. Stuffed within the stretched plastic are a multitude of toys, various building blocks and sets, play dolls with vibrant hair, and an array of sparkly dress-up items. While the objects seemed to momentarily distract Charlotte, they only fuel my rising tide of anger.

I shoot Damien a venomous glare, and he visibly flinches under the intensity of my gaze.

"What's all of that?" I demand, already certain of the answer.

He looks genuinely surprised by my hostility. "It's... uh... for the kids," he stammers, one of his large hands moving to nervously rub the back of his neck. His earlier dominant stance against his father is completely gone, the imposing figure reduced to a shy, awkward mess. A faint blush creeps across the apples of his cheeks, and his eyes nervously dart downwards. He shuffles his feet slightly, the weight of my judgment palpable.

Charlotte abruptly pulls away from me, wriggling out of my arms. Her puffy, tear-stained face brightens at the sight of the bag of goodies. I reach to steady her, but she quickly makes her way in front of Damien, stopping a few feet away to tilt her head up, regarding his intimidating form with a cautious curiosity.

Damien immediately crouches down until he is almost eye-level with her, extending his arm and offering her the overflowing bag.

Charlotte tilts her head further, her brow furrowed in innocent suspicion. "Are those really for us?" she asks hesitantly.

Damien nods slowly, a soft, tentative smile gracing his lips. He seems to be moving with deliberate gentleness, careful not to frighten her further. "Yes, these are for you," he says softly.

Charlotte doesn't reach for the bag yet, her gaze still fixed on him with wary caution. "I thought you hated us, though?" she asks timidly, the innocent question a sharp jab to my already frayed nerves.

Damien shakes his head, his eyes fills with a genuine sadness, his broad shoulders slumping almost imperceptibly. "No, I don't hate you kids. I was just… uh… sick that day," he gestures towards the bag, his voice still soft and steady. "I want you to know that I am very sorry for how I behaved. It wasn't okay for me to respond that way, and this bag is to ask you to forgive me."

A small, hesitant smile touches Charlotte's lips. "It's okay. One time my tummy hurt, and I yelled at Charlie," she offers by way of understanding, finally reaching out to grasp the offered bag.

161

She turns around quickly, her voice ringing with newfound excitement. "New toys!"

Immediately, the sound of a miniature stampede echoes through the house as Marcus and Charlie come barreling towards Charlotte, only to abruptly halt when they spot Damien. Charlotte rushes over to them, and I could vaguely hear her excitedly explaining the situation, the tension in the other childrens' small bodies slowly dissipating as the three of them began to enthusiastically rummage through the bag.

Lou and Kelsey are not far behind, little Evie perched on Lou's hip, her tiny hand reaching for the woman's pearl necklace. I notice that Lou doesn't even seem to register the grabby fingers, her gaze a hard, disapproving glare directed at both her husband and son, her displeasure with the unexpected turn of events radiating off her in waves.

I turn to Damien, a scowl twisting my features as I took in the older man's surprisingly happy expression, his eyes contentedly watching the children explore their new treasures.

Not wanting the kids to overhear, I close the distance between Damien and me.

His eyes widen slightly at my approach, and his entire demeanor seems to brighten the closer I got. A warm, hopeful smile blooms on his face, and he even straightens his broad shoulders. If I didn't know better, I would have said he subtly opened his arms in an unspoken invitation for a hug.

But I am seething with barely contained fury.

"What the fuck was that?!" I hiss angrily, trying to keep my voice low so as not to disrupt the children's newfound joy. My eyes narrow into angry slits, and my shoulders go rigid with tension.

Damien looks genuinely taken aback. "What do you mean?" he asks, his brow furrows in confusion. "I realized that my actions in the store were inappropriate, and I came to apologize," he states matter-of-factly, as if it were the most logical thing in the world.

"So you think bribing kids is the correct way to go?" I scoff, my voice dripping with sarcasm.

A low chuckle escapes Damien's lips before he awkwardly tries to suppress a smile. "Isn't that what you do at the hospital?" he asks, a hint of barely contained laughter in his voice. His large hand comes up to wipe at his mouth, but a telltale quiver at the corners of his pink lips betrays his amusement.

I all but snarl in response, my hands clenching into tight fists at my sides. "That's completely different! I'm helping children; you're trying to excuse your atrocious behavior," I whisper-yell, the effort to keep my voice down only amplifies my rage.

Damien meets my furious glare with a surprising calm. "I'm trying to take responsibility for my actions," he states evenly, his composure only serving to deepen my anger. "They weren't even supposed to see me. I was going to slowly ease my way into getting them to like me, but it seems they are far more forgiving than I anticipated."

My chest puffs out with indignation, and I took a threatening step forward. "You son of a—"

I ams abruptly interrupted by Lou's hand landing firmly on my shoulder, her grip surprisingly strong.

"Damien, this was rather inappropriate timing to try and make amends," she says flatly, her other hand running in a reassuring motion down my arm. Evie was no longer in her arms; I could only assume Kelsey had taken her.

Damien's composure finally begins to crack, a scowl darkening his features. "There wasn't another time I could do this," he argues, his gaze troubled as he looked at me. "If I had dropped off the items at the hospital, you wouldn't have given them to the kids, and I know you wouldn't have let me apologize to them in person."

I grind my teeth, my gaze flicking away from his earnest expression. What he said isn't entirely wrong. I likely would have intercepted the toys and possibly thrown them in the nearest dumpster—not to mention the silent vow I had made to myself that Damien Rockwell wouldn't come within ten feet of my kids again. If he had genuinely intended to apologize and make amends, I wouldn't have been in a receptive mood to grant him the opportunity, let alone entertain the idea.

A bitter taste rises in my throat.

Fuck, now I'm the bad guy?

A tense silence stretches between us, and I fight to keep the turmoil his words has stirred from showing on my face. It is a difficult task under his intense gaze, his dark eyes imploring me to say something, to argue against his logic. But I remain stubbornly silent.

"Are you staying for dinner?" I finally ask, the words forced through clenched teeth.

Damien inhales sharply, his expression instantly brightening with elation. He takes a step closer, his tall frame leaning slightly over my shorter one. A stray curl falls across his forehead as he tilts his head down, an unfortunately endearing gesture that softens his features. His dark eyes remain locked on mine, an almost physical intensity in their depths. Up this close, with the top of his shirt slightly open, I could see the defined lines of his chest and the powerful muscles tracing down his arms. I might have appreciated the view more if the pungent, overwhelming scent of his cologne hadn't assaulted my nostrils once again. Much to my dismay, that same spicy, warm fragrance engulfs me, causing my nose to involuntarily wrinkle.

Ugh, it's so fucking strong. Doesn't he know the two-spritz rule?

It isn't that he smelled bad, but the sheer potency of the cologne is staggering, threatening to overwhelm my senses. It is also infuriatingly unidentifiable, a complex blend that hints at spice and warmth, but with an unexpected sharp edge. Whatever ridiculously named brand it is, something like Burning Autumnal Breeze or Spicy Firewood or Caramelized Leaves, is clearly overcompensating.

I am so caught up in the olfactory assault that I startle slightly when Damien finally speaks, his voice a low, almost dreamy murmur.

"I'd love to," he replies to my curt invitation, a surprising calm settling over his features for the first time since his arrival. The tense lines around his eyes have smoothed out, and the muscles in his arms appear relaxed.

I glance over at Lou, her face an impassive mask, the same neutral expression she often wore when observing someone's questionable behavior. Al, on the other hand, seems to be oscillating between a lingering annoyance and a reluctant amusement at the unfolding drama.

A slow, wicked smirk spreads across my face.

An immense sense of satisfaction courses through me as I register the flicker of confusion that crosses Damien's handsome features at my sudden shift in demeanor.

"Hey, kids!" I yell, my voice suddenly bright and cheerful, instantly capturing their attention. My eyes remain locked on Damien's as I take a deliberate half-step back, a subtle movement that causes his brows to twitch momentarily.

"Damien just said that unicorns aren't real…"

A screech of indignant outrage erupts from Charlotte, followed by the unmistakable sound of small feet pounding on the wooden floor.

"That superheroes are lame…"

Another, equally vehement yell echoes through the room, accompanied by the determined stomping of another set of feet.

"And that comic books are terrible."

A chorus of childish profanities soon follow, punctuated by the sound of a third person rapidly approaching.

I couldn't contain the evil grin that stretched across my face as the three children, who had moments before been terrified of the brooding man in front of me, now approach with flushed, furious faces. Damien takes a hesitant step back, but it isn't nearly enough to evade the impending onslaught. Like a swarm of angry bees, the three quickly surround him, launching into a tirade of indignant accusations. The verbal abuse, a chaotic blend of three high-pitched voices, is almost impossible to decipher.

My grin widens as I watch Damien's face contort in a mixture of shock and utter helplessness. This tall, imposing man, who has exuded such a menacing aura just moments ago, now looks completely defeated by the furious onslaught of three small children. His earlier attempts to passively win them over are completely lost in the cacophony of their righteous anger.

I turn to find Kelsey watching the scene with a similar, spiteful amusement etched on her face. We share a brief, knowing look, and she gives me a small, approving nod.

Lou, however, shoots me a hard look of blatant disapproval, but I simply ignore her silent reprimand and offer her a wide, innocent smile.

"Well, let's eat. I'm starving," I announce cheerfully, turning and walking back towards the dining room. Kelsey follows, a chuckle bubbling in her throat, and I risk one last glance back at Damien.

The man is already a disheveled mess. His expensive dress pants are wrinkled from small hands desperately trying to grab his attention and make him listen to their impassioned arguments. His eyes are wide and frantic, his large hands hovering uselessly in front of him, attempting to gently fend off the tiny terrors clinging to his legs. The kids are relentless in their insults, their youthful indignation a surprisingly potent weapon. While I normally wouldn't condone such behavior, a fresh wave of amusement washes over me as I see Charlie deliberately stomp down on Damien's undoubtedly expensive leather shoes.

In utter desperation, Damien's wide, pleading eyes scan the room until they lock onto mine, and he mouths a silent, hopeless plea: "Help me."

I glance between his tormented face and the three furious children clinging to his limbs, a silent debate raging within me. Should I call them off? Or should I let them continue their torture?

He hadn't wanted them to be scared of him, well, they certainly aren't scared now.

I mouth back a concise, two-word reply: "Fuck you," and turn to join the others for dinner.

BRAYDEN

Thursday 8:10 pm

Dinner had concluded, and I was meticulously wiping down the long dining room table... again. The cloth in my hand glided smoothly over the polished surface, no longer picking up any lingering grime. The scent of wood polish, layered upon layer, now heavily permeated the air.

But I had stubbornly refused to leave this self-imposed exile.

Perhaps it was childish behavior for a guest, this silent, sulking timeout away from the rest of the group, but the thought of joining everyone in the living room, where *he* was, felt utterly unbearable.

It was all Damien's fault.

When dinner commenced, I had fully expected him to maintain a wide berth from the children after their earlier, rather... enthusiastic... reception. Instead, he had strategically positioned himself as close to the trio as possible. Somehow, with an almost unnerving patience, he had engaged each of them in individual conversations, calmly listening to their vehement arguments against his supposed opinions, genuinely hearing their perspectives. By the end of the meal, the kids, feeling validated and victorious in their intellectual triumph, had completely warmed to him, their earlier berating dissolving into excited chatter about their various passions.

Much to my profound dismay, I witnessed the kids becoming increasingly, almost alarmingly, infatuated with Damien. And once dinner was over, they had collectively pleaded with him to play.

The man, with a dazed, almost lovesick smile plastered across his face, had readily agreed.

Now, everyone was gathered in the living room, and through my frequent glances through the dining room doorway, I could see a scene of domestic bliss that made my stomach churn. Kelsey and Al were engaged in quiet conversation on the couch, while Lou sat on the floor with Charlie and Charlotte, immersed in a world of colorful building blocks. Damien, perched on a side chair, had a rapt Evie nestled on his knee, listening intently as Marcus animatedly discussed the intricacies of his newest comic book lore.

And I had chosen to hide in the supposed sanctity of the dining room.

After dinner, I had swiftly volunteered for cleanup duty, seizing the opportunity for isolation. At one point, Lou had entered, offering a hand, but after witnessing my tight-lipped demeanor and receiving my curt responses, she had wisely retreated, leaving me to my task. I had stretched the chore out with painstaking detail, meticulously washing every dish, scrubbing every countertop, and even pulling out each dining chair to sweep beneath the table.

It had taken a while, but not nearly long enough. I had finished almost ten minutes ago and was now desperately grasping at straws, searching for any plausible excuse to avoid re-entering the same room as Damien.

I look up at the sound of approaching footsteps and see Kelsey enter the room, a knowing smirk playing on her lips. She glances pointedly at the pristine table and the still-clutched cleaning cloth in my hand, her expression radiating unimpressed amusement.

"You done with your tantrum?" she asks casually, leaning against the doorframe.

I purse my lips stubbornly. "Not yet…" I reply, launching into another pointless swipe of the already gleaming tabletop.

She chuckles, pushing a stray lock of hair behind her ear. "I don't really know why you're still upset," she admits, raising an inquisitive eyebrow.

I stop my futile cleaning and spin around in annoyance. "I'm upset because that man… he's such a… he shouldn't have… ugh!" I huff, turning back to the table with a renewed scowl.

"The fucking bastard needs to just leave us alone," I finally grit out, refusing to meet her gaze.

Kelsey sighs, her tone surprisingly even. "I know you don't like him, for many reasons, and that's fine. But I think you're upset because you gave him a test, and he passed." She pauses, her words hanging in the air, causing me to finally cease my assault on the defenseless table and glare at the worn wood.

"You basically sicced the kids on him, and he handled the situation. He even gained their trust. I think there are plenty of valid reasons for you to dislike the man, Brayden, but disliking him because he managed a situation *you* instigated isn't really one of them," she responds, her logic undeniable.

I sigh, the truth of her words hitting home. Glancing through the doorway once more, I see Marcus and Al now engrossed in a game of cards, while Damien is solely occupied with a giggling Evie perched on his knee, her tiny hands tugging playfully at his dark curls. Every so often, a particularly enthusiastic tug would elicit a barely perceptible wince from him, but otherwise, his face is alight with genuine amusement.

He looks completely different than every other time I have encountered him. This calm, gentle demeanor is far more appealing than the often-brooding, volatile Mr. Rockwell I had come to know at the hospital.

I release the cleaning cloth, letting it fall onto the table. "You're right," I admit to Kelsey, "there are plenty of other reasons to not like him."

She rolls her eyes, clearly exasperated by my stubbornness. "Don't be a jackass, Brayden. He's still your boss. You need to at least be civil," she states pointedly.

I look down, a flicker of shame washing over me at her blunt assessment, but I don't offer a correction.

"Fine, I'll come out," I concede, casting an apprehensive glance towards the living room.

"There ya go, Bray. Way to take life by the balls," she says with a mocking smile.

Glaring at her, I grab both ends of the rag in my hand and begin to quickly wind it into a makeshift whip. Kelsey, recognizing my intent, lets out a playful squeal and darts out of the room, the wet cloth snapping harmlessly in the air just behind her retreating form.

I watch her disappear back into the living area, then give a resigned sigh and trudge back into the kitchen to rinse the rag in the sink.

Kelsey is right. Being petty and antagonistic towards my boss isn't a smart move, especially considering his significant contractual control over my life. I also try to remind myself that the man was, in fact, sick. It didn't excuse his past behavior, but it did offer a framework for understanding his actions a little better.

Perhaps this gentle side of Damien was his normal side? Everyone in town seemed to hold him in high regard.

Remembering his recovery actually put me a little more at ease. His freakouts were described as post-traumatic reactions, and once his therapy was complete, it sounded like he would be a much more pleasant person to be around. I wasn't entirely comfortable with him yet, but I realized my thoughts about Damien weren't as overwhelmingly negative as they had been.

I turn on the faucet in the sink, intending to rinse out the rag, when I am suddenly assaulted by a large, unexpected spray of water.

"Ah!" I yell, sputtering as the cold stream attacks my front. The water instantly blurs my vision, and the front of my t-shirt begins to cling uncomfortably to my chest. I sputter helplessly, blindly reaching out to turn off the faucet.

I take a moment to catch my breath, but the damage is already done. Greatly irritated, I glare at the sink. The top of my head is thoroughly drenched, my hair plastered to my forehead. Water streams down my face and trails across my chest, completely soaking my shirt. The fabric clings unpleasantly to my skin, a cold, wet second layer. A small puddle begins to form on the floor beneath me as I stand there, bewildered by the sudden aquatic assault.

Looking into the sink, I glare at the culprit.

A fucking spoon?!

Completely drenched and thoroughly annoyed, I grumble under my breath as I make my way back into the living room, carefully watching my step on the hardwood floors to avoid slipping.

"Hey Lou, could I bother you for a towel?" I ask, completely mortified by my sodden appearance. Lifting my head, I see that everyone in the living room stops what they are doing and stare at me. A brief moment of stunned silence hangs in the air before the kids erupt in a fit of giggles at my dripping form. While the children found my misery highly amusing, I see Lou begin to rise from the floor, a soft smile playing on her lips, clearly also finding the situation humorous.

"Sure, hun—"

Her offer is abruptly cut short as I feel a warm, strong hand wrap tightly around my bicep, yanking me forward with surprising force.

Just when I have a positive thought about the man.

Surprised, I stumble clumsily forward, my feet stomping loudly as I struggle to regain my balance. I realize the person holding me was rapidly leading me out of the living room and towards the stairs. The thudding of our feet echoes through the corridor, mingling with my startled yelp of surprise. It is difficult to keep pace with his long strides, and I scowl at the broad back steamrolling ahead of me.

Damien is rushing, not bothering to look back, forcing me to follow in his wake, his grip like a vise. Just as I am about to voice my vehement complaint, he abruptly drags us inside a room and slams the door shut behind us.

I jerk at the sudden movement, flinching as my back collides with the solid wood of the door. The cool texture presses against my wet shirt, but a sudden warmth blooms across my chest. Damien stands before me, frozen, one hand still gripping the doorknob, the other stiff at his side. He isn't physically caging me in, but he is definitely too close for comfort.

As my body registers that we are no longer in motion, I immediately sidestep, putting distance between myself and the door, and more importantly, the towering man.

Stepping back, I find myself in a large, rather plain bedroom. A big bed stands against one wall, flanked by a couple of matching pillows on a gray comforter. A lone reading chair sits in the corner. The room is clean but lacks the warmth that permeates the rest of the house, feeling vacant despite its tidiness. It could have been a rarely used guest room, and a sliver of light peeking from the crack of a door on the far side reveals a fully stocked closet.

Damien's intense gaze burns into me, and I reluctantly meet his eyes. He is breathing heavily, his mouth slightly ajar as he takes deep, ragged breaths, his focus solely on my dripping form. His hand clutches the doorknob with a painful tightness, the metal protesting with a squeak, rattling in his trembling grip.

I try to suppress a glare, remembering Kelsey's and my earlier conversation about attempting civility with my boss. But his mere presence is a constant, grating reminder of his erratic behavior. The man is truly insane.

A tense silence hangs in the air before Damien takes a shuddering breath, curses under his breath, and rushes through one of the side doors, speed-walking. Confused by his abrupt exit, I remain rooted to the spot, watching as a light flickers on beyond the door he'd disappeared through. The tiled flooring visible through the opening confirms my suspicion, an ensuite bathroom. Moments later, the sounds of banging cabinets, the clatter of falling bottles, and more muttered curses echoes from within.

Completely bewildered by the rapid turn of events, I decide I've had enough.

"So, I'm just going to go—AH!"

I jump back with a startled yelp as a towel abruptly smacks me in the face.

"Dry off, now," Damien's voice, rough and slightly strained, demands from the bathroom.

Scowling, I rip the terrycloth from my face and glare at the doorway. "Are you kidding me?!" I exclaim, irritation lacing my voice. "There was a much more polite way to get me a towel," I hiss, fisting the fabric in front of me.

Damien shrugs, his eyes fixed on me. "You were soaking the floor. Getting you off my mother's living room Turkish rug was priority one; the towel was a close second," he explains smoothly, a flicker of amusement lighting his eyes at my obvious annoyance.

I open my mouth to retort, but the logic of his statement catches me short. My eyes widen slightly.

"Thanks," I mumble, releasing my tight grip on the towel and bringing it to my face. I am not sure how to process his bizarre blend of practicality and subtle mockery. His words make sense, but the victorious glint in his eyes feels anything but polite.

Bending slightly, I roughly run the towel through my hair, trying to wring out as much moisture as possible. When I straighten up, a folded t-shirt is unexpectedly shoved into my face.

"What's that?" I ask, eyeing the garment warily.

"An old high school t-shirt of mine. Figured you'd prefer this to one of my mom's blouses," he states nonchalantly, thrusting the shirt closer.

A small smile tugs at my lips at his unexpected joke, and I quickly try to suppress it.

Too late.

The moment my lips twitches, Damien's eyes lit up. His once-stiff body seems to come alive, his chest heaving, his fingers twitching, a subtle tremor running through him for some unknown reason.

"Thanks," I simply reply, tentatively taking the offered shirt.

Without hesitation, I grab the hem of my soaked shirt and whip it over my head, eager to escape the cold, clinging fabric. As my vision is momentarily obscured, I hear a sharp, choked gasp.

I quickly pulled the shirt off and tossed it to the floor. Looking up, I found Damien even closer than before, his large frame now towering over my half-naked form, his broad shoulders leaning slightly. He remained silent, his intense gaze fixed on my face, an earnestness in his eyes that made me uneasy.

"What?" I ask, confused, slowly taking the dry shirt that hung limply in his hand.

Looking at his face, I am surprised by the raw desire burning in his eyes. I know he finds me attractive, but the sheer need in his gaze is almost unbearable. The dominant intensity might have been endearing had it not been for the faint flush of red spreading across his cheeks.

I suppress a dramatic eye roll. He is blushing.

It is rather unfortunate timing. I consider myself a submissive, though I could easily switch to dominant based on a client's preference. The idea of a lover holding complete reign in the bedroom appeals to me, the trust of relinquishing control to a true Dom who knows me intimately. As I am usually the one leading the games, the thought of surrendering that control, of giving my pleasure to someone I feel safe with, holds a unique comfort, unlike the detached interactions of work.

Damien's physique and persona certainly fits the Dom archetype. He looks the part, but his obvious inexperience shatters the illusion. He doesn't know the game, and no one could instinctively read a submissive cold-turkey without experience. It would take a miracle for him to possess the skills to safely pleasure a partner.

He probably already has a hard-on from seeing me shirtless.

Damien seems utterly lost, his eyes darting rapidly from my chest to my face. He closes his eyes briefly, his face contorting as if in physical pain.

Yep, definitely hard.

"Uh… the bathroom is right there," he rasps, weakly gesturing to the door he'd previously used, "You… didn't want some privacy?" A note of surprise edges his voice. He seems to have regained some semblance of control, though his gaze is now fixed intently on the floor. His hands clench and unclench at his sides.

At his inquiry, I roll my eyes. "I'm sure you've seen more in a men's locker room," I reply casually, grabbing the dry t-shirt and pulling it over my head. "Besides," I continue, my view of Damien momentarily obscured, "it's just a shirt. It's not like I was taking off my briefs for you."

With the oversized shirt on, I fully appreciate Damien's considerable size. I am fit, with decent muscle definition, nearly six feet tall, but the shirt completely swallows me. The sleeves hang limply past my biceps, and the collar dips low enough to reveal my entire clavicle.

Looking up, I see Damien is even closer than before. Uncomfortable with his proximity, I instinctively back away as silence stretches between us. Noticing the direction of his gaze, I try to appear nonchalant, resisting the urge to cover my arms.

Of course, he could see them now. The long sleeves I'd worn earlier had effectively concealed them, but our current closeness means they are impossible to hide.

"If you want to know, you can just ask," I say, acknowledging his unspoken curiosity, wanting to address the subject directly rather than awkwardly avoiding it.

Damien's eyes don't leave my tattoos, or more specifically, the scars beneath.

"How did you get those?" he asks, a tremor of trepidation in his voice. He doesn't seem panicked, but genuine concern is etched on his face.

Subconsciously, my right hand rubs over the tricep of my left arm, feeling the familiar ridges of my scars, slowly tracing the dark pattern tattooed over them.

"Car accident," I say, avoiding his gaze. The tips of my fingers lightly brush over the swirling black ink at the edge of my wrist. "A friend of mine offered to cover the scars, and I said yes," I explain lightly, my fingers trailing up the length of my arm.

I feel Damien hovering over me, the cool mint of his breath brushing against my face as he leans closer.

"Oh yeah?" he mumbles weakly, his body following his face.

I look up, meeting his smoldering gaze. Up this close, his eyes seem darker, or perhaps it is a trick of the light. Either way, the dark chocolate pools seem to deepen as his pupils dilate. The strong scent of his cologne returns, and for the first time, it fills the air with an almost intoxicating presence. With a deep breath, my lungs fill with the spicy aroma, and a sudden heat blooms within me. I find myself subconsciously relaxing, a strange sense of comfort washing over me that defies logic.

I don't remember that happening before.

"They cover most of my left side," I explain, trying to ignore the strange, heated atmosphere that seems to have enveloped us, but the room around us is already beginning to feel hazy, my focus narrowing to Damien.

Damien's tongue briefly flicks out to wet his pink lips, his eyes still fixed on my own. He is so close I could see the faint shadow of stubble along his jawline and the subtle flexing of the muscles beneath his shirt-covered shoulder.

"Fascinating," he mumbles, his gaze now drifting to my lips.

"Yeah, they begin on my left arm…"

Damien's left arm comes up, caging one side of my head, and my breathing hitches slightly.

What the fuck is happening…

"…and continue down the left side of my chest…"

I feel his other arm come up, mirroring the first, and a sudden chill ran down my spine.

My head feels heavy…

"…and end at the bottom of my left thigh," I finish breathlessly.

Damien's forehead leans into mine, the contact sending a strange shiver through me.

In this position, I could either tilt my head up, bringing us even closer, or tilt it down. Choosing the latter, my eyes find themselves drawn to his legs but are quickly distracted by the very prominent bulge in his pants.

Well, fuck my life. That actually looks like it could be fun. It's always the crazy ones who are blessed.

I feel his chest press against my shoulders, and my back hits the door with a soft thud. The sudden movement jolts me out of the strange, lustful fog that seems to have disoriented me. The heady scent of his cologne wanes as I rapidly blink, trying to clear my mind.

I am confused about how we'd gotten here. It was like I couldn't move… no, I had control… I think. Something smelled good, and then…

Goddamn it, Brayden! You promised yourself you would never be taken advantage of again. Take control of this now!

My hand shoots out, curling my fingers through the belt loop of his pants. I feel Damien shudder violently at my touch.

"You like being in control?" I ask, tilting my head up, softening my eyes in what I hoped is an alluring gaze.

Damien's lips part, his pupils huge and dilated. His forehead is furrows, his face and the obvious bulge in his pants straining with what look like genuine pain. He doesn't answer, but he is undeniably captivated.

"Next time you think you can take control of someone, remember never to lead with your shoulders," I murmur against his ear, my fingers stealthily grazing the top of his pant zipper. An immediate heat flares beneath my fingertips, and I feel him violently pulse under my light caress.

His body convulses under my touch, a pathetic mewl escaping his lips in response to my actions.

The distraction gives me the opportunity I need and I swiftly duck under his arms. If I had moved completely away, he might have realized I was trying to escape and attempted to coax me back, or worse, grabbed me before I could reach the door. My continued touch and the subtle rubbing against him seems to keep him locked in his lust-filled daze, exactly where I want him. I didn't let my hand stop its suggestive massage, pressing my body intimately against his hip.

"A real Dom knows that you always lead with your hips," I whisper in his ear, deliberately thrusting my hips against his.

He gasps, a sharp intake of breath, and I seize the moment to quickly open the door and slip out of the room, the soft, involuntary moans of a man coming undone echoing behind me.

I couldn't help but scowl at the closed door as I listen to the muffled sounds of his climax.

"I'm not interested in anything other than professional interaction with you, Mr. Rockwell," I state firmly through the door. "Do not try anything pertaining to sexual activities with me again." A smirk plays on my lips, even though he couldn't see it, hoping he could hear it in my voice. "I'm not interested in being your teacher."

Damien is a celibate Dom, the most unfortunate and frustrating position to be in. He craves control but has absolutely no idea how to wield it.

Poor man just needs to get laid.

A muffled groan resonates on the other side of the threshold, undoubtedly the only reaction the man was capable of after his abrupt orgasm, followed by the distinct thud of a head hitting the door.

Not wanting to push my luck, I quickly head downstairs.

There, I took control. I am in control. He doesn't have control over me... right?

BRAYDEN

Sunday 9:44 am

I tug at the collar of the button-down shirt, the scratchy fabric feeling like a noose in the growing morning heat. The long sleeves chafe uncomfortably against the raised skin of my scars and the short walk from the car to the building has left me feeling sticky and suffocated.

"It's too early for this, Brayden!" Marcus whines from behind me, the dragging of his feet against the concrete a testament to his displeasure.

"This is stupid. Who cares about a stupid person in the sky?" Charlie grumbles, crossing his arms in defiance.

I sigh, trying to maintain a semblance of calm. "It's only for today. We never have to go again after this morning." Although inside, I echo their sentiments, wanting nothing more than to whine alongside them.

Kelsey scoffs from beside me, her eyes fixed on the unassuming wooden building with undisguised contempt. "I can't believe you signed us up for this," she says bitterly.

"I didn't, not really…" I reply dejectedly. It isn't entirely my fault, but my desperate job search after Mom's passing has inadvertently led us to this unfortunate Sunday morning.

In the immediate aftermath of Mom's death, a frantic energy had propelled me to apply for jobs across the country. Location, hours, workload, none of it mattered. Hundreds of applications had been sent into the void.

And the void had largely remained silent.

Apparently, my lack of prior experience made me an undesirable candidate for entry-level positions. Desperation had begun to set in when I stumbled upon an opening at a hospital in the obscure town of Rocky Falls. The catch? It was a private institution affiliated with a religious group. In my haste to fill out the application, I had ticked a box claiming adherence to their faith, and to my surprise, I had received a call the very next day.

That minor, convenient lie in my contract had completely slipped my mind until Dr. Monroe had called me into his office the previous week to discuss my "beliefs." It had taken all of two minutes to become painfully clear that my knowledge of the hospital's affiliated religious organization and its tenets was nonexistent. Thankfully, Dr. Monroe hadn't threatened termination, but he had strongly encouraged me to familiarize myself with the religion to better understand patient terminology and potential unusual treatment requests.

I hadn't felt in a position to argue. The only truly irksome part of his suggestion was the mandatory attendance of at least one service at the so-called temple in town.

Which brought us to this less-than-holy predicament.

The six of us stand on the front stoop of the looming structure and now face two thick, imposing doors. Kelsey observes the building with quiet disdain, while the two boys continue their low-grade bickering. Evie, nestled in my arms, contentedly sucks on her bottle, her bare feet occasionally kicking against my chest. Charlotte clings tightly to my leg, perched precariously on my foot, a constant stream of complaints about the heat escaping her lips.

Odd. This is supposed to be a holy place, yet I felt closer to hell.

Turning to the disgruntled mini-mob, I try to mask my own growing irritation. "Alright," I announce, attempting to gather their attention, "when we go inside, we are all going to sit down and be quiet." A chorus of disgruntled moans follows, which I valiantly try to ignore before I succumb to the urge to join in. "After the speaker is done, we will leave as quickly as possible, so no running off after the service is over," I add, directing a pointed look at Charlie.

My gaze meets Kelsey's, and I see her already giving me a dejected look, silently mouthing, 'You owe me' from behind the kids.

I sigh, grabbing the heavy, cold metal doorknob. 'I know,' I mouth back in agreement, the unspoken understanding that our Sunday morning is destined for further unpleasantness hanging heavy in the air.

With a reluctant pull, I open the doors and blink rapidly, trying to adjust my eyes to the dimly lit interior. Despite my lack of religious inclination, the sanctuary look predictably temple-like or church-like. I consciously avoid making eye contact with anyone, not wanting to draw unwanted attention to our clearly out-of-place group.

Just stay in your seats and mind your own business. We're not regulars, and this will be the last time we're here.

I hesitate for a moment, scanning the rows of pews, when I spot Lou, Al, and Damien sitting just to the left of the stage in what appears to be designated seating. As the doors creak open, Damien's attention snaps towards us, and he immediately straightens up, his eyes locking onto mine. Even from this distance, I could see the surprise register on his face, his mouth dropping open slightly in shock before spreading into a wide, enthusiastic grin. He eagerly begins waving us over, causing several nearby congregants to turn around, curious about the source of his enthusiastic greeting.

It is obvious he wanted us to sit with them, and selfishly, I know that their presence would likely help keep the kids in line during the service... but I couldn't bring myself to do it.

After the charged encounter between Damien and me on Friday night, I had practically fled back downstairs, only to find Evie in the throes of inconsolable tears. Grateful for the convenient excuse to escape, I had quickly bundled the kids into the car and headed home before Damien reappeared. I hadn't seen him since. The thought of a confrontation this morning, especially in my already irritated state, was deeply unappealing. Not to mention, I've been sexually frustrated all weekend as I had received a text from Travis saying that he had wanted to cut ties because he was now in a serious relationship.

Yeah, dealing with Damien right now would not be good. I am far too annoyed to risk snapping at the man who owns my house.

"You want to head to the front?" Kelsey asks apprehensively, gesturing towards the enthusiastically waving man.

"No, I'd rather sit in the back for a quick escape later," I reply, already steering the kids towards the closest pew to the door, the farthest one from the stage.

"That's probably for the best," she agrees, as we maneuvered the kids into their seats and deposited our various bags of snacks and distractions. "Any closer to the altar, and you'd be struck down by lightning," she deadpans, leaning back in the pew with a lazy sigh.

A snort of laughter escapes me, but I quickly stifle it as I notice a few heads turning in our direction. Some people glance back at my sudden outburst before quickly refocusing on the front, whispering amongst themselves. It is becoming increasingly clear that the longer we remain, the more we are attracting unwanted attention.

Kelsey leans forward and grabs a pamphlet from the back of the pew in front of us before opening it with a curious frown. "Huh, they're a matriarchal religion," she murmurs, quickly scanning the information.

My eyes widen. "Really?" I inquire, leaning over her shoulder to get a better look myself. "Prophetess or deity?"

Kelsey shrugs. "I think Goddess. There's some weird stuff about her connection to the night and the cycles of the moon."

Marcus perks up from beside me, his eyes lighting up with sudden interest. "Oh, like Nyx!" he exclaims, pushing his glasses further up his nose and swiftly snatching the pamphlet from Kelsey's hands.

She shoots him a sharp glare but refrains from comment, likely wanting to avoid a public squabble.

I give him a confused look. "Who?" I ask.

He rolls his eyes, his tone condescending. "The Goddess of the night. She was worshipped in Greece for her powers over the moon," he states haughtily, clearly pleased to possess knowledge I lacked. "She's related to the myths of the underworld and other mythical creatures."

Charlie looks at him with wide-eyed curiosity. "What's the underworld?"

"It's a place full of monsters that torture people for being bad," Marcus replies, a disturbingly evil glint in his eyes.

Charlotte's eyes grow wide with alarm. "I don't want to be eaten by monsters!" she exclaims, drawing even more unwanted attention from those around us.

Marcus seems rather amused by our younger sibling's sudden fear. "Well, if you've ever lied or said a bad word, you're going to a dark dungeon after you die and—OW!" he yelps, his dark ramblings interrupted by a sharp rap on the head from Kelsey.

"Shut up," Kelsey hisses, clearly annoyed. Marcus merely rolls his eyes in response.

That little fucker.

I feel small hands grasp my arm, and I see Charlie looking up at me with wide, anxious eyes. "I don't want Brayden to be tortured after he dies!" he exclaims, his voice just as loud as Charlotte's earlier outburst.

My eyes widen in alarm. "Why would I go to hell?" I ask, aghast at the sudden theological turn.

"You swear a lot! You're going to be tortured, Brayden!" Charlotte wails, her grip on my arm tightening.

Charlotte's lower lip begins to tremble, and she joins Charlie in clinging to my arm. The two children have now created enough of a commotion that most people in the temple are openly watching us, and I could see the congregation struggling to suppress amused smiles. A wave of mortification washes over me, my blood rushing to my ears as I turn my face away, trying to hide my burning blush.

Kelsey is now berating Marcus in a low, furious whisper, the little know-it-all looking slightly ashamed by the scene he has inadvertently caused.

"No one is going to be tortured for swearing. We're not going to the underworld when we die," I say exasperatedly in a hushed tone, "especially for something as small as lying or swearing."

"Yeah, Charlie," Marcus chimes in, attempting to lighten the increasingly awkward atmosphere, "if Bray's going to be tortured, it's because he sleeps around—OW!" he yelps again as Kelsey delivers another well-aimed swat to his head.

She glares at him, while he rubs his head and mutters that he is just trying to help.

"Keep talking," she threatens him, her voice low and dangerous, "I can do this all morning."

Not wanting to get caught in the crossfire between Kelsey and Marcus, I focus on trying to console the increasingly distressed twins. "I'm not going to the underworld," I says firmly, "none of us are."

"I don't want to stay here anymore. It's scary," Charlotte whimpers, crawling into my lap and clutching my shirt.

"Yeah, the sooner we leave, the sooner the scary moon-lady forgets about us, and then we won't be tortured," Charlie agrees, his gaze fixed on the large, imposing statue of the Goddess on the stage.

"Nobody is going to be tortured!" I finally exclaim, my carefully maintained composure cracking under the weight of the ridiculous situation.

"Excuse me," a polite woman's voice says from my side of the pew. "But she was trying to make a run for it."

Startled, I look over and see a stranger holding my grinning baby sister. My face instantly flush a deeper shade of red as I realize that Evie must have quietly dashed down the pew while I was preoccupied with the twins' anxieties.

"Swearing might not send you to hell, Bray, but child abandonment probably will," Kelsey remarks dryly, her tone laced with amusement.

I give the woman a strained smile as I try not to completely lose it on my smartass sister.

The woman is striking in her own way, tall and lean with long limbs and sharp angles defining her pointy elbows and prominent cheekbones. Her smooth skin starkly contrasts the deep furrows etched around her mouth and the noticeable shadows beneath her hazel eyes, which are a little dull. Her short hair shows hints of gray, adding to an overall air of weariness that ages her features, making her appear older than she likely is.

"I'm so sorry," I say, mortified by the disruption. "This is our first time here, I promise we won't disturb you anymore."

I attempt to stand and retrieve Evie, but Charlotte remains stubbornly glued to my lap, burying her head deeper into my chest. This forces me to awkwardly reach up with only one arm to pluck Evie from the woman's grasp.

Evie immediately begins scaling my arm, wrapping her chubby limbs around my head. "We'll try to keep it down for the rest of the service," I offer with a weak, apologetic smile.

While I am speaking, Charlie decides to join the snuggle-fest, clambering onto my lap and settling himself across my legs. I wince at the added weight but couldn't dislodge him, as Charlotte has my right arm effectively pinned, and Evie is now using my left arm as a precarious perch. I try to continue addressing the woman, but my words are abruptly cut short as sticky toddler fingers invade my mouth.

I feel small hands gripping my knees and look down to see Charlie desperately clutching my pants. "Don't worry, Brayden! I won't let you be dragged away to the underworld!" he declares with fierce determination, while Charlotte whimpers softly into my shirt.

Once again, I try to offer a coherent apology, but my words emerge as an unintelligible mumble thanks to Evie's hand in my mouth.

From beside me, I hear the stranger emit an amused chuckle and glance over at her.

The thin woman stares at me, and I am slightly taken aback by the intensity of her gaze. While her lips curve in a smile that suggests amusement, there is a noticeable tightness to her features, a subtle discord in her expression. She seems genuinely entertained by the chaotic scene, yet her eyes hold a profound sadness that momentarily steals my breath.

The woman purses her lips, her gaze unwavering as she seems to probe and study me. I don't feel offended by the prolonged assessment, more just bewildered by her intense interest.

"If I could," she begins, her voice surprisingly gentle, "would you mind if I clarified some things with your... uh... kids?" she asks. "They seem to be nervous about some misconceptions of this temple."

"By all means," I reply, finally able to articulate a full sentence. If she could steer their imaginations away from the horrors of the underworld, she could tell them whatever she pleased.

The woman's smile softens, and she turns her attention to the line of children behind me. "I couldn't help but overhear that you all were concerned about the afterlife. I just wanted to say that unlike the Greek mythology of our Goddess, we don't believe she tortures any of her children. Rather, the more faithful we are in our lives, the closer we are to her when we pass on," the woman explains slowly and patiently. "Therefore, the less faithful you are in your life, the farther you will be from her presence."

Kelsey lets out a small, skeptical scoff. "So, there's even classism in the afterlife?"

The woman pauses, her gaze briefly assessing Kelsey, though the older woman doesn't seem perturbed by the blunt question. "We believe that everyone will have equal peace," she responds passively. "The closer you are to the Goddess in your faith while living is how close you'll be to her in the afterlife. Essentially, she gives you as much of her presence as you desire. We believe that everyone will have peace, although an individual's interpretation of peace is unique to them."

Marcus studies the woman, his eyes narrow with speculation. "What about murderers or really bad criminals?"

The red-headed stranger pauses, her gaze drifting towards the altar for a moment in contemplation, a weighty silence following Marcus's pointed question. "As I said, we will only be as close to our Goddess in the afterlife as we are while living. Therefore, if one of her children decides to outright reject her, she will give them peace through a means of something similar to eternal sleep," the woman replies softly, turning back to the kids with a calm expression.

Kelsey remains unconvinced, her eyes still fixed on the stranger. "Wouldn't the ones who were less faithful need to be in her presence the most?"

The woman looks down for a fleeting moment, and the same subtle sadness I had noticed earlier flickers across her face. "Our Goddess wishes for us to seek her affection through the trials she gives her children. Our reactions to the negatives help her better assess those after death," she sighs softly.

For a brief instant, I think I see the beginnings of tears forming in the corners of her eyes before she blinks, and they are gone.

"But why wouldn't she take out revenge on those who reject her? Isn't Nyx super powerful? Isn't she supposed to be a mighty and vengeful warrior?" Marcus persists, skeptical of the woman's gentle explanation.

"While Nyx is a myth based on our Goddess, they are not the same. Our Goddess is a mighty warrior, yes, but we also believe she is also the ultimate comforter," she calmly explains. "Through the trials another might impose on us, we are taught to seek her comfort and presence no matter the circumstance."

I contemplate her answer, still feeling a little confused by the nuances. "But what if someone else's blessing is another's trial?"

The woman seems startled by my question. Her eyes search my face with renewed intensity, and the sadness within them seems to deepen. I stare back, a little unsettled by the weight of her gaze.

Another pause stretches between us before she offers a somber smile. "You know, I don't care what anyone else says, I see him in you."

Her unexpected comment takes me aback, and my head whips over to Kelsey, wondering if I missed a crucial part of our earlier conversation. Seeing Kels looking just as bewildered as I feel, I turn back to the woman, a growing sense of unease settling over me. "Do I remind you of someone—"

"Brayden! I didn't know you were coming today!" an enthusiastic voice booms from behind me.

Turning to the end of the pew, I see Mr. Rockwell standing before the kids, his expression radiating delighted surprise as he looks down at us. His black hair is neatly combed back this morning, and his navy three-piece suit seems to enhance his dark tan complexion with an attractive glow.

I let out a soft grunt as the twins eagerly jump off my lap and rush to Damien, engulfing him in enthusiastic hugs. Marcus also perks up at his arrival and stands to greet him, while Kelsey offers a welcoming smile.

The large man grins down at the children's affection, his adoration for them clear on his face. However, his eyes remain fixed on mine, desperately searching my features with a look bordering on infatuation.

"Why don't you all come to the front and sit with me?" he suggest, looking at me expectantly. "It might be easier to handle the kids with more people."

I keep my face carefully neutral, determined not to betray any emotion. "Thanks for the offer, but we'd prefer to sit in the back," I reply casually. "The bathrooms are closer to this seating, and with three kids under six, there will be a bathroom request at least every ten minutes."

Damien studies my face for a moment before his dark eyes take on a playful glint, completely undeterred by my polite refusal. "I could sit here instead," he suggests, his lips twitching into a teasing smirk. "Since you're new here, there are a lot of things I could *teach* you about the service."

A shiver of unease runs down my spine, and I feel myself instinctively stiffen at his coy words. I fight the urge to glare, forcing my expression to remain passive.

The less reaction I give, the more I prove that Friday did *not* affect me.

"Actually, we've already had a wonderful teacher this morning," I say with a polite smile, gesturing subtly behind me.

Up until this point, the woman beside me has remained silent, observing the interaction. Looking over, I see that she is now timidly staring down at her feet, pointedly avoiding Damien's gaze.

Mr. Rockwell's face becomes a little more guarded as he looks at the woman, his eyes narrowing with a hint of suspicion. "Ah yes, Olivia. I'm sure you were being helpful in matters of the temple," he says, his tone slightly apprehensive.

Olivia offers a meek nod. "Yes, I've been answering some questions the kids had, strictly about the temple."

The dynamic between the two is subtly strange. While there was no overt hostility, a palpable strain hangs in the air, an unspoken conversation simmering beneath the surface that I couldn't quite decipher.

"Is there a reason why you're not in the front row with Aiden?" Damien asks, gesturing towards the front of the sanctuary. Following his movement, I notice Mr. Thompson sitting in the front pew for the first time, trying to inconspicuously glance back in our direction. The bulky man's head swivels nervously back and forth, his hands tapping agitatedly on the back of the pew in front of him.

"I felt a little more comfortable sitting in the back this Sunday," she mumbles, her arms wrapping protectively around herself as she finally meets Damien's gaze. "There are fewer eyes here."

Damien nods, seeming to understand her reasoning, and I couldn't help but feel a pang of sympathy for her. The number of eyes on us in the back is almost suffocating; I couldn't imagine the scrutiny of the front row.

Noticing the rising tension, I attempt to lighten the atmosphere. "How do you know Mr. Thompson?" I ask Olivia with genuine curiosity.

Olivia seems startled by my question, her gaze flicking away from me. "He's my husband," she replies quietly.

"That's a surprise. You're way out of his league," I blurt out with a small, genuine grin.

A moment of silence hangs in the air before the wiry woman lets out a sudden, unrestrained laugh, bringing a hand to her mouth to stifle her loud giggling.

"As you can see, Ms. Olivia and I are getting along fine, and her help is more than enough," I say, turning back to Damien with a dismissive tone. "We're fine sitting back here and don't need any extra help, and more people could be distracting for the kids."

My tone is deliberately cool, and Damien visibly deflates at my words.

"Right," he says, sounding disappointed. "I wouldn't want to create more of a problem with the kids."

He looks at me one last time, a fleeting sadness in his eyes, before turning and walking back down the aisle towards the front. As he walks away, I couldn't help but notice the impeccable tailoring of his pants, the fabric fitting attractively around his muscular legs.

He does have a nice ass—*no, bad Brayden!*

My inappropriate thought surprises me, and I am thankfully distracted by the sound of the organist beginning to play, signaling the start of the service. As the rest of the congregation begins to sing, I feel Olivia lean closer to me.

"I know the answer to your question," she states softly.

I turn to her, giving her a confused look, momentarily forgetting what I had asked.

"You asked me what happens if another's blessing becomes our trial," she says with a gentle, almost melancholic smile. There is a visible brokenness reflected in her eyes, yet slowly, the shattered remnants of pain seem to morph themselves into an even stronger emotion–

"I believe we are meant to turn that trial into our blessing."

–determination.

BRAYDEN

Tuesday 12:06 am

The fluorescent lights of the hospital hallway hum with a relentless, sterile energy, an incessant, high-pitched whine that seems to drill directly into the already throbbing ache behind my eyes. Each pulse of the harsh, unwavering light felt like a tiny hammer blow against my temples, exacerbating the dull, persistent agony. Dr. Monroe's question, sharp and sudden, sliced through the cottony fog of my exhaustion like a cold blade, making me jump, my already-tense muscles spasming as if physically prodded.

"Did you get that, Brayden?" His gaze, magnified slightly by the lenses of his thin, rimless glasses, holds an unnerving intensity and bores into me with an almost clinical detachment, as if trying to extract the last dregs of coherent thought from my thoroughly depleted brain.

"Uh, yes, Sir," I stammer, my hand jerking reflexively, the cheap, lightweight plastic of my pen digging into the thin, flimsy paper of my notepad. My fingers, clumsy and unresponsive with fatigue, struggle to translate the fragmented echoes of his previous pronouncements into legible script. Each shaky stroke sent a fresh wave of queasy nausea churning in the pit of my stomach. The air in the small office felt thick and stale, amplifying the metallic taste in my mouth.

The doctor sighs, a weary, drawn-out sound that seems to carry the accumulated weight of countless such tedious, late-night explanations. He studies me for a long, unnerving moment, his gaze lingering with a detached concern on the dark, bruised circles beneath my eyes, a silent, almost clinical acknowledgment of my evident, almost palpable exhaustion. Then, with a slow, deliberate movement, the worn leather of his executive office chair groaning in protest beneath his weight, he leaned back, the protesting springs amplifying the oppressive silence of the small, dimly lit room. The older man's gaze flickered briefly over my slumped posture, my pale, almost sickly complexion, before he finally offers a curt, almost dismissive gesture towards the closed, heavy door behind me with a languid wave of his hand, a gesture that spoke volumes about his own weariness.

"I think we're done for today," he states, his tone flat and devoid of inflection, leaving no room for argument or further discussion. Relief, sharp and immediate, floods through me, a desperate urge to escape the suffocating confines of this oppressive space. I seize the opportunity like a drowning man gasping for air, my movements jerky and uncoordinated as I practically stumble towards the door, my numb fingers fumbling with the cool, impersonal metal of the handle.

Only after I lurch out into the even brighter, relentlessly humming hallway, the heavy door clicking shut behind me with a solid, strangely reassuring thud that momentarily muffles the incessant, high-pitched whine of the fluorescent lights, did I finally allow myself to exhale the shallow breath I hadn't even realized I'd been holding, my shoulders slumping with the heavy release of tension, my muscles aching in protest. The sterile air of the hallway felt marginally less oppressive than the doctor's office, but the throbbing in my head intensifies with each step.

It is the dead of Tuesday night, and the digital clock ticks past the midnight mark, each passing second amplifying the leaden weight in my limbs. I emerge, blinking and disoriented, from yet another mandatory, soul-crushingly-dull learning session with Dr. Monroe, my brain feeling like an over-soaked sponge, saturated and utterly incapable of absorbing even a single additional drop of the doctor's late-hour religious instruction. While a small, increasingly distant rational part of me vaguely appreciates his apparent willingness to personally discuss the specific, often bizarre, religious requirements the hospital operated under, a far more dominant, all-consuming, and utterly exhausted part of me couldn't shake the persistent, bitter feeling that the majority of his rambling, often tangential explanations could have been efficiently and mercifully summarized on a simple, tri-fold pamphlet.

Or perhaps just the single, remarkably concise line that seems to underpin so many of the hospital's unusual and often perplexing protocols: "Spouses enjoy significantly more freedom and involvement in patient care here than at other, less enlightened institutions." The sheer understatement of that sentence is almost comical in the face of the reality I am slowly beginning to grasp.

According to the core, often perplexing, beliefs of the Lunar Followers, the spouse of an individual holds a unique and almost mystical ability to significantly accelerate the patient's healing process, a deeply-held conviction believed to be divinely ordained and intricately intertwined with the mysterious cycles of the moon.

This somewhat baffling belief system manifests in a series of specific, often peculiar, and occasionally logistically nightmarish hospital policies that include the exclusive and unwavering administration of the patient's spouse's blood in the event of necessary transfusions, the unrestricted and often disruptive allowance of spouses to remain at the patient's bedside past all reasonable visiting hours, and the implementation of elaborate and often logistically challenging protocols meticulously designed to prevent the patient or their spouse from ever hearing each other in distress, even if it necessitates elaborate room reassignments in the dead of night.

The actual policies themselves, while undeniably strange and occasionally incredibly inconvenient, don't particularly bother me on a fundamental level; they seem merely unusual, rooted in a belief system I don't understand and frankly don't have the energy to try to understand, but not overtly harmful or inherently illogical. However, enduring a nearly two-hour, excruciatingly detailed lecture I am left feeling physically exhausted. Every muscle in my body screaming in protest, but also emotionally drained, my empathy reserves completely tapped, and intellectually pulverized, my brain feels like a scrambled mess of useless information.

As if on cue, a fresh wave of agony pulses behind my eyes, my head throbbing in dull, insistent protest, each beat of my weary heart sending a sharp jolt of pain through my temples. The relentless hum of the lights seemed to amplify the internal pounding in my head, and I wince with each step I take down the seemingly endless corridor.

My current, self-imposed, and increasingly unsustainable work schedule only serves to amplify my profound and all-consuming exhaustion, pushing me closer to the precipice of utter collapse with each passing, dragging hour. The promise of a few extra dollars felt like a cruel mirage in the face of this overwhelming fatigue.

Maybe after this shift, I could cut back a little. It's not like the last few days have been normal, let alone sustainable.

Following the surreal and slightly unsettling church service on Sunday morning, the remainder of the day had dissolved into a chaotic and energy-draining whirlwind of antsy, sugar-fueled children, their pent-up energy unleashed in a seemingly endless flurry of running, shouting, and the inevitable minor squabbles, a miniature domestic storm that finally subsided only when they mercifully succumbed to the sweet, silent oblivion of deep sleep at bedtime.

I had then, fueled by lukewarm coffee and sheer desperation, proceeded to work a grueling, double late shift on both Sunday and Monday nights, foolishly hoping to bolster our perpetually precarious finances with a few desperately needed hours of overtime, a short-sighted decision that had come at the steep and immediate cost of only a few stolen, restless power naps in the last couple of days, leaving me feeling perpetually on the ragged edge of utter collapse, my body screaming for rest that I couldn't afford.

Utterly worn out, my vision swimming slightly, blurring the hallway's edges, I tiredly drag my heavy feet down the seemingly endless, sterile hallway, my destination the dimly lit nursing station, my last desperate hope for the life-giving elixir of strong, black coffee, the only thing that had any chance of dragging me through the rest of this interminable night.

The soft, worn rubber soles of my cheap work shoes trail listlessly against the smooth, cool tiled floor, each weary shuffle a testament to my profound fatigue, the sound echoing softly in the quiet hallway. I couldn't help but squint against the harsh, unforgiving glare of the overhead fluorescent lights, each bulb a tiny sun burning into my already aching retinas. The dull ache behind my eyes intensifies with each step, morphing into sharp, stabbing pains that radiate through my temples, and a low, persistent ringing has begun to whine in my ears, a grating prelude to the auditory assault that was soon to follow, a symphony of exhaustion building to a crescendo. My stomach churned with a queasy unease, a tight, unpleasant knot of exhaustion and gnawing hunger tightening with each step, the lack of proper food only compounding my misery.

I just need a little more caffeine, I repeat to myself like a desperate mantra, a silent, pleading prayer to my failing body, then I'll be fine. I can make it through this. Just a little more. Just keep moving forward.

A fragile wave of relief, thin and watery, washes over me as the familiar, albeit brightly lit, sight of the bustling nurses' station finally comes into view. With heavy, unsteady steps, I shuffle my way behind the long, cluttered counter, the mingled scents of stale coffee, rubbing alcohol, and antiseptic hanging heavy in the air, a familiar but not entirely comforting aroma. A few nurses and aides, their own exhaustion evident in their weary eyes and slumped postures, are hunched over their designated computer monitors, the cool glow of the screens illuminating their tired faces. Those closest to me, their movements slow and deliberate, pause their tasks, offering tired but genuinely friendly greetings, their voices a low, almost conspiratorial murmur in the otherwise quiet hum of the machinery and the occasional beep of medical equipment.

The industrial-sized coffee pot, blessedly, is full and emitting a comforting, slightly bitter and burnt, a sizzling scent that promises a temporary reprieve. I immediately reach for a flimsy, disposable plastic cup, my hand trembling with an almost desperate eagerness to fill it with the dark, steaming liquid, the promise of its bitter jolt a siren call to my flagging energy levels. As the viscous, black coffee began to flow, its rich, slightly acrid aroma momentarily cutting through the thick fog in my brain, offering a fleeting illusion of alertness, I couldn't help but notice the pronounced and uncontrollable tremor in my hands, the small, simple task of pouring the liquid requiring a surprising and disconcerting amount of conscious effort, the thin plastic cup rattling precariously against the spout. A small spill splashes onto my hand, the heat barely registering through my numbness.

Chug it down, I silently urge myself, my throat already anticipating the bitter warmth and the slight burn, You're functioning. You're still upright. You're fine. Just keep moving, one foot in front of the other.

I carefully put the empty, light coffee pot back on the hot plate. It makes a soft click in the quiet nursing station. I am finally about to drink my hot coffee. It is a small bit of hope in the long, tiring night. Then, a young nurse with kind eyes and a cheerful smile reached for the coffee pitcher. She started pouring herself a cup. The coffee makes a soft gurgling sound in the quiet room.

"Are you doing okay tonight, Brayden?" the worker asks, her brow furrowed with concern, her voice soft but carrying a genuine note of care. Her gaze lingers on my face, her expression clearly reading the exhaustion etched there.

A sharp pang of guilt shoots through me. I have absolutely no recollection of ever meeting this woman before, her face a pleasant but utterly unfamiliar blur in the swirling fog, yet she knows my name, addressing me with a casual familiarity that is both momentarily comforting and deeply unsettling. It is a peculiar and pervasive characteristic of this small-town hospital; everyone, from the seasoned surgeons to the newest, wide-eyed orderlies, seems to know everyone else. It doesn't matter which dimly lit department I find myself wandering through in my increasingly dazed state, almost every staff member greets me by name, often with a warmth and familiarity that feels both welcoming and vaguely unnerving, a constant, subtle reminder that I am still the relative outsider in this close-knit community.

Although, in my defense, I am fairly certain, or at least desperately hope, that I haven't encountered this particular nurse before this very moment.

I take another tentative sip of my drink, the hot liquid scalding my tongue slightly but offering a fleeting, almost medicinal jolt of something akin to alertness. Trying to ignore the subtle but persistent trembling causing the sloshing precariously inside the thin, flimsy disposable mug, a physical manifestation of my own internal instability.

"I'm doing well, thank you," I respond, forcing a tired but hopefully reassuring smile that probably looks more like a weak, involuntary grimace. "How are things going with you?" I add, my voice sounding distant and hollow even to my own ears, hoping to politely and swiftly redirect the conversational spotlight away from my own clearly deteriorating state, before she could scrutinize me further.

The young nurse's face brightens slightly at my weak attempt at polite conversation, her cheerful demeanor momentarily eclipsing the weariness that undoubtedly lurked beneath the surface of her own long shift, and she eagerly launches into a lengthy and remarkably detailed description of her eventful day, a torrent of medical jargon and patient anecdotes that wash over my already overloaded brain, the words blurring into an incomprehensible, buzzing stream of noise.

My head throbs in response, each syllable a tiny hammer blow.

I offer vague nods and weak, strained smiles, struggling to follow her words as my exhaustion deepens. The dull ache behind my eyes sharpens into stabbing pains that radiate through my temples.

A sudden, violent, high-pitched ringing erupts in my ears, drowning out her voice and making me wince, my hand instinctively pressing against my throbbing head. My vision wavers, the edges blurring, and her form swims before my eyes, the bright lights of the nursing station seeming to pulse with a sickening rhythm. A sharp wave of nausea churns my stomach, the half-digested coffee threatening to resurface. The air feels thick and heavy, pressing in on me, suffocating my already strained senses.

A sudden, overwhelming wave of lightheadedness washes over me, the solid floor beneath my feet tilting precariously on its axis. I instinctively reach out a trembling hand to grasp the smooth, cool surface of the counter for support, my knuckles white as I grip the edge, my vision tunneling inward. But my balance is already fatally compromised, my inner equilibrium shatters, and a dizzying, sickening vertigo spins the world around me, the bright, unforgiving lights above swirling like malevolent stars in a blackening sky. Losing all control, my legs buckle beneath me, the muscles refusing to support my weight any longer, a silent betrayal by my own exhausted body.

I begin to fall forward, my body lurching unexpectedly, my arms flailing uselessly for purchase in the empty air, a strangled gasp escaping my lips. Just as my head swims and the cold tile floor rushes up to meet me, two small, surprisingly strong arms suddenly catch me mid-descent, halting my abrupt and potentially skull-cracking plummet towards the unyielding surface. A gasp escapes my lips, a sound of pure surprise, a flicker of desperate gratitude warring with the encroaching darkness at the edges of my vision.

"Luna!?" I hear the nurse's voice cry out again, closer now, her tone laced with a sharp urgency and a strange, almost panicked note that cuts through the ringing in my ears, but I am too far gone, my senses too overwhelmed to even register the oddness of her words, let alone offer a coherent response. The world wavers in a sickening, disorienting swirl of light and shadow, the sounds around me fading in and out.

I vaguely register the nurse's surprisingly strong and determined arms gently lowering my collapsing body. The cold, hard floor meets my cheek, the smooth, unforgiving tiles pressing against my skin and sending a wave of icy chill through me. A low, involuntary groan escapes my lips with the slightest movement, each shift unleashing a fresh wave of nausea and dizzying vertigo. The room spun relentlessly around me. My body feels violently out of control, like an internal gyroscope had shattered. No matter how desperately I blink my heavy, aching eyelids, the harsh, glaring room refuses to stop its horrifying, sickening rotation. The unforgiving lights from the ceiling, now directly overhead, seem to bore into my skull like white-hot needles. I wince involuntarily, a strangled whimper escaping my dry, cracked lips as the piercing brightness intensifies the agonizing, throbbing pain behind my eyes. The ringing in my ears grows to a deafening whine that threatens to drown out all other sounds and isolate me in my suffering.

The muffled sounds of rapidly approaching footsteps, growing louder with each passing second, and increasingly frantic, overlapping yells for help barely registered in my fading consciousness, a distant, chaotic symphony of alarm and urgency. I try desperately to steady my ragged, shallow breathing.

My own breath hitches, a sharp, painful gasp in my constricted throat, as a fresh wave of icy, paralyzing fear washes over my already clammy skin, each nerve ending screaming in protest. My heart hammers against my ribs with frantic, uneven urgency, a wild, erratic rhythm that echoes the chaotic terror seizing me, each painful beat a stark reminder of my body's rapidly failing state. The edges of my vision begin to darken, and the bright, unforgiving lights of the nursing station flicker like dying embers, threatening to plunge me into complete blackness.

"Brayden, it's Dr. Monroe," I hear the familiar, authoritative voice of the doctor say again, closer now, yet strangely distant, his tone urgent and laced with a sharp edge of fear that chillingly mirrors my own spiraling panic. "Can you hear me? Squeeze my hand if you can hear me." His voice seems to echo strangely, distorted by the ringing in my ears and the encroaching darkness, as if coming from a great, impossible distance.

I try with every last vestige of my failing strength to offer a physical response, to squeeze the hand I vaguely felt pressing against mine, but my limbs feel impossibly heavy and unresponsive, filled with leaden weight, refusing to obey my frantic mental commands. The only sound I could manage is a weak, choked groan that seemed to originate from the very depths of my chest, a primal sound of utter distress and complete, bone-deep exhaustion.

Suddenly, two large, firm hands cradle my throbbing head, supporting it gently but firmly, a fleeting moment of unexpected comfort in the face of overwhelming terror, and I see the wavering, distorted form of Dr. Monroe kneeling anxiously above me, his face a pale mask of deep concern and something starkly akin to raw panic. A small penlight appears in his trembling hand, its beam once again piercing directly into my already throbbing eyes, sending a fresh, agonizing wave of searing torture through my skull, making me cry out weakly, a pathetic, strangled sound.

He slowly moves the piercing beam of light back and forth in front of my unfocused, swimming gaze, the repetitive motion making the room spin even more violently, intensifying the sickening wave of nausea that threatened to overwhelm my already fragile control. My abdomen rolls with a violent, churning force, and with the last of my rapidly fading physical control, I weakly twist myself onto my side, and the acrid, burning contents of my stomach begin to heave onto the floor beside me, the violent retching spasms shaking my already weakened body and leaving me gasping for air, my lungs burning with the effort.

The burning sensation of vomit searing my raw throat is almost secondary to the violent, involuntary convulsions wracking my abdomen as I empty the meager contents of my stomach, each heave a fresh wave of agony. Tears, hot and stinging, well in the corners of my eyes as the last bitter drops of bile drip from my trembling mouth, and beads of cold, clammy sweat pool at my temples and cling to my pale, clammy skin, a testament to my body's desperate struggle.

The sounds of panic around me seem to escalate, voices overlapping in a frantic, chaotic mirage of raw fear and desperate urgency as I collapse, my limbs feeling impossibly heavy and utterly unresponsive, as if they no longer belong to me. My eyelids feel like lead weights, impossibly heavy, beginning to drift shut against my frantic will, the oppressive darkness at the edges of my vision relentlessly closing in, threatening to swallow me whole. Through the swirling darkness of my rapidly fading consciousness, I catch fragmented snippets of rushing voices yelling over each other, their words a jumbled, unintelligible mess of raw fear and desperate urgency, a chaotic symphony of impending doom.

"Set up a room... he's been overworked... looks like extreme exhaustion... looks like he's crashing... I need fluids stat..." The fragmented phrases echo in my fading awareness, each word a chilling premonition of something terrible.

My vision flickers erratically between oppressive, all-consuming darkness and blinding, searing brightness, the transitions abrupt and disorienting, each jarring flash sending a fresh jolt of agonizing pain through my throbbing head. I couldn't quite focus on anything, the passage of time marked only by sudden, terrifying bursts of harsh, white light that sears into my retinas.

FLASH.

I feel myself being gently but firmly lifted and laid onto the crisp, cool surface of a narrow hospital bed, the rough texture of the starched sheets scratching unpleasantly against my damp, sweat-soaked skin, a minor discomfort overshadowed by the overwhelming physical distress. There is a frantic flurry of movement in the small, sterile room, the blurred silhouettes of faceless figures darting back and forth in the confined space, their hushed, urgent voices a low, anxious murmur that speaks of a crisis I was too far gone to fully comprehend. I feel a cool, soothing cloth being gently placed on my burning forehead, offering a brief, fleeting moment of fragile relief, followed by the sharp, unwelcome pinch of a needle breaking my skin, a sudden, stinging pain that signals the cold, clinical insertion of an IV line into the back of my right hand. A dull, throbbing ache begins to spread from the insertion point, a constant, unwelcome reminder of the invasive procedure.

I am drenched in a cold, clammy sweat, my thin, inadequate hospital gown clinging uncomfortably to my trembling skin, yet a deep, bone-chilling coldness seems to emanate from within, a cold that no blanket could ever touch, causing uncontrollable shivers to wrack my already weakened body, my teeth chattering violently, my entire frame convulsing with a primal, uncontrollable tremor.

FLASH.

The small room is noticeably quieter now. The initial frantic activity has subsided into a more controlled, albeit still tense, atmosphere. The number of blurred figures moving around the periphery of my fading vision seems to have diminished, leaving only a few hushed presences. However, a significant and increasingly agitated commotion, punctuated by raised, panicked voices and the distinct sound of heavy, running footsteps, is clearly audible from the hallway just outside my door, a chaotic symphony of fear and urgency. With immense, agonizing effort, my heavy eyelids flutter open, and I force myself to try and discern the source of the escalating chaos, my head throbbing in violent protest with each frantic beat of my racing heart. The ringing in my ears is a constant, deafening whine, a torturous soundtrack to my fading consciousness.

Through the slightly ajar doorway, my blurry vision catches fleeting glimpses of several medical personnel frantically rushing down the hall, their faces etched with stark worry and a palpable sense of desperate urgency, heading towards some unseen crisis unfolding further down the corridor. Their hurried movements and strained expressions paint a grim picture. I flinch involuntarily as the sound of angry, guttural yelling and the sickening crash of what sounds like heavy equipment hitting the hard floor echo into my room, which sends a fresh, piercing jolt of icy fear through my already frayed and shattered nerves. Desperate, pleading voices, filled with raw terror and unimaginable anguish, drifts through the narrow crack in the door.

"Alpha, you need to calm down... don't shift... he can't be seen at the moment... he's about to shift... please calm down... don't shift... *GROWL*... someone restrain him before he's seen!"

The fragmented words, laced with raw panic and a terrifying undercurrent of something unknown and dangerous, send a fresh, chilling wave of profound unease washing over me. Shift?

What the hell is happening in this bizarre, terrifying place?

The distinct sound of heavy, rapidly approaching footsteps, pounding against the unforgiving linoleum floor with increasing, frantic speed, grows closer and closer, accompanied by ragged, panicked breathing that sounded disturbingly animalistic, a primal sound that sends a shiver of pure dread down my spine.

My own breath hitches, a sharp, painful gasp in my constricted throat as a fresh wave of icy, paralyzing fear washes over my already clammy skin. My heart hammers against my ribs with frantic, uneven urgency, a wild, erratic rhythm that mirrors the chaotic terror seizing me. The darkness at the edges of my vision deepens, threatening to consume me entirely, pulling me down into its suffocating depths.

FLASH.

There is shouting, a chaotic barrage of panicked voices just outside my door, but a deafening, guttural growl suddenly rips through the air, a primal sound of pure, unadulterated rage and raw, untamed power that instantly silenced all other sounds in its terrifying wake, sending a visceral shiver of pure, instinctual terror down my spine, every hair on my body standing on end. My eyes widen in sheer, unadulterated horror as I see several people near the doorway, their faces contorted with abject, primal fear, cowering low to the ground, pressed against the cold, hard wall of my small, sterile room as if trying to meld with the very plaster. The hospital staff, their faces pale and contorted with terror, all had their heads bowed submissively towards the floor, their hands clasped tightly behind their necks in a gesture of utter vulnerability and desperate surrender, a silent plea for mercy from something unseen and terrifying.

Slowly, painstakingly, my blurred and unfocused vision begins to sharpen, the harsh edges of the room solidifying into horrifying, undeniable clarity. My sick, disoriented brain, struggling through the thick fog of exhaustion and the encroaching, suffocating darkness, finally begins to register the impossible, terrifying sight before me. With its broad, impossibly muscular back towards me, a creature of immense, raw power and unbridled fury stands between my trembling, fragile form on the narrow hospital bed and the petrified medical personnel huddled against the wall. There is a low, menacing growl, a deep, guttural rumble of pure, unadulterated threat, vibrating through the very air, a clear and present danger directed at their cowering, whimpering forms.

But this is no ordinary animal... This is something ancient, something wild and untamed, something ripped from the darkest, most primal corners of forgotten myth and waking nightmare.

It is a fucking wolf.

The predator's tall, impossibly imposing form looms over the whimpering, terrified figures of the nurses and aides, its sheer, overwhelming size filling the small room with an oppressive, suffocating sense of imminent, brutal danger. Its thick, coarse, dark fur, the color of a moonless, starless night, stands on end, the individual hairs along its massive spine raised in a clear and terrifying display of primal, unadulterated anger that ripples visibly between its broad, impossibly powerful shoulder blades, a living embodiment of pure rage.

Its powerful legs, thick with coiled, bunched muscle that speak of immense strength and terrifying speed, quivers slightly, the barely contained tension in its stance suggesting it is mere milliseconds away from unleashing unimaginable, brutal violence upon the cowering humans. Its paws are the size of my adult hands, each pad thick and leathery, and deadly, obsidian-black claws, sharp as shards of shattered glass and wickedly curved, tipped each of its formidable feet, the lethal weapons digging audibly into the cold, unforgiving linoleum floor, leaving faint, tell-tale scratches in their wake, a silent promise of the damage they could inflict.

A violent, uncontrollable tremor begins to shake my own fragile, exhausted body at the terrifying, utterly impossible sight before me, my teeth chattering uncontrollably, my entire frame convulsing with pure, unadulterated, fear that threatens to shatter my sanity. The rapid, erratic beeping of my heart monitor in the background, already alarmingly fast and uneven, seems to escalate into a frantic, desperate shriek, a mechanical scream mirroring my own silent, internal terror. My breath hitches in my throat, a strangled gasp caught in my constricted chest, my lungs refusing to draw in enough air as if the very atmosphere had become thick and suffocating.

As if in a horrifying, drawn-out slow motion that stretched the very fabric of time, its large, wedge-shaped head, framed by thick, bristling dark fur that seems to absorb all the light in the room, pivots slowly in my direction. The dark, unfathomable eyes of the wild creature, glowing with an unsettling, predatory intensity that sends a shiver of pure, icy dread through my very bones, meet mine, and a bone-deep, primal shudder runs through me, a cold, paralyzing wave of absolute terror washing over my already chilled and sweat-soaked body. Those eyes hold no warmth, no flicker of humanity, only the ancient, soulless gaze of a predator coldly assessing its helpless, terrified prey.

The carnivore's massive face, a terrifying mask of sharp, gleaming teeth and bristling, shadowed fur, is pulled back into a menacing, guttural snarl that vibrates through the very air, a low, rumbling sound that promises unimaginable pain and a swift, brutal end. Thick strands of saliva, glistening and viscous, drip from its open jowls, each drop a horrifying testament to its raw, untamed power and the imminent threat. The razor-sharp points of its teeth, impossibly long and wickedly white, gleam ominously in the harsh, unforgiving overhead light, the raw pink of its gums starkly visible in the wake of its lifted lip, a clear, unmistakable, and utterly terrifying threat that freezes the very blood in my veins.

I instinctively try to push myself further back against the thin, slippery pillows on the inadequate hospital bed, a futile, desperate attempt to create even a few more precious, illusory inches of distance between myself and the terrifying creature, but another deep, rumbling growl, a sound that seems to emanate from the very depths of its ancient being, erupts from the animal's massive chest, stopping me instantly in my tracks, paralyzing me with a fear so profound it stole my breath and made every muscle in my body lock in rigid, unyielding terror.

The frantic, insistent beeps on the heart monitor continue their relentless acceleration, each piercing, mechanical shriek a stark and terrifying reminder of my own rapidly escalating panic and the terrifying proximity of death as the beast seems to make a deliberate, horrifying decision. Its powerful, impossibly muscular body begins to move in my direction, each slow, deliberate, and utterly silent step across the cold linoleum floor a silent, terrifying promise of unimaginable, brutal violence. My breathing comes in short, ragged pants, each shallow inhalation a painful struggle against the crushing weight in my chest, and a cold, clammy sweat breaks out across my forehead, matting my already damp hair to my clammy skin. The unmistakable, overwhelming beginnings of a full-blown, paralyzing panic attack seize me, my entire body trembling uncontrollably, my vision tunneling inward, the edges blurring into blackness.

The animal, its dark, predatory eyes never leaving mine, seems to notice my escalating distress, perhaps sensing my utter helplessness and the raw terror radiating from me. It quickens its approach, its movements becoming more fluid, more purposeful, closing the impossible distance between us with terrifying, unnatural speed.

A strangled scream tears from my throat, a raw sound of pure agony and mortal fear, but the cry is choked and pathetic, a mere rasp due to my dry, constricted airway, barely audible above the frantic beeping of the machine beside me.

The wolf pauses mid-stride, its massive head tilting slightly, its sharp, pointed ears swiveling, as if startled by my sudden, desperate sound of terror. For a fleeting, agonizing moment, there is a tense, heart-stopping silence in the small room, broken only by the relentless, mechanical beeping of the heart monitor, each beep a stark countdown to the inevitable. I seize the minuscule opportunity, however futile, to once again try and scoot further back on the bed. My weak, trembling arms push against the slippery, sweat-soaked sheets to gain perhaps a precious inch or two of illusory safety, a pathetic attempt to escape the inescapable.

Seeing my desperate, pathetic efforts to get away, the wolf lets out another ferocious, guttural growl that vibrates through the very air.

Then it leaps.

I scream again, a high-pitched, uncontrolled shriek that echoes off the sterile walls of the small room as the large, impossibly powerful animal launches its massive, muscular body onto my narrow hospital bed with surprising agility and terrifying speed. The thin springs groan and protest violently under its immense weight. The small, sterile room erupts into a silent, internal madness, a swirling vortex of pure fear and overwhelming adrenaline as the beast swiftly brings its massive head down towards the exposed, vulnerable crook of my neck. Its wet, cold nose, surprisingly soft against my clammy skin, presses against the delicate curve, and its warm, fetid breath, carrying the raw, musky scent of something wild, something untamed, blows against my exposed shoulder, sending a fresh, paralyzing wave of icy dread washing over me. From the corner of my wide, terrified eye, I could see the animal opening its large maw, the razor-sharp points of its wickedly white teeth, impossibly long and lethal, grazing against the sensitive flesh of my neck, and in that horrifying, drawn-out instant, I know with absolute, chilling certainty that it was about to tear into me, to rip and shred.

Just as the wolf was preparing to latch its powerful jaws onto my throat, to inflict unimaginable pain and perhaps end my life, a primal surge of fight or flight reflexes, long dormant under the crushing weight of my fear, suddenly and violently kicked in, overriding the paralyzing terror.

With what little remaining strength I could possibly muster in my weakened and terrified state and fueled by pure, raw adrenaline and the desperate, instinctual will to survive, I instinctively bring my left hand up in a desperate, last-ditch effort at self-preservation, shoving it blindly between my neck and the beast's deadly, gaping mouth, just as the animal's powerful jaws clamp down with terrifying, bone-jarring force.

I wail in pure, agonizing pain as I feel the sharp, searing pressure of the animal's teeth sinking deep into the tender skin on the top and underside of my hand. The tearing sensation is immediate and excruciating, a searing agony that shot up my arm like a bolt of lightning, every nerve ending screaming in protest. Hot, sticky blood immediately wells up around the deep wounds.

Startled by the unexpected resistance and my raw, involuntary cry of agony, the animal abruptly releases its crushing hold, its powerful body recoiling slightly as it jumps back off the narrow bed with a surprised, almost yelping sound that, in my delirious, pain-filled state, sounds strangely... human, a guttural sound of shock and surprise.

Hot, bright red blood, thick and viscous, immediately spurts from the deep, ragged wound in my hand, the crimson liquid beginning to bloom across the pristine white linen of the hospital bed, staining it a horrifying, sickening crimson. Deep, ragged puncture wounds, arranged in a gruesome, half-crescent moon shape that chillingly mirrors the curve of the beast's powerful jaw, now marred my palm, a terrifying testament to the creature's savage power and the horrifying reality of what has just happened.

I scream again, a raw, primal sound of pure agony and terror that reverberates off the sterile walls of the small room, the sound raw and broken.

The wolf, its massive head now lowered, its sharp ears flattened against its skull, stares at me with an unnerving intensity, its dark eyes seeming to hold a flicker of something akin to… confusion? Or perhaps even, regret?

I cry out again, a broken, desperate plea, begging someone, anyone, for help in the silent, terrifying room, my voice cracking with hysteria, tears streaming down my face.

The wolf slowly lowers its large, powerful body to the floor, its intense, unnerving gaze never wavering from mine, its massive form radiating a palpable tension.

I begin to shake uncontrollably, violent tremors wracking my entire body, the thin hospital bed rattling precariously against the cold tile floor, amplifying the sounds of my abject, overwhelming fear. My teeth chatter like castanets.

The wolf lets out a soft, whimpering sound, a low, mournful cry that is a stark and unsettling contrast to its earlier ferocious growls, a sound that tugs at some primal, unexpected cord within me, a flicker of something other than pure terror.

I wail, and cry, and shake, and beg, and thrash weakly against the invisible restraints of my terror, my wide, tear-filled eyes lock on the terrifying animal, filled with unadulterated horror and utter disbelief.

Suddenly, an unexpected wave of warmth, strangely comforting amidst the icy grip of my fear and the searing pain in my hand, envelops my injured hand. I freeze, my body rigid with shock and a dawning sense of the utterly surreal, as I see the wolf lowering its massive head and gently, tentatively licking my shaking palm. Its large, surprisingly soft tongue laps up the sticky, warm blood, the wetness from its mouth mingling with the drying crimson on my skin, a bizarre and unsettling act of… care? Or something else entirely?

I don't dare move, my muscles locked in a vise-grip of fear and utter bewilderment, as the wolf continues its strange, almost tender ministrations on my wounded hand. After the last visible traces of blood are gone, the animal finally looks up at me, its intense, unnerving gaze now holding a strange mixture of vulnerability and… recognition?

The soulless, black eyes of the beast begin to shimmer and swirl, the darkness receding, slowly, mesmerizingly, transforming into a familiar, warm, deep brown.

The once savage-looking wolf, its fur bristling with menace just moments before, seems to ripple and flow, its powerful form subtly shifting and contorting, the impossible happening before my very disbelieving eyes. In what feels like a single, disorienting blink, the monstrous creature, the terrifying predator that has just attacked me, morphs itself into the solid, undeniably human, and utterly naked body of a very large and very familiar man.

Damien Rockwell is kneeling by the side of my narrow hospital bed, his tan skin slick with sweat, his dark hair matted against his forehead, his powerful chest heaving with ragged breaths. He cradles my wounded hand gently between his own large, trembling hands, bringing it close to his face, his expression a complex mixture of raw fear, deep concern, and something else… something akin to profound remorse and a desperate plea for understanding? He nuzzles his cheek into my bloodied palm, his touch surprisingly gentle, and the taut muscles of his broad shoulders seem to relax ever so slightly. He sighs deeply, a shuddering exhale that speaks volumes of inner turmoil, before finally raising his head, his warm, intensely brown eyes meeting my wide, uncomprehending gaze, filled with a silent, desperate plea.

"I, uh, think we need to have a talk," he mumbles, his voice rough, raw, and laced with a profound weariness and an undercurrent of something ancient and deeply unsettling.

For the first time that night, the terrifying flashing lights in my vision finally cease, the chaotic sensory overload fading away, and a strange, almost welcoming darkness begins to creep in from the edges of my awareness, a soft, enveloping void that promised oblivion, as everything finally, mercifully, goes black.

DAMIEN

Tuesday 1:00 am

My knee bounces with a nervous energy as I fix my gaze on the sterile, unyielding floor. The tips of my nails dig crescents into my palm, my white-knuckled grip tightening on the thin, scratchy sheet draped over my bare shoulders. The flimsy fabric offers little warmth against the chill that has settled deep in my bones, but it serves its purpose, a meager shield for the bare minimum of public decency. My body is stiff and coiled, every muscle tense as the chaos swirling around me continues its relentless assault, an emotional hurricane showing no signs of abating.

"What the *fuck* were you thinking?!" my mother's voice screeches, sharp and accusatory, slicing through the tense atmosphere.

I wasn't.

"He wasn't ready for this, Alpha!" Aiden's shout echoes, raw with anger and concern.

I know.

"You'll need to remain in close vicinity to the hospital. We have no way of predicting his reaction when he first regains consciousness," Dr. Monroe chastises, his tone weary but firm, a weight of medical knowledge in his pronouncements.

I will...

...I was staring out of my office's expansive window, the city skyline a distant blur as my mind drifted, inevitably, to my mate. A foolish, persistent grin had taken root on my face since yesterday, a testament to the undeniable pull he held over me.

He was at the temple. *Our* temple.

Granted, Brayden and the kids hadn't joined us on the Alpha balcony, a small sting of disappointment quickly overshadowed by a burgeoning wave of possessive glee at the sight of my mate and our family nestled amongst the pack, listening to the service. Initially, Brayden's quiet refusal to move to the front had been a minor setback, but my momentary dejection had swiftly transformed into a smug satisfaction as I realized I now had the perfect excuse to sit and unabashedly stare at him for over an hour.

And by the Goddess, did I.

Throughout the entire service, my gaze never once wavered from his presence. I devoured the sight of him handling our pups with such unexpected care and quiet devotion. Every few precious minutes, he would lean down to chastise a restless one to calm down, patiently escort another to the bathroom, or help select the perfect crayon color for their childish masterpiece. It was all so achingly glorious to witness, a domestic tableau that stirred something deep and possessive within me.

The only significant problem with my intense observation had been the continual, distracting need to try and inconspicuously shift in my seat, a desperate attempt to conceal the undeniable, massive issue that had taken root between my legs.

My persistent arousal only intensified as my treacherous mind readily recalled the deliciously naughty things my vixen of a mate had done to me on Friday night. The manipulative little tease had completely and utterly turned the situation to his advantage, and like a complete fool, I had been so willingly, so eagerly, wrapped around his greedy little fingers. Even though I had found release that night, I had been left even more frustrated after leaving his room, my body now craving the feel of his even more intensely than it had previously.

Goddess, if he was the devil himself, I would sell my very soul just to have one more night in his bed, to feel his skin against mine, to lose myself in his intoxicating scent.

"Isn't that right, Alpha?" the deep, resonant sound of Aiden's voice abruptly jerked me from my lust-fueled thoughts back to the mundane reality of the present.

I cleared my throat, the sound rough and betraying my momentary lapse in focus, as I forced myself to regain my composure and feign attention. "Yes, that is correct," I said, assertively, projecting an authority I was far from feeling, having barely registered the conversation.

It was early Monday morning, and I wished with every fiber of my being to be anywhere else other than sitting at this conference table, leading the weekly meeting with the heads of the varying pack departments. Among those in attendance were Aiden, his ever-present loyalty, a comforting anchor, Dr. Monroe, his medical expertise, often a necessary voice of reason, the Priestess, her stern pronouncements carrying the weight of ancient tradition, and my mother, her protective instincts for our pack, and especially for me, always fiercely on display. All of them held a particular, often conflicting, interest in the subject currently at hand: Brayden.

"I fail to comprehend why you don't believe he is ready. It is part of the natural order of our creation that he participates," the Priestess commented, her usually serene face hard with disapproval as she deeply frowned at me, her gaze unwavering.

"He isn't ready at all!" my mother argued back vehemently, her protective instincts flaring, a sharp glare directed at the Priestess. "He doesn't need the added stress that comes with knowing about our kind right now, let alone being forced to partake in The Run."

"I also harbor significant doubts regarding his physical ability to participate," Dr. Monroe mumbled, his brow furrowed with concern, causing several others around the table to voice their immediate disagreement at his cautious proclamation.

I sighed inwardly, a weary sound I kept carefully contained as I listened to the low rumble of the escalating ruckus around me.

This coming Saturday marked the night of the full moon, a celestial event that held deep significance for our kind. It meant that our pack would observe our monthly Run, a millennia-old tradition steeped in werewolf history.

The practice had originated as the only sanctioned time when werewolves were allowed to officially mark their chosen mates. Ancient traditions held that since the full moon was when the Goddess's power was at its zenith, her blessing of prosperity and a strong bond would be bestowed upon the mated pair at this sacred time. The ritual itself was simple: the dominant mate would chase the subordinate mate until he or she was caught, and they would mark each other as a visible sign of acceptance and lifelong commitment in the presence of the witnessing Goddess.

In modern times, we largely viewed the Run as strictly symbolic, a beautiful tradition rather than a necessary act, as most mates marked each other shortly after their initial connection, the undeniable pull of the bond too strong to resist. The Run had evolved into a vibrant symbol of the Goddess's continued blessing over the mate bond for those who chose to participate, a joyous way to celebrate newly mated couples and the vital continuation of our species. As some werewolves found their mates in other packs, this night also served as the traditional time when the official transfer of pack membership occurred, solidifying the new alliances.

The rules governing the Run were deceptively simple. At the precise setting of the sun, the subordinate mate, designated as the runner, was granted a sixty-minute head start before the dominant mate, the hunter, was allowed to give chase. There were clearly defined end zones that the runner would attempt to cross before the stroke of midnight.

According to ancient legend, if the runner successfully crossed the sacred, and blessed line before midnight, the mated pair were granted the right to part ways under the supposed blessing of the Goddess. More specifically, the runner would not have to endure the often devastating emotional or physical trauma typically associated with breaking a mate bond. However, if the runner was caught by their hunter before the midnight hour, the bond between them would strengthen exponentially, solidifying to the point where death was believed to be the only absolute option for severing the unbreakable connection.

It was an exceedingly rare occurrence for a runner to successfully cross the line. The few times I was aware of it happening were usually attributed to accidental miscalculations, and the hunter involved was often subjected to pack-wide ridicule for their perceived inability to catch their own mate. Even in these isolated instances, the mated pairs had never actually chosen to split up, opting instead to symbolically cross back over the line before midnight as a powerful sign of their unwavering acceptance and commitment to the bond.

It was considered deeply unnatural to willingly desire to break a mate bond. Doing so outside of this specific, ritualistic event would invariably plunge a werewolf into a deadly, irreversible depression, and little concrete knowledge existed regarding the long-term results of outright rejecting the bond, even with the Goddess's supposed blessing, as it was an act so abhorrent that it was virtually unheard of for someone to actually follow through with such an atrocious act.

While this annual occasion held more religious symbolism and cultural significance than actual, literal consequences, there were some undeniably barbaric and unsettling legends that clung to this otherwise happy ceremony. According to our darker folk-lore, there was a group of overzealous Priestesses in a bygone era who were fanatically obsessed with the absolute strengthening of the mate bond. Their extreme practices involved forcing one mate to partially mark the other and then cruelly withholding the completion of the mark until the rising of the rare and ominous blood moon.

As the blood moon only transpired approximately every four months instead of the regular monthly full moon, severe issues inevitably began to arise within these forced, unnatural pairings.

According to the grim fable, the werewolves who were partially marked were said to become increasingly sick and unstable once a monthly full moon had passed over them without the completion of the sacred marking ritual. Their withheld mates simultaneously descended into madness, driven to the brink by the unnatural, incomplete connection they were forced to maintain. For the un-fortunate few who actually survived the agonizing wait until the night of the blood moon, their subsequent actions were described as barbaric and utterly unhinged. The raw, untamed genetics of the wild beast was forcibly thrust to the forefront in these tormented creatures, and the mates of these cursed pairs often ended up tragically killing each other in fits of uncontrollable rage and despair.

I shuddered involuntarily at the vivid, disturbing thought, a primal fear echoing through my ancient bloodline. I offered a silent prayer of thanks that those horrific stories were widely considered to be nothing more than gruesome myths, often whispered by children around a crackling campfire to elicit shivers of fear. Such primitive and brutal actions most certainly didn't happen in our modern society, and it was highly debatable whether they had ever truly transpired even several millennia ago.

"What exactly do you mean he *can't* run?" One of the more traditional-minded men at the table asked, his tone laced with suspicion and a hint of challenge.

Dr. Monroe sighed, the sound heavy with weariness, and rubbed his tired eyes with a defeated gesture. "Our Luna has sustained some preexisting injuries that significantly affect his left side," he began to explain carefully, choosing his words with precision. "Without delving into an excessive amount of personal medical detail, the previous medical records I was able to locate on Brayden disclosed that any strenuous activity placed on his left leg would cause him an enormous, debilitating amount of pain."

A heavy silence descended upon the room at the doctor's sobering revelation, the weight of his words settling over the assembled pack leaders.

"I am not suggesting that he never participate in the Run; rather, I would strongly recommend getting him started on a comprehensive physical therapy plan to gradually improve his overall mobility and strength," Dr. Monroe clarified, his gaze sweeping over the concerned faces. "Otherwise, I sincerely feel that forcing him to participate in the Run in his current physical condition would be utterly pointless, as he simply wouldn't be able to make it very far at all without succumbing to excruciating pain."

The Priestess huffed, a sharp, disapproving sound, and the intricate network of wrinkles along the elder woman's face seemed to deepen dramatically as she scowled in barely restrained anger, her disapproval radiating across the table.

"I firmly believe that given the current, rather unusual circumstances, we must seize this opportunity to try and strengthen his bond with the pack," she seethed, her voice low and intense, sending a pointed glare directly at Aiden, her disapproval of his past actions palpable. "It is also the traditional time of initiation for any new members into our pack. Even if he won't be able to consciously feel it in the same way we do, he is still our Luna, and we currently cannot fully sense his presence within our pack bond as we naturally should."

Aiden, well aware of the severe consequences of directly challenging the Priestess's authority, wisely refrained from meeting her pointed glare, but his simmering anger could be tangibly felt in the tense atmosphere of the room as he deliberately focused his intense gaze on the far wall, his jaw tight.

"I think you're being a little… forward in your assumptions," Aiden finally ground out through clenched teeth, his voice low and dangerous. "We would essentially be forcing him to participate in a deeply significant and potentially painful tradition solely for our own selfish gain, as it wouldn't offer him any personal benefit whatsoever."

"And whose fault is *that*?!" The Priestess shrieked in righteous indignation, her voice rising sharply. "If it wasn't for your distinct lack of foresight all those years ago, he could have grown up within the embrace of our pack, surrounded by his own kind. At least then, he would have stood a far greater chance of forging some semblance of an emotional bond with our poor, isolated Alpha."

I slammed my clenched fist down onto the polished surface of the conference table, the sharp, resounding crack echoing through the suddenly silent room, effectively silencing the escalating argument.

"That's enough," I growled, my voice laced with a clear warning. The Priestess, her head bowed in reluctant acknowledgment of her overstep, wisely remained silent.

We had been going around in frustrating circles, rehashing the same core arguments, for the better part of two long, unproductive hours. The pack was clearly divided over the highly sensitive issue of whether or not to pressure Brayden into joining in on The Run this coming Saturday night.

The significant disadvantages of doing so were glaringly obvious to everyone, myself included. He was completely unaware of the existence of werewolves, emotionally unprepared to suddenly learn about such a fundamental aspect of his own identity, and, as Dr. Monroe had clearly stated, physically unable to handle the strenuous demands of the Run in his current condition.

However, there was the arguable, albeit selfish, advantage of the pack potentially being able to forge a stronger connection within our collective bond with our Luna, even though Brayden himself wouldn't necessarily consciously benefit from this forced participation.

Brayden was a unique case, a half-human and half-werewolf hybrid. Normally, this genetic makeup meant two distinct things. Firstly, he should possess some of the inherent physical attributes of a werewolf, albeit typically less intense than those of a full-blooded wolf, including a heightened sensitivity to people's pheromones, more acute hearing capabilities, and some accelerated healing advantages when faced with major physical injuries. Secondly, he should be able to emotionally feel a natural connection to his mate, me, and to the pack as a whole. While this emotional link wouldn't be as strong or deeply ingrained as that experienced by a full-blooded werewolf, it would still be undeniably present.

We knew with a reasonable degree of certainty that Brayden definitely possessed the normal range of physical attributes typically found in a half-breed. According to the limited information Dr. Monroe had been able to glean from his fragmented previous medical records, Brayden's inherent werewolf healing abilities were undoubtedly what had allowed him to survive what should have been a fatal accident years ago. There was also the subtle but undeniable fact that Brayden could subconsciously smell people's pheromones, whether he consciously recognized the scent or not. This had been subtly witnessed on a couple of occasions through his interactions with other pack members, and far more prominently whenever he was in my immediate presence, his reactions often betraying a subconscious awareness.

The emotional attributes, however… that was a far more complex and heartbreaking issue.

"Brayden was essentially secluded from any other werewolf his entire life, not to mention the fact that he is currently suffering from extreme emotional trauma," Dr. Monroe interjected, his voice low and filled with professional concern. "From my extensive assessment, Brayden appears to have adapted to his unique circumstances by basically eliminating the emotional side of his werewolf genetics," he paused, his gaze sweeping sadly over everyone in the room. "In other words, in a desperate act of self-preservation, his body appears to have survived by actively rejecting its innate need to form emotional bonds. This has tragically resulted in his current inability to consciously feel the profound bond of either a pack or his destined mate."

A heavy, somber moment of silence descended upon the room as the full weight of the doctor's devastating words sank in, the implications profound and deeply troubling.

For a werewolf, whether a half-breed like Brayden or a full-blooded member of our kind, to completely lose their innate emotional bonds, something truly horrific and deeply traumatic had to have transpired in their past. And the devastating truth was that this fundamental aspect of their being was never something that could be regained once it was lost, a permanent and heartbreaking consequence.

I cleared my throat, the sound rough and betraying the raw ache that had settled in my chest, trying desperately not to let the depth of my profound sadness show to those around me, my carefully constructed stoicism threatening to crumble. What Dr. Monroe had just articulated wasn't new information to me; I had long suspected the extent of Brayden's emotional detachment. But hearing it spoken aloud once again, the cold, clinical confirmation of my greatest fear, still cut me deeply.

I had found my destined mate, the other half of my very soul, and yet he would likely never be able to emotionally feel the profound, life-altering bond that connected us. It was a heart-wrenching, agonizing reality to face.

I was abruptly pulled from my spiraling self-pity by a thick manila folder being unceremoniously thrown down onto the table directly in front of me, the sharp thud breaking the heavy silence. Looking up, I saw Aiden standing above me, his expression expectant and his dark eyes holding a silent question.

"Those are the finalized lists of the new mating pairs from the pack's diplomatic outing to the neighboring territory this past weekend, as well as the comprehensive list of all those scheduled to participate in The Run this week," he explained, seeing my confused and slightly dazed expression. "I just require your official approval over the list of those formally scheduled for The Run this week."

I sighed, the sound heavy with the weight of my conflicting emotions, as I gathered the scattered papers and quickly began the tedious task of scanning over the official documents. The list of newly formed mating pairs was surprisingly long, a positive development that would only serve to further strengthen the crucial bonds between our pack and our neighboring allies. I retrieved a pen from my inner jacket pocket and began to carefully grant the necessary permissions where they were required, my signature a swift, decisive stroke.

It was undeniably tedious and mentally draining work. I had to meticulously look over the detailed list of all those intending to participate in the upcoming Run this week, officially granting permission for both the transferring of my own pack members out to their new mates' territories and the welcoming of new pack members into our fold. My eyes darted back and forth between the densely printed pages until a familiar name abruptly caught my attention, a sharp jolt of irritation coursing through me.

"Why isn't *he* participating in The Run this week?" I asked, my voice sharp with sudden aggravation,

the underlying possessiveness in my tone betraying the carefully constructed neutrality I usually maintained.

Aiden quickly leaned over my shoulder, his brow furrowed in confusion, to see who had elicited my unexpected reaction.

"Ah, Travis," Aiden murmured, a hint of understanding dawning in his eyes. "While he is eighteen and was indeed permitted to attend the visiting trip to the neighboring pack's territory, he is still technically enrolled in his final year of high school," Aiden carefully explained, his tone placating. "Therefore, we have him tentatively scheduled to participate in The Run after his official graduation in May. Although his chosen mate is a respected warrior from the neighboring pack and a couple of years his senior, so she has formally requested permission to visit him here until then."

Without a word, I swiftly handed him Travis's file, my expression firm and unwavering. "I deny permission for any visits. Add him to the active list of runners for this week's Run."

"But Sir, with all due respect, he is still in high school," Aiden tried to argue back, his astonishment at my abrupt decision evident in his incredulous tone. "Once he officially participates in The Run, he will be traditionally required to relocate with his mate to her pack's territory, solidifying their bond and his membership transfer."

"Now, Aiden," I demanded, my voice dropping to a low, dangerous growl that brooked no further argument, the cold authority of my Alpha command unmistakable.

Aiden, though clearly unconvinced and still visibly perplexed by my seemingly impulsive decision, wisely chose not to press the issue. He silently took the now finished pile of documents from my hand and briskly left the conference room, his footsteps echoing slightly in the sudden silence.

While I didn't possess any specific knowledge regarding the intricate details of Travis and Brayden's burgeoning relationship, I was acutely aware of one undeniable fact: my mate had found the young, eager wolf undeniably attractive.

And in my possessive, territorial heart, that single, irrefutable truth was more than enough reason to want that particular pup as far away from Brayden as possible.

A small, self-satisfied smile played on my lips as I allowed myself a fleeting thought of my own future Run with Brayden. Perhaps by next summer, he would feel comfortable enough, secure enough in our bond, to willingly participate. Over the next year, I could take my time, slowly and deliberately forging an unbreakable connection with my mate, brick by painstaking brick. It would also afford him ample time to strengthen his injured leg, ensuring his full physical participation when the time finally came. While a year stretched out like an eternity in my impatient heart, that didn't mean I couldn't officially mark him long before then, solidifying our bond in the eyes of the Goddess and our pack. Once we were fully and irrevocably marked, The Run would simply be a powerful symbol of our enduring commitment and would serve as his official, joyous celebration into the full embrace of our pack.

Yeah, a year from now would be absolutely perfect…

…"He's going to have to join The Run…" I hear Dr. Monroe mumble, his voice heavy with reluctant understanding, the weight of the situation settling upon him.

I look up for the first time since collapsing onto the uncomfortable chair, my anger flaring at his seemingly resigned statement.

"He *can't* run! You were the one who explicitly stated that he wasn't physically fit enough to be able to participate without risking serious injury!" I yell, my voice raw with a potent mix of fear and aggravated disbelief.

"You partially marked him! What the hell else is he supposed to do now?!" My mother shouts back, her own fear and frustration mirroring my own spiraling panic.

"Those are just old wives' tales! Myths!" Aiden argues, the disbelief clear and unwavering in his usually steady voice.

"We don't know that for absolute certain, Aiden," Dr. Monroe wearily counters, slumping down into the worn leather of his office chair, the springs groaning in protest beneath his weight. "All legends, no matter how fantastical they may seem, often stem from some kernel of truth, some historical event or understanding that has been embellished over time. The only thing we know for sure, without any shadow of a doubt, is that a partial mark is an unnatural occurrence within our biology. The Run under the full moon is a symbolic, natural event for those who follow the natural order and fully mark their mates. We have absolutely no concrete understanding of what unnatural consequences could potentially arise from failing to participate in the Run when one has already been partially marked." His words hang heavy in the air, a chilling premonition of unknown dangers.

"What if I fully mark him now?" I ask desperately, my voice cracking with a raw plea, frantically searching for any alternative solution to the catastrophic problem I had inadvertently created. "If I fully marked him right now, then we could just participate in the Run at any subsequent full moon."

Dr. Monroe sighs, a long, drawn-out sound of utter weariness. "From what little fragmented knowledge we possess from the ancient texts, it wouldn't make a significant difference at this critical juncture, Alpha. According to the oldest stories, the only viable time for you to now fully mark him, without risking potentially devastating side effects for both of you, is after he has been caught during The Run under the very first full moon to arise after the initial, incomplete partial mark."

"He *can't*," I mumble, my desperate arguments weakening as the terrifying inevitability of the situation becomes chillingly clear. "He's not ready to tie himself to me... permanently. Not like this." The thought of forcing him into such a profound commitment, especially under these terrifying circumstances, tears at my very soul.

"Are you truly willing to risk that those ancient legends are false?" My mother asks severely, her voice sharp with a mother's unwavering concern. "Are you willing to gamble with your own sanity, and potentially Brayden's very life, by not participating in this crucial Run? Are you prepared to be selfish enough to cling to your desire for a loving, willing mate when your impulsive mistake could very well cost him everything?" Her words strike me like a physical blow, each syllable a painful reminder of my reckless actions.

I'm not.

The devastating truth resonates deep within my core. I am not willing to risk anything where Brayden is concerned. Even if it means forcing him into a tradition he knows nothing about, a tradition that would irrevocably bind him to me. The alternative... The alternative is unthinkable.

BRAYDEN

Friday 3:26 pm

"How's your pain level?" Dr. Monroe asks, his voice calm and clinical as he stands by my side, his gaze fixed on my charts.

"Fine," I reply, the single word clipped and dismissive.

"Would you like another round of pain medication?"

"No."

"Are you hungry? Should I call up a nurse to bring your lunch?"

"No."

The doctor sighs, the sound barely audible as he puts down his clipboard, his frustration at my terse responses radiating in the tense silence that fills the small room. He reaches for my left hand, his touch impersonal as he slowly unwinds the soiled bandage, his brow furrowed in concentration as he examines the angry wound beneath.

I offer no reaction to his prodding, my body stiff and un-yielding.

"Cooperation is key to a swift recovery, Brayden," he tries again, his tone carefully encouraging as he retrieves a clean set of sterile wrap. "Your minimal eating and outright refusal of necessary medication are not going to harm anyone but yourself."

"Maybe you should just report my insubordination to your fucking Alpha," I grit out, the words laced with venom, my right hand clenching into a tight, involuntary fist.

Dr. Monroe pauses his careful treatment of my injured hand at my defiant declaration, and the already thick tension in the room palpably intensifies.

"Holding onto resentment isn't going to benefit anyone involved, Brayden," he mumbles softly, resuming his task with deliberate care, his gaze carefully averted, avoiding any direct eye contact.

I scoff, the sound sharp and dismissive, and yank my hand away from his gentle grip.

"This is all his fault! I'm lying in this damn bed because of that motherfucker!" I yell, my anger surging, grabbing the discarded bandages and choosing to haphazardly rewrap my throbbing injury myself.

"The initial wound is undeniably his fault, but you are the one who pushed yourself to the point of collapse and landed yourself back in this bed—"

"The *fuck* I did!" I yell in indignant fury, my voice rising sharply. "It was this goddamn hospital's shitty, exploitative work system that put me here in the first place!"

I can feel my face heat, the flush of anger burning against my skin.

"You deliberately went far above and beyond the permitted working hours we strictly enforce," Dr. Monroe chastises, his voice calm and undeterred by my outburst of raw rage. "In order to accrue the excessive hours you did, you knowingly manipulated the established system by deceptively obtaining permission from various superiors, all of whom were regrettably unaware as to the true extent of your dangerously overloaded schedule."

"The pathetic rules didn't explicitly forbid me from doing any of that bullshit!" I scream, angrily yanking the bandage tighter around my throbbing hand, the rough fabric chafing against my skin. "And I wouldn't have been forced to work such obscenely long hours if you actually paid me a goddamn livable wage in the first place!"

"You hear that, mighty Alpha? Some leader you are!" I shout towards the open doorway of my sterile room, my voice dripping with sarcasm and bitter resentment. "You can't even pay your own damn workers enough to survive!"

Even though I couldn't physically see him, I knew with a chilling certainty that Damien was out there, lurking just around the corner from my presence, his imposing form a silent shadow in the hallway. He had been sulking just beyond my door for the last few days, a constant, unwelcome reminder of the terrifying events, yet not daring to actually re-enter my room and face my simmering rage.

I feel a gentle touch on my left hand and see that Dr. Monroe is attempting to correct my sloppy, inadequate wrapping job. I instantly rip my hand away from his persistent grip, my irritation flaring anew at his unwavering persistence.

"I refuse any further treatment," I seethe, my glare directed at the doctor sharp enough to cut glass.

Dr. Monroe looks at me with a weary, almost defeated expression, sighing softly at my continued antagonistic behavior. "You've been trying that particular line of defiance for the past three days, Brayden. You know perfectly well that it won't work in this facility," he says dejectedly, his voice betraying his obvious exhaustion from my stubborn unwillingness to comply with even the most basic medical care.

"Get the hell out of my room," I grit out stiffly, my body rigid with barely contained fury.

The doctor pauses, his gaze lingering on my face for a long, assessing moment before he runs a tired hand down his face, a gesture of utter weariness. He studies me for another silent second before giving a small, almost imperceptible nod of resignation, finally turning and heading slowly towards the doorway. He pauses just before exiting my room, his hand resting on the cool metal of the doorframe.

"I'll be back in precisely one hour to check your vital signs, Brayden," he proclaims, turning his head back to give me one last, weary look before he finally departs.

"Get out of my goddamn room!" I shriek, my control finally snapping. I impulsively grab the flimsy plastic cup of lukewarm water from the bedside table and hurl it with all my remaining strength at his retreating form. The cup misses its intended target, splashing harmlessly against the doorframe just as Dr. Monroe quickly exits without uttering another word, leaving me alone with my simmering rage.

The door remains stubbornly open, but that was hardly anything new in this place. Even with it firmly shut, I knew the monsters lurking just outside could undoubtedly hear every single word that was spoken within these sterile walls anyway. The very concept of privacy no longer existed within these confines, only the flimsy, pathetic illusion of separation from the ever-watchful, wondering eyes that constantly tried to steal surreptitious glances into my forced confinement.

I flop back heavily onto the starched, uncomfortable hospital bed, still reeling with disbelief at the utter absurdity of what my life had inexplicably become in such a short amount of time.

After finally succumbing to utter exhaustion and passing out on Tuesday night, I had remained mercifully unconscious until late Friday afternoon. I had slowly drifted back to a jarring awareness of the unwelcome sight of Damien sitting in a chair on the far side of my sterile room, his imposing form slumped with an uncharacteristic air of remorse and guilt etched across his usually arrogant features.

While my still-foggy mind was desperately trying to grasp the multitude of bewildering questions that swirled within it, my first coherent thought, the instinct of a parent overriding my own confusion, had been frantically asking if the kids were alright. Damien had immediately assured me, his voice low and sincere, that they were perfectly fine, but a deep-seated distrust still lingered within me, prompting me to call Kelsey myself to verify his claims. Apparently, Lou had been diligently watching Evie during the day and was staying overnight at our cramped trailer in the evenings until it was time for the kids to go to bed, a comforting image in the midst of this chaos. Kelsey had mentioned that Lou had even offered to move everyone into their spacious log cabin until I was fully recovered, but Kelsey, in a rare display of stubbornness I found myself surprisingly grateful for, had firmly refused to leave our own home.

After finally being reassured that my family was safe and well-cared for, I had abruptly ended the call, the relief washing over me quickly followed by a renewed wave of anger and confusion directed squarely at the silent figure across the room. I hadn't said another word to Damien, the tense silence stretching between us like an invisible, unbreakable cord as my exhausted brain struggled to rationalize the utterly insane, terrifying events I had witnessed just a couple of nights prior, until Damien, unable to bear the oppressive silence any longer, had decided to shatter it with the most unbelievable, life-altering declaration, blurting out with an almost casual tone that werewolves were, in fact, real.

My immediate response had been to grab the nearest object, which happened to be the lightweight television remote, and hurl it with surprising force directly at his unsuspecting head, all while screeching a sarcastic, "No *shit*, Sherlock!" that echoed through the sterile room.

Things had only spiraled downhill at an alarming rate from there as he had proceeded to tell me everything.

And I mean everything.

From the general, unbelievable existence of werewolves living secretly amongst humans to the intricate, deeply held beliefs of their ancient Moon Goddess. There were vivid, detailed descriptions of what a pack truly was, a complex social structure bound by blood and loyalty, and how it fundamentally functioned within their hidden world. He had even delved into the nuances of their unique werewolf culture, patiently explaining the different rankings and hierarchical positions that were strictly upheld within their society. He had launched into long, impassioned rants on what pack bonds truly were and the profound significance they held for every werewolf, including the especially sacred and unbreakable bond that packmates held towards their revered Alpha and their chosen Alpha pair.

And then, of course, he had painstakingly explained the existence of destined mates.

I scoff derisively, the bitter sound echoing in the quiet room as I vividly remember that particular, infuriating part of our utterly unbelievable conversation.

Upon his utterly ludicrous declaration of our supposed, undeniable connection as fated mates, I had openly laughed in his face, a loud, incredulous sound that bordered on hysterical, and told him in no uncertain terms that I would rather dry-fuck a cactus in the desert heat than willingly tie myself to his arrogant, infuriating ass. To which he had proceeded to launch into a lengthy, self-deprecating explanation detailing the extensive ways in which he had royally fucked up our initial interactions, culminating in a detailed, terrifying description of a barbaric event called The Run.

When he had finally finished explaining the entirety of his unbelievable, insane story, I had simply told him to get the hell out of my room and leave me alone, the words cold and final.

I hadn't physically seen him since that explosive confrontation.

Even though his imposing form hadn't darkened my doorway in days, this didn't mean he had actually left me alone, not in the slightest. Anytime Dr. Monroe would leave after his brief, clinical check-ins, I could clearly hear the low, unmistakable reverberations of Damien's deep voice as he anxiously discussed my recovery and prognosis with the doctor just outside my room. There were also the unsettling times that I caught the distinct shadow of his large form restlessly pacing near my closed door, a silent, watchful presence that grated on my already frayed nerves. And I was almost certain that I could still faintly smell his distinctive autumnal scent, a strange mix of crisp leaves and something inherently wild, lingering in the air just as I began to stir awake this morning, a constant, unwelcome reminder of his intrusive presence.

Ugh! I hate him, I hate him! Just when his constant presence was starting to become... almost tolerable, a small, grudging part of me starting to think, *huh, maybe he isn't the absolute devil incarnate after all*, the arrogant son of a bitch goes and makes my already complicated life a goddamn living nightmare!

I'm abruptly dragged out of my spiraling thoughts by the distinct sound of someone approaching my room. My already terrible mood only darkens further as a large, imposing shadow suddenly fills the open doorway. I look up from the crumpled sheets, my eyes narrowing into a hostile scowl at the unwelcome newcomer.

Oh yeah, and one more thing...

"Does that folder come with a check worth nineteen years of child support?" I ask, my voice dripping with sarcasm, a forced, beaming smile stretching across my face, the movement pulling painfully at the still-tender bite marks on my hand.

Aiden's broad shoulders visibly slump as he hesitantly enters the room, his usual confident demeanor replaced by an uncharacteristic awkwardness. He pointedly avoids meeting my gaze as he wordlessly hands me the thick manila folder he's been holding, his movements stiff and formal.

"This contains all the pertinent information and strict regulations pertaining to your Run tonight, Luna," he says formally, his voice carefully neutral as he straightens up and clasps his hands stiffly behind his back, his posture rigid. "If you happen to have any specific questions regarding the established rules, you can directly address myself or Alpha about the official regulations."

I scan over the official papers with unconcealed contempt, pointedly pretending to be deeply engaged in the information contained within, my lip curling slightly in distaste.

"You can go," I dismiss him curtly, making no attempt to hide the disgust that colors my tone.

I see him give a quick, almost imperceptible bow of his head before silently heading back out of the door, his departure leaving a renewed tension in the air. I glare at his retreating form, a complex range of conflicting emotions churning beneath a thick, protective blanket of simmering anger.

Since I had been abruptly made aware of his biological donation to my very existence, the few strained interactions we had shared in the last couple of days had been undeniably awkward and stilted. Aiden had adopted a strictly professional approach, treating me with a formal deference and meticulously adhering to the rigid protocol that was apparently appropriate based on my supposed Luna status within their bizarre hierarchy.

This detached approach wasn't entirely unwelcome on his part, and a small, rational part of me actually preferred it to the potentially more uncomfortable alternative of him attempting to immediately forge some semblance of familial connection under the rather unbelievable pretense of newly discovered blood relations.

Part of the utterly surreal experience of finding out that Aiden was my biological father had also forced me to confront the undeniable, and equally bizarre, fact that I wasn't entirely human myself. To a degree, this shocking revelation did explain a few of the more inexplicable aspects of my life – like why I had been the fastest track runner in school without any dedicated training, why my severely broken arm at the age of eight had inexplicably healed in roughly half the expected time, or why I had always possessed an unusually heightened sensitivity to certain smells that others barely registered.

But it was still undeniably odd, deeply unsettling, to actually hear someone calmly state aloud that you weren't quite like everyone else, that your very DNA was somehow... different. For the most part, in a desperate attempt to maintain some semblance of sanity amidst this overwhelming chaos, I had consciously decided to bury my swirling thoughts and complex emotions on the truly bizarre topic, as I already had far too much immediate, pressing insanity to focus on as it was. But the underlying strangeness of it all... that was a constant, nagging undercurrent.

Although, in all honesty, that could accurately be said about the entirety of the utterly unbelievable situation I had inexplicably found myself trapped in, just pure insanity.

I begin to halfheartedly try to read over the official documents that Aiden had brought, the stark black text on the crisp white paper blurring before my tired eyes. However, it proves exceedingly difficult to focus on the dense legal jargon and convoluted rules as the persistent sound of people arguing heatedly in the hallway just outside my room continues to distract me, their raised voices carrying clearly through the thin walls.

Goddamn it, can't it just be quiet for two goddamn minutes in this insane asylum!

I give a silent, frustrated groan and throw the useless papers onto the pristine white sheets of my hospital bed, my agitation mounting. I fully anticipate hearing the low, rumbling sound of Damien's ever-present voice joining the hallway cacophony, but I am surprisingly met with the distinct sound of two distinctly female voices engaged in a rather heated argument instead. My curiosity piqued, despite my foul mood, I carefully and quietly swing my legs over the side of the bed and cautiously head towards my open doorway, my bare feet silent on the cool tile floor.

Upon reaching the threshold, I first instinctively check to make absolutely certain that Damien isn't lurking in his usual sentinel position just down the hallway, not wanting to add that particular brand of unwanted drama to my already incredibly stressful and surreal day. Happy that I don't immediately spot his imposing form, I turn my attention towards the source of the arguing women's voices.

"Who in Goddess's name allowed the likes of *you* in here?" I hear one of the nurses ask, her tone sharp and accusatory.

"I just wanted to quickly drop this off for him," the guest responds, her voice a little too quiet and slightly muffled for me to immediately identify the speaker.

"Luna is in a very sensitive and fragile state right now and desperately needs to rest as much as possible before the events of tonight," the nurse huffs, her arms crossed defensively across her chest. "He certainly doesn't need the added stress of being in the unwelcome presence of a pack member with your standing."

Growing increasingly annoyed at the unnecessarily harsh and dismissive way the nurse is treating the other woman, I finally step out of the confines of my sterile room for the first time in what feels like an eternity.

"Is there a problem here?" I ask, shooting a pointedly annoyed glare at the officious nurse. Both women seem visibly startled by my sudden and unexpected appearance, and I instantly recognize the quiet guest.

"Olivia," I exclaim, a genuine note of confusion coloring my tone at her unexpected visit.

The petite woman looks down at her feet, a blush creeping up her neck, and my eyes widen with a sudden, dawning realization.

"You just missed Aiden, he left my room a few minutes ago," I say, trying to be helpful and diffuse the awkward situation.

Olivia shakes her head gently, a small, almost sad smile gracing her lips, before stepping slightly to the side of the still-glaring nurse. It is then that I finally see she is carefully holding a delicate bouquet of pristine white flowers in her hands.

"I didn't actually come here to see him, Brayden," she explains softly, her gaze meeting mine with a surprising amount of gentle sincerity. "I just wanted to give these to you," she says, gesturing to the thoughtful gift in her hands.

The nurse's eyes narrow into angry slits, and she opens her mouth in obvious indignation, clearly about to launch another defensive tirade, but I quickly cut her off with a sharp look.

"Was there a specific reason why Ms. Olivia wasn't allowed to visit me?" I ask, my own annoyance growing on Olivia's behalf at the unnecessarily rude treatment she was receiving from the hospital staff. "I *am* allowed to have visitors, aren't I?"

The nurse's eyes widen in surprise at my unexpected intervention before she quickly bows her head in reluctant deference.

"Of course, Luna," she mumbles, her voice subdued. "My mistake." She shoots one last, lingering glare of disapproval at Olivia before huffily walking down the hallway, leaving us alone.

I offer a genuine smile to my unexpected visitor and motion her forward into my room. Olivia returns my smile with a small, grateful grin and gently hands the beautiful bouquet of white flowers over to me.

"I heard that you were being officially discharged from the hospital later this evening for… The Run," she says sheepishly, a hint of nervousness in her voice, "but I still thought you might enjoy these, even if it was only for a little while," she continues, her cheeks flushing slightly. "I also… I didn't really know which flowers or colors you particularly liked, but you were wearing a white shirt at the temple the other day… and I just… it sounds kind of stupid when I actually say it out loud…" Her voice trails off, laced with a touch of endearing awkwardness.

"Thank you, Olivia," I interrupt her gently, my gaze fixed on the delicate beauty of the white blossoms in my hands, a genuine warmth spreading through my chest at the unexpected gesture.

I awkwardly clear my throat, my gaze shifting between her kind face and the thoughtful gift I now held. I was unexpectedly touched by her kindness, especially considering the complicated circumstances, and a sudden wave of guilt washed over me for my earlier, less-than-welcoming thoughts towards her.

"I just… I wanted to say that I have absolutely no expectations from you, Olivia," I mumble nervously, the words tumbling out in a rush.

Olivia gives me a genuinely confused look, her brow furrowing slightly as I continue to stumble through my heartfelt but clumsy explanation.

"I can't even begin to fathom the incredibly difficult position you've been so suddenly thrust into," I begin rambling, my voice laced with sincere empathy. "Finding out about me and my… complicated connection to Aiden couldn't have been easy for you. I just… I genuinely don't want you to feel even the slightest bit pressured that you have to like me, or… whatever, just because I happen to be connected to your… hus– I mean, your mate," I finally manage to choke out, unable to meet Olivia's kind gaze, a deep sense of guilt twisting in my gut at what this woman must be enduring.

There's a brief moment of comfortable silence before I feel a small, surprisingly reassuring hand being gently placed on my arm. I finally look up and see Olivia smiling softly at me, the beginning of unshed tears shimmering in her warm eyes.

"I don't feel pressured at all, Brayden," she says, her voice surprisingly steady despite the emotions that clearly welled within her. A genuine, heartwarming grin spreads across her face. "The very fact that you would even take into consideration my perspective and my feelings in all of this… well, it's just continued evidence that you are absolutely worth getting to know."

A small, relieved smile finally graces my own lips in return, the weight of my earlier guilt easing slightly at her unexpected kindness and understanding.

Olivia didn't stay much longer, her visit a brief but welcome respite in the overwhelming chaos. She left just as Dr. Monroe returned to perform my final, perfunctory check-up before my impending discharge. The last couple of hours had been surprisingly quiet, the tense silence punctuated only by the relentless ticking of the clock on the sterile wall as the minutes slowly dragged by, each one bringing me closer to the terrifying unknown of tonight.

I am currently staring down at the thick manila folder containing the detailed rules and regulations for The Run, my brow furrowed in intense concentration as I tried to absorb every single word. I had meticulously read over each page, going line by painstaking line, determined not to miss even the smallest detail. Every now and then, I had made a small, almost illegible note next to one of the more confusing rules, or underlined a crucial keyword with a determined stroke of the pen.

Rules were important, after all.

My mom had always been incredibly anal about strictly following rules. She used to drill into Kelsey and me that the absolute best way to achieve the results you desperately wanted in life was to meticulously follow the established rules to the absolute letter, the proverbial "T." Follow the rules so diligently, so precisely, that you pushed them to their very limit, stretched their inherent restrictions so incredibly thin, that the very person who had initially written them would secretly wish you would just go ahead and break them already. There were always loopholes to be found within even the strictest of regulations, no matter how seemingly ironclad the rule was, but the only way to successfully uncover those hidden pathways to your desired outcome was to know the rules better, far better, than the rule-maker themselves.

I wasn't stupid. There was absolutely no realistic way that I, in my current weakened state, was going to be able to physically outrun Damien Rockwell in any kind of chase. The sheer physical difference between the two of us was almost comical, a ridiculous mismatch even with the supposed sixty-minute head start I had been begrudgingly granted. In any kind of straight footrace, I was undeniably, completely screwed. This stark reality was precisely why thoroughly understanding the intricate rules of this barbaric tradition was so critically important. If I couldn't physically outrun him, then my only viable chance of "winning" this insane game, of somehow navigating this terrifying situation without irrevocably tying myself to that arrogant... Alpha, was to exploit the very rules of the Run itself.

I just needed to follow the rules, understand them better than he did, and maybe, just maybe, I could find a way out of this nightmare without even having to participate in his ridiculous, archaic chase.

Brayden

Saturday 7:44 pm

The car I'm in smells faintly of something artificial, the kind of overpowering newness that makes you suspect they've sprayed it with a chemical cocktail. The floors are too pristine, the leather seats too unblemished, the windows reflecting the early evening sun with an unnerving clarity. It's the kind of oppressive perfection that makes me feel like a walking biohazard, terrified of leaving a single smudge on the immaculate surfaces. Even stretching my legs feels like a risky maneuver, each movement carefully calibrated to avoid any accidental damage to this ridiculously expensive vehicle.

This whole goddamn situation has me so tightly wound that I can't even find a moment's peace in this rolling sensory deprivation chamber.

It is the hazy, in-between time just before the official sundown, the sky starting to bleed into those dramatic shades of bruised purple and angry orange, and I am currently being chauffeured, against my will, to the designated location for this ludicrous "Run."

Apparently, ancient tradition dictates that once the sun dipped below the horizon, physical contact with my supposed "mate" is strictly forbidden until he inevitably "caught" me, and separate transportation is considered the height of traditional etiquette.

Which suited me just fucking fine. The less interaction I have with any of these delusional wolf-people at the moment, the better my rapidly fraying sanity would fare.

Sighing with a weariness that goes bone-deep, I stare out of the darkly tinted windows as the familiar, unsettling landscape of this cursed town whips by in a shadowy blur. The scenery triggers an unwelcome flood of memories, the most prominent being my arrival in this bizarre place. A scowl tightens my lips as a familiar wave of regret washes over me. Hindsight, that cruel mistress, whispers that I should have gunned the engine and hightailed it out of these creepy woods the second I crossed the damned county line. Turn around and never, ever look back.

It will be fine.

I have a plan A through goddamn Z meticulously formulated in your head. There is absolutely no way that arrogant bastard Damien will actually win this ridiculous game.

The soft, monotonous hum of the car engine vibrates through the seats for a while, a dull counterpoint to the turmoil in my head, until the unnatural quiet is abruptly shattered by the aggressively cheerful blare of Kelsey's personalized ringtone. I immediately lunge for the backpack wedged at my feet, a frantic rummage through its carefully chosen contents finally yielding my phone.

"Is everything Ok?" I ask quickly, my voice tight with immediate concern, the ever-present worry for my sister and the kids a knot in my stomach.

"Yeah, Bray, everything's perfectly fine," Kelsey chuckles, the sound a little too bright. "Lou just left a few minutes ago, the three little terrors have finally been wrestled into bed, and Marcus just started some brainless action movie, so I thought I'd take a quick breather and see how you were holding up."

Despite her light tone, I can still detect the subtle undercurrent of exhaustion and thinly veiled anxiety that has clung to her voice like a persistent shadow these last few days.

"Kels, we've been over this," I try to calmly reassure her, my patience wearing thin. "I am completely, unequivocally healthy. The only infuriating reason I'm not already back at the trailer is because that ridiculously archaic hospital has some asinine policy that mandates a full twenty-four hours of perfect health before they'll deign to release a patient."

As I'm speaking, the car begins to decelerate, the smooth glide gradually giving way to a complete stop. The distinct sounds of the driver's door clicking open and then firmly shutting have me instinctively reaching for my backpack, my fingers tightening around the worn straps. All too soon, an unwelcome flood of harsh sunlight spills through my suddenly opened car door. I awkwardly wedge the phone between my ear and shoulder as I ungracefully climb out, pointedly ignoring the silent, looming presence of my chauffeur.

Stepping onto the gravel, I see that we've arrived at a surprisingly crowded makeshift parking lot situated in front of a small, unnervingly still clearing that ominously backed up against the dense, shadowy expanse of a large, ancient-looking forest.

In the bustling parking lot, various werewolf family members are engaged in overly dramatic hugs and offering saccharine good wishes to the visibly nervous participating mates. Forced but ultimately smiling goodbyes are being exchanged, and the overall atmosphere feels strangely, disturbingly celebratory, a bizarrely festive air hanging over the impending, forced chase.

The open field itself is also surprisingly full of people, and a prickle of unease runs down my spine at just how many werewolves apparently participate in this archaic ritual. It is immediately obvious that those already gathered in the clearing had been separated into two distinct groups. A stark, bright white line had been painted across the middle of the field, clearly demarcating the two sides, although anyone with functioning eyeballs could have easily discerned which group is which. With their typically dominating and generally larger builds, the designated hunters are all congregated on the side of the field closest to the makeshift parking lot, while the designated runners, myself included, are huddled together on the opposite side, the side that ominously borders the dark, silent woods.

On either side of the clearly marked dividing line, various mated pairs are waving at each other with strained smiles, and some even dare to inch close to the stark white boundary to engage in hushed, overly affectionate conversations that honestly make my stomach clench with a potent mix of disgust and resentment.

The whole scene makes my teeth ache, and I couldn't help the involuntary scowl that tightens my lips as I survey the bizarrely cheerful crowd.

As I reluctantly begin to walk through the dense mass of whispering werewolves, Kelsey sighs heavily through the phone, a pointed reminder that she is still very much on the other end of this increasingly surreal conversation.

"I know you're technically healthy now, Brayden, whether it's some ridiculous hospital protocol or not, that doesn't magically stop me from worrying about you," she says, her voice sounding utterly drained, the weight of the past few days clearly taking its toll.

I frown, a familiar pang of guilt twisting in my gut at the thought of just how much additional stress and responsibility has been unfairly dumped onto my sister's already overloaded plate these last few insane days.

"Well, I'll be home first thing in the morning, and there's absolutely–" I abruptly stop walking, my attention diverted by a distinct, unsettling sound that crackles through the speaker of my phone. "What the *fuck* was that?" I ask sharply, my voice laced with a sudden spike of alarm, desperately hoping that what I had just distinctly heard was some kind of bizarre auditory hallucination.

"What was what, Brayden?" Kelsey asks innocently, her tone suspiciously even.

I hear another unmistakable clatter, a distinct scraping sound against glass, and a sinking feeling of dread settles in my stomach. I know with a chilling certainty that I had heard correctly the first time.

"Oh my God, Kelsey," I exclaim into the phone, my voice rising in disbelief and outrage, "You're in my goddamn chocolate, aren't you?!"

My sudden, indignant outburst causes some of the nearest werewolves to abruptly turn their heads in my direction, their curious gazes momentarily fixed on my outburst before they quickly, and pointedly, turn back to their own conversations, clearly not wanting to draw any unwanted attention. I shoot a venomous glare at those closest to me and desperately try to bring the phone closer to my ear, not wanting to attract any more unwanted scrutiny from these bizarre people.

"Woman, why the hell are you in my goddamn shit?!" I whisper-yell into the phone, my voice a furious hiss.

"Well, it's not like I don't deserve a little bit of comfort after the absolute hell *I've* been put through these last couple of days, Brayden," she scoffs defensively, the unmistakable sound of a spoon scraping against the bottom of a glass jar clearly audible on her end.

"The hell *you've* been put through? What about the absolute living hell *I've* been through these last few goddamn days?!" I interject, my voice rising in indignant fury. "I've been involuntarily hospitalized against my will, and you're over there delving into my personal, carefully rationed stash of goddamn serotonin!"

My increasingly agitated rant is abruptly interrupted by the silent, imposing presence of Aiden. The man's usually guarded face is carefully neutral as he approaches me, his dark eyes fixed on my backpack as he makes a subtle, almost imperceptible gesture towards it. I shoot him a venomous glare but reluctantly toss my worn backpack over to him, watching with a simmering resentment as he begins to methodically dig through its contents.

The familiar, infuriating sound of the plastic lid being firmly replaced on the telltale glass jar of my precious treasure turns my attention back to my phone conversation.

"Kelsey, if there is even a single portion missing when I get back to that trailer, I swear to God I am going to seek my vengeance upon your thieving ass," I grit out into the phone, my voice low and dangerous.

"Whatever you say, Bray," she chuckles softly, the sound undeniably smug. "We'll see you tomorrow morning. Try to get some rest, okay?"

The phone clicks abruptly, signaling that she has hung up on me, undoubtedly already savoring her ill-gotten gains.

I take a deep, steadying breath, trying to tamp down the surge of irrational anger I feel towards my sister, and slip my phone into the back pocket of my jeans as I finally give my undivided attention to Aiden, who is still inexplicably rifling through my meager belongings. There isn't even that much goddamn stuff in there to begin with. I have my carefully annotated copy of The Run's ridiculously convoluted rules, as well as a hastily drawn map of the surrounding woods outlining the supposed "safe zone" or end zone of this ridiculous chase. I also have a cheap plastic compass, a half-empty bottle of water, a small bottle of industrial-strength pain medication, and a surprisingly powerful little flashlight.

Aiden continues his silent, thorough search, and I can't help but roll my eyes at his excessive caution.

"There are literally a handful of items in there, Aiden," I tell him, my voice laced with annoyance. "If I had packed a goddamn knife with the express intention of stabbing Damien, you would have undoubtedly felt it by now, wouldn't you think?"

Besides, I have a much more satisfying and far less messy weapon in mind for that arrogant bastard than some measly blade.

Aiden finally stops his meticulous search and carefully assesses my demeanor for a long, silent moment before tossing my backpack back over to me with a soft thud.

"The designated runners are all gathered over there," he says, gesturing with a tilt of his head towards a huddled group of nervous-looking people standing near the edge of the woods behind him. "It would be in your best interest to head over to your assigned starting position now, Luna. Once you are officially entered on your designated side of the field, Damien will join the other hunters on the opposite side."

I offer no verbal response, my jaw tight with a mixture of apprehension and simmering resentment, as I reluctantly walk over to my assigned side of the makeshift field. Everyone in the immediate vicinity pointedly steps aside as I make my way towards the part of the clearing that ominously bordered the dark, silent woods. I pause for a brief, internal moment of reluctant acceptance as I reach the stark white line marking the center of the open field. I take a deep, steadying breath, the cool evening air filling my lungs, and then deliberately cross the symbolic boundary, a silent act that felt strangely like sealing my own unwanted fate as I officially entered into this bizarre, archaic ceremony.

Looking around at the other "runners," I notice that most of them are actively trying to avoid making direct eye contact with me, and a few even offer quick, nervous bows of their heads until I have passed by, their deference both unsettling and vaguely insulting. I mindlessly scan the anxious crowd until I unexpectedly spot a familiar face amidst the sea of strangers, and a surprising wave of relief washes over me as I immediately begin beelining my way over to him.

"Travis," I say, the sound of his name surprisingly comforting in the midst of this surreal nightmare. Even though I am now acutely aware that he is, in fact, a werewolf and deeply ingrained in this whole cultish community, I can't help but feel a small flicker of something akin to normalcy at seeing someone I still instinctively consider to be a part of my previous, relatively normal life.

The young man looks over at the sound of his name and visibly startles at my unexpected presence. His youthful face flushes a deep crimson the instant his eyes meet mine, and he immediately ducks his head in nervous deference.

"Luna, it's… good to see you," he greets me politely, his voice slightly trembling as he nervously shuffles his feet on the damp grass.

"So," I begin, gesturing with a subtle nod of my head over to where the imposing group of hunters have ominously gathered, "which one of those overly aggressive-looking Neanderthals is yours?"

Travis's eyes immediately light up at my casual inquiry, and his already flushed face deepens to an even more vibrant shade of red. With a shy, almost proud grin, he points just to the left side of the open field.

"That's her," he mumbles, his voice thick with a youthful pride as he openly gazes at his chosen mate.

I follow his gaze and my own eyes widen in genuine surprise. Travis's mate was a strikingly tall woman, easily towering over most of the other werewolves gathered. Her undeniably athletic build was all lean, hardened muscle that put my own form to shame. Even as she casually conversed with some other werewolves, her posture was ramrod straight, and her overall stance exudes a quiet but undeniably dominating presence that I could clearly sense even from this distance.

"Well, that's a sadist if I've ever seen one," I say appraisingly, playfully bumping Travis's shoulder with my own. "Good job, kid."

The brunette's flush deepens even further, and he self-consciously looks down at the ground, unable to meet my amused gaze.

"Uh… yeah… I mean, we haven't explicitly, like, discussed… that particular aspect of our… dynamic, but… yeah…" He rambles out awkwardly, his gaze fixed on the damp grass, and he nervously wipes his sweaty palms on the tops of his worn jeans.

I can't help the small chuckle that escapes my lips at his obvious unease, finding his youthful embarrassment strangely endearing in the midst of this otherwise terrifying situation.

"I haven't actually seen her around town before," I comment, my curiosity piqued.

Travis rubs the back of his neck self-consciously and looks back up at his imposing mate, a soft smile spreading across his face as he takes the opportunity to enthusiastically discuss his new partner. "She's actually from a neighboring pack, about an hour's drive from here," he explains proudly. "She's also the youngest werewolf to ever successfully pass the rigorous warrior training program in her entire pack, and she's already in line to receive a significant promotion even though she's only in her mid-twenties."

"So, you're now officially in the long-distance relationship club," I joke lightly, offering him a small, sympathetic smile.

Travis's expression suddenly becomes noticeably sullen, the previous excitement and youthful enthusiasm he had been displaying slowly beginning to diminish, replaced by a quiet resignation. "Actually, I'll be moving in with her permanently as soon as all of this... Run... is over."

"Really?" I exclaim in genuine surprise, my eyebrows shooting up. "I mean, I'm still incredibly new to all of this bizarre werewolf stuff, but... is that actually normal protocol?"

"Uh, no, not really," he admits quietly, his gaze dropping back down to the ground. "Normally, mates who are still enrolled in high school don't actually participate in The Run until after they officially graduate, but... Alpha thought it would be best for me to participate now, apparently."

An uncomfortable silence hangs in the air between us after his quiet, revealing answer.

Although he didn't explicitly say it aloud, I can't shake the nagging feeling that this sudden, unwelcome change in his plans is somehow indirectly my fault. I don't know the specifics of how Damien would have found out about my brief, ill-advised physical relationship with Travis, but a dark, cynical part of me can't help but suspect that this is some kind of petty, vindictive retaliation on Damien's part.

"Do you... do you want me to try and see if I can somehow get your Run postponed, Travis?" I offer hesitantly, feeling a confusing mix of guilt and genuine pity for the only person in this bizarre town I could even remotely consider a friend. Honestly, I had absolutely no idea if I even possessed the authority to make such a request, or even how one would go about postponing a centuries-old werewolf tradition, but it still felt like the right thing to at least try and offer some kind of assistance.

Travis shakes his head slowly, a small, weary smile gracing his lips. "No, Luna, it's… it's okay. I've already inadvertently caused enough problems for myself by getting involved with you. This is actually a pretty mild punishment compared to what Alpha could have potentially done," he shrugs with a forced nonchalance that doesn't quite reach his eyes. "Besides," he continues, trying to sound more upbeat, "we were planning on officially moving in together anyway, it's really only a few months earlier than originally planned," he says, the forced cheerfulness in his tone not entirely convincing.

While his words don't outwardly express any anger or resentment towards me, I still can't shake the persistent feeling of guilt that gnaws at my conscience.

Ugh, this whole situation isn't even remotely my fault!

Travis and I didn't actually do anything inherently *wrong*, and yet he's somehow the one paying the goddamn penalty for it.

As I'm about to offer Travis some kind of inadequate comfort, I suddenly notice just how eerily quiet everything has become. The once bustling area, filled with the murmur of hushed conversations and nervous laughter, has gone completely silent. A sudden, unwelcome chill runs down my spine, a primal instinct already anticipating the reason behind everyone's abrupt stillness.

Turning back towards the imposing group of hunters gathered on the opposite side of the field, I see that Damien has finally arrived.

BRAYDEN

Saturday 8:11 pm

Damien's arrival didn't go unnoticed.

The once-bustling clearing of excited werewolves and loud conversations fell silent. Every person present acknowledged the arrival of the Alpha, turning to give him their undivided attention. On both sides of the small clearing, the werewolves lowered their gazes, bowing in deference.

Damien slowly surveys the bowed heads of his followers, his gaze sweeping across the crowd. His eyes were hard, and his intent was clear. He scans the area for only a few seconds before his gaze locks onto its target.

Our eyes meet.

It is unsettling how strongly Damien's presence affects me. An uncomfortable jolt shot down my spine. While I want to claim the upper hand, to deny his effect on me, to feign indifference... I couldn't.

I hate it, I hate everything about the bond. Despite my attempts to deny any feelings for Damien, something is there. Not attraction, relief, or a void only he could fill; rather, a physiological pressure seems to build in my chest the longer we are separated. It is as if an invisible line tied us together, growing tighter and tighter over the past few days, straining against me.

And just by looking into his brown eyes, I feel that line loosen to a more bearable level.

My reaction to the bond seems more influenced by my werewolf genes than my human ones. A full-blooded human wouldn't have felt any differently. From what I understood, the physical tightness in my chest is even more intense for a werewolf, intertwined with an emotional yearning. This means Damien should have felt suffocated by his need for me during our time apart.

Hopefully, the bastard has been suffering the last few days.

Damien begins walking toward me, and everyone raises their heads as he passes. I maintain eye contact as he approaches. His movements are almost in slow motion as I absorb every detail. Each step is calculated and purposeful, every breath deliberate in his mission to get as close to me as possible.

I take the opportunity to assess my mate. The first thing I notice is his surprisingly casual attire: loose sweatpants and a plain t-shirt. Clothes that would normally make someone appear more relaxed look out of place on him. His back is too straight, his shoulders too rigid. His walk is too determined and authoritative. He looks like he is wearing a costume rather than simple loungewear.

Damien stops just before the line dividing the field.

Neither of us speaks, a moment of silence hanging between us as we both seem to struggle with what to say.

I want to yell and scream at him. To shout about how unfair this whole situation is. I want him to know exactly how much I hate him. How I loathe the tense feeling he has forced upon me the last few days, and how I especially hate the way that feeling dissipates in his presence. I want to say something, anything, the perfect words to make him regret ever meeting me.

But I remain silent.

It became obvious that Damien is also experiencing inner turmoil. His eyes dart across my face, and his lips remain down-turned in a hard frown. The Alpha is as lost for words as I am.

Damien is the first to break our staring contest, but instead of addressing me, he turns slightly toward the crowd.

"I want to thank everyone for coming and participating in this month's Run!" his voice booms across the field.

A loud roar of adulation and applause follows his announce-ment. The energy of those around me seems to surge in anticipa-tion of the event.

"As always, the runners will have a sixty-minute head start after the sun goes down, before the hunters are released, per our ancient traditions sanctioned by our Goddess. Runners, this is your thirty-minute warning for the start time! Good luck, everyone!" he yells, and another round of applause and excited shouts erupts as the crowd resumes its previous chatter with renewed vigor.

Damien remains still, watching me from across the line. His attention is solely on me, and it is clear he wouldn't break eye contact anytime soon. We are probably only a few yards apart, close enough for conversation, but far enough that he couldn't touch me if he reached out.

As I watch the sun slowly dip behind the silhouettes of the hunters, I know it is time to put my plan into action.

Dropping my backpack onto the grass at my feet, I look away from Damien. While remaining within his line of sight, I angle my torso slightly away from him. I want him to see me, but also to convey my indifference to his presence.

I lower myself to sit on the dry grass. My legs are protected from any bristles or scratchy blades by my jeans and sneakers, but the hardness of the ground is still a little uncomfortable.

I spread my legs out in a wide "Y" shape and reach my fingers toward my foot, holding the position for about fifteen seconds before switching sides.

Travis looks down at me, a little confused, as he watches me repeat this process a few times.

"What are you doing?" he asks, sounding bewildered.

"I'm stretching out my muscles before The Run," I state casually with a shrug. "The last thing I want is for my legs to seize up." I switch to the other side, making sure my movements are slow and purposeful. "I already have enough working against me."

Travis nods and remains silent. I am glad he'd asked, knowing Damien could also hear our conversation.

Glancing up briefly, I see Damien is still watching me intently. Good, keep your eyes on me.

After a few more minutes of stretching my legs, I slowly stand up. Similar to when I was sitting, I stretch one arm high above my head before dropping it and stretching the other. I repeat this process for a while before subtly changing things.

This time, when I bring my arm down, I run my fingers through my hair, tousling my locks.

Damien's eyes are locked on me.

When I raise my other arm, I let my fingertips catch the hem of my shirt, raising it slightly and exposing the front of my toned stomach.

His stare intensifies.

Up and down go my arms, stretching my limbs high above my head. I rotate my wrists and tense my muscles subtly. I tease my viewer with quick glimpses of my skin and chest, gently grazing my hands across my face and hair. My movements are subtle but calculated.

Time to escalate.

In one swift motion, I reach down and remove my t-shirt, earning a growl from Damien, which I ignore.

Travis's eyes widen at my action.

"It's hot as balls out," I nonchalantly answer his unspoken question. "I don't want to overheat before The Run even starts." I sigh. "Wouldn't it be awful if I didn't take proper precautions and ended up passed out from heatstroke in the middle of the woods?" I ask rhetorically.

While facing Travis, I am really talking to Damien. The growling from across the field stops, confirming he's heard everything.

No longer subtle, I brazenly meet Damien's gaze. He seems startled by my initiative but doesn't look away. With our eyes locked, I resume my movements.

This time, I rub my palms all the way up my torso as I stretch. Touching my exposed stomach and chest, up to my neck, and through my hair. I flex my fingers as I raise my hands above my head and lean my body from side to side.

The heat of Damien's stare intensifies, and I note with satisfaction that his chest is rising and falling faster than before. Inhaling deeply, I notice his autumnal scent has also become stronger, almost nauseatingly so.

I now understood that the spicy scent I always smelled near Damien are his pheromones. This scent is unique to him, just like everyone has a unique smell. While I couldn't identify other people's scents as clearly, being Damien's mate means his pheromones are strong enough for easy identification. This became clear after we met in the grocery store when our interaction solidified my scent as Luna and Damien's mate.

While his scent has always irritates me, I now revel in its pungency.

Swiftly, I sit back on the ground and spread my legs again, careful not to break eye contact with Damien. This time, I lean forward, reaching out in front of me. I place my palms on the ground and push off slightly, arching my back. As I do this, I straighten my legs behind me.

Keeping my eyelids heavy, I stare at Damien and give a sultry smile as I lower my chest to the ground, grazing it against the scratchy blades of grass before pushing myself back up.

My mate is enthralled. His eyes are wide as I continue, and I notice him take a step closer.

I quickly swing my legs back in front of me and run my hand down my naked chest.

He takes another step.

I run my fingers up toward my mouth and lightly wet their tips, showing the alpha wolf the pink of my tongue as I trail the wet fingers down my chest.

He lifts his foot to take another step… but pauses.

I freeze.

No, just one more step, you son of a bitch!

I maintain my sultry smirk, but my face tightens as he slowly sets his foot back a step… and then another… and another.

With a big sigh, the man runs a large hand through his hair and rubs his neck in exasperation.

"If you wanted me that bad, Brayden, you should've stayed longer on Friday night," he said, his eyes defeated.

Fuck, I knew that'd come back to bite me in the ass!

"Whatever you're doing now, I know it's not sincere," He clenches his fists and looks away. "If your goal is to taunt me, congratulations, it's working."

I immediately drop my act and scowl at him as I stand up from the ground and glare at the bright white line dividing the field.

He was so fucking close! Just one more step, and he would've officially been on the runner's side!

I don't fully understand how this werewolf-mate-bond stuff works. I know I could feel a pressure within me that somehow ties me to Damien. I also know that without breaking the bond, prolonged separation from Damien would lead to a slow decline into depression and eventual death. And I know that during The Run, these special lines allow me to officially break the bond without that consequence.

Maybe they have a Priestess bless the lines? Or the paint used for the lines is mixed with the blood of their enemies?

"Why are you doing this, Brayden?" Damien asks, his voice strained and tired. For the first time tonight, I see his hard shell begin to crack.

Looking back at him, I couldn't hide the devious smirk that stretches across my lips.

"Let's be honest, everyone knows I'll never make it to the end zone of The Run," I say, gesturing down to my left leg. A moment of silence follows, and I feel a surge of satisfaction at seeing Damien's confusion.

According to the rules, the runners have two definitive advantages: breaking the mate bond by crossing the line at the end of The Run, and a sixty-minute head start. I know reaching the finish line is highly improbable, so I focused on the fine print regarding the head start. If a hunter pursues the runner before their head start, it is considered a forfeit of their right to Run. This is monitored by the line dividing the clearing where The Run is held.

My face splits into a wide grin as I stare into his pain-filled eyes.

"But I don't have to," I exclaim, relishing the moment as I watch Damien slowly grasp my meaning.

He looks down at the ground and took another cautionary step back from the line.

"You can try all you want, mate, but I'm not crossing this line," Damien grits out, his tone hardening, his previous sadness replaced by a fit of promising anger.

"You say that now," I reply, with an indifferent wave of my hand, "but I still have another twenty minutes."

I let out a mocking laugh, hissing my next words, "And I've had men do a lot more for me with a lot less time."

Damien curses under his breath, running a hand through his hair again. He begins pacing in front of the dividing line in agitation, mumbling to himself while occasionally glancing at me.

Let the real game of the night begin, Alpha.

BRAYDEN

Saturday 8:57 pm

I watch with a smug satisfaction as Damien's composure visibly crumbles, his frustration with my blatant display growing. Despite the confident front I was projecting, a knot of anxiety tightens in my stomach. Time is definitely not on my side, and the window of opportunity to get Damien to cross that dividing line is rapidly closing.

Taking a deliberate moment to compose myself, I mentally debate my next move. Getting Damien to breach that boundary is proving to be a significantly more challenging endeavor than I have initially anticipated. My ego has perhaps overestimated the raw, untamed nature of his supposed lust, naively assuming that my impromptu mini-striptease would have been enough to send him charging across the field like a lovesick idiot.

Turns out the bastard possessed a stronger will than I had given him credit for.

There is always what I internally label my "last resort" option, the nuclear button in my arsenal of manipulative tactics. But I am reluctant to deploy it so soon. While I am reasonably confident in its effectiveness, life has taught me that nothing was ever truly guaranteed. It would be far more prudent to concoct another, less drastic plan, and to do it quickly.

While my mind races through potential strategies, I consciously try to project an air of bored indifference to my increasingly precarious situation. My gaze lazily drifts over the assembled crowd of imposing hunters. A subtle movement to the left of Damien catches my attention, and I see Travis's imposing mate casually conversing amongst a small group of equally intimidating-looking wolves.

A spark of inspiration ignites in my mind, and my eyes widen as a sudden revelation hits me.

I spin around abruptly, ready to locate Travis and put my impulsive new plan into motion, only to startle slightly as I realize he is already standing right next to me, his presence so quiet I've momentarily forgotten him. I am not the only one caught off guard by my sudden movement; the perpetually flustered brunette eyes me carefully, a mixture of confusion and apprehension in his gaze.

"Is it true that after The Run, a werewolf will experience physical pain if they become intimate with someone other than their mate?" I blurt out in a rushed, urgent tone.

Travis's eyes widen, though I couldn't decipher if it is the specific nature of my question or the sheer intensity with which I've posed it that has elicited such a strong reaction. I am sure my own eyes look a bit wild at the moment, and the underlying desperation fueling my inquiry isn't even remotely concealed to my own ears.

"Uh… yes…" he answers hesitantly, a note of apprehension in his voice as he seems to process the unexpected nature of my question. "Although, since you seem to take predominantly after your human genes, I wouldn't think it would affect…"

"No," I quickly interrupt him, shaking my head emphatically to convey my earnestness. "I'm not concerned about myself in this scenario. I need to clarify that once a werewolf participates in The Run, they will feel physically ill if they attempt to be sexually intimate with anyone other than their designated mate."

Travis nervously darts his gaze across my face several times, his apprehension seemingly growing with each passing second. "Yes," he finally answers, his tone a little more certain this time.

I release his arm, a devilish grin slowly spreading across my face as my new, potentially disastrous plan solidified in my mind.

"Then," I purr, leaning in closer with a suggestive smirk that I hope conveys just the right amount of scandalous invitation. "Would you be interested in some hardcore foreplay with me before your little run tonight?"

"What?!" Travis loudly exclaims, his voice cracking with a mixture of shock and disbelief before he nervously glances over at both of our respective mates.

I follow his gaze, but I already instinctively know that both of the wolves in question are too preoccupied to have overheard our hushed conversation. Travis's imposing mate seems to be engaged in a lighthearted conversation with a group of individuals who look like close friends, and Damien is in an intense, one-sided discussion with the ever-stoic Aiden.

"Are you actively trying to get me killed, Brayden?" he asks in a hushed tone, this time leaning in conspiratorially closer to me, his wide eyes darting nervously back towards Damien's imposing figure.

I shake my head with an exaggerated air of innocence. "No, Travis, darling. I'm merely offering you a once-in-a-lifetime, truly unique proposition of voyeuristic play," I answer, my suggestive smirk firmly back in place.

Travis doesn't look remotely convinced, his gaze hardening into a glare. "I'm already in enough deep shit as it is for getting involved with the Alpha's Luna at work," he mutters with a sigh of exasperation. "I really don't want to give Damien any more reasons to get even angrier at me than he already is."

I shake my head dismissively. "Damien isn't as dense as he sometimes appears. It's abundantly clear that my current goal is to get him to cross that line by any means necessary, so he's not going to genuinely believe that you're the one coercing me into this... display. Therefore, his considerable wrath will be solely directed at me, which I can definitely handle," I try to assuage his legitimate concerns. "Besides, you're leaving the pack tonight, remember? He can't exactly retaliate against you once you're no longer under his jurisdiction."

Travis gives me a conflicted look, his brow furrows with indecision, and remains stubbornly silent.

"Listen, Travis," I continue, softening my tone slightly, "I'm absolutely not going to push you to do something you're genuinely uncomfortable with," I try to reassure him, although a significant part of me is desperately hoping for his agreement. "But I do know a few pertinent things. One," I begin to list, holding up a finger for emphasis, "your mate is undeniably a sadist, and therefore, she will likely derive a considerable amount of perverse pleasure from executing such a deliciously large punishment on your wayward ass."

Travis looks down at the damp grass but pointedly doesn't refute my rather accurate assessment of his mate's... proclivities.

"Two," I continue, holding up a second finger, my suggestive smirk returning with full force, "you, my friend, will secretly find the ensuing harsh punishment to be hella fun, despite any outward protests you might feel obligated to make."

I receive another silent response, but this time Travis finally meets my gaze, a flicker of intrigued curiosity in his eyes, silently probing me to continue my persuasive argument.

"And three," I conclude, finally putting my hand down with a dramatic flourish, "you will literally never, in your entire werewolf existence, have another golden opportunity to be legitimately punished for adultery quite like this specific moment in time."

"You do realize that you'll likely get into a considerable amount of trouble for this little stunt too, right?" Travis asks, looking at me with a wary skepticism.

I smile, a genuine, unrestrained grin spreading across my face as I realize his response isn't an immediate, outright refusal.

"I'll only be punished if my current strategy doesn't actually work, Travis," I reply, my voice laced with a newfound confidence.

Travis's gaze drifts back over to his imposing mate, his eyes studying her from across the bustling clearing. A subtle, almost imperceptible upturn appears at the corners of his mouth as he nervously rubs his arm with one hand.

"It's really a rather unique opportunity, isn't it?" he muses aloud, a hint of reluctant excitement creeping into his tone.

"If you're willing, great. If you're not, it's absolutely fine," I try to assuage, not wanting him to feel unduly pressured but also desperately hoping for his enthusiastic agreement.

Travis takes a deep, fortifying breath, his gaze still fixed on his formidable mate.

"She is going to whoop my ass real good," he says with a surprisingly eager smirk as he straightens his back, a newfound resolve hardening his features.

He suddenly looks me directly in the eyes, a mischievous glint dancing within them.

"Alright, Brayden," he says with a genuine smile, a hint of reckless abandon in his voice. "I'll do it."

I don't waste a single second.

I let out a loud, theatrical laugh that immediately draws Damien's attention, his head snapping in my direction with a look of bewildered fury. Travis gives me a slightly confused look at my sudden outburst, but his eyes quickly widen with dawning realization as I deliberately trail my hand up his arm, my touch lingering suggestively.

He glances over briefly at his formidable mate, a nervous but excited giggle escaping his own lips.

I lean down close to his neck, my breath warm against his skin as I whisper my next set of instructions.

"If I go too far for your comfort level, tap me twice firmly. Do so now, just so that I know you understand the signal," I demand in a low, urgent tone.

I immediately feel two firm taps on my forearm, a silent confirmation of his understanding and reluctant agreement.

With a predatory smile, I continue trailing my hand up and down Travis's arm, before slowly moving my caress down his side, my fingertips lightly tracing the contours of his lean torso.

From the corner of my eye, I see that Damien has abruptly stopped his intense conversation with his stoic beta and has resumed his agitated pacing in front of the dividing line, his movements jerky and filled with barely suppressed rage. Travis's imposing mate has also finally taken notice of our scandalous display, and the heated glare she was directing my way could practically melt steel, even from this considerable distance.

Because another mated couple is now involved in my desperate scheme, I know I am going to have to handle this delicate situation with a slightly more nuanced approach. Unlike my previous, more direct plan of blatant sexual provocation, I am now primarily playing with Damien's possessive jealousy and simmering anger. If I could successfully stoke his territorial instincts and make him feel possessive enough about me, he would, in theory, be compelled to cross that forbidden line in order to stake his claim and put an immediate stop to my perceived infidelity. However, the presence of another equally possessive mate in the equation adds a significant layer of complexity. I absolutely do not want to push Travis's formidable mate so far that she herself crosses the line in a fit of protective rage. This is going to be a precarious game of balance, a high-stakes tightrope walk, and I desperately hope that the scales would ultimately tip in my favor.

While I continue to caress Travis's side with one deliberately suggestive hand, I bring my other hand up to his head and aggressively pull on his short hair, sharply jerking his head back. He lets out an audible whimper at my sudden, rough movement, and soft, involuntary pants escape his slightly parted lips.

I deliberately met Damien's furious gaze. The Alpha has completely stopped his agitated pacing and is now frozen in front of the dividing line, his entire body rigid with barely suppressed rage at the scene unfolding before him.

"Brayden, stop this right now!" Damien roars across the clearing, the fabric of his plain t-shirt straining against the tense muscles in his arms. His knuckles are white as he clenches his fists, the intensity of his fury visible even from where I am standing. Travis's formidable mate is also visibly tense, a low, guttural growl of pure anger rumbling in her chest from the sidelines. I see a few of the calmer werewolves around her have placed restraining arms on her shoulders, as if they are already anticipating the need to physically hold her back.

While I couldn't bring myself to genuinely give a damn if Damien's overly dramatic feelings are hurt, I don't want to push the poor, albeit intimidating, female wolf too far and risk her intervention.

Maintaining unwavering eye contact with the enraged Alpha, I deliberately pause my scandalous ministrations for a brief, tantalizing second.

I could see the raw hurt swirling in the depths of his usually confident brown eyes—the blatant betrayal of witnessing my feigned intimacy with another so brazenly displayed before him, seemingly without any remorse whatsoever. His handsome face is already contorted into a grimace of pain and fury, silently begging me to cease my provocative actions. I see his full mouth downturn into a hard, unforgiving frown. My attention is involuntarily drawn to his lips, and I notice the soft pink of his lower lip slightly part in an inaudible plea. I couldn't help the unwelcome tug of... something... as I imagine his tongue wetting those same lips and...

Fuck, Brayden, get a goddamn hold of yourself!

My unwelcome, wandering thoughts only fuel my simmering anger, and I glare at Damien with renewed, laser-like determination.

Without another moment's hesitation, I smash my lips against Travis's. I deliberately maintain unwavering eye contact with Damien as I roughly open my mouth and plunge my tongue into Travis's. The kiss is wet and sloppy, devoid of any genuine pleasure for either of us. This isn't an act of passion; it is a calculated, theatrical performance for our captive audience.

The instant our lips make contact, a primal, guttural roar of anguish rips through the sudden silence as Damien drops to his knees, his large hands clawing at his own hair. Several concerned-looking wolves on either side of him instinctively move as if ready to physically restrain him, but even I could see that their intervention wouldn't be necessary. Damien sits rocking back and forth on his knees, his eyes squeezed tightly shut against the painful reality unfolding before him. Although the bastard undoubtedly knows exactly what is happening behind his closed eyelids, it seems that by refusing to look, he is erecting a flimsy but apparently effective enough barrier to prevent himself from crossing over that crucial line.

I notice that Travis's formidable mate is now actively pulling against the werewolves who are attempting to restrain her, her low growls escalating into full-throated snarls of fury. I decide that it is probably time to bring this particular act to a close before I inadvertently trigger a full-scale werewolf brawl.

With a theatrical sigh of feigned boredom, I release my rather forceful hold on Travis, allowing him to stand upright, his lips slightly swollen from our decidedly unromantic encounter.

He glances over at the kneeling, visibly distraught Damien, a conflicted expression flickering across his youthful features as he seems to process the bizarre events that has just transpired.

Much to both Travis's and my considerable surprise, Damien immediately stands up, his movements stiff and jerky, and marches directly over to Travis's enraged mate, his imposing figure towering over the poor warrior. The she-wolf, clearly caught off guard by his sudden shift in focus, quickly begins to vehemently refute whatever Damien is saying to her. I would have described their interaction as a heated discussion except for the fact that Damien was the only one doing any of the talking. The she-wolf initially looks furious, but her expression slowly morphs into something disturbingly close to fear as Damien continues his intense, low-toned monologue.

Fuck, I fully expected him to start a yelling match with me. What the hell is he saying to her?

"I probably better head over there," Travis says, eyeing our respective mates with a palpable apprehension.

"I'll come too," I offer, wanting to make sure Damien isn't being a complete dick, especially since this whole chaotic mess has been entirely my impulsive idea.

Travis immediately shakes his head vehemently. "No, Brayden. I honestly think your presence will only exacerbate the situation. I'm not going over there to try and calm Damien down; I'm just going to talk with Ellen," he shrugs his broad shoulders with a surprising air of nonchalance. "As you so helpfully pointed out earlier, I'm leaving the pack tonight anyway. Since he won't technically be my Alpha after this little ceremony, he can't actually touch me."

With that surprisingly logical and self-assured statement, Travis heads over to the dividing line where Damien is still engaged in his intense conversation with Ellen. Damien briefly glances at Travis as he approaches, a flicker of something unreadable in his eyes, before quickly turning and abruptly walking away, disappearing into the growing shadows near the edge of the woods.

I let out a breath I hadn't even realized I was holding. I had fully expected Damien to unleash his considerable fury on Travis, and I couldn't help but feel a little disoriented by his unexpected lack of reaction to Travis's presence.

I guess he really is only mad at me.

Across the field, Travis and Ellen are now conversing, and the raw anger that had initially contorted her features is slowly giving way to a rather smug expression as Travis continued to talk with her, his tone earnest and placating. While a new, almost devilish glint has appeared in her eyes, I could still detect a subtle undercurrent of worry beneath the surface. She opens her mouth as if to say something, but I deliberately stop watching them, already making a fairly accurate guess that they are now discussing the intricate details of their undoubtedly... interesting... evening together.

If I had to hazard a guess, I'd say I probably only have another ten minutes left before this whole ridiculous Run was officially set to commence. It is a little peeving that Damien still hasn't crossed over to my side of the clearing. I had at least expected him to have to be physically restrained from doing so, but the stubborn bastard has just... endured. He had sat there, facing his own apparent torment, and stubbornly refused to break his self-imposed boundary.

I scoff, a sound of pure annoyance.

I guess it is officially time for my last resort.

BRAYDEN

Saturday 9:17 pm

While Travis continues his hushed conversation with his imposing mate, I deliberately lower myself to the damp ground and snatch up my discarded t-shirt. With the thin fabric clutched in my hand, I give a harsh, impatient tug at the collar, tearing it right down the center until I am left with two ragged halves. I then repeat this destructive process several times, the tearing sound a small act of rebellion in the tense silence. The task is slow-going and undeniably tedious, my fingers fumbling with the stubborn cotton, but I soon hear the unmistakable sound of approaching footsteps, and without even bothering to look up, I already know who it was.

"So," I ask Travis, injecting a healthy dose of smugness into my tone, "is she just as... *enthusiastic* about your evening after The Run as you are?"

There is a noticeable pause, the silence in response to my pointed question prompting me to finally look up, a flicker of genuine concern replacing my earlier amusement. Travis stands next to me, his expression strangely thoughtful as he stares down at me in contemplation. The intensity of his gaze is a little off-putting, not because there seems to be any aggression lurking there, but more of a solemn, almost mournful quality as he looks down at my messy handiwork.

"Did she not understand the nuances of the situation?" I ask, confusion creeping into my voice.

I fully anticipated Ellen being furious, but all the subtle cues pointed towards her channeling that anger into a night of enthusiastic retribution.

I stop tearing my shirt, the unnerving lack of response from Travis starting to prickle my already-frayed nerves.

"No, she understood perfectly," he mumbles, his gaze still fixed on me, "I mean, she's pissed as hell, which, you know, isn't necessarily a bad thing in this specific context."

His cryptic response only leaves me more perplexed. This is precisely the scenario he had seemed to be looking forward to. Although his words are meant to be reassuring, there is an odd, almost melancholic edge to his tone that I couldn't quite decipher.

"So, was Damien being a complete dick about the whole thing?" I ask, still trying to understand Travis's sudden shift in demeanor.

Travis silently shakes his head, his gaze distant.

"No, apparently he just flat-out told Ellen that as soon as our respective runs are over, he wants us both off his goddamn land," he says with a shrug of his broad shoulders, his tone surprisingly devoid of any real emotion. "Ellen and I then talked some more about this pack and, you know, everything…" he responds, his voice trailing off into an uncomfortable silence.

I scrunch my forehead in confusion, still completely failing to grasp his strangely subdued attitude. Damien's rather blunt response isn't exactly shocking news, and from what I understood, Travis was slated to leave immediately anyway. Whatever is causing this shift in his mood must have stemmed from the latter part of his conversation with his formidable mate.

Not wanting to push him any further down this unexpected rabbit hole of somber reflection, I refrain from asking any more probing questions and silently resume my tedious task. He gives me one last, thoughtful look, his eyes lingering on my face for a moment longer before finally focusing on the strips of torn fabric in my hands.

"What exactly are you doing now?" he asks, quickly changing the subject, his gaze finally averting from my face and settling on my lap.

By now, I have successfully ripped my already ruined shirt into several long, uneven strips of fabric. For the last few minutes, I have been carefully filling the center of each strip with handfuls of loose dirt and tightly knotting the corners around the soil to create crude, makeshift weighted sacks.

"I'm winning," I answer him with a bright, albeit slightly manic, smile. Travis merely shakes his head slowly at my overly optimistic assessment, and for a fleeting moment, I think I see something akin to regret flash across his usually cheerful face. However, he doesn't offer another comment about my increasingly bizarre actions as I gather up my pathetic collection of weighted fabric scraps and begin walking over to where Damien stood, a brooding silhouette against the fading light.

As I approach the Alpha's imposing figure, I consciously try to reign in the swirling vortex of conflicting emotions churning within me.

I keep my expression carefully neutral as I pause a deliberate step away from the stark white dividing line.

With a look of utter weariness etched onto his handsome features, Damien slowly lifts his eyes to meet mine. I can see that my previous theatrical display with Travis has clearly taken its toll on him, draining him in a way I hadn't fully anticipated. The man looks like he has just emerged from a brutal, drawn-out fight, and come out on the decidedly losing end. There is a palpable sense of hopelessness clinging to him, and the fierce determination I had witnessed just moments ago has dimmed considerably, flickering like a dying flame.

The seemingly impenetrable wolf is breaking.

I let out a sigh, allowing my own genuine exhaustion with this whole ridiculous situation to seep through my carefully constructed neutral expression.

"What exactly are we doing here, Damien?" I ask quietly, my voice surprisingly devoid of any sharp edge or accusatory tone. Instead, my question came out sounding almost... gentle.

Damien's brow furrows in confusion, and he opens his mouth in what appears to be a silent, desperate plea, before quickly snapping it shut again, his jaw tight.

I let my head drop slightly, pretending to intently examine the pathetic scraps of fabric in my hands, lightly pulling at the frayed ends of my ruined shirt.

"Please, Brayden," Damien begs softly, his voice raw with a desperate vulnerability I hadn't heard before, "whatever you need me to do after tonight, I'll fucking do it. Just please... stop this madness."

I keep my expression blank, refusing to meet his pleading gaze as he continues to speak, his voice laced with a growing desperation.

"If either of us crosses these lines you're not going to feel the bond break..."

Yep, no personal loss there for me, buddy.

"I'll feel the full, unadulterated effect of a broken mating… all of the pain and anguish…"

Frankly, my dear, I really don't give a damn.

The Alpha pauses, his gaze sweeping across the assembled werewolves in the field. In a gesture of utter desperation, he gestures vaguely to the silent, watchful wolves around us with a heavy, defeated hand.

"If that happens, then all of the pack–"

I don't give him a chance to finish his dramatic pronouncement, cutting him off abruptly, not wanting his self-pitying rant to consume any more of my rapidly dwindling time.

"But," I interject, finally looking up at him, my eyes wide and deliberately doe-like, "would you *really* feel all of that… if I chose to eventually accept you later down the line?"

My unexpected question visibly startles him, and he seems utterly at a loss for words, his handsome face a mask of wild desperation as he tries to process the implications of my sudden shift in tone.

I raise my hand slightly, pretending to sheepishly show him the pathetic scraps of torn fabric.

"I… I tore up my shirt, Damien," I say with a pitiful little laugh that sounds surprisingly genuine even to my own ears. "I tore it into strips because… I wanted to leave scraps of my scent around the woods." I let my gaze drift over to the looming, imposing trees that mark the edge of the clearing, attempting a helpless gesture towards the vast expanse of land behind me. "I'm so… desperate to not participate in this whole ridiculous charade that I'm literally tearing my own clothes apart in a pathetic attempt to buy myself a little extra time."

Damien opens his mouth as if to offer some sort of comforting platitude, but I steamroll right over his intended words, pressing my advantage.

"All of this... it's so new to me. I don't even know how to begin to handle everything yet," I choke out, widening my eyes and trying to project an image of utter vulnerability. "Everything about werewolves... it's completely foreign to me, and honestly... I'm completely terrified right now."

"Brayden, please..." Damien gasps out, his voice thick with emotion, and I could see the internal struggle etched on his face.

"I'm just... not ready, Damien," I beg him, my gaze locked on his, trying to convey the depth of my supposed fear and uncertainty. "But... What's to say that I won't eventually be ready? What if... with a little more time..."

The Alpha takes a deep, shuddering breath, and his entire body goes rigid, his muscles visibly tensing. A palpable stillness seems to descend over the entire field, and several of the wolves around him shift, their bodies tensing as if preparing to intervene. It is abundantly clear that our conversation has taken an unexpected and potentially volatile turn, and Damien's loyal pack is poised to step in if their Alpha isn't able to think rationally. I am not the only one who notices the subtle change in the hunters' demeanor, and Damien lets out a low, warning growl, presumably commanding those around him to remain where they are. The wolves don't move closer, and I take this as my cue to press my advantage.

"I know that we can't postpone The Run indefinitely because of this... partial mark," I say, allowing a dramatic pause to let my carefully-chosen words sink in. "But right now... I'm simply not ready to choose you, Damien." I give another, more significant pause, letting the harshness of my words hang in the air between us. "Don't you *want* me to choose you?" I ask, dropping my voice to a soft, almost breathless whisper. My eyes are wide and pleading, and I try to force an innocent, almost childlike look upon my face.

Damien's eyes become unnervingly glossy, his breath catching in his throat as he gives a jerky, almost imperceptible nod. "Of course... of course I want you to choose me, Brayden!" he gasps out, his large hands desperately scrunching the fabric of his sweatpants in a shaky grip.

"Then... who's to say that I won't... if you just give me a little more time?" I ask, finally dropping the carefully constructed bomb I had been holding in reserve.

And there it is. My trump card, deployed with what I hoped was just the right amount of calculated vulnerability. While I have previously been attempting to play off Damien's more primal, instinctual desires, this is a direct appeal to his more rational side, the part of him that desperately craves a genuine, willing connection. The proposition of a future together, however vague and non-committal, allows him to build in his mind the long-cherished illusion of his fantasy, the possibility of finally hearing the words he has undoubtedly longed to hear for so long.

"Brayden..." The man rasps out, his voice barely more than a choked whimper of my name, completely unable to articulate anything more coherent.

I offer what I hope was a compassionate, understanding smile, trying to project an air of fragile hope.

"I know that there will be a lot of pain and immediate consequences right after you cross that line, Damien," I explain softly, my voice gentle and persuasive, "but by giving me a little more time... that pain could ultimately be temporary. You wouldn't be forcing me to irrevocably tie myself to you against my will, which means you could give me the genuine opportunity to get to know the real you better. We could get closer with time, and as time passes, I could potentially become more comfortable with the idea of… us."

Damien's eyes visibly fill with unshed tears as I paint him a picture of his deepest desires, a fragile possibility of the future he so desperately craved.

"You would be giving me the opportunity to choose you, Damien," I said softly, my voice barely above a whisper.

Making sure to take a small, almost imperceptible step forward, I deliver my final, carefully aimed blow.

"And with more time you would be giving me the opportunity to choose to love you," I whisper out gently, my gaze locks onto his tear-filled eyes.

I see the tears finally spill over and freely flow down his pale cheeks at my carefully chosen words, and the raw, unguarded emotions etched on his face pierces my own heart for a fleeting, unwelcome second. I quickly try to push away the sudden, unexpected assault of guilt that rips through my carefully-constructed defenses. Technically, I haven't actually lied. I *could* do all of those things… but I had never explicitly promised that I *would*.

Damien takes a deep, shuddering breath, and I notice a subtle flurry of movement coming from behind him, but I deliberately pay it no mind, my focus entirely on Damien's clearly imminent decision.

"Alright," he says, his voice thick with exhaustion and a fragile hope, "you win, Brayden."

My heart soars at his proclamation, a surge of triumph coursing through me. He is mere moments away from crossing that line, from forfeiting the Run. He slowly shuffles his feet forward, a hesitant, almost weary movement, but stops abruptly just before the stark, white line.

Our eyes meet, and I am taken aback by how quickly the previous look of raw sorrow and vulnerability has vanished from his face, replaced by a steely resolve.

"I'm not doing this solely because of everything you just said that would benefit me," Damien tells me, his voice surprisingly firm despite the tears still glistening on his cheeks. "I'm doing this so that you know that, although there are undoubtedly others who are going to be affected by this, I choose you first, Brayden."

I try my best to suppress a cynical scoff.

Just as Damien takes his final, decisive step forward, he suddenly lets out a sharp, involuntary hiss of pain, his hand immediately flying to clutch his neck. In utter disbelief and dawning horror, he spins around just in time to see Aiden swiftly pulling a large, ominous-looking syringe from the precise area of obvious pain. Damien stumbles backward in shock and surprise, his eyes wide with betrayal, but quickly loses his balance. Whatever potent drug has just been injected into his system takes immediate effect, his knees buckling as he drops to the ground, his eyes fluttering shut, and his body going limp.

A surge of raw fury, unlike anything I have ever experienced before erupts within me, my teeth grinding together with an ungodly amount of force.

"What the *fuck*, Aiden?!" I scream across the suddenly silent field, spittle flying from my lips in my incandescent rage.

Aiden completely ignores my furious outburst, his focus entirely on checking over Damien's now unconscious form. While crouching on the ground, his cold, calculating eyes never leave his task, but there is a rigid tension in all of his movements.

"This is so much bigger than just you and him, Brayden," he says tersely, his voice low and dangerous. "If the bond were to break and never be properly repaired..." He finally looks up at me, his gaze filled with a vicious, unwavering intensity. "…which we all know, deep down, is the most likely outcome. Other lives would be irrevocably affected, far more than just the two of yours."

"This is a goddamn mate bond, you interfering bastard! It was between him and me, and absolutely no one else!" I yell back, my voice thick with indignant fury. "This had everything to do with his own goddamn choice to cross that line!"

I am absolutely seething, my rational thought completely clouded by a blinding rage. I don't even begin to understand what he meant by Damien and my relationship affecting others, but I don't have a second to spare, to demand an explanation.

Just at that precise moment, the piercing shriek of a loud alarm rips across the clearing, its shrill tone signaling the official start of this barbaric game. All around me, the designated runners take off towards the dark, ominous woods, and my heart plummets like a lead weight as I realize the sun has finally set.

"After he wakes up, the primal instincts of The Run will completely cloud his judgment, Brayden," Aiden explains stiffly, his gaze still fixed on Damien's prone form. "He won't be able to consciously reign in those instincts until after you cross the designated finish line."

A chilling silence descends as I desperately try to process the full implications of his words. In other words, Damien wouldn't just stand idly by and help me cross the finish line; he is going to wake up with a single-minded, instinctual drive to hunt me down and prevent me from reaching it.

My breathing hitches, a wave of panic washing over my body. My eyes widen in dawning horror, my entire body freezing as I stare at Aiden, a cold, clammy sweat breaking out across my forehead.

The Alpha's stoic beta simply gives me a cold, indifferent look, devoid of any sympathy or remorse.

"The specific drug cocktail in his system will be fully effective for another two and a half hours," he states bluntly, his tone flat and devoid of emotion. "Congratulations, Luna. You've just bought yourself an extra ninety minutes of head start."

He doesn't offer any further explanation or attempt at reassurance, and it is chillingly clear that he didn't intend to. My mind reels with this devastating, new information, and like a brutal bolt of lightning searing down my spine, the full, terrifying reality of my current predicament finally hits me with brutal force.

With a jerky, almost frantic movement, I quickly reach down to grab my battered backpack, and with a somewhat shaky start, I turn my back on the unconscious Alpha and the smugly indifferent beta and head off into the dark, foreboding woods with every ounce of self-preservation I possess.

My Run has officially started.

Brayden

Saturday ?:?? pm

I run.

Blind panic is the only thing I feel. I genuinely hadn't anticipated this outcome.

No, this shouldn't have happened.

My mind spirals with the events that just unfolded, and the same thought relentlessly loops through my head.

Damien was going to cross the line. He *should've* crossed the line.

The moment I burst into the woods, the thunderous pounding of my own heart is the only sound that registers. As my legs pump and the soles of my shoes slam into the unforgiving dirt of the forest floor, I feel each surge of blood coursing through my veins, and it isn't long before the familiar, unwelcome heat begins to build within me.

My feet find an automatic rhythm, my knees lifting almost independently as my arms swing uselessly at my sides. The ingrained mechanics of proper running form take over in a subconscious moment, and I reluctantly allow the familiar sensation of the sport to lead my battered body. My breathing evens out slightly, and I settle into a strained pace, a muscle memory from countless past sessions of brutal training kicking in.

I let my body run on autopilot, my mind mercifully shutting down for a few precious minutes.

As I run, the darkness feels absolute, a suffocating blanket. The tendrils of the night seem to stretch out from every direction, enveloping me in a shadowy, claustrophobic tunnel. The unforgiving ground beneath my feet blends seamlessly into the treacherous roots that crisscross the forest floor, their gnarled fingers snagging at my shoes every few steps. The trees are the worst offenders in this assault, their sharp, skeletal branches brushing against my bare skin in a thoroughly unpleasant manner, and it isn't long before I can feel the raw skin of my chest and arms chafing painfully against the dry, unforgiving leaves.

I can't stop running.

A sudden, chilling realization pierces through my panicked haze: I have absolutely no idea where the hell I'm going. I just bolted without a single coherent thought. I'm smack-dab in the middle of unknown woods, and it's pitch black out.

I can't stop running.

This stark realization doesn't cause me to slow down; rather, the more I dwell on my utter helplessness, the more my speed increases in sheer terror. My feet begin to stumble with increasing frequency, and I realize that my previous, somewhat steady rhythm of breathing is devolving into ragged, desperate gasps. My arms begin to tremble uncontrollably as I feel myself physically being overwhelmed by this rapidly escalating nightmare.

I can't stop running.

My eyes dart wildly around, fear now firmly in control of the helm, but all they can register is the suffocating, all-encompassing darkness.

Darkness everywhere, trying to cage me within its suffocating grasp. The long, skeletal tree branches scrape against me like grasping claws, trying to reach for my flesh and hold me back. The gnarled roots of the forest reach out like grasping hands, ready to lock around my legs and keep me hostage in this verdant prison.

I can't stop running.

I stumble once more, but this time my already precarious balance completely gives way. I crash heavily to the ground on my knees, the impact jarring my already aching joints, and I realize with a fresh wave of terror that the darkness around me is intensifying. The edges of my vision begin to swim and fade to black, my breathing escalating into frantic, desperate gasps as my lungs savagely cry out for air. I can't focus on anything but the raw, primal fear ripping through my entire being.

I can't stop running.

I'm all alone. I'm trapped in the thick, suffocating darkness that surrounds me. I can't escape. There's nowhere that's safe anymore... I'm all alone. I'm trapped–

SLAP!

My head snaps violently to the side from the sudden, unexpected impact. My face stings with a sharp, burning sensation as I feel my cheek heat up, and my previous internal, panicked rambling comes to an abrupt, screeching halt.

There's a disoriented moment of stunned silence as I tentatively raise my hand and feel the throbbing heat on my cheek before my vision clears enough to take in my surroundings.

Travis stands above my shaking form, one hand still raised in the air, the seemingly obvious culprit of my current, stinging pain.

His eyes are wide with a stark mixture of shock and concern as he stares down at me. When my blurry gaze finally meets his, he immediately crouches down next to me and grips my shoulders tightly with surprising strength.

"I need you to take a deep breath," he commands gently, his voice surprisingly calm amidst my chaotic unraveling, and it's only then that I consciously realize my breathing has slowed down fractionally, although it's still far from normal.

I do as he instructs, my mouth falling open as I inhale a big, shuddering breath before slowly, shakily exhaling through my nose.

"Again," he commands, although this time his tone is a little more stern, his intense gaze drilling into mine.

I repeat my previous actions a few more times, and I find myself slowly, reluctantly beginning to regain a semblance of control. The violent tremors racking my body gradually subside, and the suffocating tension in my muscles begins to ease.

When Travis is finally satisfied that I have, at least superficially, calmed down from my full-blown panic attack, he moves back a couple of feet, giving me some much-needed personal space. We both sit on the damp ground in a strained but comfortable silence for a few moments as I desperately try to claw my way back to some semblance of mental stability.

"Thanks," I manage to croak out, although my voice sounds surprisingly raspy and tight. I vaguely remember that I have some precious water stashed in my backpack and quickly reach in, fumbling with the straps, before finally pulling out the life-saving liquid.

Travis merely nods curtly at my mumbled gratitude but remains stubbornly silent as I greedily chug down half of my bottle in desperate gulps.

Guess rationing for the night has officially been thrown out the goddamn window.

"You're really that scared of the mate bond?" Travis asks, his tone tinged with disbelief.

I immediately look away, a wave of shame washing over me at my recent display of utter vulnerability. The call-out stings, and I can't help but feel a profound sense of embarrassment.

With a heavy, defeated sigh, I can't bring myself to do much more than give a small, reluctant nod.

"I honestly thought this was all just some elaborate act of stubborn defiance," he admits softly, his gaze thoughtful. "I didn't actually think you harbored a genuine fear of it."

I shake my head slightly, not entirely agreeing with his assessment, although he's not that far off the mark.

"I'm not specifically scared of the bond itself," I try to explain, my fingers nervously fiddling with the condensation on the plastic water bottle in my hands. "I'm terrified of what it represents."

"It represents eternal security in a life partner, Brayden!" Travis exclaims, his voice filled with an almost evangelical fervor. "I mean, sure, there are those of us who fool around a bit before we meet our destined mate – your very existence is a rather glaring testament to that."

I can't help but crack a small, involuntary smile at his surprisingly dry joke.

"But once we finally find our true mate, there's no longer that gnawing worry about what the future holds," he takes a deep breath, his gaze drifting off with a blissfully vacant look towards the surrounding, menacing woods. "It's... safety. Unwavering, absolute safety."

I let out a short, disdainful huff at his idealized pronouncement. He looks at me in genuine surprise, and as a mocking, disbelieving smile slowly spreads across my face, Travis's eyes widen in dawning comprehension.

"No," I refute bitterly, my voice laced with a venomous edge. "It's the insidious promise of safety cleverly wrapping the toxicity of restriction."

Travis visibly flinches at my harsh declaration before the same unsettlingly solemn look from earlier on the field settles back onto his features.

"Then," he states flatly, his gaze unwavering, "I strongly suggest you get back to running, Brayden." He pushes himself to his feet with a fluid, athletic grace.

I look up at him, surprised to see a stark intensity of grim determination now hardening his usually affable features. Travis turns as if ready to take off into the darkness, before abruptly pausing and giving me one last, piercing look.

"Whatever happens next out here," he says stiffly, his voice devoid of any warmth, "isn't personal, Brayden. Remember that tonight is bigger than just you and him."

A cold shiver runs down my spine at his ominous words, and the perpetually flustered brunette disappears into the oppressive darkness just as quickly and silently as he had first arrived.

With shaky legs that still threatened to buckle beneath me, I force myself to stand up, taking another slow, deliberate deep breath. I look around my immediate surroundings, and unlike my previous panicked perception, I don't find the looming forest quite as overwhelmingly intimidating. What I had initially perceived as an absolute, suffocating void, I now realize is actually a surprisingly well-lit area, the full moon casting long, ethereal shadows that allow me to make out the distinct silhouettes of all the surrounding plants and trees.

I need to refocus–and fast. I had blindly bolted into the woods in a fit of pure, unadulterated panic and, in doing so, had undoubtedly wasted precious time traveling who knows where.

Opening my backpack with fumbling fingers, I throw my half-empty water bottle back inside and grab my ridiculously crude map as well as my cheap, unreliable compass. It takes me a few frustrating minutes of squinting in the moonlight, but I'm finally able to get my bearings of the immediate area and realize, with a surge of relief, that I have thankfully been headed in the general right direction and haven't been running in aimless circles as I had initially feared. With a renewed, albeit fragile, sense of motivation, I quickly swing my pack back over my shoulder, ready to take off once more.

I'm abruptly stopped as my foot connects with a soft, yielding object on the ground. Looking down, I see all of my pathetic little dirt-filled shirt sacks scattered haphazardly in front of me. I vaguely remember clutching them tightly in the field, and must have dropped them during my less-than-graceful tumble. I take another brief moment, staring down at the useless scraps of fabric.

It's bittersweet in a way, a twisted irony. I had only ever intended to use these ridiculous items as a manipulative prop in order to sway Damien. There's a certain dark humor in the fact that they will now be used for the very purpose I had so dramatically claimed to have created them for.

With a sigh of reluctant acceptance, I quickly bend down and begin collecting the lumpy sacks in one hand, carefully holding the flimsy map and compass in the other.

I'm ready to start again, this time with a modicum of actual direction.

Looking down at the wavering needle of the compass, I take off in the direction of the elusive end zone. I consciously allow my body to once again find its strained rhythm. I deliberately control my aching legs and force myself to pay attention to my ragged breathing. I'm acutely aware of my surroundings, and every once in a while, I'll slow down my pace just enough to toss one of my pathetic weighted sacks in a completely opposing direction, a desperate attempt to confuse my undoubtedly superior pursuer.

The next couple of hours pass in a blur of exhausting exertion, punctuated only by the rhythmic pounding of my feet and the increasingly labored sound of my own breathing. Every so often, I'll force myself to take a brief, grudging break in order to gulp down a meager mouthful of water or swallow a couple of pain pills. All in all, the seemingly endless night drags on with agonizing slowness, while the bright, judgmental moon continues its steady ascent above me.

By the time I'm getting reasonably close to the supposed end zone, I'm bone-deep tired. Although I had tried to pace myself throughout the long, grueling night, my body is still screaming in protest, every muscle burning with exhaustion. My clothes are plastered to me with sweat, and no matter how desperately I try to regulate my breathing, I can't seem to quell the agonizing burn in my lungs. In addition to my overall physical misery, the pain medication had started to lose its grip about thirty minutes ago, and my left side is beginning to flare up with a severe, stabbing agony that threatens to buckle my already-weakened legs.

I realize I'm probably only about a quarter of a mile from my destination, and the wave of relief that washes over me is immense, almost overwhelming. I genuinely hadn't thought I would make it this far, but the extra, ill-gotten time I had managed to buy myself seems to be just enough. A fragile bud of hope tentatively blooms in my chest as the reality of potentially being free from Damien's unwanted bond begins to solidify into a tangible possibility.

I could actually do it.

From the oppressive darkness ahead, a screeching, bloodcurdling howl suddenly pierces through the relative silence of the night air. The violent reverberations of the impossibly loud sound echo through the towering trees, and my entire body stiffens involuntarily, every muscle locking in primal fear. My body's immediate, visceral response to the sound is all the horrifying information I need to know exactly who, or rather *what*, is closing in.

Damien was gaining on me, and fast.

With a renewed surge of adrenaline-fueled desperation, I try to pick up my already faltering pace, my legs beginning to shake uncontrollably with the sheer effort. I desperately try to shut down every non-essential thought, focusing solely on the elusive goal ahead of me. My injured side flares in violent protest as I force my weary body to accelerate.

I see the stark, glaring white line a few hundred agonizing yards ahead of me.

The unmistakable sound of a massive, powerful creature pounding into the soft dirt bed of the forest floor suddenly erupts from directly behind me, the earth vibrating with each thunderous step. I stubbornly refuse to look back, my gaze locked with a desperate intensity on the beckoning white line in front of me. The end zone, so tantalizingly close yet still impossibly far, almost mocks me from the distance, the stark white reflecting the cold light of the moon and taunting me with promises of a freedom that feels increasingly out of reach.

The low, guttural growls emanating from the creature rapidly closing in behind me increase in volume, and I can now physically feel the heavy, earth-shattering steps of the beast reverberate through the very ground beneath my pounding feet.

The line gets closer.

Another ear-splitting howl tears its way through the silent woods, and my heart nearly stops dead in my chest as the terrifying sound comes from what feels like mere yards behind me.

The line gets closer.

The hair on the back of my neck prickles with a primal fear as I realize the monstrous proximity of the beast is now only a few terrifying feet away. I can feel the hot, fetid breath of the animal graze against my trembling calf, and at that precise, horrifying moment, I realize the stark white line is directly in front of me. Summoning the very last dregs of my rapidly depleting strength, as my lungs scream in agonizing protest and my overexerted legs quiver uncontrollably, the last tiny spark of my rapidly fading energy is desperately gathered.

I leap.

BRAYDEN

Saturday ?:?? pm

I cry out as my left shoulder slams into the unforgiving dirt. My skin grinds against the dried earth, and I can feel some of my older scars stretching and tearing open from the brutal friction. My old injury absorbs the brunt force of my body weight, and another groan escapes my lips as a fresh wave of agony washes through me.

I keep my eyes squeezed shut, simply lying sprawled on the ground, too utterly exhausted at that moment to even begin to think or attempt any movement.

I'm in a lot of pain.

Everything seems to hurt, from my strained, screaming muscles to my burning, aching lungs. My skin feels as if it's been rubbed raw by the relentless underbrush of the forest, and the sweat trickling down my body stings with vicious intensity in the areas where sharp branches had ripped open my flesh.

I'm in pain, but–

My eyes snap open immediately in utter shock.

I take several deep, shuddering breaths as I stare up at the bright, almost accusatory moon above me in bewildered disbelief. A few silent seconds pass, stretching into an eternity. The night almost seems to hold its breath at my unexpected revelation, granting me a brief, surreal moment to process my current condition and the undeniable reality of the situation.

I'm in pain, but I'm alone.

In a surge of desperate hope, my head whips to the side, and a silent gasp of utter disbelief catches in my throat at the sight that greets me.

Lying parallel to my disheveled body, mere inches away, a stark white line fills my vision. I stare at the line for what feels like an eternity, completely unaware of how much actual time passes. It feels as though this damned white line has been at the forefront of my thoughts all night. From my initial, reluctant entry into the field, to the desperate, ill-conceived attempts to get either Damien or myself to cross it. It has been a constant source of trouble, a heavy weight that seemed to relentlessly hold me down with anxiety and worry throughout the seemingly endless night. But for the first time since this whole nightmare began, this cursed white line fills me with an unexpected, overwhelming sense of relief.

An incredulous laugh bubbles up from my chest, and once it starts, I can't seem to stop the hysterical outpouring. All of my pent-up anxiety and bone-deep worry filter out through my loud, unrestrained cackling, and the surrounding forest eerily echoes my moment of utter lunacy. I feel something wet stream down my face, and I can't discern if it's just more sweat mingling with dirt, or if tears of both bitter anger and a strange, almost giddy joy have finally broken free from their emotional dam.

I have no idea how long my descent into temporary insanity lasts, but a loud, pitiful whine abruptly drags my attention to a creature just across the stark white line.

A few feet in front of me, a large, heavily panting wolf stares intently at my sprawled form. Unlike my terrified reaction at the sterile, brightly lit hospital, I feel no immediate fear of the imposing beast, and surprisingly, I can't even muster up any lingering anger.

I simply feel nothing.

My own detached reaction to the creature surprises me slightly. With a blank, almost clinical stare, I watch as the wolf paces restlessly in front of the line a few times, its large tongue lolling from its open mouth as the powerful jaws greedily gulp down air. Every once in a while, a soft, pitiful whine escapes the wolf's throat, but other than that, there isn't any overt aggression in its movements, merely an endless, repetitive pacing back and forth, walking the length of my prone body from the other side of the symbolic end zone.

With a loud, involuntary groan of protest from my abused muscles, I decide to push myself off the cold, damp ground and attempt to maneuver my aching body into a more upright position. Every single muscle and joint practically screams at me in furious protest, but with a monumental effort of sheer willpower, I'm finally able to sit up, my body trembling with the exertion. Very slowly and deliberately, I straighten my aching back and gingerly stretch my protesting legs out in front of me as I desperately try to grant them a temporary reprieve from their brutal ordeal. I reach for my discarded backpack and quickly rummage inside–ready to drink the last precious drops of my dwindling water supply.

While I'm fumbling for my chosen item, I hear a low, guttural grunt coming from just beyond my immediate periphery, and I instinctively flinch as the following sound, the distinct shift of weight and rustle of movement, brings back the unwanted memories that had set this entire disastrous evening into motion. I pointedly avoid looking to my side as I finally locate my water bottle, twist off the cap, and greedily finish off its remaining contents in a series of desperate swallows.

Another stretch of strained silence descends, and the more time that passes, the harder it becomes to keep my gaze averted from the large creature still pacing restlessly across the white line. As I tip the last meager drops of water back into my parched throat, my eyes unconsciously drift over.

Damien is crouched low on the ground, his palms pressed flat against the cool dirt in front of him, the lower half of his powerful body supported on his bent knees. The man's entire physique is glistening with sweat, mirroring my own exhausted state, and the bright moonlight reflects off the naked sheen of his tanned skin.

His head hangs low as he heaves in desperate gulps of air, his whole body visibly quivering from the sheer physical exertion of his relentless pursuit.

"Don't... don't..." Damien gasps out something unintelligible, his voice barely a strained whisper, making it difficult to discern his intended words.

I lean in a fraction closer, straining to hear, when the Alpha's head suddenly snaps up with a jerky, almost violent movement, and his wide, desperate eyes lock onto mine.

"Don't cross back over!" he yells with raw earnestness, his voice hoarse and strained.

I flinch involuntarily at his sudden and loud exclamation, and a stark, almost deranged desperation is clearly displayed across his handsome, sweat-streaked face.

His eyes look unnervingly wide, and from this close proximity, I can see that his pupils are slightly more dilated than those of an average man. All of his features seem to be subtly sharpened, from the prominent angles of his cheekbones and the bridge of his nose, all the way to the tips of his canines that I can see just barely poking out from beneath his slightly parted lip.

While his subtly altered features momentarily intrigue me, it's not what truly surprises me in the next disorienting second. His dark eyes suddenly roll back into his head, the whites briefly visible, and his large, muscular form crashes heavily to the ground with a dull thud.

I'm stunned into momentary paralysis as he lies face first in the dirt, completely unmoving besides the shallow, ragged rise and fall of his labored breathing. For a fleeting moment, a cynical part of me wonders if this is just another elaborate ploy, a desperate attempt to make me worry about his well-being enough that I'll foolishly cross back over the safety of the white line, but as the silent minutes continue to tick by, I realize with a growing certainty that he has genuinely passed out, his exhausted body finally succumbing to the extreme physical and mental strain.

A sudden rustling sound emanating from the woods directly behind Damien draws my attention away from the prone Alpha, and I see several shadowy figures of wolves cautiously emerge from the darkness. I don't recognize the majority of them, their forms indistinct in the moonlight, and I don't pay them too much mind as they begin to cautiously crowd up to the edge of the dividing line.

However, amidst the anonymous gathering, one looming figure strides forward with a distinct air of authority. Aiden walks ahead of the hesitant crowd with long, confident strides, his imposing form almost making as grand of an entrance as Damien had earlier in the evening when he first dramatically entered the field.

Even with their Alpha lying unconscious in the dirt, the established hierarchy of those present is undeniably clear. The alpha is the closest to the line, albeit horizontal and unresponsive, and Aiden stands just off to the side, a silent sentinel directly behind his fallen leader. From there, the other mated couples have cautiously gathered, their forms scattered amongst the shadows of the trees, not daring to approach the stark white boundary.

The stoic beta seems to be in a significantly better state than his exhausted superior, as he walks with purpose towards the line. As he approaches, he casts me a disdainful look, a silent judgment that I gladly reciprocate with a tired glare of my own, before the larger man crouches down next to Damien's unmoving form and begins a cursory examination.

"I didn't do anything to him if that's what you're checking for," I spit out, my voice still rough and laced with lingering annoyance.

"I know," he replies, his gaze flicking up to meet mine briefly before returning to Damien. "The moment he regained even a sliver of consciousness, his base instincts took over, but that doesn't necessarily mean the residual effects of the drugs have fully left his system," he explains, his voice surprisingly clinical as he slowly stands back up after his brief examination. "After you successfully crossed into the end zone, his more primal instincts were finally able to be pushed aside by his exhausted mind, resulting in the... state you see him in now. His physical and mental strength won't be at full capacity for the remainder of the night."

I ponder his somewhat convoluted explanation for a moment before merely shrugging, my exhaustion overriding any real concern for the unconscious Alpha.

"That's one hell of a hangover he's going to have tomorrow," I jab at Aiden, sending a tired, sarcastic smile across the dividing line.

A muscle in Aiden's jaw twitches almost imperceptibly at my pointed comment as he presses his lips into a thin, irritating scowl but pointedly refrains from offering any further retort. With a heavy sigh, the beta looks up at the slowly ascending moon before leveling his gaze once again on me, his expression unreadable.

"Midnight is in approximately fifteen minutes," he comments stiffly, his tone devoid of any warmth.

My eyebrow raises slightly at his seemingly random comment, but otherwise, I give no other outward reaction to his unsolicited information. I'm a little surprised by how much time I had left, as I had believed that I wasn't going to make it to the end zone within the designated time limit in the first place. But other than that minor surprise, the information doesn't really affect me in any significant way.

I casually lean back on my elbows, letting my head fall back against the cool earth, and bask in the unexpected quiet of the night. Even though the woods surrounding the clearing are undoubtedly filled with the other participants of the brutal Run, it is surprisingly silent as those around me watch with a hushed, almost horrified fascination at the sight of their Alpha couple lying forever separated by the stark white line in front of them.

A sudden, shrill sound abruptly breaks through the stillness of the evening causing several of the shadowy figures around me to jump at the unexpected noise. I instantly recognize the irritatingly familiar sound and instinctively reach for my backpack, fumbling with the zipper as I desperately search through my few remaining belongings.

Where the hell is it? I know I packed it in here earlier.

The insistent ringing continues, and a dreadful, sinking realization washes over me: the sound isn't coming from my backpack.

My heart plummets like a lead weight at the sight before me. I can feel my blood immediately run cold, a wave of icy dread washing over me as my whole body freezes and a sudden light-headedness threatens to overwhelm me.

I mouth a helpless, silent 'no'.

From amongst the hushed ranks of the mated werewolf couples, a small, familiar figure confidently walks out from the shadowy group. The smaller wolf, his perpetually flustered brown hair illuminated by the moonlight, walks with a determined gait towards me until he's standing directly behind Aiden's imposing form.

I see my phone raised high in Travis's hand, Kelsey's annoyingly cheerful ringtone continuing to shatter the fragile peace of the night.

With utter disbelief, a choked, incredulous "Why?" escapes my lips.

Travis doesn't offer any verbal response. His gaze is fixed on the ground, a clear look of guilt etched on his features.

"Why!" I yell, the unanswered question ripping from my throat with a raw, desperate edge.

Travis stubbornly refuses to meet my furious gaze.

"Even though they weren't allowed for personal use when we were at work, you always kept your phone on you, Brayden," he says quietly, deftly avoiding my direct question, his voice barely above a whisper. "And every single time that specific ringtone would start, you'd immediately excuse yourself from whatever you were doing to answer it without hesitation."

He finally lifts his gaze, his eyes meeting mine for the first time since his betrayal.

"I saw it had fallen out of your pocket earlier, during your… dramatic exit from the woods, and I took my chance," he says softly, his expression conflicted. "I care for my family too, Brayden."

There's a sharp, almost desperate edge to his voice, a silent plea as if he's desperately hoping I'll somehow understand the impossible position he believes he's in at that exact moment—but I don't. Not even remotely.

Upon his damning declaration, Travis bows his head in a gesture of reluctant deference towards the beta and hands my ringing phone over to the larger man.

Just then, the insistent ringing of my phone abruptly stops, and my heart skips another terrified beat.

Maybe she won't call back? Maybe it isn't an actual emergency, and it is just accidental?

Just as soon as those fleeting thoughts of desperate hope enter my mind, my phone begins ringing again, the cheerful, oblivious melody slicing through the tense silence.

"It's almost midnight, Brayden. We're rapidly running out of time on our end," Aiden says impassively, palming my device as if it were a dangerous weapon. "Judging by the sound of this second call, you're also running out of time on yours."

I offer no verbal response, slowly pushing myself to a shaky standing position, my hands clenching into tight, trembling fists at my sides.

"This isn't personal, Brayden," Aiden tries to placate, his tone surprisingly devoid of any real malice.

I let out a short, bitter scoff, the hollow sound echoing in the stillness. I've heard that particular line way too goddamn much this evening. There's a tense, solemn pause as I glare down at the dirt beneath my feet, already knowing with a chilling certainty what must happen next.

"I wish I had the luxury of time to go into more detail about the specific reasons why I'm doing this, but that particular conversation will just have to wait for another, undoubtedly less stressful, time," Aiden says with a heavy sigh, his gaze momentarily drifting towards the unconscious form of his Alpha. "As the beta of this pack, one of my primary responsibilities is to always put the well-being of the pack first... no matter the personal cost."

I finally lift my furious gaze to meet Aiden's impassive stare, but I don't even have the energy left to voice my burning frustration. Screaming and yelling wouldn't change the inevitable outcome unfolding before me right now; it would only postpone the unavoidable, and we both know, deep down, that I am going to do whatever it takes to answer my relentlessly ringing phone.

"I want to be able to answer that call without any further disturbance," I say, gesturing with a pointed look over to Damien's still-unconscious form lying just across the white line. "I know that the moment I cross back over, he'll probably be forced to wake up by the remnants of the bond, but I need to finish that call before he... marks me again."

Aiden follows my gaze to his fallen Alpha before gesturing curtly for some of the surrounding, watchful wolves to cautiously approach.

"We'll hold him off until you're done with your call," he promises, his voice flat but firm.

With a heavy, resigned sigh, I refuse to let my mind wander down the treacherous path of 'what ifs' or dwell on the bitter regrets and seething anger that threaten to consume me. This is not the time to ponder the myriad how's and why's that have led to this disastrous culmination of the evening's events. I would undoubtedly begin to spiral down a dark, suffocating hole of unending questions and burning resentment towards all those present tonight. But now, right now, is simply not the time for such self-destructive indulgences.

I take a deliberate, heavy step back over the stark white line. Almost immediately after my foot crosses back over the forbidden boundary, Damien's eyes shoot wide open. His irises are their regular, familiar shade of warm brown, simple in their own way, but undeniably familiar to me at this point. For the briefest of disoriented moments, a look of utter disbelief flickers across his handsome features before it's quickly replaced by a dawning, gut-wrenching dread. The Alpha gives a small, almost imperceptible shake of his head as if silently pleading with me to turn back, to undo my rash decision… but all of that fleeting vulnerability vanishes from his face as quickly as it had appeared.

His pupils dilate rapidly, swallowing the warm brown of his eyes, and his features subtly sharpen, mirroring his briefly altered appearance from earlier. There's an untamed, almost feral wildness emanating from the man, or beast, before me, and almost as soon as this primal being comes back to life, several of the surrounding werewolves lunge forward with surprising speed to restrain him.

I don't waste another precious second. Snatching my relentlessly ringing phone from Aiden's impassive grasp, I quickly answer the call.

"What's wrong, Kelsey?" I answer, my tone deliberately neutral as I'm not angry at her, but I can't completely mask the raw edge of exhaustion that clings to my voice, no matter how much I desperately wish to.

"Brayden!" she exclaims, and a fresh wave of concern washes over me as I can clearly hear that she's on the verge of tears. "Charlotte just woke up from one of her really bad nightmares, and I can't find the damned paper with the list of ways to… you know… put her back down," she explains, her voice thick with unshed tears. "I'm so sorry, I know you're still recovering and everything, but I'm just completely at a loss," she says, a hint of utter desperation lacing her tone.

In the background, I can clearly hear Charlotte's heart-wrenching sobs, and my chest aches with a sharp pang of guilt and helplessness that I can't be there in person to handle the situation, to offer them both the comfort they desperately need.

For the next couple of strained minutes, I talk calmly and reassuringly to both Kelsey and a still-sobbing Charlotte; I manage to gradually soothe both girls before offering Kelsey some practical advice on what she should try next to help Charlotte settle back down. While my voice remains steady and calm on the phone, I consciously shut out the chaotic, terrifying scene unfolding before me, refusing to allow myself to fully react to the horrifying reality of what I'm witnessing.

Damien is being held down on the ground, albeit not very successfully. Several burly men attempt to restrain him but are all visibly sweating and grunting with the immense effort required to keep him from lunging after me. Even with so many of his pack members desperately clinging to his powerful limbs, it's a jarringly clear display of his raw, untamed strength that Damien is only just barely being subdued. The man, or beast, is thrashing wildly on the ground, his powerful body convulsing with uncontrolled fury. Viscous saliva is dripping from his open, snarling mouth, his elongated canines remaining permanently visible in a terrifying display of his altered state. He's emitting a continuous stream of guttural growls and enraged screeches, the primal sounds chilling me to the very bone.

The terrifying sight doesn't exactly fill me with optimism for my immediate future.

It takes only a couple more agonizing minutes of talking with Kelsey, my voice a carefully constructed mask of calm, to finally get Charlotte calmed down enough that her sobs begin to subside into tired whimpers, and eventually, to the soft, rhythmic breathing of approaching sleep.

"I'm really, really sorry, Brayden," Kelsey whispers into the phone, her voice thick with lingering emotion. "She's been completely fine all week, but tonight was just… different."

"Hey," I quickly interrupt her, my voice softening with genuine affection. "You're never a bother, alright? Never."

I glance over at the still-foaming werewolf currently trying with terrifying strength to rip away from the desperate hold of his pack.

"I'll always choose you guys first," I say, the raw emotion I've been desperately trying to suppress finally seeping into my voice, a testament to the unwavering love I hold for my makeshift family.

There's a brief, poignant silence on the other end of the line before Kelsey lets out a small, watery chuckle.

"Well, duh, you would," she replies with a hint of her usual faux arrogance, a small, familiar light in the surrounding darkness. "We're the best, after all."

With that simple, heartfelt declaration, I hear the faint click of her ending the call… and the dreaded sound of the connection severing rings in my ears, a finality to this brief moment of normalcy. I choose not to look up at the struggling werewolf as I numbly hand my phone back to Aiden.

I clench my eyes shut tightly, my hands balling into shaking fists at my sides. The loud grunting of the restraining men resonates loudly in my ears, a grim soundtrack to my impending doom. There's the brief, muffled sound of a scuffle, a desperate attempt to maintain control, before an ominous, heavy silence descends over the clearing.

I suddenly feel a warm, ragged breath against the sensitive skin at the base of my neck, the familiar scent of pine and something wild and untamed sending a shiver down my spine.

An odd sense of detached acceptance washes over me—not an acceptance of Damien or of the unwanted bond that fate seems determined to force upon us but the kind of weary acceptance that comes with the stark realization that at this precise, terrifying moment, everything is completely, irrevocably out of my control.

Sharp, elongated teeth sink deeply into the flesh of my neck, the searing pain a brutal punctuation mark to this disastrous night.

And then, I welcome the darkness.

BRAYDEN

Sunday 7:57 am

My eyes open on their own, much to my displeasure. I can feel the crust of oversleeping stubbornly clinging to the corners of my eyes, which makes my lids part with a slight, unwelcome stickiness. I'm lying flat on my back, and the vaulted ceiling above me is a familiar sight, the sturdy beams of aged wood instantly recognizable.

For a few moments, I simply remain unmoving, allowing the lingering fog of sleep to dissipate. The bed beneath me is a touch too firm for my liking, and the grey comforter has me bordering on uncomfortably warm. I can feel the absence of my jeans from the previous night, leaving me indecently bare beneath the scratchy linen sheets, save for my underwear and the thick, slightly itchy bandage wrapped firmly around the right side of my neck.

With a sigh of resignation, I throw the blankets off and attempt to swing my legs over the side of the bed. The sheer effort required just to force myself into a sitting position is borderline shameful, and it takes several clumsy tries before I finally manage the feat.

A quiet groan escapes my lips as the events of the previous night crash down on me with the force of a physical blow. My muscles ache in protest with every minute movement, and I take a moment to rest my elbows heavily on my knees and gather what little energy I can muster to actually get off this damn bed.

My body hangs forward in this slumped position for a while, my gaze drifting around the familiar details of my surroundings.

From my left, a flood of sunlight streams in through a window, its bright intensity more than enough to illuminate the entire room. Dust motes dance and swirl in the golden rays, and if it were any other unremarkable morning, I might have found this tranquility a welcome relief from the usual, chaotic activity of my everyday existence.

Across the rumpled grey comforter, a closet door stands ajar, revealing a haphazard collection of old t-shirts that dredge up hazy memories of a night that feels like an eternity ago. I vaguely recognize the bathroom door next to it, and as my eyes continue their reluctant survey of the room, I spot a few small, insignificant trinkets that spark fleeting, indistinct recollections.

From somewhere below the aged floorboards, the muffled sound of someone moving drifts upwards. I hear the distinct pattern of their movement before it abruptly stops for a couple of tense minutes, only to resume again. A couple of dull thuds signal the unmistakable sound of cupboard doors opening and closing which tells me with a weary certainty that Damien, the infuriatingly persistent werewolf, is in the kitchen.

With another sigh, this one laced with a heavy dose of impending doom, I decide that I can't remain sequestered in this bedroom indefinitely. Sooner or later, reality, in all its messy, unwelcome glory, has to be faced, and at the very least, I need to leave this room, if not the entire damn house, and attempt to return to some semblance of my normal, pre-werewolf-induced-chaos life.

Standing up with a groan that seems to emanate from the very depths of my soul, I lean heavily on the edge of the bed for support as my bare feet make contact with the cool wooden floor.

The distinct sounds from downstairs abruptly cease, and I presume that Damien is now acutely aware of my awakening.

My gaze sweeps around the bedroom, but my pants from the previous night are conspicuously absent. With a mental shrug, I decide to head over to the slightly ajar closet. Upon attempting to walk freely, my left leg immediately begins to tremble uncontrollably, and I'm forced to quickly grab the wooden bedpost before I completely collapse in a heap of aching limbs. With a considerable, and frankly embarrassing, amount of effort, I use the bed and then the adjacent wall to slowly, painstakingly stabilize myself as I shuffle forward.

A frustrated scowl tightens my features as I realize with a grim certainty that I'll be sporting a rather undignified limp for the next few days while my abused muscles slowly regain some semblance of their former strength.

Upon finally reaching the closet, I grab the first pair of soft lounge pants I see and carefully, deliberately pull them on, wincing slightly at the necessary movements. With the same level of utter carelessness, I grab an old, faded t-shirt before beginning my slow, arduous journey out of the familiar room.

Passing the bathroom door, I briefly entertain the notion of indulging in a long, hot shower. I can still feel the sticky residue of sweat and the gritty film of dirt from the previous night stubbornly clinging to my skin in a thick, unpleasant layer of grime, but I simply can't bring myself to care how utterly disheveled I must look or about the undoubtedly offensive smell currently emanating from my person.

With my mind firmly made up, I continue my slow, deliberate trek towards the bedroom door.

My pace is agonizingly slow. I have to keep at least one of my hands pressed firmly against a wall for much-needed support, and every few steps, I'm forced to pause, catching my breath in ragged gasps or simply taking a brief respite from the searing, relentless pain that seems to radiate from every fiber of my being. Even with the majority of my weight carefully shifted to my right side, by the time I finally reach the arched entryway to the kitchen, my left leg has begun to shake uncontrollably, threatening to give out completely.

The moment I finally enter the familiar, sun-drenched kitchen, Damien's head snaps up with an almost violent jerk, his intense gaze immediately locking onto mine. The infuriatingly handsome werewolf instantly freezes at my arrival, his entire muscular body going rigid as he stares at me with an apprehension that, for once, I find somewhat gratifying. He's currently standing near the stovetop, positioned kitty-corner to the large kitchen sink that sits beneath the bright window. Even in the early hours of the morning, Damien is impeccably dressed in his signature crisp button-down shirt and tailored dress pants. His long sleeves are neatly rolled up along his powerful forearms, and a neatly folded towel is draped casually over his broad shoulder.

Looking around the otherwise familiar kitchen, I take in the distinct remnants of a rather extensive cooking session. Scattered eggshells litter the polished countertop alongside a chaotic assortment of various food items and measuring powders. The large farmhouse sink is overflowing with a jumbled mess of dirty dishes and cooking utensils. The only relatively clean surface is the expansive central island, which is completely bare except for two meticulously arranged plates piled high with fluffy scrambled eggs, golden-brown pancakes, and a vibrant assortment of fresh fruit.

The bastard has actually made breakfast for me.

I pointedly don't acknowledge the presence of the overly attentive werewolf, and I certainly don't offer any reaction whatsoever to the carefully prepared food laid out on the pristine island. Instead, I pass the tempting display with an air of complete indifference and head directly over to one of the sleek cabinets positioned next to Damien before quickly pulling out a clean glass and filling it with cold water from the faucet. Turning slightly to my side, I eye the tense Alpha with an almost bored, utterly unimpressed expression.

"I need pain meds," I demand flatly, my voice still rough from the previous night's ordeal.

At my abrupt and rather blunt request, Damien visibly jumps, his frozen posture instantly shattering as he practically flees the immediate vicinity of the kitchen and disappears through the arched doorway with surprising speed.

I lean my weary body heavily against the cool countertop; I do not even flinch as I feel the sharp edge of the stone dig into my already sore back muscles. As I wait for Damien's inevitable return, I casually take a slow sip of the refreshing water from my glass and revel in the cool sensation as it soothes my parched throat.

I don't have to endure his absence for long. It takes only a few short moments to hear the heavy, rapid pounding of his footsteps ascending the stairs and even less time to hear them pounding back down towards the kitchen. Damien stops abruptly on the other side of the central island, and without a word, I reach out my hand, palm open, a silent but crystal-clear demand.

Stay on your side of the damn island.

Damien quickly drops a small bottle of pills into my out-stretched hand, and I waste no time in unscrewing the cap and tossing back a couple of the hard tablets. I remain stubbornly silent throughout the entire exchange, not once acknowledging the werewolf's overly eager attempt to fulfill my simple request or offering any further commentary on the rather extensive nature of my injuries.

Once I've swallowed the pills, a heavy, uncomfortable silence descends over the kitchen, the quiet almost echoing in the otherwise bright space. Almost as if we had somehow planned it, Damien and I speak simultaneously, our voices overlapping in the tense air.

"I need to get home–"

"Help yourself to the food–"

Realizing the utterly ridiculous nature of his well-intentioned but completely unwelcome suggestion, I glare at the meticulously arranged plates of breakfast as if their very presence is a personal affront.

"I'm not hungry," I grit out through tightly clenched teeth, the lie feeling heavy and bitter on my tongue.

Damien pauses, his intense gaze dropping to the elaborate meal he had probably spent close to an hour painstakingly preparing.

"I... I didn't use any meat products. I remembered you're a vegetarian," he says softly, finally looking up at me with a surprisingly gentle and earnest gaze.

"I don't have an appetite," I reply, my voice flat and undeterred. That is a blatant lie. Truthfully, my stomach is currently twisting itself into painful knots of hunger, and the perfectly fried eggs and buttery pancakes, glistening with warm, sugary syrup, are undeniably, torturously tempting.

"You really need to get some nutrients into your system," he tries to coax gently, his voice laced with a hesitant concern. Damien pointedly doesn't make any move to walk around the expansive island, but he does lean slightly over the polished countertop, attempting to get a fraction closer to me. "After you've had some breakfast, I can take you home and—"

"I said I'm not hungry, damn it!" I scream at him, my control finally snapping as I violently hurl my now-empty water glass across the kitchen.

Damien doesn't even flinch, his reflexes honed by his supernatural nature. My pathetic attempt at assault is woefully inaccurate; the cup sails harmlessly over his broad shoulder and bounces off the wall behind him with a dull thud. I wait, a perverse part of me actually hoping to hear the satisfying crash of shattering glass, a visual and audible representation of the roiling anger currently threatening to consume me.

But nothing comes.

Utterly confused, I peer over Damien's shoulder and see the cup lying fully intact on the cool tile floor.

With a choked sigh of utter frustration, something inside me finally breaks.

"What kind of grown-ass man doesn't even own a single piece of goddamn glassware?!" I yell, all of my pent-up rage and frustration finally exploding in a torrent of pure, unadulterated fury. Damien seems genuinely taken aback by the sheer intensity of my outburst, but he valiantly attempts to remain calm, probably hoping to somehow soothe my rapidly escalating hysteria.

"Plastic is more durable," he explains slowly as if he's trying to appease a frightened, cornered animal. " I got tired of having glasses shatter every time I accidentally placed them a little too hard on the counter."

With a large, shuddering intake of breath, I fill my lungs to their capacity with air and then unleash a roaring, primal screech that seems to come from the very depths of my tormented soul. I squeeze my eyes shut tightly and frantically fist my hair in both trembling hands to release every ounce of pent-up frustration, pain, and sheer, rage.

I have absolutely no idea how long this uncontrolled outburst lasts, but it isn't long before I feel a large, warm hand tentatively settle on my trembling shoulder, and the unwelcome warmth of my unwanted mate's touch only seems to drive me even deeper into the blinding depths of my fury.

Whirling around with a guttural snarl, I blindly reach into the overflowing kitchen sink and immediately grab a handful of used kitchen utensils. Fueled by nothing but pure rage, I begin throwing them with violent force at the taller, infuriatingly patient man.

"You! Motherfucking! Bastard!" I yell, whipping the silverware and various other implements at him, one right after the other, each projectile punctuated by a fresh, venomous curse.

Damien, doesn't fight back in any meaningful way. Instead, his large, muscular body instinctively bends over at the waist, his hands shooting up to instinctively cover his head from my increasingly dangerous assault.

"I don't ask for much, you overgrown wolf!" I continue my furious barrage, blindly reaching back into the sink for more makeshift weapons. "But you can't even give me the simple satisfaction of a goddamn broken glass!" I spit at him, my voice hoarse and cracking with the intensity of my rage.

There's a brief, tense moment of strained silence as I finally run out of cutlery and other throwable items within easy reach. My chest is heaving with the exertion, and I gulp down desperate lungfuls of air and try to catch my breath after my sudden, explosive burst of manic energy. Damien remains frozen in his defensive crouch in front of me, his large hands still protectively curled over his head, his wary face just barely peeking out from around his bent arm.

He gives me a look of apprehension.

"Are you... are you done now, Brayden?"

Another raw, furious scream rips from my throat at his seemingly innocent question.

Reaching blindly onto the countertop, I grab the closest object within my immediate reach, which just happens to be a soft, absorbent kitchen towel. With a surge of adrenaline-fueled strength, I launch myself onto his already crouched back with a surprising agility.

His back muscles instantly stiffen beneath my unexpected weight, and his broad shoulder blades dig uncomfortably into my chest as the startled Alpha instinctively tries to twist me off of him. I quickly curl my legs tightly around his hips, effectively locking myself onto his broad back. I bring my arm up and around his thick neck, securing him in a semi-chokehold.

With the soft towel fisted tightly in my right hand, I begin using my weapon to repeatedly beat Damien's head, all while screaming like a banshee. The Alpha lets out a surprised, involuntary yell of his own as he tries unsuccessfully to reach back and dislodge my tenacious hold, probably at a complete loss on how to do so without actually causing me any real harm.

He thrashes his powerful body violently to and fro around the relatively confined space of the kitchen while desperately trying to buck me off his back as I continue my furious assault, screaming a litany of creative curses with every blow I manage to land on his head. The restrained wolf doesn't offer any real offense and merely matches my furious curses with yelps of pain and grunts of discomfort while unsuccessfully attempting to dodge my increasingly wild punches.

Just then, I hear the distinct sound of approaching footsteps from the adjoining dining room.

"Boys? I just wanted to check and see how everything was going—" Lou's soft, familiar voice abruptly trails off, her tone laced with a growing concern as she pauses, her eyes widening in comical disbelief in the arched doorway between the two rooms at the utterly chaotic sight before her.

By now, the once relatively tidy kitchen is a complete and utter disaster. Kitchen utensils and various other implements are strewn haphazardly across the tiled floor, casualties of my earlier, explosive tantrum. Open containers of food have also been either carelessly toppled onto the countertops or are currently spilling their contents onto the already messy floor, all the unintended result of Damien's earnest, and unsuccessful, thrashing attempts to dislodge his incredibly angry, human backpack.

I'm also fairly certain that both the infuriated wolf and his tenacious rider are quite a sight in themselves.

I can feel that my oversized borrowed clothes are now hanging loosely on my sweat-soaked, crazed form. Lingering sweat and grime from the previous night still stubbornly clings to my face and arms, and my hair is sticking out at odd, angry angles. Not to mention, the undoubtedly wild, unhinged look in my eyes and my aggressive, primate-like hold on Damien probably give me more of an animalistic appearance than a human one at this point.

Damien's once impeccably crisp shirt has also popped several buttons from our roughhousing, revealing glimpses of his toned chest. His once perfectly manicured hair is now a tangled, knotted mess from my frantic pulling and ineffective hitting, and I can clearly see that his cheeks are now flushed a bright red from his vigorous, involuntary tour of the kitchen with me clinging to his back.

There's a brief, surreal moment of absolute silence as all three of us abruptly pause our respective activities. Lou stands frozen in her spot in the dining room doorway, her eyes wide with a mixture of shock and exasperation. Damien remains crouched low to the ground, his hands still instinctively raised to protect his head. And my own hand is suspended mid-air, the soft towel clutched tightly in my fist as I stare wide-eyed at the unexpected arrival of the Alpha's mother.

Lou lets out a long, weary sigh, pinching the bridge of her nose with a delicate hand as she closes her eyes in utter, defeated exasperation.

"Now," she says tiredly, her voice laced with a weary resignation, "this is what I like to categorize as a prime example of... *unhealthy* communication."

DAMIEN

Sunday 8:42 am

Brayden and I are seated side by side on the long couch in the front living room. Although, he isn't really sitting beside me so much as actively occupying the furthest possible point on the opposite side of the cushions. His tired form is practically listing off the arm of the couch, and his legs are crossed at an awkward angle, pointed away from my very existence. He isn't even attempting subtlety; his actions are so deliberately exaggerated that there is absolutely no way he was remotely comfortable.

My mother sits across from us, perched precariously on the edge of one of the floral accent chairs. Her back is ramrod straight, and her hands are folded meekly in her lap. She is the picture of poised expectation, her eyes sharp and keen as she surveys the two of us.

I, on the other hand, am a complete and utter mess and flounder helplessly in the awkward silence. My agitated state does absolutely nothing to improve matters. I don't know what to do with my own limbs. My feet tap an incessant rhythm against the floor, my legs bounce with nervous energy, and my hands keep folding and unfolding in my lap; my elbow, a shaky anchor on my bouncing knees.

Everything feels frustratingly out of my control.

Last night, despite the gut-wrenching difficulty, I had finally made the conscious decision to let Brayden do as he ultimately pleased. No matter how much it was going to tear me apart, no matter what the potential consequences were for myself or the pack. Witnessing the extreme lengths he was willing to go to in order to be completely separate from me was enough to finally force my hand and give him the one thing he so desperately desired: my reluctant freedom.

I vividly remembered his pleading eyes, the raw sincerity etched on his pale face as he begged me to let him go. I remembered the agonizing moment of decision, the conscious act of putting his desires before any of my responsibilities as Alpha. I remembered approaching the stark white line that separated us. And then–

Everything beyond that point becomes frustratingly fuzzy and disorientated, like trying to grasp smoke.

I had fleeting snippets of recollection from the rest of the seemingly endless night. There were shadowy impressions of me running in my wolf form through the oppressive darkness of the forest, my primal instincts growing more and more desperate with each agonizing second that ticked by. I vaguely recalled seeing Brayden's prone form lying still on the cold ground in front of me and the brief, almost overwhelming wave of relief that washed over me with the knowledge that he had finally achieved what he so desperately wanted in the end.

But after that... nothing. A gaping void in my memory.

The next coherent thing I remembered was standing over Brayden, the metallic scent of fresh blood thick in the air as it dripped from the newly formed mark on his neck. Due to a potent cocktail of both physical and mental exhaustion, I vaguely recalled that his slender form was completely limp in my arms, utterly passed out after my possessive bite, and I held him cradled in my own shaking limbs, a profound sense of wrongness settling deep in my gut.

I remembered a surge of panicked confusion. A complete and utter despair as the horrifying realization of what I had irrevocably done crashed down on me. There was a chilling moment of dread as I looked up at Aiden, who had merely shaken his head solemnly, offering a curt, apologetic bow of his head.

There was no flicker of remorse on my beta's face, and I knew with a sinking certainty that he didn't regret a single one of his calculated actions throughout the long night. For Aiden, the well-being of the pack had always, and would always, come first. Duty and unwavering loyalty to those we, as leaders, were sworn to watch over and protect. In his pragmatic mind, he was simply fulfilling the obligations of his position, no matter the devastatingly costly results those obligations entailed.

Betrayal of both his Alpha, his Alpha's mate, and his own offspring.

At that moment, everything had felt completely, terrifyingly out of my control. I didn't understand the full scope of what was happening, and to a frustrating degree, I couldn't quite comprehend the explanations being offered to me through the lingering haze of the drugs still coursing through my system. I didn't have a solid grasp on anything that was going on, which is precisely why the following morning I had been so desperately driven to try and regain some semblance of the control that had been so brutally ripped away from me.

I had decided to try and cook.

I knew, deep down, that Brayden was likely going to vehemently refuse anything that I painstakingly laid out for him, but the act of preparing that breakfast was as much for my own fractured sanity as the misguided intention had been for him. While I was meticulously cooking, I was in control of that small, contained area, in control of the ingredients and the process.

It was a desperate, futile act to try and reclaim the control I had so carelessly lost the previous night. But that, too, had quickly spiraled into another chaotic situation that I couldn't seem to keep a firm grasp on.

"Alright," my mother's soft, yet undeniably stern voice cuts through the heavy, suffocating silence in the room, effectively dragging me from the swirling vortex of my guilt-ridden thoughts. "I don't think either of you are remotely ready to have a productive conversation with the other, but you both desperately need to talk."

Her gaze is severe, her sharp eyes darting back and forth between Brayden and me, giving us both an equal measure of her unwavering attention.

"Therefore, I want to begin with you both taking turns and asking questions that I can answer," she uncrosses her legs, shifting slightly in her seat as if preparing for a lengthy interrogation. "We'll start with you, Brayden, and after he asks one question, we can move on to you, Damien."

Her demand leaves absolutely no room for argument or refusal.

Brayden remains stubbornly in his self-imposed exile on the far end of the couch. He's completely still now, curled tightly into his little corner, his gaze fixed intently on the blank expanse of the sidewall as he refuses to make any form of eye contact with either my mother or me. A tense moment of silence stretches out, and for a fleeting second, I actually believe that he isn't going to say a single word.

"Why am I in your house?" he finally asks, his voice devoid of any inflection, flat and utterly monotone.

My mother seems genuinely pleased by his reluctant participation and offers him a small, encouraging smile.

"This is the official Alpha house of the pack, Brayden," she calmly explains, making sure to maintain unwavering eye contact with him as she answers his question. "After it was decided that you had to participate in the Run, Al and I temporarily moved out, and Damien moved in. However, the move was primarily for political appeasement within the pack rather than out of any practical expectation of… this."

Brayden doesn't inquire further, retreating back into his silent, guarded shell after her surprisingly straightforward answer.

My mother turns her full, unwavering attention to me, and I struggle to come up with a coherent question under her intense scrutiny. I end up mumbling some vague inquiry about the general well-being of a few peripheral pack members, which my mother answers concisely before it is once again Brayden's turn to speak.

"What did it mean when people were saying last night wasn't just about me?" he asks, this time turning his head slightly to finally face my mother directly. His blue eyes are sharp, narrowed with suspicion, and his jaw is visibly stiff with tension.

I grimace almost imperceptibly as I can hear the faint grating of his teeth as he rubs them together in barely suppressed anger.

"You are mated to an Alpha, Brayden," my mother explains honestly, yet with a calming tone. "Therefore, while, yes, the intimate ties of the mate bond are solely between the two individuals of a mated couple, Damien's position as Alpha meant that there would have been wider consequences for the entire pack."

Brayden's brow furrows in genuine confusion as he stares intently at my mother, completely absorbed by her unexpected explanation.

"More specifically," my mother continues patiently, "Damien, as your mate, shares a unique bond with you. However, Damien, as the active Alpha, also shares a profound and vital bond with every single member of our pack. Therefore, by irrevocably breaking your mate bond, every single pack member would have felt Damien's deep sorrow, his anguish, and his profound loss through the intricate network of the pack bond."

She lets out a long, weary sigh, and I instinctively look away, bracing myself for the difficult part of the explanation that I know is inevitably coming next.

"The pack bond is considered sacred as it intimately ties all of the members to the active Alpha and Luna. This bond allows for both the leaders and the pack members to have a deep, almost symbiotic connection, a level of intimate care and understanding that humans aren't quite able to fully comprehend," she pauses, allowing Brayden the necessary time to absorb the weight of the information she is sharing. "Therefore, whenever a pack loses either their active Alpha or their Luna, it is a devastating blow to the entire community. Packs with strong bonds to both their active Alpha and Luna couple will statistically lose forty to fifty percent of their pack members to suicide as they are simply unable to cope with the overwhelming anguish and despair of the loss if one half of the mated pair were to die."

I hear Brayden take a sharp, audible breath of shock, the sound echoing in the otherwise silent room.

"As you hadn't yet fully formed your Luna bond with the pack, our potential losses weren't going to be quite as... *egregious*, but—"

"How many?" Brayden whispers, his question barely audible, the shock evident in his hushed tone.

My mother presses her lips together, a flicker of internal debate crossing her features as she considers whether or not to give him the precise information he is seeking.

"How many pack members would you have lost had I successfully broken the bond between myself and Damien last night?" Brayden asks again, this time with more strength and clarity in his voice. His pronunciation is precise, and his tone is completely clear, underscoring his sincere desire for a direct answer.

My mother turns her gaze towards me, and I can tell she is deliberately giving me an opportunity to speak, to shoulder some of the responsibility for the truth.

"Fifteen... to twenty-five percent," I mumble, the words feeling heavy and shameful on my tongue.

My palms are clammy with nervous sweat as I speak, and I subconsciously begin wringing my hands together in front of me, a futile attempt to quell the rising tide of my anxiety.

A heavy, oppressive silence descends upon the room, the unspoken weight of the potential loss hanging in the air. Brayden doesn't ask another question immediately, and I can see the impact of the information clearly etched on his pale face. A foolish, hopeful part of me dares to hope that he will take this devastating information and finally understand just how intrinsically important he is to me, to the entire pack. I desperately want him to realize that even with the potential for such catastrophic loss, I was still willing to give him the one thing he so desperately craved: his freedom.

But I know better. Brayden's perception of me is too deeply ingrained.

Brayden won't see my actions as some grand act of selfless romanticism. This devastating revelation will simply be another damning reason for him to look at me with disdain, another excuse for him to paint me as a monster, someone who was willing to let a significant portion of his community die for the sake of his own selfish, "wanton desire."

"I... I need some time," Brayden mumbles from beside me, his voice barely above a whisper.

There's a small, tense pause before my mother clears her throat, the sound surprisingly loud in the quiet room.

I look up and see her rather blatantly shifting her pointed gaze from me back to Brayden. Surprised by this unexpected shift in attention, I look over at Brayden and see that he is already staring directly at me with a look of quiet inquiry. The tired blues of his eyes seem to implore mine for an answer, his lean body having subtly turned itself ever so slightly in my direction.

I have to consciously fight back a flinch at his sudden, direct attention, belatedly realizing that what I had initially interpreted as a general statement of needing space from the situation had actually been a direct question aimed squarely at me.

"Take all the time you need, Brayden," I tell him with complete and utter sincerity, the words genuine.

I seize this brief, unexpected moment of openness from Brayden to quickly assess his reaction. As I had fully expected, Brayden's response to the devastating information seems to be... neutral. He doesn't look to be swayed in the slightest by anything he has heard today. There isn't a sudden softening in his guarded gaze, no flicker of appreciation for finally understanding the gravity of the circumstances; rather, he remains just as wary and emotionally distant as before. His face is impassive, a carefully-constructed mask. If there are any discernible changes at all, it could perhaps be argued that he has merely lost a fraction of the intense hatred that usually burns in his eyes whenever he is forced to look at me.

Some of it, but certainly not all.

"How long until I start to feel the physical effects of being away from you?" Brayden asks, a distinct edge of cold contempt lacing his weary voice.

I instinctively clench my sweaty hands together once again at his pointed question, the anxiety tightening its icy grip around my chest.

"At the most, ten days. At the very least... three," I mutter, the summarized version of the brutal truth feeling inadequate and dismissive, even though it was the stark reality.

After three agonizing days of separation, he would likely begin to experience significant trouble falling asleep, an unsettling, unsatisfied restlessness beginning to plague his waking hours. After a few more torturous days apart, he would start to feel the undeniable physical pressure of the bond straining and stretching, an invisible cord pulling him inexorably towards me in a near-painful manner. Within two weeks, he would likely have to fight down bouts of physical sickness, and after a few more weeks of continued separation, the insidious tendrils of depression and potentially self-destructive urges would begin to take root.

The explicit, gruesome details of the prolonged separation could be relayed to Brayden during a later, undoubtedly more unpleasant, conversation.

After my brief, clinical response, Brayden doesn't say anything further, and my mother, sensing the tension in the room, brings our strained conversation to a close. The two of them begin to discuss the logistical details of getting him back to his own home, and it feels far too soon when they both stand up, preparing to walk out the front door together.

With one last, awkward parting, Brayden walks out of the living room, not granting me so much as a fleeting backward glance as he heads towards his waiting car. Right before quietly shutting the front doorway behind him, my mother pauses, her gaze locking onto mine, offering me a knowing look. The kind of look only a deeply concerned mother can give to her child when she wants to convey both profound disapproval and genuine worry all at once.

I look away from her first, unable to meet the weight of her silent judgment, and she lets out a soft, resigned sigh as she finally closes the door, the gentle click echoing in the sudden silence of the house. I understand perfectly the unspoken meaning behind that look; it wasn't so much a direct warning, but a somber, unavoidable reminder of the harsh reality that awaited me.

The agonizing physical symptoms of our forced separation would inevitably begin to affect me in roughly half the time it would take for Brayden to feel their full, devastating impact.

BRAYDEN

Sunday 9:36 pm

Lou and I didn't exchange much conversation during the drive back to the trailer, but there wasn't any lingering animosity between us either. I was quick to get out of her car, and she was just as quick to pull away, granting me the much-needed time alone with my family.

The sight of the familiar, slightly dilapidated trailer is surprisingly welcoming as I step onto the warped wooden steps just outside the screen door. The dingy, faded metal siding even managed to coax a small, genuine smile from my lips. Even from outside, the wild cacophony of sounds emanating from within the cramped space is unmistakable. Shouts and unrestrained hollering echoed from the small living room, punctuated by muffled taunts that would momentarily silence the ruckus before a loud thud would follow, and the joyful screams would erupt anew.

The broken screen of the door stares back at me like a tired, vacant eye as I grip the slightly rusted handle and pull it open.

A momentary hush falls over the chaotic scene at my entrance.

The twins stand frozen mid-leap on the faded futon that serves as our couch in the living room. Their flushed cheeks and wildly tangled hair are clear evidence of their previous enthusiastic jumping session on the wilted cushions. It appears they had been in the midst of a dramatic game as Charlotte is wielding an empty cardboard paper towel tube like a fearsome weapon over Charlie, who is dramatically sprawled beneath it with a lopsided plastic crown drooping precariously over one side of his head.

Just below their energetic antics, Marcus is sprawled out on the worn linoleum floor, lying flat on his back. The quiet pre-teen doesn't seem remotely disturbed by the previous, or current, rambunctiousness of his younger siblings above him. He is completely engrossed in one of his beloved books, the colorful cover obscuring his entire face with only the thin edges of his glasses peeking out from under the well-worn pages. It isn't immediately clear whether his complete lack of reaction is due to the sheer shock of my unexpected arrival or his typical teenage obliviousness to any changes in his immediate surroundings.

Off to the side, Kelsey is in the cramped kitchen. Several paper plates laden with finished deli sandwiches are neatly lined along the cluttered counter next to an open bag of cheap bread and a collection of empty plastic cups. A well-used cutting board sits in front of her, evidence that she has been in the process of slicing up some apples to add to the plates of food; however, that domestic task is momentarily forgotten as her attention snapped up to my arrival.

The only distinct sound that could be heard above the general stillness is little Evie's insistent grumbling. She is securely strapped into her highchair just beside Kelsey and wiggling indignantly in her seat, her small face red and contorted in an angry frown. Her loud, unhappy noises make it clear that she is less than thrilled at being forced to remain confined while the other kids gleefully play and food is being prepared, seemingly without her direct input.

Just as suddenly as the room had fallen into a brief, stunned silence, it erupts once again into a flurry of loud, joyful activity. Excited screeches fill the small space, and I can't help the wide grin that spreads across my face at the sight of the beaming faces around me. The twins each grab one of my legs and latch onto them with surprising strength as they both try to excitedly pull me in opposite directions, their small bodies wriggling with unrestrained joy.

Kelsey gives me a small, relieved smile as she comes over and offers me a tight side-hug, and I can physically feel the tension drain from her small frame at my return home. Marcus remains sprawled on the floor, but he pulls his book just far enough away from his face to offer me a brief, almost shy greeting before immediately retreating back into his literary world. By the time I finally manage to navigate the enthusiastic chaos and make my way over to Evie, her angry red face has softened into a wide, gummy grin; however, as I reach down and scoop her up from her confining highchair, I immediately realize, with a familiar sense of weary resignation, that she has thoroughly peed through her diaper.

The rest of the day dissolves into a completely delightful, utterly hectic blur. All the kids are far too overstimulated by my unexpected return to even consider sitting down for a proper lunch, so we opt for a more wild picnic out on the overgrown lawn.

While the oppressive summer heat is finally beginning to wane, it is still more than warm enough to leave all of us red-faced and uncomfortably sticky by the time our impromptu outdoor meal has finally concluded.

The twins proceed to completely monopolize my afternoon and are determined to show me everything they have accomplished during my week-long absence. Charlie proudly presents a slightly ripped plastic grocery bag that he has diligently filled with an impressive collection of rocks over the past seven days. We are required to examine each individual pebble with the utmost seriousness as he painstakingly explains, in great and often repetitive detail, what he personally finds so uniquely special about each discarded piece of the earth. Charlotte, then, produces a surprisingly large pile of drawings she has been diligently working on in her kindergarten class. Each brightly colored creation is described to me with an intense level of detail as she perches comfortably on my lap and meticulously explains the profound artistic reasons behind her specific color choices.

After a surprisingly calm dinner, I navigate Evie's lengthy nighttime routine, and it isn't too long before the three youngest members of our chaotic little clan are finally tucked snugly into their beds, the trailer blessedly silent. Marcus, who has remained uncharacteristically quiet and withdrawn around me all day, suddenly appears in the dimly lit living room clutching one of his well-worn favorite movies. Even though Kelsey and I are attempting to have a quiet conversation, he wordlessly proceeds to put on his chosen film before settling down next to me on the worn couch and pointedly shares a corner of his threadbare blanket.

While he doesn't need to articulate his feelings out loud, I know that my unexpected absence has been emotionally taxing on the quiet teenager, and this silent gesture is his awkward way of processing the unsettling events of the past week. This is precisely why, when the movie finally ends, I know he is genuinely glad to have me back when he deliberately leaves his soft blanket draped over the arm of the couch for me to use rather than taking it with him to his own small bed.

It is now fully dark outside, the trailer casting long, distorted shadows in the pale moonlight. I am currently perched on one of the warped wooden steps of our small, rickety stoop, my gaze turned upwards towards the vast expanse of the night sky.

It is a remarkably clear night. The distant stars are twinkling with a brilliant, almost defiant light, and the moon is beginning its slow, steady ascent into the inky blackness. A cool, gentle wind sweeps through the stillness for a fleeting moment, ruffling my hair and carrying with it the earthy scent of the surrounding wild-life. The peacefulness momentarily engulfs my senses with a false, fragile feeling of normality.

Behind me, I hear the familiar creak of the screen door open-ing, and Kelsey quietly walks out. Clad in a pair of ridiculously fluffy fleece pajama pants and her perpetually oversized sweatshirt, which may or may not have originally belonged to me, she casually sits down on the step next to me, her small frame slumped with exhaustion. The young teenager looks utterly worn out. Familiar dark circles have begun to heavily line the delicate skin beneath her tired eyes, and the persistent, downturned set of a frown on her lips seems to have taken permanent residence there since the beginning of my unwelcome absence. Her usually stringy, unkempt hair is even more stubbornly grungy than its normal state and is hastily swept back from her pale face in a tight, unflattering ponytail.

I haven't managed to spend much quality time with Kelsey this evening as the younger kids had understandably monopolized my attention, but I have a strong feeling we will more than make up for that lost time through the unspoken questions swirling in her tired eyes.

"So," she begins, drawing out the single word with a weary sigh, "you want to maybe… tell me where you've *really* been?"

I let out a long, drawn-out sigh of my own. "I've been in the hospital, Kel. Recovering from…"

"Oh, cut the bullshit, Brayden!" Kelsey scolds sharply, rolling her dark eyes with an exasperated flick of her head. "Someone who's recovering from a supposed stay in the hospital for mere exhaustion doesn't return home with brand-new injuries on their neck or come hobbling back with a limp."

There is a frustrated edge to her usually quiet voice, and a deep scowl has firmly replaced her earlier weary frown. The dark coloring of her small eyes give me a direct, accusing glare as she silently waits for my response.

For a long moment, I honestly don't know what to say. She is right, of course. I can see the simmering frustration brewing in the depths of her tired eyes, and the unmistakable, borderline emotion of betrayal playing across her usually stoic features. It is strangely disconcerting to witness Kelsey displaying the same turmoil and sense of being kept in the dark that I had found myself feeling just a few short, chaotic days prior, and the unsettling familiarity of her emotions is enough to finally push me towards a decision.

I decide to hold nothing back.

Maybe it was selfish of me to suddenly dump the entire, unbelievable truth onto Kelsey's unsuspecting shoulders. I knew firsthand just how utterly overwhelming the information was when it was abruptly thrust upon you, but that initial shock was nothing compared to the profound sense of clarity that followed when all the seemingly random puzzle pieces that hadn't quite fit together around you suddenly clicked into place, confirming that you weren't, in fact, just losing your damn mind.

She let me ramble on, only interrupting a time or two for brief clarification on something particularly unbelievable that I had said. I continued to talk and explain, reciting everything that Damien had awkwardly confessed to me earlier in the day and catching her up on the bizarre, terrifying events of the previous night. The only detail I deliberately kept vague was the specific, gut-wrenching reason why I had ultimately made the fateful decision to cross back over that stark white line, but other than that significant omission, everything else, no matter how insane it sounded, was laid bare.

She remained understandably skeptical at first, her brow furrowed in disbelief, but the undeniable proof etched onto my own skin. Both the fresh, angry scar on my left hand and the disturbingly fresh bite mark on the right side of my neck was more than enough irrefutable evidence that I was, against all logical reasoning, telling her the truth.

Kelsey absorbed the unbelievable information in silence, her sock-clad feet tapping a nervous rhythm against the warped wooden step below her as she thoughtfully processed everything I had just confessed.

I honestly didn't know what kind of reaction to expect. There was a very real chance she would erupt in anger and begin yelling at me for not having confided in her sooner, or she might be visibly terrified at the sudden, undeniable realization that the impossible was now, apparently, very much possible. I knew, deep down, that whatever her eventual reaction was going to be, it was ultimately going to be better for me to tell Kelsey everything now rather than leaving her to fester in the dark, having some inkling that something was terribly wrong but not understanding the terrifying, unbelievable reality.

"I guess," she finally mumbles out, her gaze blankly fixed on the overgrown expanse of our small yard, "you can now officially add 'willing to do furry play' to your business cards."

I sputter out a surprised, slightly hysterical half-laugh, and a small, genuine smile flickers across her tired lips at her own dark humor. Her unexpected joke, as morbid as it is, manages to put me slightly at ease, a strange, twisted way of her telling me that she is, somehow, going to be alright, even if absolutely nothing feels even remotely alright at that particular moment in time.

"So," she inquires after a moment of contemplative silence, mindlessly pulling at a few loose strings dangling from the worn hood of her oversized sweatshirt, "what exactly is the brilliant plan now, oh fearless leader?"

I let out a long, weary sigh, resting my head heavily against the rough, splintered wood of the trailer as I close my aching eyes.

"I honestly don't know, Kel," I mumble out, utterly exhausted by the sheer weight of everything.

"I mean, realistically, we're kind of stuck here, right?" she says, her thoughts beginning to tumble out in a rapid, almost frantic stream. "We can't exactly leave without you literally dying a slow and agonizing death. But... I guess settling down here isn't the absolute worst-case scenario. For the most part, we all actually like our schools here. Charlie and Charlotte have somehow managed to make a surprising number of friends in their classes, and even Marcus brought up the other day that he's considering joining the school's chess team. And you... well, you actually like your ridiculously underpaid job, although I'm sure you'll have a few choice words to say when it comes to negotiating your new, supernaturally-mandated working hours and pay."

She pauses, her rapid train of thought seemingly slowing down as she finally takes a deep breath.

"There's also... nothing, that explicitly states you actually have to be in a *relationship* with the beast, right?" she mumbles out her last, surprisingly insightful comment, and in genuine surprise, I finally look over at her to see her gaze thoughtfully fixed on the slowly rising moon.

At her sudden, surprisingly astute statement, a dawning realization washes over me. She is absolutely right. The only concrete piece of information we know for certain is that I am now irrevocably bound to remain within the pack's territory due to my newly formed, unwanted bonds, but absolutely nothing has been explicitly stated about having to actually play house, or any other kind of domestic charade, with the infuriatingly persistent werewolf.

I sit for a long moment, lost in the sudden whirlwind of my own thoughts at this unexpected, potentially life-altering revelation, and vaguely register Kelsey quietly getting up and heading back inside the trailer. I hear her shuffling around in the cramped space for a moment before she reappears in the doorway while holding a somewhat dusty glass bottle filled with a dark, amber liquid.

"Where the actual fuck did you get *that*?!" I immediately ask, genuinely surprised and slightly alarmed, that my usually mousy and fiercely introverted younger sister would somehow be running with a crowd capable of acquiring such an item underage.

I honestly don't know whether to be impressed or appalled.

She rolls her eyes with teenage disdain as she wordlessly hands me the bottle. "It's literally still sealed," she says defensively, and looking down, I can see that she is indeed correct. I give her a look of utter confusion.

"I... uh... I walked into the grocery store the other day, and I must have gotten completely lost in thought in front of the liquor aisle," she begins explaining sheepishly, a small, embarrassed smile playing on her lips. "Next thing I know, this overly helpful store associate comes over and starts helping me pick something out, completely under the mistaken impression that I was picking something up for you, and then he just... let me have it for free," she shrugs her small shoulders with a wry smile. "His actions make a hell of a lot more sense now, in hindsight."

With a tired sigh that seemed far too heavy for someone her age, she lifts her small hands and begins rubbing her tired eyes vigorously. When she finally stops, the delicate skin around her eyes is red and irritated from her ministrations, and she blinks heavily, clearly displaying her own mental and emotional exhaustion.

Getting ready to head back inside for the night, she turns around in the open doorway before pausing, her small frame silhouetted against the dim interior light. "Mom's biggest mistake," she says quietly, her gaze far too knowing and heavy for a girl her age, "was thinking that if she felt fear, she no longer had control." She looks back at me, her dark eyes filled with an unsettling wisdom. "It's okay to have both, Brayden."

My own eyes unexpectedly fill with tears at her surprisingly profound words as she finally pushes open our creaky metal door and disappears into the dark interior of the trailer.

After Kelsey leaves me alone on the stoop, I honestly couldn't recall what I did during the rest of the seemingly endless night. My thoughts would swirl in a dizzying, anxious whirlwind of unease, and then there were moments when my mind felt completely still, utterly exhausted and numb, beyond the capacity for any coherent thought. There were times when I vaguely registered the wetness on my cheeks, although the specific memory of when I had started crying, and more importantly, when I had finally stopped, remained unclear. Tears for myself, for my siblings, for the uncertain weight of my past actions and the terrifying unknown of my future, all silently trailed down my face in the cool night air.

The long night slowly wanes, the unopened bottle clutched loosely in my hand gradually feeling a little less heavy, and the silent, watchful moon continues its steady rise into the vast, indifferent sky.

BRAYDEN

Monday 7:57 am

I t is cooler out this morning, a welcome shift as the weather has been steadily dipping in temperature recently, the full swing of the season's change undeniably upon us. The sun is just beginning its slow ascent, painting the sky in soft hues, and I enjoy the cool breeze that sweeps across my face as I wait with bated breath for the imposing establishment before me to officially open its doors.

While the building isn't enormous, it is undeniably the most impressive structure on the entire block. It honestly looks like a stereotypical government building, all stark concrete and imposing authority. Massive, unfluted columns adorn the sides of the building beneath the surprisingly large awning, adding to the air of gravitas. Ornate, vaguely intimidating embellishments wrap around the top of the structure, and the stylized sign of the Goddess rests as the prominent center crest just above the heavy main doorway, a silent declaration of purpose.

Standing in front of the two large, impersonal glass doors, my own reflection stares back at me with a critical eye. I am decidedly more dressed up than my usual casual attire, and I am desperately hoping my carefully chosen outfit conveyed the level of professionalism I am aiming for.

I am sporting my one-and-only pair of slightly wrinkled khakis paired with my equally lonely pair of stiff dress shoes. On top, I have reluctantly chosen to wear a long-sleeved navy button-down shirt, the sleeves rolled up to my forearms, which is a direct result of a breakfast-related syrup incident, rather than any conscious stylistic choice. For the first time in a while, I have also attempted to style my stubbornly straight hair, but the cheap product has unfortunately resulted in a look that is more aggressively messy than sleekly sophisticated.

Even if my overall appearance doesn't quite achieve the pristine level I had envisioned, the underlying message is still undeniably clear.

I am not here for a friendly chat or a casual visit; I am here for business.

The only thing that seems to slightly diminish the severity of my carefully-constructed attire is the cane propped awkwardly next to my side.

After I had begrudgingly woken up on my first morning back in the familiar chaos of the trailer, Kelsey had relentlessly pestered me to go and get my throbbing leg properly checked out. I had adamantly refused, stubbornly resistant to any further medical intervention, but after the younger kids were finally wrangled and sent off to school, I had begrudgingly swung by the local hospital. My visit there was blessedly short as I had been pointedly reluctant to engage with the overly cheerful Dr. Monroe about anything beyond the bare minimum of logistical information. After a brief, perfunctory examination, he had prescribed me some surprisingly effective painkillers and sternly instructed me to utilize a walking aid for the next couple of weeks.

It was now a full week after that unwelcome appointment, and while I personally felt that I was more than strong enough to walk perfectly fine without the damn thing, Kelsey had made me solemnly promise,with the kind of intense, unwavering stare that brooked no argument, to strictly adhere to Dr. Monroe's diagnosis until my arbitrary two-week sentence was officially up.

In addition to my stubbornly aching leg, all of my other more... *supernatural* injuries seemed to have healed remarkably well. I had a small, pale scar on both the top and bottom of my left hand, a permanent memento of Damien's partial, possessive bite, and other than a slight, almost imperceptible irritation when the skin gets particularly dry, the old wound was hardly even noticeable. The undeniably more significant mark on my neck had also mostly healed, much to my grudging relief. The noticeable swelling around the distinct canine punctures had completely vanished, along with any lingering redness or inflammation. All that remained was a faint, soft pink outline of his teeth marks, which would undoubtedly fade to a less conspicuous white in the near future.

The heavy door in front of me suddenly emits a soft, electronic click, and I see a startled-looking pack member quickly fumbling with the deadbolt of the entrance. I don't pay them much mind as I stride purposefully past them, their wide, gaping mouth and stammered apologies for not realizing I was standing there sooner going in one ear and promptly out the other. The flustered worker trails awkwardly behind me as I enter the surprisingly spacious lobby, and the other early-morning administrative employees abruptly cease their hushed conversations to stare openly at my unannounced arrival.

Walking directly up to the imposing front desk, I see the middle-aged secretary's carefully neutral expression crumble into one of blatant shock as I simply meet her wide-eyed gaze with a deliberately blank stare of my own.

"Where's his office?" I ask flatly.

The startled secretary immediately scrambles to her feet and begins leading me down a surprisingly long side hall. As we walk in silence, I deliberately choose to quietly observe the sterile, government-esque interior of the building rather than engage in any pointless, polite conversation.

The floors are covered in shiny, almost aggressively clean tiles, their deep cream color bordering on a sickly yellow rather than a more neutral, inoffensive shade. The walls are painted a matching, equally uninspired dark beige, while the trim around the doorways and the heavy, imposing doors themselves are all glossy wood stained a rather dated, bright cherry red. While I am fairly certain the individual materials had likely been quite expensive at some point in the distant past, the overall aesthetic feels distinctly out-of-date—like stepping into a poorly maintained time capsule.

At the very end of the long, echoing hall, two heavy double doors stand proudly, exuding an air of self-importance. I notice a small, polished gold plaque affixed just above the ornate door frame, which reveals the full, official name and title of the man I am here to see. As I stare at the formal inscription, the flustered secretary quickly mumbles an excuse and hastily retreats back down the hall to leave me standing alone before the imposing entrance.

I take a deep, steadying breath and attempt to collect the scattered fragments of my composure.

You can be both scared and in control, Brayden. Remember that.

Without bothering with the polite formality of a knock, I swing the heavy, double doors wide open with a decisive push.

Upon entering the surprisingly spacious office, the first thing I notice is that Damien is already looking directly at me. This isn't particularly surprising; I am fairly certain the hyper-aware Alpha could likely hear my approach from halfway down the hall, or, failing that, he could undoubtedly smell my distinct scent, even through the thick, solid wood of the closed doors.

The attractive wolf is standing in front of a massive, floor-to-ceiling bookshelf that dominates one entire wall of the office. The densely packed shelves are overflowing with numerous leather-bound volumes, interspersed with a surprisingly eclectic collection of personal trinkets.

Damien's large, imposing desk sits just in front of the towering bookshelf; the polished wood piece of furniture is surprisingly clean and uncluttered. In front of the desk, two plush accent chairs and a low-slung lounge chair surround a low, equally polished coffee table. The rich patterns on each piece of furniture are all deep, regal colors, and the expensive upholstery is just beginning to show the faintest signs of wear and fading. To the side of the room, a wall lined with large windows overlooks the grounds with a long, formal conference table dominating the space in front of them.

Walking directly up to his expansive desk, I deliberately throw two folded pieces of paper onto its polished surface and assess him with what I hope is a cool, calculating gaze.

His impeccably groomed appearance isn't particularly surprising. He is dressed to the absolute nines, impeccably adorned in a perfectly tailored black three-piece suit; his dark, almost black hair is ruthlessly slicked back from his handsome face.

Although his overall demeanor was... a little off.

Damien's usually expressive face is completely devoid of any discernible emotion. The sharp lines of his mouth and the intense gaze of his dark eyes stare back at me with a hard, almost aggressively business-like expression, and his eyes seem more hollow and empty than usual with noticeable dark bags of exhaustion lining the skin beneath them.

I am a little surprised by how outwardly composed Damien appears, considering we have been forcibly separated for a full week. After only a few short nights apart, I had experienced increasing trouble sleeping, eventually resorting to taking strong sleeping pills just to achieve a few hours of restless unconsciousness. By the end of the week, a heavy, oppressive weight had begun to settle in my chest, and my muscles had started to ache with a persistent stiffness as the unnatural separation began to physically pull against me, an invisible tether constantly reminding me of his absence.

I could only vaguely imagine what the forced separation has been like for the powerful werewolf.

Damien clears his throat, the sound a bit rough and scratchy to my ears, no doubt the lingering remnant of several sleepless nights, as he gingerly reaches over to the two documents I have unceremoniously flung onto his pristine desk. He gives me a sharply inquisitive look as he picks them up to examine their contents.

"What exactly are these, Brayden?" he questions, his usually smooth baritone voice sounding slightly strained.

I straightened my own aching back and consciously school my expression into one of cool indifference.

"The first one is an invitation from the twins," I explain, gesturing one hand towards the top pamphlet.

Damien's dark eyes rake over the brightly colored paper in quick succession and efficiently take in the childishly scrawled information.

"They're… inviting me to their elementary school performance of the Blood Moon Celebration in a couple of months?" he asks, a hint of uncertainty in his tone, although I couldn't miss the slight, almost imperceptible quirk of his lips as he visibly fights back a genuine smile.

"They were informed by a classmate that when you invite someone to such an auspicious event, you traditionally receive gifts," I cross my arms firmly across my chest, straightening my shoulders for added emphasis. "They're expecting candy."

Damien's dark eyebrow arches sharply, and the corner of his full lip twitches almost imperceptibly as one of his large hands comes up to casually cover his mouth, a clear attempt to conceal the genuine grin that threatens to break across his stoic facade.

"Then, I shall certainly come prepared," he replies quietly, a hint of amusement finally coloring his deep voice as he gingerly sets the childish pamphlet down to the side.

His intense gaze then moves to the second, more official-looking piece of paper.

My own heart inexplicably begins to beat a little faster as his dark eyes slowly, deliberately read over the contents of the second document, but I stubbornly refuse to back down from his unwavering stare as his gaze finally meets mine.

"Those," I state firmly, answering his unspoken, quizzical look, "are my demands."

Damien's eyes widen almost imperceptibly as he glances back down at the document in his hands.

"Ah," he mumbles softly, a flicker of something unreadable crossing his usually impassive features.

The powerful Alpha takes a deep, steadying breath before leaning back in his large, expensive leather office chair, his intense gaze fixing expectantly on me.

"What we have here is not personal, Damien, and I don't have any emotional attachment to the overall situation," I begin speaking, my voice deliberately cool and business-like. "However, there are undeniably certain aspects of our lives that now make us, to varying degrees, dependent on each other."

Damien turns his head slightly to look out of the large office window, his impeccably styled dark hair catching the early morning sunlight. His dark eyes remain open and completely unblinking as he stares intently at something outside my line of sight.

"So," he inquires, his tone carefully neutral as he refuses to meet my gaze. The powerful wolf rests one large hand on the polished surface of his desk, his long, elegant fingers flexing back and forth with a barely concealed agitation. "You're proposing the equivalent of a formal business contract?"

"Yes," I state firmly, my voice leaving no room for argument. "I took the liberty of visiting the local library this past week and diligently read up on some of the fundamental pack laws as well as more specific details regarding the... intricacies of mating. So, I am now reasonably well-informed about what I am, theoretically, entitled to."

My unexpected excursions to the surprisingly extensive local library had actually been one of the few things that had managed to keep me from completely losing my already tenuous grip on sanity during the forced separation. Because the immediate future had felt so incredibly uncertain in the aftermath of the disastrous Run, I had been granted an indefinite leave of absence from the hospital, contingent on my eventual return, whenever that might be. It hadn't taken long for me to become overwhelmingly agitated and restless without the familiar routine of work, so I had deliberately utilized my newfound free time for intensive research. I had spent countless hours poring over surprisingly detailed werewolf literature, ranging from anatomical studies to historical accounts to surprisingly candid personal memoirs. I had finally decided that I wasn't going to simply sit idly in the dark any longer, waiting for answers that might never come. The information I desperately craved slowly began to clarify as I finally took matters into my own hands, or rather, into the surprisingly well-organized library's archives.

Upon my pointed comment, Damien remains outwardly stone-faced, his intense gaze finally turning back towards me. The powerful wolf doesn't betray a single one of his thoughts as he sits perfectly still in his imposing chair and offers me a small, almost imperceptible gesture to continue with my demands.

"First," I begin, my voice firm, "I want to continue working at the hospital. I genuinely like the people I'm able to help while I'm there, but I want my work hours significantly reduced, and my current pay is, frankly, absolutely atrocious and no longer acceptable."

I haven't quite worked out the specific details of the compensation I now expect. From my extensive research, I know that the Luna traditionally has a monthly spending budget allocated to them, and that basic necessities like food and utility bills are automatically covered for the Alpha couple. I am not entirely certain how these established rules would integrate into our current, decidedly unconventional situation of living separately, but I am still begrudgingly willing to work for at least some of the benefits I am now theoretically entitled to.

Damien offers a small, almost imperceptible nod but otherwise maintains his carefully-constructed, stoic facade. His surprisingly reserved reactions are slowly starting to put me on edge; I have never witnessed this particular side of him before. The stiff, formal presence. The almost palpable weight of his inherent dominance in this setting. It is almost suffocating, making it surprisingly difficult to simply remain standing upright.

It takes me a brief moment before the somewhat unsettling realization finally dawns on me: I am finally seeing the Alpha of the powerful Rocky Falls pack in his element. Not just the man awkwardly claiming to be my unwanted mate. Not the love-sick fool from the woods or the man prone to nervous, awkward antics.

Damien is deliberately allowing me to witness him in his full, unadulterated position of power and authority. Surprisingly, it isn't as oppressive as I might have initially expected; instead, I find a strange sort of comfort in his professional demeanor as this detached treatment subtly implies he is granting me a certain level of respectful space in our undeniably personal, albeit unwanted, situation.

It is this unexpected professional courtesy that gives me the unexpected courage to continue with my demands.

"I would also like to continue seeing Lou, without your… direct involvement," I state firmly and quickly continue before Damien has a chance to interrupt my carefully constructed train of thought. "I have read the relevant pack law regarding this particular aspect. I am not entirely certain what specific documents you might need to sign to officially authorize this, but that is entirely up to you to figure out."

Damien once again offers a small, almost imperceptible nod and doesn't voice any immediate objection to my second, non-negotiable request. My confidence begins to build ever so slightly as I move on to the final, and perhaps most personally significant, item on my carefully prepared agenda.

I deliberately remain silent as I watch the powerful wolf carefully read the final piece of paper, his long fingers tapping a slow, rhythmic strum against the polished surface of his desk. I could clearly see the almost imperceptible clench of his strong jaw as he absorbs the information.

"For the absolute bare minimum, I will require one hour, twice a week," he finally states, his intense gaze still fixed on the document in his hands, pointedly avoiding any direct eye contact with me.

The deep baritone of his voice resonates throughout the large, surprisingly quiet office, and the serious weight of the topic hangs heavy in the air between us.

"One of those designated hours," he continues, his warm brown eyes finally lifting to meet mine with an unexpected intensity, "I will leave entirely up to your discretion. We can either spend that time in a neutral, public setting, such as grabbing coffee or a quick lunch, or you could simply come to my office here, and we can… work on whatever it is you deem necessary."

I nod my head slowly, finding that proposal surprisingly reasonable. One measly hour of my undoubtedly precious time a week wouldn't actually kill me, and the flexibility is… surprisingly appreciated.

"What about the other mandatory hour?" I inquire, my voice carefully neutral.

"For that one," he replies, leaning back slightly in his imposing chair, his gaze unwavering, "I would strongly prefer you attend at least one of the weekly pack meetings that are held here."

Leaning back further in his expensive chair, he reaches down and smoothly pulls open a discreet drawer in his desk before reaching inside and carefully passing me a small stack of neatly organized papers.

"Those are the comprehensive list of the various weekly meetings I currently lead. Simply pick one that best suits your schedule, and your attendance can count towards the second required hour," he explains, his tone surprisingly reasonable.

I nod again, briefly scanning over the small pile of official-looking documents now resting in my hands.

"You do realize, Brayden, that by proposing this arrangement, you are implicitly agreeing to everything we have just discussed as well as your regular attendance and at least partial administrative involvement in pack affairs," Damien states, his deep voice carrying a subtle undercurrent of apprehension.

"I'm effectively stuck here anyway, aren't I?" I reply with a deliberately nonchalant shrug of my shoulders, tucking the small pile of documents securely under my arm. "I might as well attempt to make the absolute most of whatever this position has to offer me."

A tense moment of silence hangs in the air as my somewhat cynical comment echoes in the otherwise quiet office. I am not going to vehemently deny my unwelcome, newfound position within the pack any longer. To a certain, undeniable degree, I physically couldn't. Over the past week, I had found myself inexplicably drawn to taking long walks around the town or even deliberately seeking out crowded public places. Much like Damien's undeniable physical tie to me, I also seemed to have developed a similar, albeit less dramatic, connection with the pack itself. An unsettling unease would begin to build in my chest if I deliberately secluded myself away for too long, a feeling of being slightly off-kilter that could only be remedied by the ambient presence of those within the town's borders.

I am not going to deny my unwanted position, but I also stubbornly refuse to be pushed into yet another metaphorical corner. I will begrudgingly accept this unwelcome roll but strictly on my own meticulously outlined terms.

"I'll have someone draw up an official, legally-binding contract containing all the explicit details of our agreement," Damien says, turning his gaze back towards the window, his profile sharp against the muted daylight. "This conversation can certainly count towards this week's mandatory personal hour."

Nothing more is said by either of us, and I take that as my clear cue to finally leave his imposing office. Turning around, I deliberately make my way towards the heavy double doors.

"One last thing, Brayden," Damien's deep voice stops me just as my hand reaches for the cool metal of the door handle.

I don't bother turning back around, but I freeze in my spot, listening intently to his carefully neutral tone.

"The Alpha house is far too large for just one person. If you want," a flicker of something that sounded suspiciously like genuine emotion briefly slips through his carefully-constructed voice at the mention of the kids, but it is quickly masked by a return to his previous tone of detached indifference "you and the kids can certainly move in here while I find a smaller, more suitable place for myself."

"I'll think about it," I reply, my voice equally noncommittal as I finally turn the heavy knob and head out of the imposing office.

The rhythmic clack of my stupid cane against the polished stone floor echoes in the long, silent hall as I make my way back towards the lobby. The unexpected meeting had gone surprisingly well. In fact, Damien had been far more open and amenable to my demands than I had initially anticipated. I would hazard a guess that the terms we had discussed would be officially drafted no later than this afternoon with the final, excruciating details to be hammered out sometime shortly thereafter. There was still a considerable amount that needed to be explicitly written down and legally codified but that could all wait for another day. For now, Damien and I were, somewhat unbelievably, on the same page.

We had a set, mutually agreed-upon framework for what our contractually obligated responsibilities were to each other, and that was a structured, controllable situation that I could, perhaps begrudgingly, handle. The impending contract would finally allow me to exert some semblance of control over a life that had been so violently thrust upon me, and it would, hopefully, provide some clarity on how to navigate the increasingly bizarre landscape of my future.

As I finally reached the heavy exit doors, one of the overly eager workers immediately rushes forward to open them for me. I don't acknowledge his help, nor do I offer any response to his deeply bowed head of forced respect as I pass him by.

A small, almost involuntary smirk finally tugs at the corner of my lips once I step out into the relatively normal morning air.

The esteemed pack had ultimately gotten exactly what they had so desperately craved: a Luna. While there had been undeniably extenuating circumstances surrounding the disastrous Run and more than enough blame to go around amongst several key individuals, they had still ultimately manipulated and forced me into this unwanted position of leadership. Decisions had been made that were now, for all intents and purposes, irreversible. Well, I would give this demanding pack exactly what they had so pointedly asked for. They had collectively wished for me to lead, and by damn, here I was.

I was now in control.

I am Luna.

www.ingramcontent.com/pod-product-compliance
Lightning Source LLC
Chambersburg PA
CBHW030345120726
47901CB00007B/1925